Apollodorus' *Library*

and

Hyginus' *Fabulae*

Two Handbooks of Greek Mythology

Apollodorus' *Library*

and

Hyginus' *Fabulae*

Two Handbooks of Greek Mythology

Translated, with Introductions, by
R. Scott Smith and Stephen M. Trzaskoma

Hackett Publishing Company, Inc.
Indianapolis/Cambridge

Printed in the United States of America

10 09 08 07 1 2 3 4 5 6 7

For further information, please address
Hackett Publishing Company, Inc.
P.O. Box 44937
Indianapolis, IN 46244-0937

www.hackettpublishing.com

Cover design by Abigail Coyle
Interior design by Elizabeth Wilson
Composition by Agnew's, Inc.
Printed at Edwards Brothers, Inc.

Library of Congress Cataloging-in-Publication Data

Apollodorus.
[Bibliotheca. English]
Apollodorus' Library. And, Hyginus' Fabulae / translated, with introductions by R. Scott Smith and Stephen M. Trzaskoma.
p. cm.
Includes bibliographical references and indexes.
"Two handbooks of Greek mythology."
ISBN-13: 978-0-87220-821-6 (cloth)
ISBN-13: 978-0-87220-820-9 (pbk.)
1. Mythology, Greek—Early works to 1800. I. Smith, R. Scott, 1971–. II. Trzaskoma, Stephen M. III. Hyginus. Fabulae. English. IV. Title.
PA3870.A55A285 2007
292.1′3—dc22

2006031184

The paper used in this publication meets the minimum requirements of American National Standard for Information Sciences—Permanence of Paper for Printed Library Materials, ANSI Z39.48–1984.

∞

CONTENTS

GUILLELMO CALDERO
QUI NOS MULTA ET VIR ET PER LIBROS ADHUC DOCET.

PREFACE

Apollodorus and Hyginus have both been translated into English before, but never in their entirety in the same volume. Their appearance here seemed a logical next step after we had already produced translations of the bulk of these two authors for the *Anthology of Classical Myth* (2004). That book was designed to bring as many interesting primary sources before new audiences as possible; this one is designed to make two of the most important of those sources even more accessible by providing up-to-date and high-quality translations in an inexpensive volume. The *Bibliotheke (Library)* and *Fabulae (Myths)* ought to be read more widely both by those with a general interest in the subject and students approaching it in an academic environment. The only other English translation of Hyginus' *Fabulae,* that of Grant (1960), has some flaws and is out of print; that was our primary impetus. Apollodorus' *Bibliotheke,* though already published in several translations, seemed a natural partner.

In our English translations we have aimed above all at accuracy and clarity, although "accuracy" and "clarity" must be qualified. In some places there are serious questions as to what the Greek and Latin of Apollodorus and Hyginus mean or imply, but we hope that we have not intentionally rendered anything perfectly intelligible into gibberish or made our authors say things they never wrote. Neither of the works in question is of interest for its literary qualities, and we have not attempted to transform them into something they are not. If the translations often reveal a certain awkwardness, one can be quite sure that it is representative of the general qualities of their originals.

To the translations themselves we have added a General Introduction that treats the wider context and development of mythography in some detail; those more interested only in issues specifically related to the authors at hand can turn directly to the introductions provided for each, which follow the General Introduction. All of the introductory matter is geared toward the general reader or student but, we trust, not so much so as to be entirely devoid of interest to specialists.

Footnotes have been designed to provide immediate clarification on content, but in the interest of space we have not included full mythological notes—one can easily find full discussions of these myths in the many excellent handbooks available. To reduce the clutter of footnotes and cross-references, we have provided full indexes for the names, places, and authors cited, containing enough detail, we hope, to answer many questions that might occur to readers.

Technical and textual matters that will generally be of interest to a more limited audience have been relegated to endnotes (marked in the text by asterisks). In the *Anthology of Classical Myth,* where much of the translations originally appeared, we resolved to stick as closely to the texts printed in the scholarly editions on which the translations were based (Frazer's for all of Apollodorus; Marshall's first edition for Hyginus). Here we felt no such compunction, but more than that, we keyed the first three books of Apollodorus to Wagner's critical edition instead of Frazer's Loeb (though the latter remains the basis for the combined texts of the epitomes of Apollodorus) and updated Hyginus to reflect Marshall's second edition. With the opportunity to comment more fully in our endnotes here, we freely consulted all available editions, not only accepting the conjectures of other scholars but also suggesting many of our own as we felt the need. In fact, we thoroughly revised our earlier translations and reconsidered the whole of both works, and there are as a consequence many deviations from our versions in the *Anthology,* most of them quite minor but several of great significance—all of them improvements, we hope. We have endeavored in the endnotes to document and provide rationale for every deviation from Wagner, Frazer, and Marshall, and we beg the indulgence of other scholars if we have missed any.

In terms of a division of responsibility, Trzaskoma translated Apollodorus, while Smith translated Hyginus, and we each provided the section of the Introduction devoted to our respective author. We carefully worked through each other's translations and introductions, however, and the improvements of the nontranslating partner are present on every page. The General Introduction was initially written by Trzaskoma but thoroughly revised and expanded by Smith. The indexes were a joint project, as were the footnotes and endnotes (it should be noted, however, that wherever only one of us is responsible for a textual conjecture discussed in the endnotes, this is indicated by our initials).

Like all books, this one is a product of more than just the authors whose names appear on the cover, and there are many people whom we must thank for their support, wisdom, and help during its preparation. In particular, we would like to thank Stephen Brunet, our colleague and collaborator in *Anthology of Classical Myth,* for his collegiality and useful discussions. Likewise, we extend our gratitude to our editor at Hackett Publishing Company, Rick Todhunter, who encouraged the project, and to the production staff that shepherded it to fruition. We would also like to thank Michelle Cain, the publisher's copyeditor, whose diligence saved us from many errors and inconsistencies. We should like to extend our gratitude to William Nelson, whose attractive and accurate maps add great value to the volume. Also thanks are due to the two anonymous readers, whose comments improved the Introductions.

The Dean's Office of the College of Liberal Arts at the University of New Hampshire generously provided funding to each of us in support of this project, as did the university's Center for Humanities and the Department of Languages, Literatures, and Cultures. The Graduate College of the University of New Hampshire facilitated much of the initial work on Hyginus with the award of a summer fellowship to Smith in 2005. In August, 2005 the Fondation Hardt pour l'étude de l'antiquité classique in Vandoeuvres, Switzerland, allowed us to work for a worry-free three weeks in an excellent library surrounded by brilliant and stimulating international colleagues. Our visit there was subsidized by the William A. Oldfather Research Fund at the University of Illinois at Urbana-Champaign. Without this financial support the volume would not have been possible. Likewise, without the timeliness and efficiency of the Interlibrary Loan Office of the Dimond Library, this project might have languished interminably.

We would also like to thank Piero Garofalo, our colleague in the Italian Program at UNH, for his invaluable assistance in acquiring the image of the bronze Chimera di Arezzo that graces the cover. Our thanks also to Daniela Selisca for the wonderful photo and permission to reproduce it, as well as to the Soprintendenza per i Beni Archeologici della Toscana for access to the piece in the Museo Archeologico Nazionale di Firenze.

Finally, we owe special thanks to our wives, Maggie Smith and Laurel Trzaskoma, who suffered many indignities as work on this book progressed, not least being forced to read drafts of the General Introduction. They indulged us with kindness and understanding, all the while reminding us that there can be such a thing as too much mythography.

GENERAL INTRODUCTION
What Is Mythography?

Of the many gifts passed on to us from the Greeks and Romans, their myths are surely one of our most enduring and important cultural legacies. Because of the perennial appeal of these traditional stories about gods and heroes, modern audiences are exposed to a steady supply of mythically inspired popular and highbrow culture in a variety of media, from animated movies to operas. With surprising regularity, modern audiences also still turn directly to an ancient source for their myth. Somewhere in the world right now a play of Euripides is being staged, the appearance of new translations of Homer's epics can still cause critical and popular stirrings (and sell a lot of books), and visitors to museums gaze daily in rapt fascination at Greek and Roman sculptures and painted vases depicting mythical figures. Herein lies the rub: for all their beauty and importance, all those plays, poems, and artworks from the ancient world can be remarkably inefficient vehicles for imparting basic knowledge about the myths. But what is contained in this book—the two most important surviving ancient works of mythography ("writing *about* myth")—was deliberately designed to do just that, to provide clear, straightforward accounts of the myths without pretense or adornment.

Before we get into what mythography is all about, let's back up just a moment. *What is the myth of Oedipus?* This is the sort of question that people ask us all the time because they are curious and because we get paid to talk about Greek myth. If you know someone like us, or have a friend who loves Greek myths, watch him or her carefully the next time you ask something like this. There will be an uncomfortable pause, eventually broken by a "Well . . ." or a good, long "Um . . .". Your question, it turns out, is remarkably complex for two reasons. First, the word "myth" is notoriously difficult to define for scholars (we'll leave that controversy aside, but the definition most likely to be given by a layperson, "a false story," is the one least likely to be given by a scholar who works on myth). Second, deciding what constitutes a myth is just as complicated because one myth might be told differently in various places, times, and contexts, and your acquaintance might be trying to decide which version to tell, which details to include, and what information to leave out.

Once the hemming and hawing is done, your question might be answered in a minute or two in a bare-bones account that glosses over most if not all the difficulties. Your other option is to go read Sophocles' *Oedipus Tyrannus,* a Greek tragedy of some 1,500 lines of poetry, and gather the relevant information yourself; most of the relevant information is there, although you'll learn nothing about Oedipus' life after he blinds himself and leaves the city (for that you'd also have to read Sophocles' *Oedipus at Colonus,* an even longer play!). Which method is better? In most ways, of course, the second is. You will read one of the most influential and brilliant literary works human endeavor has ever produced, for one thing. But if you are simply trying to satisfy idle curiosity, just following up on a quick reference to Oedipus in a book you are reading, or merely reminding yourself of the main outlines of the story, the first method, turning to a bare-bones account, is clearly superior in a variety of ways.

The problem here is not just Oedipus. The same essentially goes for all the hundreds of Greek myths. For example, the recent appearance of the film *Troy* made a lot of people curious about the Trojan War in Greek myth. Most of those people, of course, were not going to set aside a week to read through Homer's *Iliad* to learn more. Should people read the *Iliad?* Obviously they should—though we might be prejudiced in this regard since our careers revolve around trying to get people to read it! But should they read it just to answer their basic questions about the Trojan War? Most certainly not, and if they do, they would probably be mightily angry at whoever suggested they read more than 15,000 lines of poetry to discover one inescapable fact: the *Iliad* does not tell the whole story of the Trojan War. It doesn't even tell most of it, only a month or two toward the end of a ten-year war. Some of the most important features of the Trojan War tale have no place in it. If you are already something of a mythology buff, you might remember that the ultimate cause of the war was the goddess Strife throwing a golden apple (with "For the most beautiful" written on it) into the middle of a wedding reception to which she was not invited. Not in the *Iliad.* There's no Trojan horse, either, and the Trojan horse is a pretty big deal. And it is not just the big wooden horse that's missing from the end of the war. When the poem comes to a close, Achilles has not yet been shot (in the heel or anywhere else) by Paris, Paris has not yet been killed in an archery duel, Troy still stands, and Odysseus hasn't yet set off for his ten years of wandering before he can return home.

What we are getting at here is the problem we raised above: delineating *a* myth—that is, answering a question like "What's the myth of Oedipus?" or "What's the story of the Trojan War?"—is tricky business, particularly when it comes to Greek myths, since evidence for them comes from a complex literary and artistic tradition that spans almost two millennia. All the information about a myth has to be organized, the different versions evaluated for reliability and interest, the contradictory bits accounted for somehow (or smoothed over to give a better presentation), and a decision reached as to how much detail to include—the alternative is simply to collect all the ancient quotations that mention Oedipus and put them together in one place and let the person who asked the question sort it all out. For Oedipus, that would entail an enormous amount of material (including the two *Oedipus* plays of Sophocles in their entirety). For other mythical figures there might be nothing more than a few sentences.

Another problem is evaluating all those sources. Is an earlier source better than a later one? Is a poetic source better than a prose one? Is a longer source better than a short one? More fundamental than such questions, however, is the very nature of *all* our sources for Greek myths. Myths are, at least in some scholars' minds, properly regarded as traditional stories that depend to some extent on oral transmission. In other words, myths are the stories that members of a society tell each other, passing those stories along by retelling what they themselves have heard, all the while altering here, cutting there, even inventing entirely new stories or elements of stories. What we have from the ancient Greek world is, by contrast, a literary tradition, and that involves an entirely different sort of transmission. Is Sophocles' *Oedipus Tyrannus* the same thing as the "myth of Oedipus"? Not really. Instead, it's just one very highly literary *version* of the myth. The myth, in turn, doesn't really exist at all. If you could gather everything ever written about Oedipus, and gather everything the ancient Greeks ever said about Oedipus, then you would have "the myth." That's impossible to do, of course, and certainly would not be very user-friendly, so when one puts forward the question "What's the myth of Oedipus?" to even the most knowledgeable and sophisticated scholar, we are likely to get something relatively straightforward and pithy after the initial hesitation. Somewhere in the back of his or her brain that scholar might be thinking, "How can I answer that when I don't know precisely what 'myth' means?" or "How can I possibly convey all the wealth of material we know about Oedipus?" but you're not likely to have to suffer through lengthy discussions of those questions. You'll hear about the oracles, the exposure of Oedipus, his unwitting killing of his father, his solution to the riddle of the Sphinx, his marriage to his mother, the discovery of his true identity, and his blinding himself. In short, in reply to a query like "What is the myth of Oedipus?" you will receive a reply that aims at simplicity, accuracy, and completeness balanced against brevity and practicality.

People have been asking questions in the form of "What is the myth of X?" for centuries. What is important to grasp here is that the Greeks themselves asked that question countless times. When an ancient wanted to know what Oedipus' story was, he did not go to a performance of *Oedipus Tyrannus*. That would have been as inefficient for him as reading the play would be for you. In many cases, he turned to a reference work that provided a simple, accurate, complete, brief, and practical account of the myth. He turned, in other words, to a work like those in this volume, Apollodorus' *Bibliotheke* or Hyginus' *Fabulae*. That is, he turned to mythography.

When consulting our works he would have found the following accounts of the Oedipus myth (Apollodorus' [2.48–56] is on the left, Hyginus', which is split into two stories, on the right):[1]

After the death of Amphion, Laios succeeded to the kingdom. He married Menoiceus' daughter, whom some call Iocaste and others Epicaste. They received an oracle not to have children (for their offspring would be a patricide), but Laios got drunk and slept with his wife. After boring through its ankles with pins, Laios gave the child to a shepherd to expose. But although

66 Laius: Laius son of Labdacus received a prophecy from Apollo warning him to beware death at the hands of his own son. So, when his wife, Jocasta, Menoeceus' daughter, gave birth, he ordered the child to be exposed. It just so happened that Periboea, King Polybus' wife, was at the shore washing clothes, found the exposed child, and took it in. When Polybus found out, because

1. One of the obvious differences is the spelling of the proper names. In the translation, introduction, and the endnotes of Apollodorus, we transliterate directly from the Greek, which often differs slightly from Hyginus' Latinate spellings.

the shepherd exposed it on Mount Cithairon, some herders of Polybos, the king of the Corinthians, found the infant and brought it to the king's wife, Periboia. She adopted it and passed it off as her own. After treating its ankles, she called it Oidipous, giving this name because its feet had swollen. When the boy grew up, he surpassed his peers in strength. Out of jealousy they mocked him for not really being his parents' son. He asked Periboia, but was not able to find out the truth. So he went to Delphi and inquired about his own parents. The god told him not to travel to his country, for he would kill his father and have sex with his mother. When he heard this, he left Corinth behind, believing that he had been born from those who were said to be his parents. While riding in a chariot through Phocis on a certain narrow stretch of road he ran into Laios driving in a chariot. Polyphontes, who was Laios' herald, ordered Oidipous to get out of the way and killed one of his horses because of the holdup caused by his refusal to do so. So Oidipous became enraged and killed both Polyphontes and Laios. Then he arrived in Thebes.

Now, Damasistratos, king of the Plataians, buried Laios, and Creon son of Menoiceus succeeded to the throne of Thebes. While he was king, a great misfortune befell the city; Hera sent the Sphinx, whose mother was Echidna and whose father was Typhon. She had the face of a woman; the chest, feet, and tail of a lion; and the wings of a bird. She had learned a riddle from the Muses, set herself up on Mount Phicion, and proposed it to the Thebans. This was the riddle: What is four-footed and two-footed and three-footed though it has but one voice? The Thebans had at that time an oracle that they would be rid of the Sphinx when they solved her riddle. So they gathered together often to search for what the answer was. And when they did not find it, she would snatch and devour one of them. After many had died, and last of all Creon's son Haimon, Creon proclaimed that he would give both they had no children, they raised him as their own, naming him Oedipus because his feet had been pierced.

67 Oedipus: When Oedipus, the son of Laius and Jocasta, reached manhood, he was the strongest of all his peers. As they were envious of him, they accused him of not really being Polybus' son because Polybus was so gentle yet he was so brash. Oedipus felt that their claim had some merit, so he went to Delphi to inquire about his parentage. Laius was experiencing ominous signs that told him that death at his son's hands was near. So he too set out on his way to Delphi, and Oedipus ran into him on the way. The king's guards ordered him to make way for the king. Oedipus refused. The king drove the horses on anyway and ran over Oedipus' foot with the wheel. Oedipus grew angry and threw his father from the chariot, killing him without realizing who he was.

Upon Laius' death, Creon son of Menoeceus took power. Meanwhile, the Sphinx, the daughter of Typhon, was running loose in Boeotia and destroying the Thebans' crops. She issued a challenge to King Creon: if someone solved the riddle she posed, she would leave the area; if, however, the person did not solve the riddle, the Sphinx said she would devour him. Under no other circumstances would she leave the territory.

When the king heard these conditions, he made a proclamation throughout Greece. He promised to grant his kingdom and his sister Jocasta in marriage to the man who solved the riddle of the Sphinx. In their desire to be king many came and were devoured by the Sphinx. Oedipus son of Laius came and solved the riddle, upon which the Sphinx threw herself to her death. Oedipus was given his father's kingdom and, not knowing who she was, his mother as wife. By her he fathered Eteocles, Polynices, Antigone, and Ismene.

Meanwhile, Thebes was stricken with a crop failure and a shortage of grain because of the kingdom and Laios' wife to the man who solved the riddle. When Oidipous heard this, he solved it, saying that the answer to the riddle spoken by the Sphinx was a human being, because a person is four-footed as an infant carried on four limbs, two-footed when grown up, and in old age takes a staff as a third foot. Then the Sphinx threw herself off of the acropolis, and Oidipous both received the kingdom and unwittingly married his mother. With her he had sons, Polyneices and Eteocles, and daughters, Ismene and Antigone, though there are some who say that the children's mother was Euryganeia daughter of Hyperphas.

When what was hidden was later revealed, Iocaste hanged herself in a noose, and Oidipous put out his eyes and was driven out of Thebes. He laid curses on his sons because they watched him being banished from the city and did not come to his aid. He came with Antigone to Colonos in Attica, where the sanctuary of the Eumenides is, and sat down as a suppliant. He was received as a guest by Theseus and died not long afterward.

Oedipus' crimes. When he asked Tiresias why Thebes was plagued with this, he responded that if a descendant of the Sparti was still alive and died for his country, it would be freed from the plague. Then Menoeceus, Jocasta's father, threw himself from the city walls to his death.

While all of this was going on in Thebes, Polybus died in Corinth. When Oedipus heard this, at first he took it badly because he was under the assumption that it was his father who had died. But Periboea informed him that he was adopted, and at the same time the old man Menoetes (the one who exposed him) recognized from the scars on his feet and ankles that he was Laius' son. When Oedipus heard this and realized that he had committed so many horrible crimes, he removed the brooches from his mother's dress and blinded himself. He then handed his kingdom over to his sons to share in alternate years and went from Thebes into exile with his daughter Antigone as his guide.

In about 600 words, both Apollodorus and Hyginus give perfectly competent answers to anyone who wonders what the myth of Oedipus is, and they cover essentially the same material. But there are differences too, usually matters of detail. For instance, Apollodorus gives the Sphinx's riddle, but Hyginus does not. Apollodorus describes how Jocasta killed herself, but Hyginus does not mention her death at all (though it can be assumed). On the other hand, Apollodorus leaves out the story of Jocasta's father entirely and is quite vague about how the whole sordid affair came to light, while Hyginus describes it in some detail, even giving the name of the servant who exposes the infant Oedipus and recognizes him as an adult. Such differences are to be expected given the nature of the process: boiling down multiple, often conflicting, sources into a single account. Apollodorus even occasionally allows different details to emerge; for instance, many who are familiar with the Oedipus myth or even the Freudian Oedipus complex might be surprised to read in Apollodorus that some Greeks thought that the mother of Oedipus' children was not his own mother Jocasta, but a woman named Euryganeia!

Mythography and the Study of Myth

From the brief examples of the Oedipus myth above, you can glimpse the nature of mythography and what ancient mythographers were aiming at: *retelling or paraphrasing* myths to capture their essential features, or at least their essential plots, and provide a reliable version without embellishment. To this we should add that there is a second kind of mythography, concerned with *interpreting or analyzing* myths to explain their origin, function, inner logic, hidden meanings, and so on, but since Apollodorus and Hyginus are predominantly engaged in the first type, we will only lightly touch on this kind in the course of our discussion. Both sorts of mythography, however, share one overriding feature: they approach myths from an external and essentially nonartistic perspective in an attempt to make sense of them.

Because of this conscious detachment from the subject matter, mythographic works never did and never will compete with the vivid and imaginative creations of the great poets—such as Homer, Sophocles, or Ovid—and have therefore been relegated to a second-class existence. Up until recently few of the mythographic works that have survived from antiquity had been translated into English. And while many people at least recognize the great names of Homer, Sophocles, and Ovid, few have heard the word "mythography" or understand the genre of writing associated with it, and even most professional classicists would be hard pressed to come up with more than a couple of ancient mythographers off the top of their head. The two names most likely to occur to those classicists are Apollodorus and Hyginus, an indication of these writers' importance.

To be sure, mythography will never appear on anyone's top ten list of great achievements from the ancient world, but that does not mean that it is of limited value in the modern study of myth. On the contrary, we rely a great deal on ancient mythographers precisely because they were not trying to enchant or entertain but organize and simplify. To take the works translated here, the *Bibliotheke* and the *Fabulae* attempt to organize and recapitulate the entire vast array of stories that constituted what the ancients thought of as the body of Greek myth (there is nothing of what we might call Roman myth in the former, and precious little in the latter, though it is written in Latin). This project in and of itself was impossible, of course, in works as brief as these, but Apollodorus makes a more credible job of it than many modern equivalents, and Hyginus would perhaps appear at least a little more successful if the text of his work had not suffered so much in coming down to us (more on this in the introduction to the *Fabulae*). These writers' testimony is invaluable, not least because of their attempt to be exhaustive.

In short, anyone interested in Greek myth profits through an understanding of the mythographic writings that survive from antiquity, and those of Apollodorus and Hyginus most of all. A modern anthropologist working in a contemporary culture might have access to live retellings of stories in an ongoing mythical tradition to help put his or her analysis in a wider context. We, unfortunately, have absolutely no such access to the myths of the Greeks and Romans, so we use all the evidence at our disposal, from dramatic productions (perhaps a Greek tragedy), to references found in other works (say, Aristotle's discussion of that Greek tragedy in his *Poetics*), to artistic representations (for instance, a painted Greek vase showing a scene from the play). Works of mythography—with their discussion, categorization, paraphrase, and interpretation of myths found scattered in the rest of ancient literature—are immensely valuable witnesses. If the myths and the justly famous literary tellings of those myths are among the most important parts of the artistic and cultural legacy that has come down to us from the Greeks and the Romans, we ought not to despise what the ancient mythographers wrote about them, and we have much to learn by looking at the mythographers' explicit and implicit criteria of inclusion, what they find most important when summarizing, how they attempt to reconcile variants or relate two different myths, and their place in transmitting myth in the wider culture.

In a more basic way, we often rely heavily on mythographers for the very content of the myths. In most literary works we usually do not get narration of a myth in its entirety but rather incomplete references or passing allusions, and in many instances we have no literary versions of a myth at all, either because none was ever produced in antiquity or because, like so much ancient literature, it was lost. It is mythographers who continually fill in the details or give the entire scheme of a story. The debt we owe the mythographers, and Apollodorus and Hyginus above all, can be seen in scholarly footnotes and source citations in just about any book having to do with Greek myth. Just to give one example, Timothy Gantz's invaluable *Early Greek Myth: A Guide to Literary and Artistic Sources* (The Johns Hopkins University Press: Baltimore, 1996), though particularly concerned with finding the earliest attestations for myths and their details in the tradition, cites for specifics our two authors over and over despite their late dates (at least seven centuries after the earliest surviving Greek literary works).

Modern Mythography

What makes the undervaluation of ancient mythographic works more surprising is that modern books paraphrasing or interpreting myths—corresponding to the two kinds of mythography discussed above—enjoy great popularity, not to mention robust sales. We generally do not call these modern books "mythography" (or their authors "mythographers") because we use the term in a restricted sense, to refer specifically to ancient writing about myth. There are differences, of course, between ancient and modern mythographers, but most of these stem from the obvious fact that ancient mythographic works were written for ancient audiences, and their requirements and tastes were different from our own. But the basic impulse, method, and execution remain the same.

Examples of modern mythography are not hard to find. In the United States Thomas Bulfinch's *The Age of Fable* (1855) and Edith Hamilton's *Mythology* (1942) were both designed for comprehensive retelling of myths in a form palatable to contemporary American audiences and have captivated generations. In fact, though these two venerable volumes have had many imitators, they still sit perched atop the heap—to give an indication of their enduring popularity, as this General Introduction was being written, they occupied the top three slots in sales rankings in the category of "Mythology, Classical" at the website of the bookseller Barnes & Noble (two different printings of Hamilton hold the top two places). As time goes on and both the audience for Greek myth and our understanding of the ancient world change, new treatments will no doubt strive to displace these by recapitulating the myths in new and different forms, just as Bulfinch and Hamilton pushed aside their predecessors, and just as Apollodorus and Hyginus varied in how they approached their task. Sometimes the authors of this sort of book attempt to provide interpretation as well as paraphrase, but they often date themselves quickly as scholarship and society evolve. Robert Graves' *The Greek Myths* (1955), for instance, has not held up as well as Bulfinch and Hamilton, mostly because of the rather idiosyncratic interpretations woven throughout the book. It remains to be seen whether more recent efforts at paraphrasing will stand the test of time. The best of these in English, Richard Martin's *Myths of the Ancient Greeks* (New American Library: New York, 2003), an excellent overview, adds evaluative comments in a responsible but light-handed way.

No less numerous are modern interpretive books on myth, which investigate the nature and origins of myths; their place in ancient thought, literature, and religion; and even their continued relevance to the contemporary world as narrative models or as stories with hidden, deeper meanings—witness the phenomenal success of Joseph Campbell's books. Some of these are written by specialists for other scholars, some for use in classrooms (where courses in classical myth are often some of the most popular on campus), and some for consumption by the public. Of those in English directed at a nonspecialist audience but written by scholars, G. S. Kirk's *The Nature of Greek Myths* (Overlook Press: Woodstock, NY, 1974) and Fritz Graf's *Greek Mythology: An Introduction* (The Johns Hopkins University Press: Baltimore, translated from German in 1993) are the best examples. Broadly speaking, we might say that these modern treatments correspond reasonably well to ancient mythographic works of this second sort—that is, those interested in providing interpretation and evaluation, not paraphrase—but the resemblance between ancient and modern examples of this type of mythography is not nearly as close as that of the other kind. Since the act of interpretation is tied so closely to contemporary intellectual currents and there is a vast gulf between those of antiquity and today, modern scholarly analysis of myth and ancient interpretive mythography are very different enterprises, sharing only a common intent.

The Development of Mythography

What unites the two different strains of ancient mythography? Above all, both are fundamentally concerned with bringing order to the chaotic Greek mythical traditions handed down by oral, literary, and artistic traditions. This is immediately obvious in the interpretive works, but it should not be forgotten that behind the apparently simple task of retelling there is an attempt to take incomplete, contradictory, and often remote traditional stories and produce an account of Greek myths that is at once reasonably comprehensive, reasonably consistent, and reasonably accessible. Although it is impossible here to provide a comprehensive treatment of mythography, a brief survey of the main developments and some of the more important mythographers is worthwhile, if for no other reason than because the *Bibliotheke* and *Fabulae* are products of this long and rich tradition.

Considering that the underlying impulse of mythography is to make sense of what seems at first intractable, we ought not be surprised that we can trace mythography back to the sixth and fifth centuries BC. During that period thought was being revolutionized in many ways as the Greeks began to search for rational and consistent explanations for everything from natural phenomena to the various aspects of human society, leading to the development of early science and new forms of critical literature. Much of this new literature began for the first time in Greek culture to be written in prose—as opposed to poetry—and prose became the normal mode of expression for these pursuits in the centuries to come. The two most important literary genres to arise from this ferment were history and philosophy, but right alongside them arose mythography, which similarly attempted to organize and explain the world in rational ways. In fact, mythography, even if it has not fared as well in esteem or interest among later generations, nonetheless shares more than a general intellectual background and outlook with its more prestigious cousins—it often overlaps them and is intertwined with them, particularly history.

That overlap is sometimes so strong when it comes to history that perhaps initially we ought to think of mythography not as a separate genre of writing but as one differing only in the kind of material the authors were working with. Let us turn for a moment to Herodotus' *Histories* (written in the mid-fifth century BC about the Persian invasions of the 490s and 480s), often regarded as the first history proper—in fact, the word "history" ("inquiry") in that more limited sense derives from Herodotus' opening sentence. The work begins by giving a striking and fascinating version of the origins of the conflict between Greece and Persia, or more broadly, between Europe and Asia. Persian storytellers, Herodotus reports, say that the struggle can be traced back to the events recounted in some of the most famous of Greek myths—those of Io, Europa, Medea, and Helen—which are linked into a chain of reciprocal abductions that increasingly raise tensions between East and West. Herodotus then declares that he will not analyze these stories, but rather begin his account with the earliest individual he himself *knows* to have harmed the Greeks in a way and at a time that were connected directly to the later conflict, King Croesus of Lydia (a historical king in what would today be western Turkey, who reigned from around 560 until 546 BC).

Thus Herodotus implicitly recognizes categories that we might think of as *prehistorical* and *historical,* but the first member of the pair might just as easily be thought of as *mythical.* What is most interesting here for a discussion of mythography is not just that Herodotus treats something mythical at the start of his history, or that he relays Persian accounts (which he very well may have invented), but the particular form these accounts take. His original audience knew the stories intimately, but even today they are not unfamiliar: Zeus, in love with the mortal Io, princess of the Greek city of Argos, lures her away from home and transforms himself into a thundercloud to hide his dalliance with her; Zeus again, this time disguised as a bull, abducts the Phoenician princess Europa and carries her off to Crete; Medea leaves Colchis in Asia with Jason when the Argonauts bring the Golden Fleece back to Greece; and Paris takes the Spartan queen Helen back home with him to Asiatic Troy, an event that directly leads to the Trojan War. But Herodotus relays very different forms of these stories. Phoenician traders kidnapped Io. As payback, some Greeks abducted Europa. It might have ended with that tit-for-tat, but the Greeks then practically guaranteed a further decline in international relations by carrying off Medea. The Greeks refused to make recompense, so Paris resolved to commit an equally brazen act and took Helen. At this point, open warfare erupted, creating a grand East versus West conflict that Herodotus saw as directly connected to the Greek versus Persian wars of his own day.

What we have here in Herodotus is nothing less than mythography, or at least a particular type of mythography—rationalizing—that exists later as a distinct and separate form, best known from the writings of Palaephatus, whom we will discuss briefly below. The basic method of rationalists is to remove all supernatural elements from a myth in order to transform it into something entirely ordinary, or at least something somehow explicable by common sense about what constitutes normal cause and effect. The underlying assumption is that myths as they have come down to us are the products of successive misunderstandings (and distortions intentionally introduced by storytellers or poets) that have metamorphosed perfectly normal events into fantastic tales of gods, heroes, magic, and monsters. And Herodotus is not the only historian to engage in rationalizing of myth; as we will see below, the few fragments that remain of his predecessor Hecataeus also show signs of rationalizing.

Herodotus' own attitude toward the mythical and divine is complex, not least because of his habit of attributing mythical stories to other people and begging off fuller discussion of his thoughts of such matters. A generation later, the attitude of the historian Thucydides, who wrote an account of the Peloponnesian War between Athens and Sparta, is crystal clear. His absolute rejection of anything mythical as a secure basis of determining fact makes him widely regarded as the first practitioner of objective history. Nevertheless, Thucydides too began his history by engaging with the mythical. Why? Because, simply put, he had to. As with Herodotus and the history of warfare between Europe and Asia, Thucydides could see in his analysis of developments in Greece a reasonably clear dividing line between an earlier time from which evidence was primarily in the form of mythical accounts and a later time in which there was a multitude of different kinds of evidence. Both kinds of evidence could be subjected rigorously to rational evaluation, but only the application of such methods to the evidence from the later periods was properly history, for only in that case was there enough context to permit strong confidence in the results. Still, the basic point here is that myths, when critical methods were applied to them, could reveal something useful to the historian in the ancient world, and when it comes to the early history of Greece—the history of Greece, that is, before history was invented!—the strongest evidence was the content of the myths passed down from previous generations.

So the Greeks, at the beginning of critical inquiry, faced a past that was entirely mythical. That is not to say that it was a fictional past, but a past that contained fiction and truth in various proportions and that was to differing degrees subject to rational analysis. It is really no surprise, then, that historians were occupied with myth. The entire body of Greek myths could not simply be ignored or swept away—no society can wave a wand and have its past disappear—but myths could be made the object of study in an attempt to understand that past. Herodotus and Thucydides did not develop their attitudes about and methods of analyzing myth in a vacuum, but very little remains of their contemporaries and immediate predecessors. We consider Herodotus and Thucydides historians because they were concerned primarily with events on *this* side of the dividing line between mythical prehistory and history. There were early writers—mythographers—concerned solely or overwhelmingly with events on *that* side of the divide. Although we have only meager fragments of their work, it is clear that there was essentially no difference between what a mythographer did and what a historian did—there was merely a difference of material—and the same individual might just as well be both.

Important Early Mythographers

The two most important early figures in prose mythography, Acusilaus and Hecataeus, are excellent illustrations of this. Before their time, the cataloging and organization of Greek myths was done entirely by the same poets who were creating and transmitting them. The best-known example, of course, is Hesiod. His *Theogony* not only tells the story of the creation of the gods but is arranged such that genealogical connections provide a framework. So too the *Catalog of Women,* a later continuation (perhaps not by Hesiod) of the *Theogony,* which traces the lineages of the great heroes. But the perspective is entirely internal—it is organization subordinated to artistic intent and storytelling—in such works as this. The prose mythographers, by contrast, wrote from the outside looking in. Acusilaus flourished just before the Persian Wars that broke out in the early fifth century BC. Later Greek tradition sometimes identifies him as "the first historian," but the subject matter of this work, to judge by the surviving fragments, was solely mythical: the origin of the gods, Heracles, the battle of the gods and giants, the children of Deucalion, and so forth. Perhaps this is an indication that the ancients were not so rigorous about making the distinction between mythographers and historians as we are. Later generations applied two titles to this book, *Histories* and *Genealogies.* The organization, to judge by the latter title and by the surviving fragments, was strongly based on lines of descent—just the sort of organization Apollodorus was to employ centuries later. The scope, like Apollodorus', was broad, covering the origins of the gods down to the various legendary heroic myths, and so it is perhaps not surprising to find that Apollodorus cites Acusilaus by name several times (though this does not mean he read Acusilaus directly; he may have been working with intermediary sources). Since there is only the slightest trace of interpretation present in the surviving fragments (see *fr.* 32 Fowler), perhaps Acusilaus was mostly interested in reconciling the conflicting genealogies present in the contemporary oral tradition and inherited from the earlier poetic tradition, and that was method enough to be revolutionary. Acusilaus, then, was clearly one of the originators of the first sort of mythography we have delineated, namely, that which aimed at organization and recapitulation.

Hecataeus was active perhaps just a decade or two after Acusilaus and personally involved in the Ionian revolt that led to the Persian Wars. He too, like Acusilaus, is called by some ancient authorities the "oldest historian." He was famous in antiquity for his *Journey around the World,* a geographical survey that treated the known world, and, more importantly for us, a work variously known as *Histories, Genealogies,* or *Heroology,* which survives in thirty or forty fragments. Like Acusilaus' *Histories/Genealogies,* Hecataeus' book traced myths via lines of descent, even connecting them to the contemporary world. But he was not just interested in mere recapitulation of family trees embellished by stories, valuable as that activity was. His opening sentence is justly famous: "Hecataeus the Milesian says this: I write what follows as it seems to me to be true, for the stories [*muthoi*] of the Greeks, as I see them, are many and laughable." A few of the fragments reveal that this skepticism flowered into outright rationalizing, which influenced Herodotus and others. For instance, Hecataeus evidently thought the three-headed Cerberus, canine guardian of the underworld, was beyond belief, and he explained away the creature as a "terrible serpent" known as the "hound of Hades" from the fatal effects of its venom (*fr.* 27 Fowler). Most of the fragments do not, however, contain such strongly defined tendencies, even when the material is as unbelievable as Cerberus. More often found is a kind of contrarianism that does not blossom into rationalizing. When Hecataeus disagrees about the number of sons of Aegyptus: "there were, as Hesiod had it, fifty of them, or as I do, not even twenty" (*fr.* 19 Fowler). Fifty sons are simply too many to believe. This interest in the "truth" behind myths and their origins pointed the way toward the second type of mythography, the interpretive, and may explain why Apollodorus never refers to Hecataeus as an authority. Although most of the fully surviving mythographers (who are many centuries later) belong clearly to one type or the other, there is no inherent reason why a mythographer should be interested only in summarizing or interpreting but not both. In fact, it is obvious that at the early period they could be comfortably mingled within the same work.

Pherecydes, who was writing around the second quarter of the fifth century BC, is the mythographic authority cited most often by Apollodorus, and even Hyginus, whose text contains far fewer source references, names him in *Fab.* 154. Pherecydes' work, like that of the other early mythographers, is fragmentary, but it was obviously of tremendous influence. The surviving fragments reveal several characteristics that would have commended him to later authors: a straightforward and lively style that can be glimpsed in the longer fragments, an admirable and detailed comprehensiveness, and a knack for presenting the stories smoothly. The overall organization of the work is difficult to grasp in its current state, but genealogy was a prime focus here too. Once again, we find an early mythographer straddling the lines of myth and history (Pherecydes is referred to by later sources as both a genealogist and a historian), and one of the notable features of his writings was an attempt to tie the mythical genealogies into contemporary ones. One fragment, for instance, traces the lineage of the fifth-century Athenian politician and general Miltiades step-by-step back to the son of Ajax, one of the heroes of the Trojan War.

Hellanicus of Lesbos, another fifth-century mythographer of importance, is never named by Apollodorus as an authority, but scholars have identified a few places in the *Bibliotheke* where material derives ultimately from him (particularly the section on Trojan genealogy). The fragments of his many works, though quite numerous (thereby attesting to his importance as a source for later authors, who cite him frequently), do not allow us to form a judgment with certainty. Still, it is clear that Hellanicus treated myth in what might be said to be a complete fashion, covering almost every major region and lineage of the Greek world, and that his work was of particular importance for his treatment of the myths of Athens, as well as for Troy and the Trojan War, including events such as Aeneas' flight after the city's fall. A contemporary of Herodotus, and often mentioned together with him, Hellanicus was also a figure of tremendous importance for the development of the writing of history. In particular, his interest in establishing secure chronologies gave a firm foundation to dating the events of Greek history. That interest in establishing systematic and consistent chronology seems to have carried over also into his mythographic works. Intriguingly, his *Atthis,* the first attempt to tell the entire history of Athens, involved arranging prehistorical (i.e., mythical) "events" into a coherent narrative, after which followed more securely attested historical data in a seamless whole. Although his style does not seem from the fragments to have been anywhere near as appealing as Pherecydes' or Herodotus', his encyclopedic mix of breadth and detail, as well as his reliability, meant that his work was later mined continually as a source.

Theagenes of Rhegium, a fifth-century BC scholar who worked on the Homeric epics, is traditionally credited as the first intellectual to analyze poetry allegorically by discerning beneath Homer's descriptions of gods references to the interaction of the elements of the physical world. Allegory of that sort, as well as moral and ethical allegory, became tied up intimately with larger developments in Greek philosophy, and so mythography developed a philosophical side. The earliest mythographer we know to have taken a consistently allegorizing approach is Herodorus (fifth to fourth century BC), who seems to have been primarily interested in heroic myths. The story of Heracles' holding up the sky in Atlas' place was an allegory of Heracles' mastery of astronomical knowledge. That same hero's famous lion skin was not to be taken literally; the lion skin, rather, was the impenetrable "noble purpose" that Heracles armored himself with by practicing philosophy. Herodorus seems to have been tremendously innovative, and in addition to allegory we find rationalism as well as skepticism of the most basic premises of the traditional stories. For instance, Herodorus, after carefully studying the myths of Heracles, seems to have come to the conclusion that there were at least eight different men named Heracles. The myths about the hero, he thought, resulted from the conflation of all of them combined with deliberate allegorizing on the part of poets and storytellers as well as the obscuring effects of time and misunderstanding.

In the fourth century BC Asclepiades of Tragilus in his *Subjects of Tragedies (Tragodoumena)* systematically studied the myths that were found in the plays of the tragedians. He is cited by Apollodorus twice, both times as the source of minor variants—not surprising, since Asclepiades was interested both in retelling the versions of myths found in tragedy, as well as discussing how these intersected with the earlier accounts of epic and lyric. As the tragedies, particularly those of Aeschylus, Sophocles, and Euripides, attained the status of classics during their lifetimes and immediately thereafter, Asclepiades became a valuable source for many later writers on myth. In roughly the same time frame, another scholar, Dicaearchus, produced *hypotheseis,* or "summaries," of Greek tragedies, which supposedly also evaluated the innovations of Sophocles and Euripides in their use of myths. Although these do not themselves survive, we do have other, later *hypotheseis.* Despite being little more than summaries, they are of immense value in the case of tragedies that are now lost. If they formed a coherent collection in antiquity, as seems to be the case, that would have been a quite valuable mythographic source, and some scholars see just such a source behind some of Hyginus' *Fabulae.*

Hellenistic and Imperial Mythographers

The conquests of Alexander the Great in the late fourth century BC fundamentally altered the Greek world. Greek culture, language, and ideas spread over a vast area, all of which was already inhabited by other civilizations, some of them of tremendous sophistication and prestige (one thinks particularly of Egypt). The subsequent era of Greek kingdoms thriving in non-Greek areas has become known as the Hellenistic ("Greekish") Period. Greek political and cultural dominance around the Mediterranean and in the Near East produced a vital culture with strong interests in its Greek past. It is not surprising, therefore, that the Hellenistic Greeks defined the idea of the preceding period as the Classical Age and devoted tremendous energy to studying the literature and myths of earlier times. Great centers of learning arose in Alexandria, Pergamum, and other important cities, and these in turn led to a newly professionalized scholarly class that took the Greek world to new heights of science, history, and other intellectual pursuits. When the Romans conquered these Greek kingdoms (the last, Egypt, fell in 31 BC) and incorporated them into their empire, these pursuits continued, albeit sometimes in changed form. Mythography shared in all these developments, representing, as it did, the study of one of the most important cultural elements the Hellenistic Greeks and Romans inherited from the ancient civilization of Greece.

With Palaephatus we finally come to an author whose work survives in a reasonably full state of preservation. We cannot date this author with any precision, but he may be as early as the fourth or third century BC (and thus would have lived at the very beginning of the Hellenistic Period). His *On Unbelievable Things (Peri Apiston)* has come down to us not in disconnected fragments but in a (possibly abridged) form consisting of fifty-two entries (the last several are not genuine and look little like the others). Each of these introduces a myth, usually a well-known one, and then goes on to explain the "real story" behind it. The technique is everywhere insistently rationalizing, and Palaephatus relentlessly strips the miraculous and supernatural from the story and replaces it with everyday occurrences. The results are sometimes absurd since the miraculous is often traded for the quotidian but utterly improbable. One is shocked to learn that Medea's killing of Pelias by convincing his daughters to boil him was nothing more than a spa treatment gone horribly awry. The collection also contains a preface with a clear programmatic statement of purpose explaining its author's intellectual stance: myths are distortions of certain events that have been altered beyond recognition either accidentally by the passage of time or a misunderstanding of language, or deliberately by poets and prose writers.

A particular kind of rationalizing is attributed to Euhemerus (fourth to third century BC), who was in antiquity identified variously as historian, geographer, philosopher, and poet. Euhemerism, named after the man to first employ it, essentially argues that the gods arise from the glorification of early kings and other great individuals who because of their benefactions merited immortalization by their subjects—that is, distortions of perfectly normal human affairs. Thus Demeter was immortalized as the grain goddess because she was the first human to gather, store, and cultivate grain; Zeus was worshipped as king of the gods because during his reign he was a great conqueror and provided the greatest and most numerous benefits for humankind. Euhemerus' *Sacred Treatise (Hiera Anagraphe),* which sets out the basis for his theory, is unfortunately lost. From the fragments it seems to have been a fictitious travel narrative to a utopian island in the Indian Ocean, on which Euhemerus claims to have found an inscription in the temple of Zeus revealing this "truth" about the origins of divine worship. None of this is true, of course, since it was invented (with lots of details) to give Euhemerus' radical beliefs an air of authority. Yet, this particular type of rationalism was later employed by the fragmentary mythographer Dionysius Scytobrachion (second century BC), by the historian Diodorus of Sicily (first century BC), and even later by Christian apologists grappling with pagan stories. Apollodorus cites Dionysius Scytobrachion once, a reference to his work on the Argonauts, in which he rationalized the adventures of the heroes as they sought the Golden Fleece.

Apollodorus of Athens (second century BC; not the author of the *Bibliotheke*) was one of the greatest scholars of the Hellenistic Period, and among his works one of the most widely read was his late book *On the Gods (Peri Theon).* Though it is now lost, it was of incalculable influence on later authors who considered Greek myth and religion. Taking as its starting point the names and cult-titles of the gods in Homeric epic, the work ranged over almost every conceivable related topic as it sought to explain their origin, development, and significance. Apollodorus' methods were scholarly and rationalizing, and he was used as a source both for his analysis and for basic information.

Surviving in an epitomized form are the *Constellation Myths (Catasterismoi)* of Pseudo-Eratosthenes ("pseudo" because, although these myths have come down under the name of the great Hellenistic scientist Eratosthenes, they are not genuinely his). This collection of forty-five stories belongs, like those of Apollodorus and Hyginus, to the paraphrasing strain of mythography, but its purpose is rather more limited: to tell only myths that have to do with heavenly bodies. The abridged work that we have is dated to the first century BC or AD, but the original work is some centuries earlier. This original work was also the source for the second book of Hyginus' *On Astronomy (De Astronomia),* and as it turns out, this Latin translation preserves more of the original than these epitomized Greek *Constellation Myths.*

One of the few mythographic works to survive essentially intact, Parthenius' *Sentimental* or *Unhappy Love Stories (Erotica Pathemata),* is also one of the few that we can precisely date. Parthenius, a popular Greek poet of the first century BC (we have, unfortunately, only a few fragments of his poetry), was captured by the Romans, reduced to slavery, and brought to Italy. There he regained his freedom and established relationships with some of the most important Latin poets of the age, including Vergil and Gallus. In the third quarter of the first century Parthenius compiled a brief collection of prose summaries of interesting myths—all of them having to do with love gone wrong—that had been alluded to or told in earlier Greek poetry. The compilation is prefaced with a letter from Parthenius to his friend Gallus that explains the point of the summaries: to provide raw material in the form of interesting stories for Gallus to recast and retell in his own poetry. Since only a few lines of Gallus' poetry have come to light, we have no idea whether he took up Parthenius' offer. Nonetheless, the *Erotica Pathemata,* written by a highly educated and talented poet for another cultured and famous poet, should caution us against viewing late mythography as just the ancient form of *Mythology for Dummies.* Mythography, even of the paraphrasing sort, was woven into the culture in fascinating ways and at the highest levels of society.

Conon's *Stories (Diegeseis)* is another work that survives, but only in a summary made by the ninth-century AD scholar and patriarch Photius (he found a copy bound into the same volume as the *Bibliotheke*). The original work, which is not securely datable but is probably from the first century BC or AD, contains fifty individual myths. Unlike the collections of Parthenius and Antoninus Liberalis (for the latter see below), there is no single criterion that unites these myths, though they tend toward local myths and stories that treat foundations of cities and institutions, as well as tales that contain unusual features. The approach taken in the retellings is, like that of Apollodorus and Hyginus, mostly centered on simple narration and summary, but a few of the stories show strongly rationalizing tendencies. The diversity of myths and the uneven approach, coupled with their existence only in epitomized form, make evaluation difficult.

The *Compendium of the Traditions of Greek Theology* (commonly referred to as the *Epidrome* from the first word of its Greek title) is the sole surviving work of the first-century AD Stoic philosopher Cornutus. The work does not bother to retell myth and is entirely interpretive, employing allegory and etymology to explain myth in terms of Stoic philosophy. Unlike their philosophical rivals, the Epicureans (who dismissed myth as absurd and even dangerously misleading), the Stoics had a long history of analyzing myth in this way, for they saw it as a kind of "philosophy before philosophy" (cf. the idea sometimes voiced in modern times that myth is a form of primitive science). Myths, according to this view, encoded scientific observations and moral truths behind the facade of storytelling. The proper method, however, could reveal those hidden meanings. To give but one example of Cornutus' interpretive strategy, we might point out his analysis of Zeus (2)—"Just as we are governed by a soul, so too the cosmos has a soul that holds it together, and it is called Zeus"—and he analyzes Zeus' name etymologically by deriving it from the Greek word *zen* ("to live"), asserting that "it is through Zeus that all living things have life."

Another work of allegorical mythography from approximately the same time frame as Cornutus is Heraclitus' *Homeric Problems (Homerica Problemata).* Since the time of Theagenes of Rhegium and Herodorus, allegorical interpretation had been used to defend myths against the charge of being morally corrupt or meaningless. The *Homeric Problems* is a late example of the rich intertwining of mythography and philosophy, but it is a fascinating one. Heraclitus' narrowly defined purpose is to defend Homer's *Iliad* and *Odyssey.* Heraclitus works his way through the episodes of the two poems that had been criticized, providing allegorical analysis showing that these episodes should never be taken literally but contain hidden philosophical lessons about the physical universe or moral truths. As with Cornutus' interpretive mythography, the *Homeric Problems* also relies heavily on Stoic thought and on etymologizing.

Antoninus Liberalis' *Collection of Metamorphoses (Metamorphoseon Synagoge)* is, like Parthenius' work, an example of a work of noninterpretive mythography centered on a particular theme, in this case myths involving transformation. Forty-one individual stories are contained in the collection, many of them mined from now lost poetic works. There are some general similarities with Conon's *Diegeseis,* including strong interests in local myths and unusual variations from the standard versions. We cannot date the work with any certainty, but it is probably from the second or third century AD.

Latin Mythographic Collections

We now turn to the few collections of myths written in Latin that have had the fortune to survive other than Hyginus' *Fabulae* and *On Astronomy.* The first of these is an anonymous collection of some 200 transformation stories found in Ovid's *Metamorphoses* but not entirely derived from that poem (called today the *Tellings of Ovid's Myths* or in Latin *Narrationes Fabularum Ovidianarum*). The author of the text followed the sequence of stories as they appear in the *Metamorphoses* but added details taken from other mythographic sources, one of which was Hyginus' *Fabulae.* It was once thought that this collection was composed very late, perhaps in the fifth or sixth century AD, but recently a persuasive case by Alan Cameron (see Further Reading at the end of this General Introduction) has been made for a date as early as the second or third century.

Fulgentius the mythographer was a Christian writer of the fifth or sixth century AD, possibly identical with a North African bishop of the same name who lived AD 467–532. In Fulgentius' *Myths (Mitologiae)* we find allegorical interpretations of pagan myths (although the interpretations themselves are surprisingly not overtly Christian), and like Cornutus, he consistently employs etymology to find the significance or origin of mythological names. Fulgentius separately analyzes fifty myths in three books, moving from the gods to familiar myths, often prefacing his interpretation with a retelling of the myth (some in more detail than others) before explaining its origin, meaning, or significance. Although both his Latin style and interpretation are sometimes impenetrable, he was immensely popular in the Middle Ages.

We should also mention the three Vatican Mythographers, so-called because the first editor used only manuscripts found in the Vatican Library. Despite the misleading name, these medieval collections were assembled separately at different times (ninth to twelfth century), using different sources, and containing different selections of myths. The first two Vatican Mythographers only provide straightforward accounts of stories (the first contains 234 entries in three books, the second a preface followed by 230 entries) and shun interpretation altogether. By contrast, the third Vatican Mythographer, who used Fulgentius as one of his sources, adds much allegorical interpretation. Although the authors of the first two remain anonymous, it is now generally believed that the third Vatican Mythographer was Master Alberic of London, who wrote at the end of the twelfth century. Surprisingly, none of them seems to have used Hyginus' *Fabulae.*

This catalog of mythographers records only those early fragmentary examples and the later (primarily Hellenistic and Roman) works that have survived intact. But surely there were many more handbooks and collections that have been entirely lost. It is likely that behind many *scholia*—ancient explanatory notes to texts that elaborate on mythological and other matters—lie mythographic collections that otherwise have been lost. Scholars working on Homer, for example, noted that some of the *scholia* to the *Iliad* seemed to draw consistently on the same mythographic collection now lost, and papyrus fragments have recently come to light that prove the existence of this independent collection, which circulated separately as a book in antiquity (the unknown author is designated as *Mythographus Homericus,* or the Homeric Mythographer). Other papyri containing mythological lists, summaries of tragedies, or narrative material like the *Mythographus Homericus* suggest that we have only a small fraction of what was once available to the Greeks and Romans—the proverbial tip of the iceberg.

Further Reading

Mythography has enjoyed a recent surge in scholarly interest, resulting in a greater availability of texts, commentaries, and English translations. For the early Greek mythographers there is still too little, but Robert L. Fowler has collected and re-edited for a scholarly audience the relevant Greek fragments in *Early Greek Mythography;* vol. 1, *Text and Introduction* (Oxford University Press: Oxford, 2000). He plans a second volume that will contain extensive commentary and discussion. On its appearance, we will at last have a fundamentally sound basis for future work.

The Hellenistic and Imperial mythographers have fared better. Alan Cameron's learned *Greek Mythography in the Roman World* (Oxford University Press: Oxford, 2004) contains invaluable discussion on the subject, but it is geared more for scholars than those without knowledge of Greek and Latin. An important book bringing together the Greek texts of many papyri with mythological content and providing excellent commentary on them is Monique van Rossum-Steenbeek, *Greek Readers' Digests? Studies on a Selection of Greek Sub-literary Papyri* (Brill: Leiden, 1997).

Most of the surviving collections discussed in this General Introduction are now thankfully available in English. Jacob Stern's excellent *Palaephatus: On Unbelievable Tales* (Bolchazy-Carducci Publishers: Wauconda, IL, 1996), contains faithful translation, Greek text, and a fine introduction to the author and rationalizing. Those interested in star myths may consult Theony Condos, *Star Myths of the Greeks and Romans: A Sourcebook* (Phanes Press: Grand Rapids, MI, 1997), though the translations of Ps.-Eratosthenes and Hyginus' *On Astronomy* in it are not always accurate. Parthenius' neat collection of unhappy love stories has now been fully treated in J. L. Lightfoot's scholarly *Parthenius of Nicaea: The Poetical Works and the* Erotika Pathemata (Oxford University Press: Oxford, 1999), which contains the Greek text, translation, commentary, and introduction (an earlier English translation can be found in Jacob Stern, Erotika Pathemata: *The Love Stories of Parthenius* [Garland Publishers: New York, 1992]). The fifty stories of Conon are treated at length in the scholarly work of Malcolm Brown, *The Narratives of Konon* (Saur: Munich, 2003), which provides an English translation. Unfortunately, the only translation of Cornutus into English is the unpublished doctoral thesis of R. S. Hays, *Lucius Annaeus Cornutus' Epidrome (Introduction to the Traditions of Greek Theology): Introduction, Translation, and Notes* (Diss. Univ. of Texas at Austin 1983). Heraclitus' *Homeric Problems* can now also be read in translation with the recent appearance of Donald A. Russell and David Konstan, *Heraclitus: Homeric Problems* (Society of Biblical Literature: Atlanta, 2005), which has the original Greek and a facing English translation, along with detailed commentary and an excellent introduction. Antoninus Liberalis is translated in Francis Celoria, *The Metamorphoses of Antoninus Liberalis* (Routledge: London and New York, 1992), which also contains informative and witty introduction and notes. A reader content with only samples of the mythographers may wish to consult S. M. Trzaskoma, R. S. Smith, S. Brunet (eds.), *Anthology of Classical Myth* (Hackett Publishing Co.: Cambridge, MA, 2004), where all these mythographers are represented in extracts.

INTRODUCTION TO APOLLODORUS' *BIBLIOTHEKE (LIBRARY)*

Author and Date

The author of the *Bibliotheke* is completely unknown to us. The work has come down to us attributed to Apollodorus the Grammarian, that is, Apollodorus of Athens, a second-century BC scholar and author of *On the Gods (Peri Theon)* (see the General Introduction for this scholar and the other authors mentioned below). However, it is certainly not by him, and it may well not even be by someone else named Apollodorus. The reputation and influence of Apollodorus of Athens was so great that most modern scholars suspect that it inspired someone later to use his name as a *nom de plume* in imitative flattery, a phenomenon not unknown in other genres of ancient writing. Other scenarios likewise have parallels and have been suggested: first, it may be that our author tried to pass his work off initially as an authentic work of the famous scholar, his forgery passing unremarked until modern times—it was only in 1873 that Carl Robert proved the work could not be even a mangled version of *On the Gods* or any other work of Apollodorus of Athens, and although there have been some holdouts against this position, few if any now doubt it. Second, it is perfectly plausible that the name Apollodorus simply displaced that of the real author or was attached to an anonymous work as it was transmitted through the centuries, as commonly happened. This is not to say that our author could not have been named Apollodorus, but it seems unlikely in the circumstances. Our author is, as a consequence, often referred to as Pseudo-Apollodorus, a convention we do not follow here because the writings of the genuine Apollodorus have been lost to us and there is little chance for confusion.

What else do we know about our author? Almost nothing. The date of his work can only be generally fixed. In 2.5 he refers to "the chronicler Castor" as one of the sources for a variant in Io's parentage. This is Castor of Rhodes, an author of the first century BC who constructed an international historical chronology that was widely consulted. The latest date in his chronology was 61/60 BC, and Castor was presumably writing soon after this, so we have a reasonably firm *terminus post quem* (date after which it must have been written) for Apollodorus, since he could not refer to Castor unless Castor's work was available. Pinning down a date on the other side—that is, a date before which the *Bibliotheke* was written—is rather more difficult, though there is no reason to suppose that it could be later than the beginning of the third century AD.

Attempts have been made to refine this broad range by analyzing the vocabulary and style of the author. Unfortunately, such stylistic arguments cannot provide precise answers for Greek prose of this period, though it can be helpful in other time periods and genres. The prose writings in Greek from the last century BC and the first two centuries AD simply have not been studied or statistically analyzed enough. There are too few texts of this nature from the early part of the period to provide comparison, and from the later part there are too many that are themselves undatable. The problem, in other words, is not confined to Apollodorus. He is one of many Greek authors from the Imperial period who are little more than names to us and for whom we have no biographical knowledge to anchor our researches. The accepted dates of these authors sometimes become fixed by scholarly consensus and the accumulation of circumstantial evidence, but smoking guns are rare and even so tentative a statement on our part as "probably first century AD" is to be taken as a best guess.

Anything else said about Apollodorus is pure speculation. For example, that he ignores Rome and the Romans has been used to argue for a particular date (the second century AD, when the Greeks were supposedly ignoring the Romans in their literature more than they did earlier and later) and a particular geographic origin (the eastern Mediterranean, which accounts for the lack of interest in myths about Italy). Scholars arguing in this fashion might have occasionally stumbled on the truth, but we have not been able to confirm their hypotheses. Perhaps in the future someone will notice a telling detail that has escaped previous researchers or new evidence will be uncovered that will allow us to say more.

Title, Purpose, and Audience

On the positive side of the ledger, we have no reason to doubt the authenticity of the title *Bibliotheke* (Latinized *Bibliotheca*), that is, *Library.* The title implies first of all that the contents are the results of research, that is, of the reading of other books, the knowledge from which has been brought together into one place—a whole library, in other words, in one book. It also indicates an attempt at completeness. Diodorus of Sicily's partly surviving first-century BC *Historical Library (Bibliotheke Historike),* for instance, tries to cover the entire history of the world in forty books. The beginning of Diodorus' work, which survives, contains a clear statement of his purposes, the most basic of which was characterized in the following manner by a modern scholar: "He set out to present the world with a clear, concise account of all its history, thereby obviating for the reader the necessity of contending with numerous isolated and disconnected treatises" (R. Drews, "Diodorus and his Sources," *American Journal of Philology* 83 [1962] 383). If one replaces the word "history" with "myths," the first part of the formulation provides a fair description of what Apollodorus seems to have been after: a clear, concise account of the whole of Greek myth.

As for the further purpose of the *Bibliotheke,* it seems absurd to imagine that its author really supposed it would replace the reading of the mythical narratives of epic, lyric, and tragedy, a rather incredible goal. But in this regard it must be noted that when Photios, the ninth-century Byzantine patriarch and scholar, came across and read the *Bibliotheke,* his copy included an introductory poem (we have printed it at the start of the translation) that, if it is genuine and meant in earnest, explicitly claims for the work the virtue of supplanting the great poetry of earlier Greek literature. Most modern scholars, however, do not believe the poem is the original preface of the author. If it is a later addition to the text, we can consequently suppose, more charitably, that our author intended his work to be nothing more than an introduction and an aid to the cultural masterpieces, in other words, as an encouragement to read literature rather than an attempt to replace it.

For whom was the work written? This is yet another question we cannot answer with certainty. If the *Bibliotheke* was designed for people who could read earlier Greek literature but did not want to, then the answer to our question is: the lazy, of whatever age and circumstance. If it was designed for people who could not read earlier Greek literature but wanted to or at least wanted access to the cultural content, then other answers suggest themselves: students, say, or a general audience with some formal education at a relatively low level. There is also the possibility that the *Bibliotheke* was designed as a handy guidebook for the educated. Its purpose in that case would simply have been to help remind these people of the generally accepted "standard" versions of myths and how they all fit together genealogically and chronologically, without presuming to be their only source. Professional educators might well have kept, as their modern counterparts do, a copy of a work such as this to answer questions quickly and to help prepare lectures.

All these possibilities are not mutually exclusive, and perhaps without good evidence to unlock the mystery of the author's intention we ought to focus on what uses the book might have been put to. The only audience for which it seems originally to have been unsuited is the advanced scholarly one. The work lacks any analytical interest and is neither consistently encyclopedic enough to have competed with, say, the work of Apollodorus of Athens, nor specialized enough to have garnered the kind of interest that Parthenius' collection of unhappy love stories did. That last example should give us pause. If the *Erotica Pathemata* had survived without its introductory letter and with no indication of who the author was, would modern scholars have correctly divined that it was written by one of the leading Greek poets of the first century BC and was specifically intended to provide raw material for the Latin poetry of a friend? Almost certainly not.

Even if we grant that the *Bibliotheke* was not originally viewed as a product of a brilliant mind engaged in imposing scholarly industry or as a scholarly tool for high-level research, it is a perfectly competent work and would have been well suited to all the potential audiences outlined above. Furthermore, in the changing cultural, educational, and literary circumstances of the early centuries AD, it is possible that the book itself became perceived differently by different readers. We can certainly say that by the Middle Ages it represented for Byzantine scholars a work of great scholarship (the attribution to Apollodorus of Athens would not have hurt in this regard) since so much else had been lost, and it is quoted many times in their work as an authority.

This inconclusive stance on our part is not necessarily shared by other scholars, some of whom feel more comfortable identifying one of these audiences as *the* audience. J.-C. Carrière and B. Massonie, for instance, in the introduction to their French translation (*La Bibliothèque d'Apollodore,* Les Belles Lettres: Paris, 1991) argue that the *Bibliotheke* was intended for the general literate public, but not for use in schools. M. van der Valk, in a learned and important article treating many matters having to do with Apollodorus (see Further Reading), argued that because our author has a tendency to shy away from indecent matters the book was intended "for young readers let us say for use in schools." One might object, as van Rossum-Steenbeek has recently, that plenty of indecent sexual and violent material remains, and that any self-censoring tendency is so inconsistently applied as to be almost impossible to discern. For every explicit reference to a rape that Apollodorus might have removed, we have several more left in the text. This is fatal for the specific form of van der Valk's analysis (as is the fact that as so often in such cases, the one making the argument is the one deciding what is indecent), though the general thesis that the book was a school manual, which has been put forward by other scholars before and after van der Valk, may well be correct.

Content and Organization

The *Bibliotheke* is the surviving ancient mythographic work with the widest scope, treating practically the whole of mainstream Greek myth down to the death of Odysseus after his return from the Trojan War and reliably hitting the highlights along the way. Thus, a reader will find the birth of the Olympian gods, the myths of the major heroes (Jason, Heracles, Bellerophontes, Theseus, Perseus), the stories that focus on various local dynasties (at Argos, Thebes, Athens, etc.), as well as a variety of other myths, many of which are rather less familiar today than they were in antiquity. Apollodorus does not begin, as Hesiod did in his *Theogony,* with the creation of primordial deities such as Chaos, Ge, and Ouranos, but with Ouranos' kingship and marriage to Ge, for this is the beginning of narrative myth. There is no story to tell of Chaos, just that it was. There is nothing to say of Earth's coming into existence other than that it did so. Beginning with Ouranos allows Apollodorus immediately to introduce genealogy (Ouranos and Ge have their first children in the second sentence of the book) and dynastic succession (Ouranos is designated in the first sentences as the first to rule), which are the two main intertwined organizing principles that Apollodorus will use to structure the whole. Who gives birth to whom and who succeeds whom to the throne of which country or city are the questions that move the narrative forward through time.

We divide the *Bibliotheke* today into three books, but the third book is broken off and the remainder of the work exists only in an abridged form (we will return to this below). These book divisions were introduced into the first modern edition of the work and do not occur in the surviving manuscripts, but we do have external evidence in the form of citations (specifying, for instance, that a certain story was found in the first book of Apollodorus) that the work in fact was broken up into three books in antiquity.

Book 1 covers the gods as well as the mortal lineages that spring from Deucalion, the mortal son of the Titan Prometheus. Book 2 covers the lineage of Inachos, the Argive river god. Book 3 and the surviving epitomes of the end of the work cover the lineage of Agenor, the mortal son of Poseidon, until 3.96, when Apollodorus loops around to begin gathering all the loose ends and stray genealogies in order to prepare for his account of the Trojan War, the culminating event, as the Greeks saw it, of their mythical heritage. The overall arrangement is as follows (the numbers referring to subsections within each book and the epitomes are entirely modern in origin):

I. Theogony 1.1–44
II. Lineage of Deucalion 1.45–147
III. Lineage of Inachos 2.1–180
IV. Lineage of Agenor 3.1–95
V. Lineage of Pelasgos 3.96–109
VI. Lineage of Atlas 3.110–155
VII. Lineage of Asopos 3.156–176
VIII. Kings of Athens 3.177–218, plus E.1.1–24
IX. Lineage of Pelops E.2.1–16
X. Events of the Trojan War before the *Iliad* of Homer E.3.1–35
XI. Summary of the *Iliad* E.4.1–8
XII. Events of the Trojan War after the *Iliad* of Homer E.5.1–25
XIII. The Aftermath of the Trojan War E.6.1–30
XIV. The Wanderings of Odysseus E.7.1–40

There is admirable genealogical economy in this scheme, with the myriad figures of myth fitting into a relatively few main genealogies. The three lineages of Deucalion, Inachos, and Agenor take up the bulk of the work, but then it becomes quite complex.

The hinge here is the figure of Pelasgos. Although he is first mentioned in 2.2 in his appropriate genealogical place as an early descendant of Inachos, Apollodorus delays the discussion of Pelasgos (3.96) a full book and a half until after the lineage of Agenor. This displacement of Pelasgos, which might at first sight seem surprisingly unmotivated, is, in fact, crucial, for it sets up the entire rest of the narrative as we move toward the Trojan War and introduces another secondary organizational principle: the geographic. Genealogy and dynastic succession are still the dominant modes, but not all major figures of Greek myth (and certainly not all stories) easily connect into the preceding genealogies, and so other considerations take precedence. Pelasgos' descendants will populate Arcadia—Arcadia, in turn, allows us to transition (in 3.110) to the myths of the daughters of Atlas, who are born there. But all this is not random. Pelasgos has been carefully delayed because of Arcadia, and Arcadia becomes the link (via Atlas' daughter Taygete) to Sparta (3.116–128). The Spartan genealogy brings us to Helen, which brings us to her suitors and marriage (3.129–137), which bring us to the Trojans (in 3.138), and thence ultimately to the Trojan War, though other major characters in the war need to be brought onto the stage before we get there. This is cleverly arranged and as seamless as one could possibly expect under the circumstances. Above all, Apollodorus has an end point in mind, namely, the Trojan War, and at 3.96 we turn the corner and head toward the finish line. Genealogy is never abandoned, but other priorities are allowed to come to the fore when a purely genealogical approach would be unproductive.

The dominance of genealogy throughout the bulk of the early portion of the narrative, as we have seen, is not unique to Apollodorus and was by no means his invention. Most of the connections and chronology had been established by earlier mythographers such as Pherecydes and Hellanicus (see General Introduction) long before Apollodorus wrote. In fact, the genealogical impulse combined with narrative appears strong and early in Greek literature even before the development of scholarly mythography as such, and is ultimately the product of poetic tradition. In the fifth book of Homer's *Iliad,* when the heroes Diomedes and Glaucos meet, the latter gives a rapid but complete account of his family history (he was the son of Hippolochos son of Bellerophontes son of another Glaucos, the son, in turn, of Sisyphos), taking the time to tell the story of Bellerophontes in full. Not much later than the *Iliad,* the *Theogony* of Hesiod gives an account of the origins of the universe and the gods that weaves narrative around a genealogical framework, concluding with some heroic genealogy. Its continuation, the poetic *Catalog of Women,* though probably not by Hesiod, carried the scheme even further into heroic genealogies, and this work probably inspired the large-scale mythographic attempt to organize myth in coherent ways.

One element of genealogical organization is, of course, the chronological. As we pointed out above, the focus on genealogy and dynastic succession creates a built-in chronological scheme (parents come before their children, after all, just as a king comes before his successor). But each lineage has its *own* chronological scheme, and Apollodorus adopts a practical solution. We begin with the gods and end with post–Trojan War events, so the overall sweep of the narrative is from earlier to later, but at the start of each new lineage we must move back in time. This works out quite nicely, and Apollodorus may deserve credit for the specifics of this admirable organization (it may be, of course, that he took it over in detail from an earlier mythographer). To be sure, there is some repetition and some unexplained anticipation where a myth or character not yet treated crops up, but this is absolutely unavoidable. The first mention of Heracles, for instance, is in 1.14, where he is mentioned as the killer of Linos—because Linos fits genealogically here. The full story will have to wait, however, until 2.63, when it occurs in the narrative of the myths of Heracles. In 1.19 there is a slight digression in which we are told that Zeus had suspended Hera from Olympos "for sending a storm against Heracles when he was sailing away after capturing Troy." That story will not be fully told until 2.137. In 1.35, by contrast, a full account is given of Heracles' role in the gods' battle against the Giants, while in 2.138, where it fits into the section on Heracles, there is only a single sentence that implicitly looks back to the fuller narration ("After plundering Cos, he came to Phlegra at Athena's request and alongside the gods defeated the Giants."). In each case the more detailed version of the story is told in the more appropriate location.

Apollodorus occasionally makes some use of cross-references (as with Pelasgos), which clarify how a story fits into one lineage while pointing the reader to where it is told more fully in another. These hints are often not enough for the average modern reader, but we do not generally have any idea whatsoever of how the figures of the Greek mythical system fit together. We suspect that the cultural knowledge most people in antiquity would have brought to reading the work—they certainly knew more about Heracles (that, for instance, he was related to Perseus) than the average person off the street today—would have mitigated the confusion caused by jumping around and perhaps helped them locate the major figures in the appropriate genealogy more quickly than we could without the benefit of an index such as the one in this book. The real point, however, is that Apollodorus creates a narrative that not only has a sense of momentum but is based on clear organizational principles and a sense of appropriateness. Those principles, in turn, are not rigidly or foolishly adhered to. The material at the start of the *Bibliotheke* is unlike the material at the end. Apollodorus accordingly modifies his principles as necessary and does an admirable job in making the transition. The care with which he positions certain elements of the narrative (delaying Pelasgos, for example, and using his Arcadian connection to tie in to the daughters of Atlas and then to Spartan genealogy) is really quite impressive, and we ought to admire how he does this, rather than assume that something has gone awry when he does not tell a story in its "proper" place.

Method and Sources

It is clear that the *Bibliotheke,* like all our examples of late mythography, is derivative, so the real issue is generally not whether but in what manner and to what degree it relies on its sources, though the discussion in the previous section does raise the question of whether Apollodorus himself or an earlier source deserves credit for the merits of this specific organization. There were obviously many sources that Apollodorus might have relied on, but the neatness of the whole organization and the care with which it is deployed convince us either that he is entirely responsible for it or that he took the specific scheme wholesale from an earlier source. In the latter case, the *Bibliotheke* would be in essence an abridged version of a longer work with exactly the same form, and this position has been advanced in the scholarship. The former scenario would not imply that the work is wholly original or the information was gleaned entirely from original research, but only that Apollodorus fit information he took from an earlier source or sources into a narrative that in the specifics of its overall plan was essentially and originally his. We incline toward this view, but either one would account for the fact that the cross-references show that Apollodorus had a good sense of the scope and organization of his work as he was producing it and that he did not just pick a random point and proceed from there. He either had the entire scheme worked out well in advance or had it worked out for him.

If we cannot be sure whether the organization of the whole relies on a single earlier source, we do know that the organization of individual portions and the information contained therein go back to numerous sources, both literary and mythographic. Modern scholarship has devoted a great deal of energy trying to determine the nature and extent of Apollodorus' dependency on these earlier sources. Many of the references are vague. The first occurs, for example, in 1.18: "Euterpe and the river Strymon had Rhesos, whom Diomedes killed at Troy. According to some he was Calliope's son." There are more than 130 places where Apollodorus attributes alternative stories or genealogies to unnamed sources in this or similar fashion ("some say," "according to others," "they say," and the like). While it is sometimes possible to identify specific authors that may lie behind these variants, Apollodorus' lack of precision is probably a conscious choice to indicate sometimes that the view in question was held widely enough not to bother associating it with a single individual and sometimes that the information was not ultimately attributable to a source of major importance. In this case, for instance, Rhesos' mother was never mentioned by Homer in the *Iliad,* where his story is first told. In the extant tragedy *Rhesos* (which has come down to us under the name of Euripides, though there are doubts about the attribution), Rhesos' mother is designated simply as one of the Muses. The unnamed Muse was later identified variously (and Euterpe and Calliope were not the only Muses designated for this honor, merely the two most frequently chosen), but no major literary or mythographic writers are ever credited with these identifications in any of our sources.

Another possibility, of course, is that Apollodorus did not provide specific references because he could not. In other words, if Apollodorus were simply taking his information from another source or sources that did not provide names, he could not provide names even if he wanted to. In this view, Apollodorus would have been working with one or more earlier mythographic manuals, simply transferring the information into his own work. This has implications not just for the anonymous references but also for the many places in which Apollodorus cites a source by name, either a literary source (the first: "According to Homer, however, she had him [sc. Hephaistos] with Zeus." 1.19) or a mythographic source (the first: "They say he [sc. Orion] was an *autochthon* and had a gigantic body. Pherecydes says he was the son of Poseidon and Euryale." 1.25). In the case of the Homeric reference, it is difficult to imagine that Apollodorus would not have been able to provide this reference himself since the first book of Homer's *Iliad,* where the story occurs, was one of the most widely read works of literature in the ancient classroom. But other literary references in the work are more *recherché* (Telesilla in 3.47; Philocrates in 3.176). Did Apollodorus know them directly or take them from intermediary sources? The same question applies to the mythographic sources. Did Apollodorus get his Pherecydes and Acousilaos directly or by reading mythographic manuals that had already distilled these earlier writings?

As with so much else having to do with Apollodorus, we cannot be entirely certain. At one extreme we can form a picture of an industrious Apollodorus with access to an excellent library containing everything he might want. He read widely in literary and mythographic sources of all ages, including ones rarely read in his day, taking copious notes on the origins of various myths, tracking their variations among different authors, and compiling an original account. At the other extreme we can imagine Apollodorus with a single work in front of him, a large and encyclopedic mythographic manual that contained many references gleaned from earlier mythographic works and literary texts; Apollodorus' job in this scenario is to turn this huge work into something more digestible. These are not the only two alternatives, merely the end points on a continuum, and just about any intermediary position can be imagined (and has probably been proposed by a modern scholar).

Our own feeling is that Apollodorus was utilizing several sources, but that these were generally mythographic in nature rather than literary. The occasional reference to a well-known work might come from Apollodorus' firsthand knowledge, but mythography had been practically an industry for centuries by his time. The stories told (or sometimes purportedly told—just as in modern times, mistakes are made and then passed on) in Homer, Hesiod, the tragedians, and a host of other literary authors had been collected countless times before, and the earlier mythographers' views had been rolled into this mix, so that Hesiod and Acousilaos, despite their very different natures, could be treated equally as sources (cf. 2.5 "Hesiod and Acousilaos say . . ."). It is conceivable, of course, that Apollodorus might have done all this work over again, but it is extraordinarily unlikely, even if we allow for the occasional bit of original source research.

There are still many questions that remain, however. Were Apollodorus' mythographic sources all late, or did he turn at least sometimes and in some cases to the works of Pherecydes, Acousilaos, and Hellanicus directly? A. Cameron's recent book *Greek Mythography in the Roman World* (Oxford University Press: Oxford, 2004) gives us little reason initially to think that the latter alternative is the correct one. Although Apollodorus is not the main focus of Cameron's arguments, the general impression gained from Cameron's work is that late mythography was essentially derivative and cannibalistic and that the source citations found in it, even when made in good faith (and some are most definitely not made in good faith but are clearly fraudulent, invented to add authority to the author's views), are overwhelmingly more likely to come from intermediary sources, rather than to be the result of primary source research, and inserted to give greater intellectual authority to a work. Still, some mythographers are better than others, and some sources more reliable than others; Apollodorus, it seems to us, used his sources intelligently and cogently, and to our benefit his *Bibliotheke* seems based—even if not always directly—on excellent and well-informed works. Apollodorus and his book, then, are no doubt part of the trends that Cameron describes, but they avoid the worst characteristics of the genre.

Our Index of Authors collects Apollodorus' source citations, but he is not a modern scholar and so makes no attempt to provide exhaustive source citations for every section of his work, much less for every individual piece of information. We also face a problem of preservation—there are no specifically named sources in the epitomes, so it is likely that the name of Hellanicus, probably a source for much of the Trojan material now found in the epitomes, does not appear in the *Bibliotheke* because it has been removed by the epitomators, who seem to have eliminated many references or, at the least, reduced them all to the "some say" type.

History of the Text

The earliest secure reference we have to the *Bibliotheke* dates to AD 858, when the Byzantine scholar Photios read a book that contained it (and Conon's *Diegeseis*). After summarizing Conon's work, he goes on:

> In the same volume I also read a little book by Apollodorus the Grammarian. Its title is *Bibliotheke*. It contained the ancient stories of the Hellenes about gods and

> heroes that time gave them to believe, as well as the names of rivers, countries, peoples, and cities, and also everything else that goes back to antiquity. It goes down to the Trojan War, summarizing the battles and deeds of some of the warriors with each other and some of their wanderings from Troy, particularly Odysseus', and it is with him that the book's account of antiquity ends. Most of the book is paraphrase and quite useful for people who think it worthwhile to remember the ancient world. The little book also has the following epigram, which is not inelegant. [The epigram is printed at the start of our translation.]

Photios' judgment that the work was "quite useful" proved true. Scholars in the next several centuries mined the *Bibliotheke* to produce *scholia,* explanatory notes to various texts. This activity culminated in the twelfth century with John Tzetzes, who used the *Bibliotheke* as a source to elucidate the mythological details of the notoriously difficult third-century BC poet Lycophron. Tzetzes also incorporated some material from Apollodorus into his own long poem *Chiliades.* The *Bibliotheke* afterward seems to have fallen out of favor, for it is not discussed or cited again until the fourteenth century, when John Pediasimus used its account of the labors of Heracles as the basis for a little prose summary and a short poem on the same subject. This is the last appearance of Apollodorus in Byzantium.

Photios and Tzetzes both had complete copies of the *Bibliotheke* at their disposal, but we do not (which makes Tzetzes a valuable witness in helping reconstruct some of the missing material). Our earliest surviving manuscript of the work dates to the fourteenth century (around the time of Pediasimus, and perhaps his copy), but it is incomplete, now missing several pages, and it seems to have never contained the end of the *Bibliotheke.* This manuscript made its way to Italy after the fall of Constantinople in 1453. There are other, later manuscripts of the work, all missing the end, and it turns out that all of them are copies ultimately derived from this fourteenth-century copy. Thus, despite the utility of Apollodorus, his work came very close to being lost entirely.

As it stands, none of these manuscripts contain the end of Book 3 (the text breaks off abruptly in the middle of Theseus' adventures). Tzetzes, however, had a complete text, and in 1885 R. Wagner realized that a manuscript in the Vatican Library containing excerpts of some of Tzetzes' work also contained large abridged excerpts drawn from across the whole of the *Bibliotheke*—including the lost ending. This abridged version (or epitome), known now as the Vatican Epitome, is invaluable, but it is not our only witness to the last part of the book. Only a few years after Wagner's discovery, A. Papadopoulos-Kerameus discovered in Jerusalem a manuscript that contained another set of abridged excerpts, all from the third book and the portion known only from Tzetzes' epitome. This became known as the Sabbaitic Epitome (from the monastery of St. Sabbas, where the manuscript was discovered). Thus, although the *Bibliotheke* was first printed in a modern edition in 1555, it was only with Wagner's edition of 1894 that we had a complete, or at least nearly complete, text. To give you some idea of how much is omitted in the process of abridgment, the following is a translation of a section from the surviving part of the *Bibliotheke* (3.206–207, left), as well as the equivalent section from the Vatican Epitome (right):

While Pandion was in Megara, he had sons, Aigeus, Pallas, Nisos, and Lycos. However, some say that Aigeus was Scyrios' son and that Pandion just passed him off as his own. After Pandion's death, his sons marched against Athens and cast out the sons of Metion. They divided the leadership four ways, but Aigeus had all the power. He married Meta daughter of Hoples first and then Chalciope daughter of Rhexenor second, but when he did not have a child, he was afraid of his brothers and went to Pytho and consulted the oracle about having children.

Pandion's sons were Aigeus, Pallas, Nisos, and Lycos, who after the death of Pandion marched against Athens and cast out the sons of Metion and divided the leadership four ways. But Aigeus had all the power. He, lacking a child, consulted an oracle about this.

The bones of the story remain, but most of the details have been stripped out. The epitomizing is not entirely consistent—sometimes there is a detail left out in one place, but an equivalent sort of detail slips through in another—but the overall effect is to make a short and straightforward narrative even shorter. But shorter is not always more straightforward, and there are places where the removal of detail creates a less coherent narrative than the original.

The two epitomes were made at different times by different people, and when they overlap they do not always preserve the same material or details. We have chosen in this book to translate a combined version of them (created by J. G. Frazer for his 1921 Loeb edition), which stitches the separate epitomes together to create a fuller and more connected account that presumably resembles the unepitomized original more closely than either of the two individual abridgments. Although we will not recover the exact wording of the whole end of Apollodorus without new discoveries, the two epitomes together are a reliable guide to what stories were covered and how they were organized in this section. And where the epitomes happen to coincide exactly, as they do with some frequency, we can be sure that we at least have something reasonably close to the wording of the original.

The *Bibliotheke* and This Translation

The *Bibliotheke* is written in a homely but correct Greek. Its style is extremely unadorned, but in vocabulary and syntax there is nothing else to make it stand out from the typical prose of the first century BC or the first two centuries AD. Perhaps the best way to describe Apollodorus' writing is "workmanlike," for it has a job to do and it does that job adequately and efficiently, even well, but no instructor of ancient Greek would ever put it before his or her students and ask them to emulate it as a model of brilliant style, for it is too pedestrian and awkward to make any pretense toward artistry. It does veer very occasionally toward the artistic, and there are a few recondite vocabulary items scattered here and there, but these are not consistent and are possibly places where we glimpse our author being tempted by his sources to the occasional flourish. We have tried to be clear and straightforward in our translation while remaining faithful to the somewhat awkward style of the original. Our goal, in other words, was to capture in English what Apollodorus reads like in Greek. Our rendering is close, therefore, but not literal, and we have done a fair amount of recasting without "prettying up" our author into something he is not.

It is worth mentioning again that the translation of Books 1–3 is based on Wagner's text, though we do accept conjectures, adopt alternate readings, and make a few emendations of our own. The epitome is based on Frazer's combined text, but there again we felt free to vary from it. There are two competing systems used by scholars for dividing up the books into sections, the traditional one that goes back to early editions and the new numbering of Wagner's edition. We print Wagner's section divisions in the text. We abandoned the traditional numbering scheme with reluctance, since it is in wider use in the English-speaking world. It is also, however, irrational and cumbersome. Many scholars today provide double citations, using both systems. Likewise, we have printed the major section numbers from the traditional system in the margins, so a reader faced with a citation of Apollodorus in this form should be able to find the right general portion of the text being sought, and the indexes provide a convenient way to locate the major characters and places throughout the *Bibliotheke.* We have inserted into the text subheadings (printed in boldface) to break up the narrative in logical places; these should not be mistaken for an original part of the text—they are entirely our own in placement and wording.

Greek names have, for the most part, been transliterated directly from the Greek, although we use *c* instead of *k* for the Greek letter kappa in most places. We have made some exceptions for certain familiar names, such as Athena (not Athene here) or Achilles (not Achilleus here). This is not a scholarly edition, and we do not consistently indicate every textual supplement. Rather, <angle brackets> enclose only restored material that Wagner did not accept and print in his text, or for the epitome, Frazer (scholars should note, therefore, that everything that is in angle brackets in Wagner is not in angle brackets here). <*Angle brackets*> enclosing text in italics are used to indicate the nature of missing material. Angle brackets enclosing an ellipsis < . . . > indicate gaps in the preserved material. [Square brackets] indicate material that is transmitted in the manuscript but which we judge to be later additions to the text. Expository material to clarify etymologies and wordplay is enclosed in {braces}.

Further Reading

There is, unfortunately, very little in English on Apollodorus that is aimed at or accessible to the general reader. "Very little," in this case is almost a euphemism for "nothing." There have been four earlier translations into English, and each of these has been accompanied by an introduction and notes that might be consulted. They are:

J. G. Frazer (ed. and trans.), *The Library,* 2 vols., Loeb Classical Library (Harvard University Press: Oxford/New York, 1921).

K. Aldrich (trans.), *The Library of Greek Mythology* (Coronado Press: Lawrence, 1975).

M. Simpson (trans.), *Gods and Heroes of the Greeks: The Library of Apollodorus* (University of Massachusetts: Amherst, 1976).

R. Hard (trans.), *The Library of Greek Mythology* (Oxford University Press: Oxford, 1997).

Of these, Aldrich is now out of print, and Simpson is generally inferior to Hard. Frazer's translation and introduction are somewhat dated, but the main attraction of his two volumes is the extensive notes, including those marking parallels in other sources (as well as, quite fascinatingly but irrelevantly, a massive amount of comparative anthropological material). The notes contained in the three more recent translations also concentrate more heavily than our own on identifying other sources from antiquity that tell the stories contained in Apollodorus.

In the bibliography around Apollodorus, there are only two articles in English that are simultaneously important and of broad enough scope to interest the ambitious nonspecialist reader—though, it must be noted, that neither was written for such an audience and they contain much that will be opaque to general readers. They are:

A. Diller, "The Text History of the Bibliotheca of Apollodorus," *Transactions of the American Philological Association* 66 (1935) 296–313.

M. van der Valk, "On Apollodori *Bibliotheca,*" *Revues des études grecques* 71 (1958) 100–168.

Some comments on Apollodorus can be ferreted out in the books of M. van Rossum-Steenbeek and A. Cameron that are listed in the Further Reading section of the General Introduction. These, like the scholarly articles noted above, are not designed for the general reader, but the sections on Apollodorus are not so overwhelmingly technical as to be entirely useless to the interested nonspecialist.

Absolutely invaluable is M. Huys' website devoted to Apollodorus (http://abel.arts.kuleuven.be/). This is a constantly updated searchable database that comprehensively indexes all scholarship on the *Bibliotheke* (based on two extensive bibliographic articles he earlier published).

INTRODUCTION TO HYGINUS' *FABULAE (MYTHS)*

Author, Title, and Date

As in the case of Apollodorus' *Bibliotheke,* we know little to nothing about the collection of myths that goes under the title *Fabulae,* about the person who wrote it, and about its date of composition. For this Latin collection there are further difficulties: over the course of its existence the original work has been modified, reorganized, abridged, and again expanded, all while suffering mutilation and corruption along the way. All this, and much else, make seemingly simple questions like "Who wrote the *Fabulae?*" or "When was it written?" extraordinarily difficult. Since the collection as we have it is the result of so many modifications, we are better off speaking about *authors* rather than a single author, and *dates* instead of a single date. Simply put, the collection of myths we possess under the name *Fabulae* is likely so far removed from the author's original that, we suspect, he would have scarcely recognized it as his own.

Of course there must have been a point of conception and an original author—whatever form that original composition took—and we have no reason to suspect that the name of that author was not Hyginus. That is, after all, the name given in the sole ancient reference to the work, and probably also in the now lost single manuscript that survived into the modern era. Neither of these witnesses, however, adds the other two names Romans were normally endowed with, so that we cannot determine which Hyginus we are talking about. It would be like someone today talking about a book written by someone with the last name Jones or King. Hyginus, like both of these names, was not uncommon, and many books on extremely diverse subjects, ranging from pedestrian surveying manuals to literary treatises on Vergil's poetry, are attributed to one or another person by this name.

Can we be more specific? At first glance, perhaps so. Jacob Molsheim (he is usually referred to by his Latin name, Micyllus), the editor of the first printed edition of the *Fabulae* in 1535, gives as the full title *The Book of Fabulae by Gaius Julius Hyginus, the Freedman of Augustus.* But since the manuscript of the *Fabulae* was lost soon after publication, we cannot be certain that it gave this full name, and in fact it is quite doubtful (Micyllus implies in his introduction that only "Hyginus" was found in the manuscript). So why did Micyllus specify our Hyginus as Gaius Julius Hyginus? Because that Hyginus, who really did exist, seemed to him a logical candidate. Suetonius (ca. AD 70–130), the famous Roman biographer, devotes an entire section to him in his treatise *On Famous Grammarians.* According to Suetonius, this Hyginus, a native of Spain, became the freedman of the Roman emperor Augustus (reigned 31 BC–AD 14) and served as the head of the extensive Palatine Library (containing both Greek and Latin texts), a position that no doubt required broad expertise and a scholarly interest in many fields. This Hyginus was also a close friend of, among other literary luminaries, Ovid, the author of the great mythological poem *Metamorphoses.* Micyllus, then, seems to have simply taken it for granted, as many have done subsequently, that our Hyginus is this particular Hyginus, and what better candidate could we hope for? He was a scholar and closely connected with literary giants of his time, just the sort of person we would expect to be engaged in composing a mythological handbook.

But as we have seen in the General Introduction, mythography was not conducted solely by bookish scholars consulting vast tomes of Greek epic and tragedy in the original. Mythography was a continuous tradition, and we should not assume that each compiler of myths was a scholar independently verifying the truth of earlier works by consulting the originals—that in fact is a modern notion of scholarship. There would have been available to Hyginus, whoever he was, a multitude of accessible texts from which any literate person could reproduce this material. Thus, while it is not impossible that the Palatine librarian is the author of the original *Fabulae,* we should not feel inclined to make the association *because* of his academic interests, and although a few scholars have continued to try to identify the Palatine librarian as our Hyginus, the vast majority now reject the identification.

If Gaius Julius Hyginus did not write the work, then we run into the problem of dating its original composition. Gaius lived in the first centuries BC and AD, but our unknown Hyginus could have been a rough contemporary or even from the next century. Luckily, we do have one securely datable reference to the work that lets us know that the *Fabulae* cannot have originally been written after the end of the second century. On September 11 in AD 207, a schoolteacher today known as Pseudo-Dositheus (once falsely identified as the more famous grammarian Dositheus, hence Pseudo) decided to excerpt passages from Hyginus' *Genealogy* (a translation is provided in the Appendix), which he characterized as "world-famous." Since the work must have been in circulation for some time before achieving the status of a classic, we can with some confidence establish the late second century AD as a *terminus ante quem* (a time before which it must have been written)—that is, for *one* version of the collection. But the situation is yet more complicated, for we would still have to contend with the numerous later changes and additions—all anonymous—that the collection experienced. The problem is essentially this: although the passages excerpted by Ps.-Dositheus demonstrably prove that his copy of Hyginus' *Genealogy* is a relative of the extant *Fabulae,* the two collections are by no means the same. The excerpts contain some intriguing lists (e.g., an efficient account of the Muses, their craft, lovers, and children) that are not to be found in the *Fabulae.* Conversely, the *Fabulae* contains material added later, some of it coming as late as the fifth century AD. Thus, at best we can only say that one version of the collection, loosely related to the extant *Fabulae,* was available and well known in the early third century AD.

Narrowing the date of the original composition further is a purely hypothetical enterprise, though this has not prevented scholars from hazarding guesses, usually based on intelligent but unverifiable argumentation: first, the Antonine period (middle to late second century AD), based on Hyginus' use of archaic language in vogue at the time and the availability of certain mythographic sources; second, the late first century AD, based on a possible reference to Marcus Fabius Quintilian (ca. AD 35–95) in *On Astronomy,* generally regarded to be by the same Hyginus who authored the *Fabulae;* finally, there are those who still doggedly hold that the *Fabulae* was composed by the Palatine librarian (ca. 27 BC–AD 14). Any one of these positions may represent the truth, but we will likely never know for sure.

The title *Fabulae* is probably a modern one, given to it by the first editor, Micyllus, in 1535—modern, that is, by classicists' standards. In antiquity the collection circulated under the title *Genealogy* (or *Genealogies*), which implies a very different sort of organization than the *Fabulae* exhibits and raises all sorts of questions about the original format of the work. We'll reserve that discussion for a later section (see History of the Text), but the fact that Micyllus did not publish the collection under its ancient title *Genealogy* probably indicates that it was not to be found in the manuscript, and since he makes no mention of any title for that work in his introduction (as he does for the other mythological works he publishes in the same volume), we can be nearly certain that Micyllus was dealing with an untitled collection. Since it is the usual practice to refer to the surviving collection by its modern title, in this book we too use this title unless we are specifically referring to the ancient versions.

What does *Fabulae* mean? What it does not mean in this context is "fable," although the Latin word *fabula* could be used specifically to denote that literary form. The word, like its Greek counterpart *mythos,* covers a wide range of meanings in addition to "fable," from "story" and "myth" to "dramatic play." The Romans themselves could and did use the word specifically to describe the myths of Hercules, Theseus, the Trojan War, and the like, and by the Middle Ages it became the standard word for "myth" or "story," especially one that was relatively short and self-contained, such as those we find in Hyginus' collection. Thus, *Fabulae,* either *Myths* or *Stories,* accurately describes the surviving collection—more accurately, in fact, than the ancient title *Genealogies.*

Contents and Organization

Unlike Apollodorus' *Library,* which presents its material in continuous narrative form, Hyginus' *Fabulae* offers discrete stories or lists, each with its own title. Overall, the collection falls into three sections: (1) a short theogony (literally, "birth of the gods") providing a genealogy of gods; (2) narrative accounts of myths (*Fab.* 1–220); and (3) lists compiled from different myths under an individual category (*Fab.* 221–277). But we also find lists in the narrative section, and narrative accounts amid the lists, adding to the impression that the book is a collection composed and reworked many times during its existence.

The organization of a mythological handbook into individual entries is not unique to the *Fabulae.* Other mythological handbooks present collections of individual myths, but those are narrowly focused on a particular type of myth, such as transformations, star myths, or love stories. The *Fabulae,* by contrast, does not exhibit such specialization or consistency. The entries vary greatly in length, form, and content. Some are no longer than a few sentences (e.g., 5, 11, 17, et al.), while others occupy several pages (e.g., 125). Some are merely lists of names (e.g., 11,

48, et al.), others recount famous myths and sagas (e.g., 12–27), and still others treat historical or geographic material (e.g., 223, 276).

Accompanying the collection was a table of contents (which we have not reproduced here), which conveniently indexed the *Fabulae* and was keyed to titles given before each entry. Whether this helpful tool was original or a later addition is impossible to say for certain, but a collection as eclectic as this one clearly benefits from some guide to its contents. Without such an aid, who could readily find what one was looking for? Even Ps.-Dositheus felt inclined to provide an index to the thirty or so lists and stories that he excerpted so that the reader "might easily find them." It might be pointed out, however, that even without a table of contents readers of Hyginus enjoyed an advantage over those trying to find material in the unbroken narrative of Apollodorus' *Bibliotheke* (which we felt compelled to break up into more user-friendly pieces): with a bit of work one could find the desired stories in the *Fabulae* from the titles heading each entry.

The *Fabulae* opens with a theogony. This section's aim, like all theogonies, is to give an account of how the gods and other worldly forces came into being. There were many such accounts found in ancient literature—none more famous, of course, than Hesiod's poetic treatment the *Theogony*—but most of them have been lost. These accounts often varied greatly from one another, but the one attached to the *Fabulae* may be the most bizarre (not to mention corrupt) of those that survive. For instance, by the usual ancient account, Chaos is the first being that comes into existence. Surprisingly, however, in the theogony in Hyginus there is an even earlier being, Mist, listed, which is unknown elsewhere. Moreover, the theogony is neither headed by a title in the text (the title "Theogony" in the translation is our addition) nor mentioned in the table of contents, and on those grounds we may suspect that it was added later, perhaps because the *Fabulae* otherwise devotes few entries to the gods and virtually nothing to the early gods (cf. Apollodorus' comparatively extensive treatment at 1.1–44).

The rest of the *Fabulae* consists of individual, self-contained entries, and it is the variety and scope of these that make them most interesting. Although at times there seems no rational order to the stories, generally speaking there is a concerted effort at some sort of organization. To take the narrative portion separately (*Fab.* 1–220), we can discern numerous clusters of entries organized thematically, most concerning heroic myth:

1–11	Early Theban Myth
12–27	Jason, the Argonauts, and Medea
29–36	Hercules
37–48	Athens and Crete (loosely organized)
49–51	Apollo, Admetus, and Alcestis
63–64	Perseus (miserably abridged)
66–76	Theban Myth from Laius to the Epigoni
77–127	The Trojan War
168–170	Danaus and His Daughters
171–175	Calydonian Boar Hunt and Aftermath

We can also detect clusters concerning individual gods (129–134 Liber; 164–166 Minerva; 176–179 mortal loves of Jupiter) or containing related lists (155–162 children of male gods). Still other criteria can be discerned, although some may be accidental and not intended: 52–53 island names; 57–59 women unlucky in love; 60–62 impious men (two punished in the underworld); 194–197 star myths; 198–205 transformations (200–203 pertaining to Apollo's love affairs); 204 and 206 incestuous affairs. The inorganic placement of some stories suggests that at some point the order has been altered, the book has been abridged, or both. *Fab.* 28 ("Otos and Ephialtes"), for instance, is strangely inserted between the Argonaut adventure and the account of Hercules, apparently without reason.

The lists are one of the most exceptional features of the *Fabulae*. While they occur sporadically throughout the whole text (11, 14, 30, 31, 38, 48, 70, 71, 76, 81, 90, 97, 112–115, 124, 128, 151, 155–163, 170, 173, 173A), at 221 a continuous series of lists begins that runs virtually unabated until the end. Unfortunately, some thirty-three entries have been lost; their titles, however, have survived in the table of contents (which we provide in the footnotes to the translation). The lists, like the narrative *Fabulae,* are mostly grouped together thematically (e.g., 234–245 murderers and suicides), but now and again there seems no rhyme or reason to the order: for instance, after encountering the miraculous at 252 ("Those Nourished by the Milk of Wild Animals") and the tabloidesque at 253 ("Those Who Committed Incest"), we then turn to noble deeds at 254 ("Exceptionally Dutiful Women and Men").

Lists of names are common in mythographic texts—see, for instance, Apollodorus' lists of the 50 sons and daughters of Aigyptos and Danaos (2.16–21), the 51 sons of Heracles by Thespios' daughters (2.161–164; by other women see 2.165–166), the 50 sons of Lycaon (3.96), the 31 suitors of Helen (3.129–131), the 55 sons of Priam (3.147–153; cf. the 54 sons at *Fab.* 90), and the 136 suitors of Penelope (E.7.26–30). Recent papyrus finds have also provided us with numerous examples of mythological lists from otherwise lost mythographic sources; among others we find catalogs of Argonauts (cf. *Fab.* 14), the names of Actaeon's dogs (cf. *Fab.* 181), and a list of mothers who killed their own children (cf. *Fab.* 239).

Greek Sources and Romanization

Although the *Fabulae* as we have it is in Latin and draws to a limited degree on Latin sources (see more below), it almost exclusively encapsulates Greek myth. Little of what we might call Roman myth—and there was plenty available—has been preserved in the collection. In several places we can clearly demonstrate where Hyginus translated a Greek text into Latin, betraying the direct use of Greek sources (for examples see the endnote to *Fab.* 14.17 and the footnote to 186). Elsewhere etymologies relying on a knowledge of Greek are frequently left unexplained in the Latin translation, and at times even a familiarity with the Greek myth is expected. For instance, when Hyginus explains the origin of Oedipus' name at the end of *Fab.* 66 we read, "When Polybus found out . . . they raised him as their own, naming him

Oedipus *because his feet had been pierced.*" To understand this completely a reader must not only have a familiarity with the Oedipus story to know that he was exposed as an infant on the mountainside (with ankle-pins attached to thongs to prevent his wandering off), but also enough knowledge of Greek to unpack the supposed significance of his name (Greek *oid-,* "swollen," and *pous-,* "foot").

As for the specific sources of the *Fabulae,* it is not possible to determine what Greek work or works Hyginus turned to, not only because Hyginus is extremely reticent about his sources, but also because so many Greek mythographic works have perished. It was once fashionable to think that Hyginus simply translated a single Greek handbook of mythology into Latin, but it is now generally recognized that Hyginus himself may have used multiple sources and that the work has gone through many different phases of reworking during which other sources were tapped as well. Certainly the stark differences in form among the theogony, the narrative accounts, and the lists suggest that at some point someone fused together different types of mythographic forms into a single body.

Although the specific forms that most of these sources took are unknown, there were numerous works to cull from, and in one case at least we have a pretty clear picture. Some of the narrative *Fabulae* probably draw on the so-called "Tales from Euripides" or some other source book on tragedy. It has been long recognized that because of their dramatic nature many of the narrative *Fabulae* probably derive from Greek tragedies (or Latin adaptations thereof), in particular those of Euripides. The titles of *Fab.* 4 ("Euripides' *Ino*") and *Fab.* 8 ("The Same Play of Euripides, [Which Ennius Wrote]") point to Euripides as the source, though we cannot determine how closely Hyginus' accounts follow these plays since they are unfortunately lost. A recent study lists no fewer than forty entries that may derive ultimately from either Sophocles or Euripides (Breen 44–46). It is unlikely that Hyginus (or his source for that matter) pored over innumerable tragedies in the original just to glean the basic plot outlines; nor did he have to. The work had already been done for him, in the form of tragic *hypotheseis,* short summaries of the plots containing pertinent background to the myths and often prefixed to the plays as a sort of introduction. It is not implausible that some form of these summaries made their way into the collection.

Over the past century, however, papyri have been found that prove conclusively that the *hypotheseis* of Euripides circulated as a book separately from the plays themselves, a work that is today given the name "Tales from Euripides." In a few cases the language seemed so similar to that of the *Fabulae* that some scholars have asserted that Hyginus consulted these *hypotheseis* directly and translated them. Unfortunately, upon reexamination this position can no longer be maintained: the places where Hyginus may have translated a *hypothesis* are actually few and even then not certain, and a recent careful study of the correspondences concludes that there is in fact no direct relationship between these "Tales from Euripides" and the *Fabulae* (Huys I, II). Thus, although many narrative *Fabulae* almost certainly derive from a specific Greek tragedy, we still have not found the magic missing link that connects those plays to Hyginus' *Fabulae,* even if we know generally what it looked like.

Although the *Fabulae* is at its core based mainly on Greek sources, it has been to some degree adapted for a Latin audience. When this adaptation took place—that is, whether it is owed to Hyginus himself or belongs to a later stage—is uncertain. Some scholars have even gone so far as to state that everything Roman is a later addition to an original work. We would argue, however, that this statement is too sweeping and inflexible. Could it not be that Hyginus' innovation was specifically that he compiled various Greek myths from Greek sources but then translated them for a Latin-speaking audience, as was clearly his intent in *On Astronomy?*

We find in the *Fabulae* occasions when Hyginus, or perhaps a later scribe, attempts to provide assistance to the non-Greek speaker. At *Fab.* 87 we are helpfully told that "in Greek the word for 'she-goat' [Latin *capra*] is *aega*" in order to explain Aegisthus' name. We are also given such help again at *Fab.* 52 (Myrmidons), 96 (Pyrrha), 143 (Hermes), 151 (Chimaera), 153 (*laos-laas*), and 166 (Erichthonius). Latin equivalents of Greek names and words are sometimes added, often with the first-person "we": *Fab.* 2, "Liber ordained that she be called Leucothea (we call her Mater Matuta) and that Melicertes be called the god Palaemon (we call him Portunus)"; *Fab.* 53, "So he turned her into an *ortyx* bird (what we call a quail)"; *Fab.* 92, "Jupiter summoned all the gods to the feast except for Eris (that is, Discord)"; *Fab.* 183, "Bronte and Sterope, whom we call Thunder and Lightning." Since we see similar patterns in Hyginus' *On Astronomy,* some of this Latin material may have been included by Hyginus himself in places where a Latin audience might be expected to have difficulty.

Roman legends (*Fab.* 252, 255, 256) and Roman cultural institutions (*Fab.* 80, 261, 274, 277) have also been inserted from time to time. Many of them have been simply added to the end, mere appendages of a preexisting list of Greek material. Some information from Latin mythological poems too has been added, but the infrequency with which it is employed ought to alert us to the fact that it was not systematically employed in the original composition of the *Fabulae.* In a few places Ovid's *Metamorphoses* is used, almost all mere lists of names (*Fab.* 134 [Tyrrhenian sailors], 181 [Actaeon's dogs], 183 [horses of the Sun]). Elsewhere Vergil's *Aeneid* has been cursorily mined (243, 251, 254, 273). Upon closer examination, however, the Vergilian material might not even come from Vergil's poem, but rather from Servius' commentary on Vergil's *Aeneid,* compiled in the fourth century AD. A small group of tales near the end of the collection (*Fab.* 258–261) was certainly taken directly from the first two books of that commentary.

On two occasions an etymology relying on a Latin word betrays a specifically Roman origin. *Fab.* 220 (*Cura;* "Worry") is a charming myth describing the creation of humans, one found nowhere else. Its main purpose, it seems, is to give an account of why humans are consumed with worry during their lives. Nothing until the end of the tale suggests a purely Latin origin, but there the author happily tells us where the name human (*homo*) came from: because Worry had fashioned the first human out of earth (*humus*) it received a similar name. That the clever tale hinges entirely on Latin wordplay points to a purely Roman origin. A Latin etymology also occurs at 274.22, where a strange derivation is given to explain the origin of the Latin word for "war," *bellum:* it is said to come from the Greek mythical figure Belus (note one *l*), who was the first to fight with a sword. The position of these two items amid predominantly Greek material is again important. The former falls at the end of the narrative portion and just before the lists, suggesting that this particularly Roman tale was simply added to the end of the existing narrative portion before, or perhaps when, the lists were sutured on. The latter stands at the end of a long list of otherwise Greek inventors and discoverers, as if attached to a preexisting list of Greek items.

History of the Text

The earliest reference that we have to Hyginus' mythological work comes from *On Astronomy (De Astronomia),* a detailed treatise bearing the name Hyginus, who is generally believed to be the same as the author of the *Fabulae.* We find in the second book a reference to the *Fabulae* under its original name (2.12.2): "But, as Aeschylus the tragedian says in his *Phorcides,* the Graeae were the Gorgons' guardians; we wrote about this in the first book of *Genealogies.*" We are again faced with a problem: the *Fabulae* as we have it is not divided into books and contains no mention of the Graeae, the Gorgons, or—more shocking still—Perseus' killing of Medusa, the most famous part of the myth!

The original title *Genealogies* and the cross-reference may provide insight into the original form of the *Fabulae.* If the title accurately describes the original contents, Hyginus' work was organized in a fashion similar to the Greek mythographers such as Pherecydes or Hellanicus, or even the later Apollodorus, all of whom arranged myth on genealogical principles, in narrative form, and in multiple books. Certainly, it is hard to imagine that *Genealogy* or *Genealogies* was a natural title to give to a collection of individual stories arranged eclectically such as the *Fabulae.* Presuming that Hyginus knew what he was doing when he titled his work, we might imagine that originally it was a continuous narrative organized by family lineage rather than the collection of self-contained stories we now have. There are, of course, serious objections that can be raised against this position; for example, if the original was a complete narrative, how do we reconcile Hyginus' presumed use of tragic summaries as a source, which almost beg for separate entries?

Whatever the original form, by the early third century AD Hyginus' *Genealogy* had taken on a form somewhat like what we have today. Here we return to Ps.-Dositheus, whom we met earlier in our discussion of the date, for a fuller discussion (one can read a translation of the relevant section of Ps.-Dositheus in the Appendix). In a desire to help Greeks learn Latin (or vice versa), Ps.-Dositheus provided both a Greek and Latin version of four lists and twenty-eight separate stories taken from the *Genealogy.* Unfortunately, we do not know whether his copy of Hyginus was Latin or Greek (it was possibly both), but we can compare the contents of the entries he transcribes to the extant *Fabulae.* Although none of the lists are found in the *Fabulae,* most of the stories he indexes do have similar entries in the *Fabulae,* and the three full narratives that have survived in Ps.-Dositheus look similar enough to those in the *Fabulae* to prove that Ps.-Dositheus' text was an ancient relative of our text (Prometheus = *Fab.* 144; Philyra = *Fab.* 138; Sirens = *Fab.* 141).

Strangely, the collection still bore the name *Genealogy* even though it was no longer appropriate for the form it had, although it should be noted that just possibly the change from the plural ("*Genealogies*" in *On Astronomy*) to the singular may indicate a revision from numerous books to just one. Perhaps the full form of Hyginus' (narrative) *Genealogies* was, so to speak, dismantled and refashioned into self-contained, individual entries, still retaining the original title despite the obvious incongruity.

The act of abridgement and reshaping would have afforded ample opportunity for omission of material and the introduction of mistakes. For instance, we mentioned above that the *Fabulae* does not mention Perseus' killing of Medusa although it was found in the original *Genealogies.* It is conceivable that this episode was somehow simply left out during this initial reshaping of the long narrative account of the Perseus myth into discrete entries—not hard to do if one was working quickly and assumed ancient readers would remember (as most surely would) that Perseus killed Medusa. Now, this omission may have occurred at a later stage of transmission when the *Genealogy* was further modified and transformed. The main point to remember here is that at every stage of transmission mistakes are possible, and for our author, probable.

After Ps.-Dositheus, the *Fabulae* occasionally turn up elsewhere in late antiquity (third to fifth centuries AD), mostly in *scholia* to Latin mythological poems. Roughly equivalent to modern footnotes or endnotes, *scholia* were often added to explain unelaborated mythological allusions, and Hyginus' collection was seen as an authority for mythological lore worth quoting. But when we compare the language of the scholiasts to that of the *Fabulae,* we discover that, again, the scholiasts were using a copy of Hyginus' work that was significantly different from the surviving *Fabulae* and that our collection had not yet reached its final form.

Surprisingly—given that the *Genealogy* could be called "world-famous" in the third century AD—the influence of Hyginus in late antiquity was limited. Nothing of the *Fabulae* is found in Servius' extensive fourth-century commentary to Vergil's *Aeneid* (in fact, as we have already pointed out, the opposite is true, for at some point material was taken from Servius and added to Hyginus' collection) or the three other vast mythological compilations known under the title of the Vatican Mythographers (post-ninth century AD; see General Introduction).

Apart from these few references, however, we cannot trace the fate of this handbook until the 16th century, when the *Fabulae* were first published. Micyllus, the editor mentioned earlier, had found a barely legible and damaged manuscript from around AD 900 written in Beneventan script, which is notoriously difficult to read. He had such a difficult time deciphering the letters that he resorted to using a partial transcript of the same manuscript made by an unknown scribe, whose copy Micyllus followed, as he himself wrote, "like some thread." Since no other manuscript has come to light (although we have found fragments of an "abridged" *Fabulae;* see below), the only source for the *Fabulae* is that solitary, debased, hardly legible manuscript that Micyllus transcribed with difficulty.

Still worse, by 1558—less than twenty-five years after publication—the manuscript was dismantled and reused for other purposes. Although scholars subsequently recovered a few pages of it in 1870 and 1944, we cannot for the vast majority of the *Fabulae* assess Micyllus' accuracy (recall our discussion of the author and title). When we do compare the recovered fragments with his transcription, it is clear that Micyllus simply could not read the words very well and on occasion may have silently made changes to the text he could read—again, adding to the potential sources of Hyginus' mistakes. Perhaps one day a scholar will find a substantial part of this manuscript, so that we can further judge Micyllus' accuracy.

Let us now turn briefly to what we have referred to above as the "abridged" *Fabulae.* In 1820 the German classicist B. G. Niebuhr found some fragments of a shortened form of the *Fabulae* in a palimpsest of the fifth century AD. *Palimpsest* (literally "scraped again") is a technical term given to a manuscript in which the original writing was scraped off so that the writing surface could be reused for other purposes. Occasionally, we can recover the original text that was scraped off, and in this case we were fortunate enough to reclaim versions of *Fab.* 67–71. While the palimpsest version of 67 is substantially the same as that of the *Fabulae,* we do see some differences and abridgments in the other versions (in our translation these palimpsest texts are numbered 68B, 69A, 70A, 71A). As one might imagine, some of the letters that have been scraped off have been lost for good, so here as with other palimpsests we have had to provide supplements (noted by <angle brackets>). Be that as it may, it is interesting that an abridged copy of Hyginus seems to have been circulating as late as the fifth century, the same time, perhaps, when the *Fabulae* was reaching its final form. Perhaps we are to conclude that numerous copies or editions of Hyginus circulated in antiquity, of which ours is but one.

The *Fabulae* and the Modern Study of Myth

Using Hyginus' *Fabulae* as a source for the study of mythology is much like walking through a briar patch. No matter how carefully one treads, one simply cannot avoid the inevitable snags sure to occur along the way. Although undeniably rich as a mythological source, the *Fabulae* unfortunately presents us with difficulties no matter which way we turn, and like those thorny vines in the briar patch many of the problems are intertwined in such a way that when dealing with one issue others are sure to tear at us as well. Readers should not take this rather gloomy warning as a sign to stop reading immediately, put the book down, and forget about Hyginus' *Fabulae* forever. Rather, we want those meeting Hyginus' *Fabulae* for the first time to understand that Hyginus needs to be used with caution. But if one is prepared to proceed cautiously, and untangle some bramble along the way, Hyginus' *Fabulae* can be remarkably fruitful as a source in the study of mythology.

As you have probably surmised by now, there were numerous occasions where the "original" text of Hyginus' work could have been, and often was, altered, abridged, distorted, or, at worst, corrupted beyond recognition. In other words, some "authentic" versions—by which we mean ones we can use to reconstruct genuine stories told by the Greeks—are no longer authentic because they have been compromised as the *Fabulae* has come into our hands. It should be remarked here that we firmly believe, unlike some scholars, that Hyginus was not some hack and was honest in his attempt to record his stories accurately, and that many of the problems arise not from the ignorance of the author but from the circumstances of transmission, right up until the moment it entered the printing press in 1535.

But Hyginus does provide authentic but otherwise unknown variants, and it is precisely in these cases that the dubious reliability of the text presents us with real problems of interpretation. If the text commonly transmits erroneous or garbled accounts (and it often does), what is to say that another account, unable to be checked because it is unique, is not simply an error, a product of a faulty text?

Perhaps the best way to clarify what we mean is by a specific example. In *Fab.* 25 we are treated to a relatively straightforward account of the Medea myth, derived ultimately—but probably indirectly—from the most famous account, Euripides' *Medea.* Several unique (to use an optimistic word) features can be observed in this short account: (1) an outright mistake: Creon, the king of Corinth, is here identified as the son of Menoeceus, but Creon son of Menoeceus is the king of Thebes familiar from the Oedipus myth; (2) an internal inconsistency: Creon's daughter is first called Glauce, then Creusa; (3) a deviation from Euripides' play: the *Medea* reports both a poisoned crown and robe, whereas the *Fabulae* only speaks of a crown; and (4) another, more substantive deviation from Euripides' play: Jason is said to have been consumed in the fire that took the lives of Creon and his daughter.

The first can be explained easily, and there is no reason to suppose it is anything but an error: at some point only the name Creon was found in the text, and someone out of ignorance supplied the wrong lineage. So can the second: some ancient versions call the daughter Glauce, others Creusa, and someone conflated the two traditions. As for the third, what we have is a simple omission of the robe in the account, a not unexpected result of summarization, and it hardly registers as consequential. The fourth, however, is indeed remarkable. No other account has Jason die in this way; usually Jason either hangs himself or is killed by the falling prow of the deteriorating *Argo.* Where does this detail come from?

There are four possibilities. First, and most favorably, Hyginus found this version in a source and reports it; second, Hyginus invented this detail out of thin air; third, the text of the *Fabulae* once transmitted the Euripidean events (where virtually everyone but Jason dies), but it somehow became corrupt, and by mere chance Jason's name became included among the victims of Medea's rage; finally, Hyginus or a later scribe could have simply made a mistake, which for all intents and purposes is the same as the third possibility. Obviously, although we can make reasonable claims about the likelihood of this or that, we are in no position to decide for certain.

Let's see what might be going through a scholar's mind as she or he tries to sort it all out using all the available evidence. Early in the Euripidean play, Medea in her unquenchable anger proclaims that she will produce three corpses—the king, the daughter, and Jason. Of course, she later changes her mind, only to produce *four* corpses (the king, the daughter, and Medea's two sons by Jason), but Jason himself does not die at her hands. One might imagine a scenario where her intent to kill Jason was recorded in a commentary or summary and was subsequently taken out of context and treated by Hyginus as a "true" variant (so an unintentional mistake). But one can just as easily imagine that Euripides himself was alluding to a version in which Jason too was consumed by the flames that killed the king and his daughter, and that somehow Hyginus is the only source that preserves that tradition in full. After all, if Medea's killing of her children is Euripides' innovation, as appears likely, is it not a brilliant touch to suppress Jason's death to achieve a more dramatic finale—to have him, still alive, watch as his children are murdered? Then again, someone ignorant of the story might simply have added Jason's name to the mix. And so on.

If the text is so problematic, why not simply jettison the *Fabulae* completely and turn to so-called reliable accounts? If only it were so easy! Leaving aside the issue of what constitutes a "reliable" tradition, sometimes Hyginus is the *only* tradition (since most mythography has been lost), and simply because the *Fabulae* at any one time might transmit a false or unreliable text does not imply that it *always* does so. On the contrary, we can verify in most places accounts that are entirely consistent with known literary accounts. There is nothing unusual or objectionable about Hyginus' account of Nessus' attempted rape of Hercules' wife Deianira in *Fab.* 34, to take just one example of many. And on other occasions, when we might have our doubts because one of Hyginus' stories is unattested in other literary accounts, it might still be corroborated by nonliterary evidence. For instance, on a vase found in Apulia in south Italy (ca. 340 BC) we find a representation of the characters and action in *Fab.* 72, both perhaps deriving from Euripides' lost *Antigone,* a tragedy that offered a markedly different perspective of the events than Sophocles' surviving play of the same name.

Given just how much mythography we have lost, there's no telling how many unique variants will be supported by new archaeological finds. Recent papyrus discoveries have already confirmed the accuracy of some parts of the *Fabulae* that once might have seemed suspicious. Let us take as an example *Fab.* 14, which is a catalog of those who participated in the voyage of the *Argo.* In many places the account is corrupt, sometimes desperately, and we ourselves have proposed many possible solutions where we think we can remedy the situation (documented, like all textual matters, in the endnotes). Yet, even in this context we find authentic material. The first section of the list closely follows the catalog set out in Apollonius Rhodius' great Hellenistic poem *Argonautica,* with only a few deviations. Following this, the account provides still other names, some of which are found in other lists of Argonauts (e.g., in Apollodorus), others of which, until recently, appeared nowhere else. Four of the Argonauts' names once only known from Hyginus (14.19 Phocus and Priasus; 14.20 Thersanor; 14.22 Iolaus) have now been confirmed by a second-century AD papyrus found in Oxyrhynchus, Egypt (*POxy* 61.4097).

Suffice it to say in summary that although the *Fabulae* presents quite significant challenges of interpretation, it is an invaluable source for those interested in Greek myth—if used with caution. But its importance is not just confined to transmitting unique variants of early myth or summaries of lost Greek tragedy. That sort of approach —using the *Fabulae* merely as a means to retrieve *real* myth from pure and golden times of yore—minimizes its distinction as being the only surviving example of its kind, a handbook of Greek myth, written in Latin, aiming at something approaching comprehensiveness, and containing a multitude of forms (e.g., genealogies, narratives, *and* lists) and types (e.g., star myths *and* transformations). No doubt the *Fabulae* will never compete with Homer or Sophocles or Ovid in artistic presentation of myth, but that was never the point in the first place. The *Fabulae* were composed, revised, and continually updated in order to preserve Greek myth in easily digestible form, as a touchstone of culture and as a sort of encyclopedia of cultural literacy. Every Roman who wished to be considered "cultured" was expected to know Greek mythology. The *Fabulae* helped meet that need.

The *Fabulae* and This Translation

Despite the apparent simplicity of Hyginus' Latin, his crabbed and clumsy language presents all too many challenges to the translator, as does the mangled state of the text. There are late Latin expressions, telegraphic compression of language, strange combinations of subordinate clauses, unintelligible phrases, and corrupt passages (see *Fab.* 157 "Neptune's Children" for an extreme example of the last). In a desire to make the *Fabulae* more accessible to a general audience, we have ironed out as many rough patches as we could without misrepresenting what (we think) Hyginus wrote. When the text does present gaps we have noted them with <angle brackets>, but in the many cases where names are clearly wrong and we cannot securely correct them, we have nevertheless decided to print them instead of burdening the book with the cumbersome phrase <*unintelligible name*> or some other notation again and again. Approach names in particular, as everything else, with caution.

For the longer entries such as 125, *The Odyssey,* which runs for several pages, we have added paragraph numbers. As a rule, we have added them in entries where P. K. Marshall's text marks seven or more such sections. We have tried to standardize names, although among so many some unstandardized names may have slipped through.

Further Reading

Despite the important position Hyginus holds as a mythographer, he has not been well served in English, due, presumably, to the great difficulties surrounding the text. The only full-length study of the *Fabulae* in English is Anthony Breen's unpublished 1991 dissertation (University of Illinois at Urbana-Champaign). The best recent treatment in English are those sections of Alan Cameron's *Mythography in the Roman World* (Oxford University Press: Oxford, 2004) that deal with Hyginus, but the *Fabulae* is hardly the focus of that study and the book is geared toward a scholarly audience. The bulk of the work on Hyginus is either in languages other than English—such as A. Werth, *De Hygini Fabularum Indole* (Teubner: Leipzig, 1901) and the introduction and commentary of H. J. Rose, *Hygini Fabulae* (A. W. Sijthoff: repr. Leiden, 1963)—or it appears in specialized journals, for instance, M. Huys, "Euripides and the 'Tales from Euripides': Sources of the *Fabulae* of Ps.-Hyginus?" Part I, *Archiv für Papyrusforschung* 42 (1996) 168–178; Part II, 43 (1997) 11–30.

To our knowledge the only other translation of Hyginus in English is Mary Grant, *The Myths of Hyginus* (University of Kansas Press: Lawrence, 1960), now long out of print. Her work is, moreover, derivative and almost entirely dependent on Rose's edition (first published in 1927), which itself was vitiated by numerous inaccuracies and is now outdated. One of the most pressing needs in classical studies is an updated commentary on Hyginus' *Fabulae.* Our translation is based on P. K. Marshall, *Hygini Fabulae* 2nd ed. (Saur: Munich, 2002), which is vastly superior to the other current edition, that of J.-Y. Boriaud, *Hygin. Fables* (Les Belles Lettres: Paris, 1997), but certainly much work remains to be done on the *Fabulae.* In those places where we diverge from Marshall's text (noted by asterisks in the translation), we have tried to document our changes and the reasons for those changes in the endnotes.

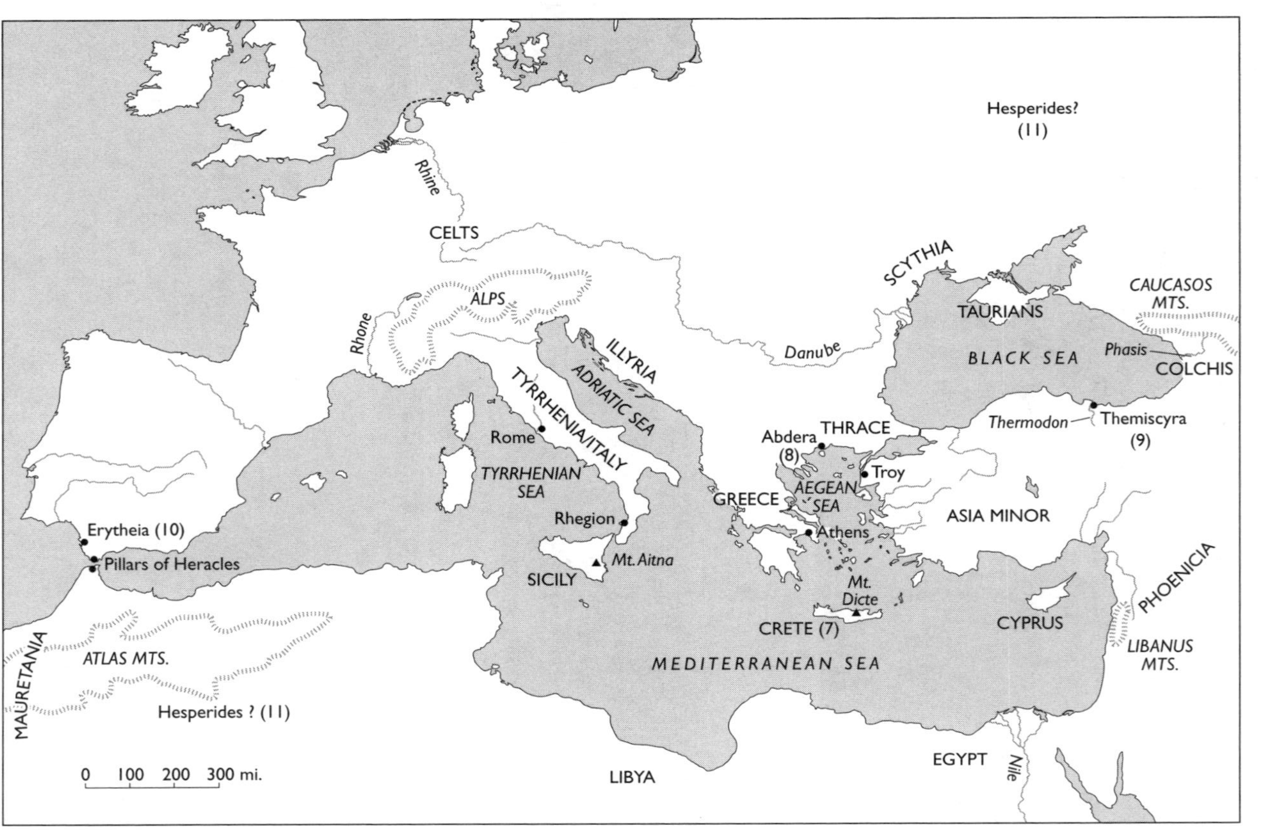

The Mediterranean World. *(Numbers indicate Heracles' labors outside of Greece.)*

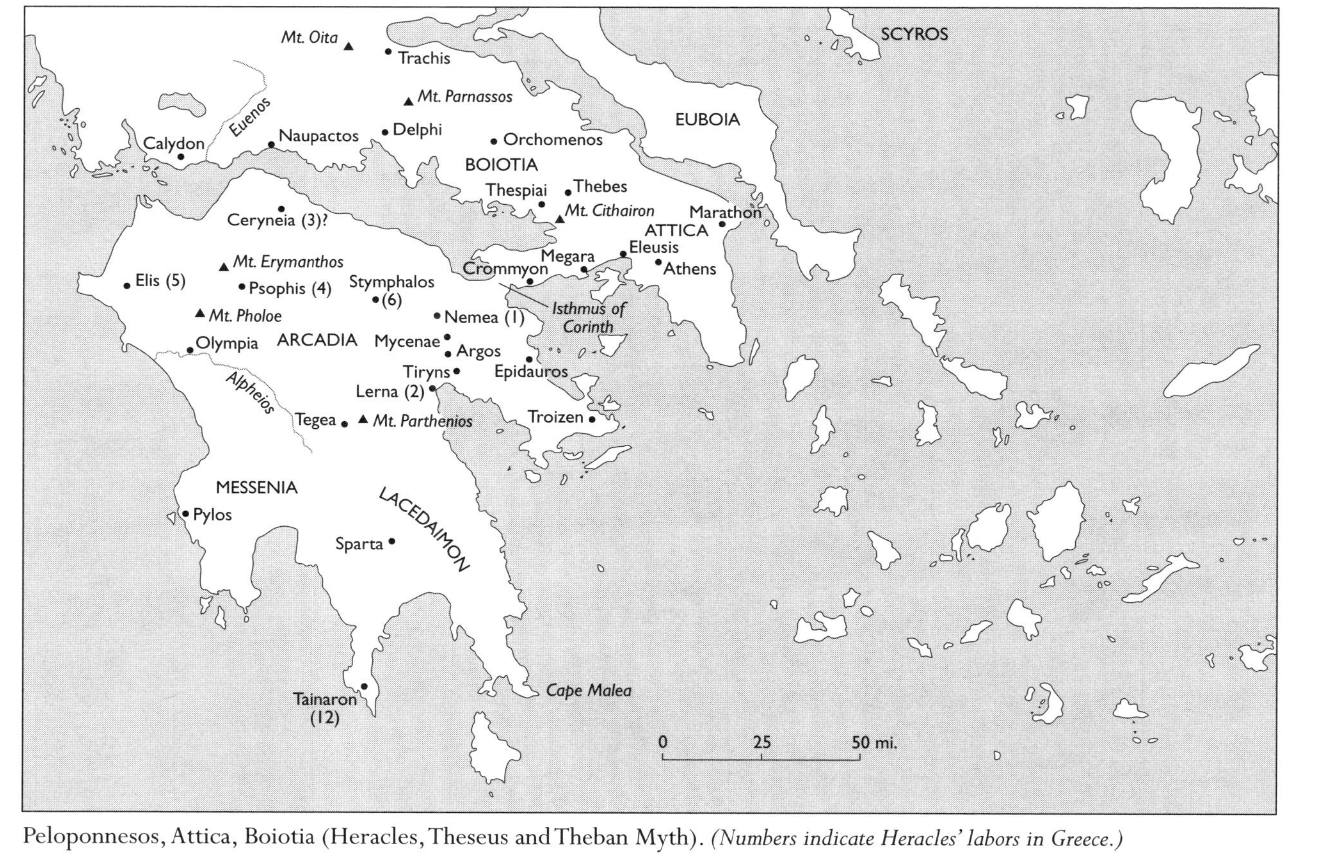

Peloponnesos, Attica, Boiotia (Heracles, Theseus and Theban Myth). *(Numbers indicate Heracles' labors in Greece.)*

Greece and the Aegean. *(Names in parentheses indicate gods and heroes associated with the area.)*

GENEALOGICAL CHARTS

The following nineteen charts represent the main lines of most of the major lineages in Apollodorus' *Bibliotheke*. They are not meant to be complete (the result would be unusable for most purposes), nor do they take into account variants and alternate accounts. Hyginus does not factor into these charts, though there are, of course, many points of agreement between the two authors. Where a name appears in parentheses, the same individual will be found elsewhere on the same chart in his or her place of birth. Cross-references connect many of the charts, but something like "see chart 5" means only that that individual is to be found somewhere on chart 5, not that chart 5 begins with that individual at the top. The charts appear in roughly the order the lineages are introduced, with charts 1–6 covering Book 1, charts 7–9 covering Book 2, and charts 10–18 covering Book 3 and the epitomized material (chart 19 combines material from Books 1 and 2). This division is approximate, however, since there is much overlap in the family histories of the major mythical figures, and Apollodorus sometimes jumps back and forth between lineages as his narrative progresses.

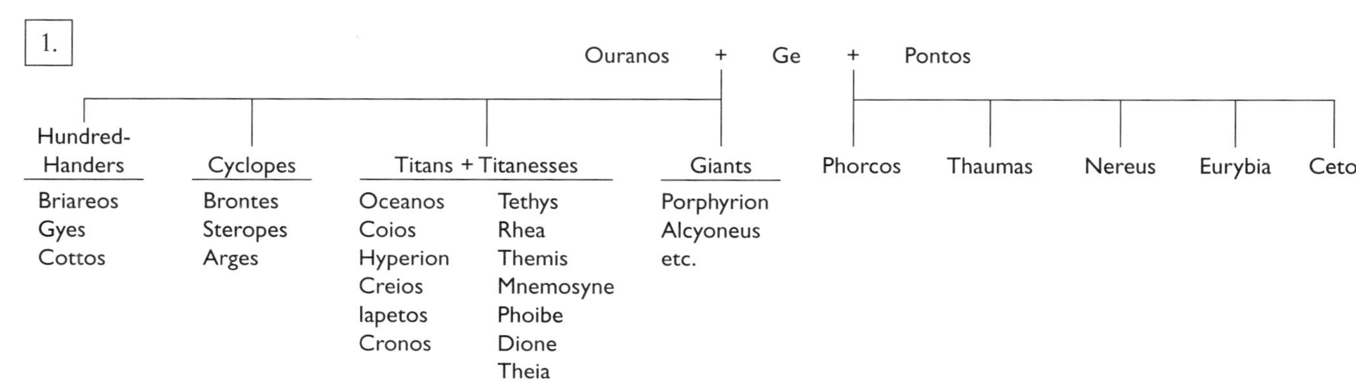

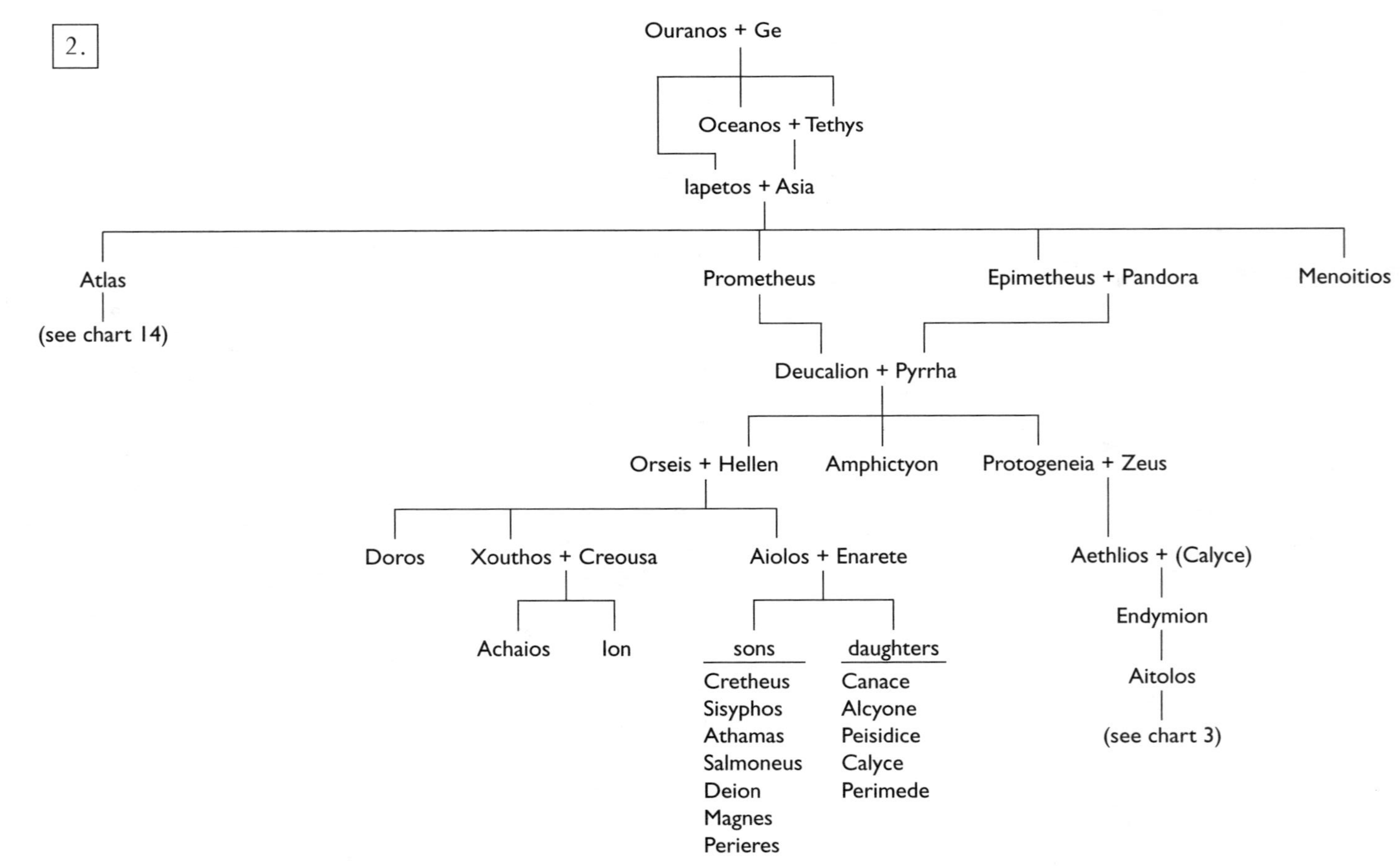
2.
Ouranos + Ge
Oceanos + Tethys
Iapetos + Asia
Atlas
(see chart 14)
Prometheus
Epimetheus + Pandora
Menoitios
Deucalion + Pyrrha
Orseis + Hellen
Amphictyon
Protogeneia + Zeus
Doros
Xouthos + Creousa
Aiolos + Enarete
Aethlios + (Calyce)
Achaios
Ion
sons
Cretheus
Sisyphos
Athamas
Salmoneus
Deion
Magnes
Perieres
daughters
Canace
Alcyone
Peisidice
Calyce
Perimede
Endymion
Aitolos
(see chart 3)

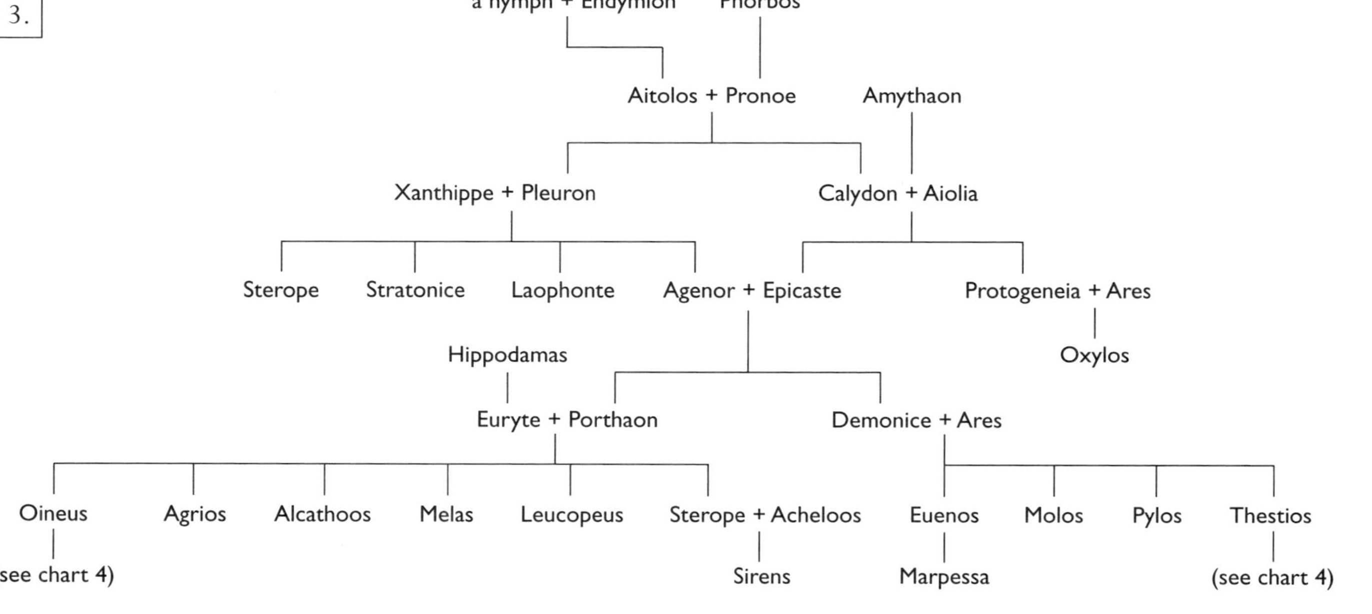
3.
a nymph + Endymion
Phorbos
Aitolos + Pronoe
Amythaon
Xanthippe + Pleuron
Calydon + Aiolia
Sterope
Stratonice
Laophonte
Agenor + Epicaste
Protogeneia + Ares
Oxylos
Hippodamas
Euryte + Porthaon
Demonice + Ares
Oineus
Agrios
Alcathoos
Melas
Leucopeus
Sterope + Acheloos
Euenos
Molos
Pylos
Thestios
(see chart 4)
Sirens
Marpessa
(see chart 4)

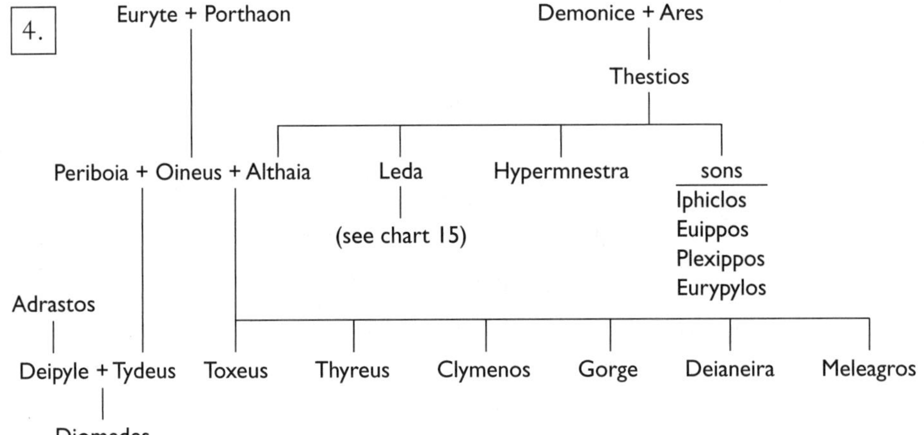
4.
Euryte + Porthaon
Demonice + Ares
Thestios
Periboia + Oineus + Althaia
Leda
(see chart 15)
Hypermnestra
sons
Iphiclos
Euippos
Plexippos
Eurypylos
Adrastos
Deipyle + Tydeus
Diomedes
Toxeus
Thyreus
Clymenos
Gorge
Deianeira
Meleagros

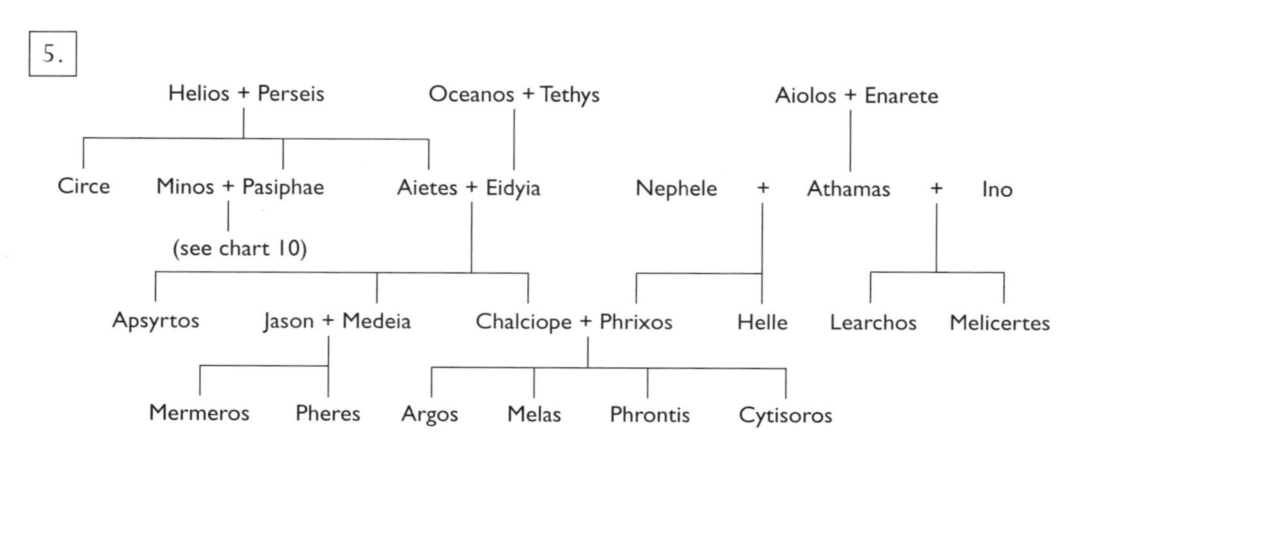

5.
Helios + Perseis
Oceanos + Tethys
Aiolos + Enarete
Circe
Minos + Pasiphae
Aietes + Eidyia
Nephele
+
Athamas
+
Ino
(see chart 10)
Apsyrtos
Jason + Medeia
Chalciope + Phrixos
Helle
Learchos
Melicertes
Mermeros
Pheres
Argos
Melas
Phrontis
Cytisoros

6.

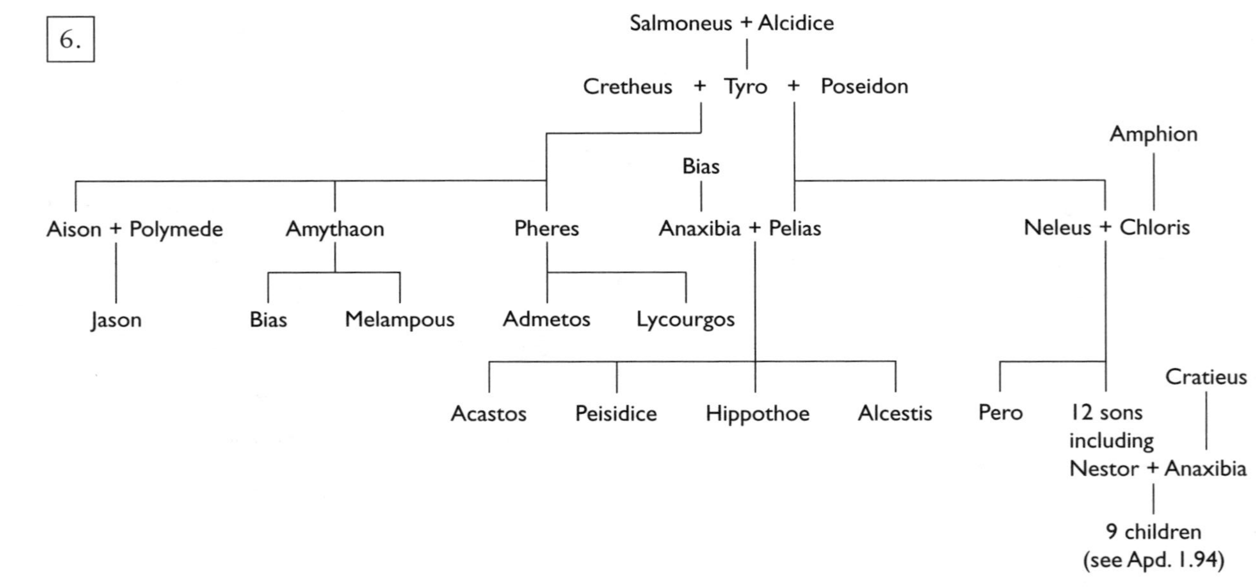

Salmoneus + Alcidice
Cretheus + Tyro + Poseidon
Amphion
Bias
Aison + Polymede
Amythaon
Pheres
Anaxibia + Pelias
Neleus + Chloris
Jason
Bias
Melampous
Admetos
Lycourgos
Cratieus
Acastos
Peisidice
Hippothoe
Alcestis
Pero
12 sons
including
Nestor + Anaxibia
9 children
(see Apd. 1.94)

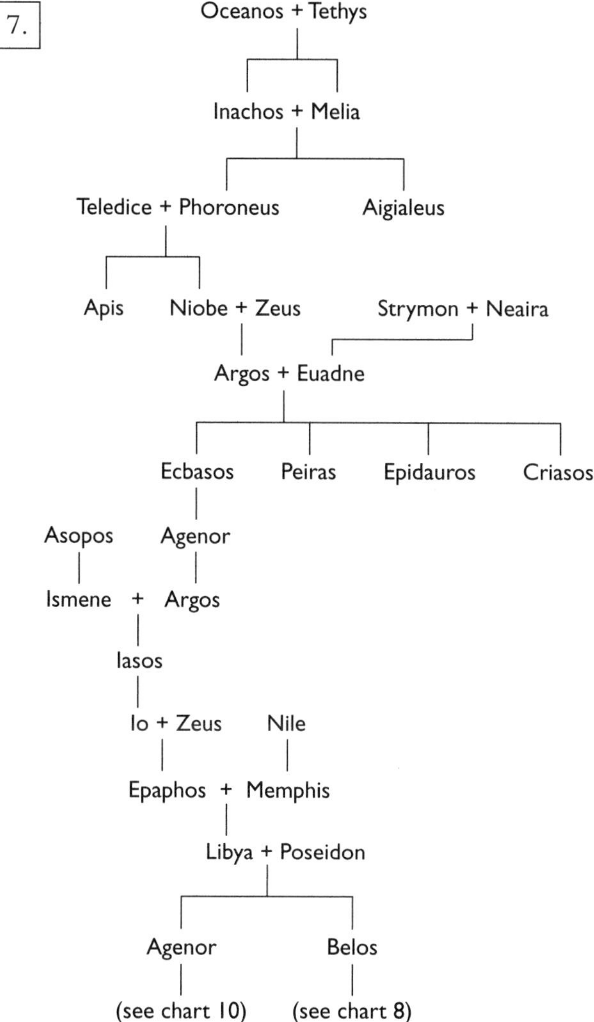
7.
Oceanos + Tethys
Inachos + Melia
Teledice + Phoroneus
Aigialeus
Apis
Niobe + Zeus
Strymon + Neaira
Argos + Euadne
Ecbasos
Peiras
Epidauros
Criasos
Asopos
Agenor
Ismene + Argos
Iasos
Io + Zeus
Nile
Epaphos + Memphis
Libya + Poseidon
Agenor
Belos
(see chart 10)
(see chart 8)

8.

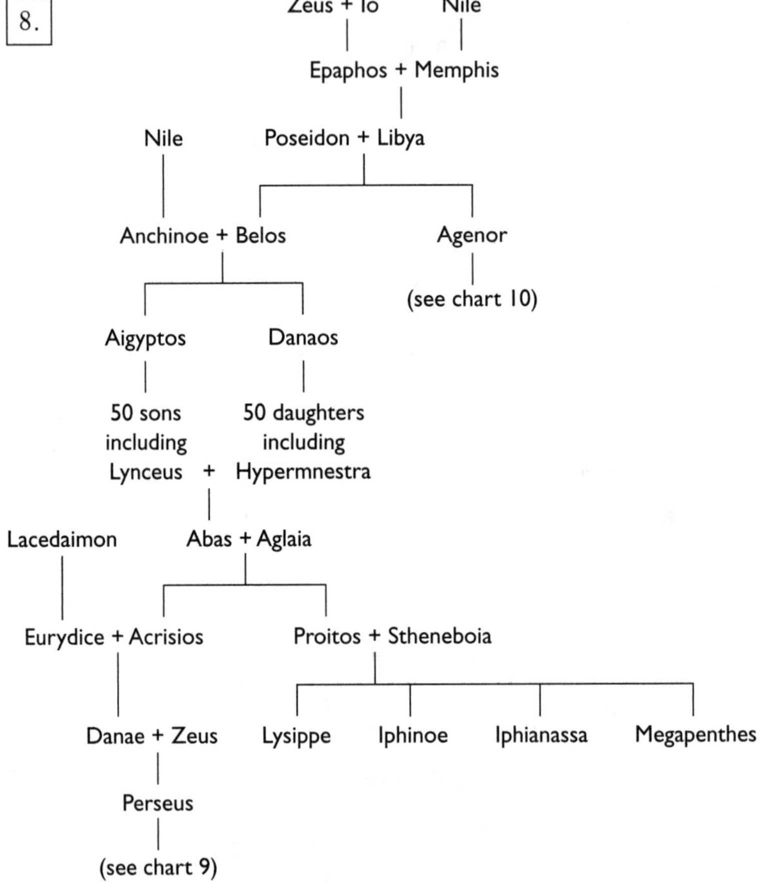
Zeus + Io
Nile
Epaphos + Memphis
Nile
Poseidon + Libya
Anchinoe + Belos
Agenor
(see chart 10)
Aigyptos
Danaos
50 sons including Lynceus
+
50 daughters including Hypermnestra
Lacedaimon
Abas + Aglaia
Eurydice + Acrisios
Proitos + Stheneboia
Danae + Zeus
Lysippe
Iphinoe
Iphianassa
Megapenthes
Perseus
(see chart 9)

9.

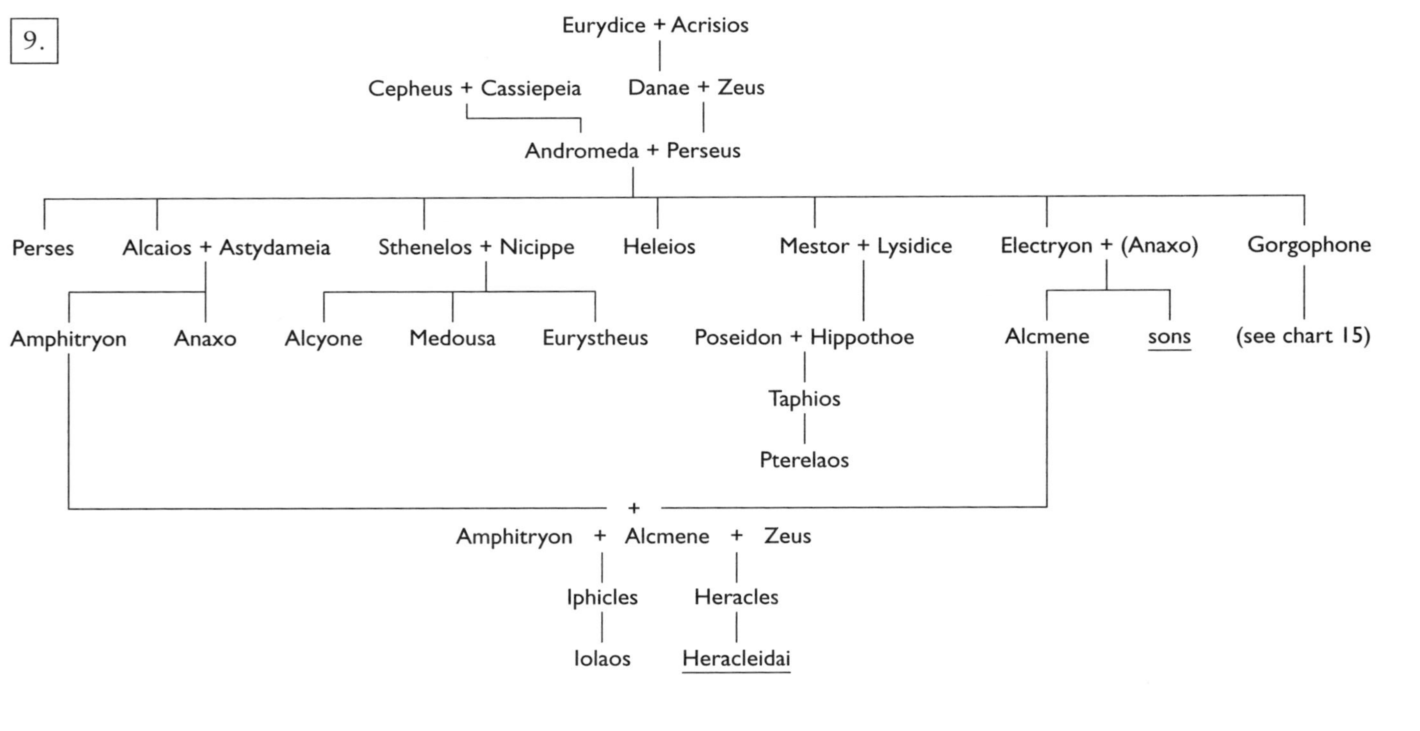
Eurydice + Acrisios
Cepheus + Cassiepeia
Danae + Zeus
Andromeda + Perseus
Perses
Alcaios + Astydameia
Sthenelos + Nicippe
Heleios
Mestor + Lysidice
Electryon + (Anaxo)
Gorgophone
Amphitryon
Anaxo
Alcyone
Medousa
Eurystheus
Poseidon + Hippothoe
Alcmene
sons
(see chart 15)
Taphios
Pterelaos
+
Amphitryon + Alcmene + Zeus
Iphicles
Heracles
Iolaos
Heracleidai

10.

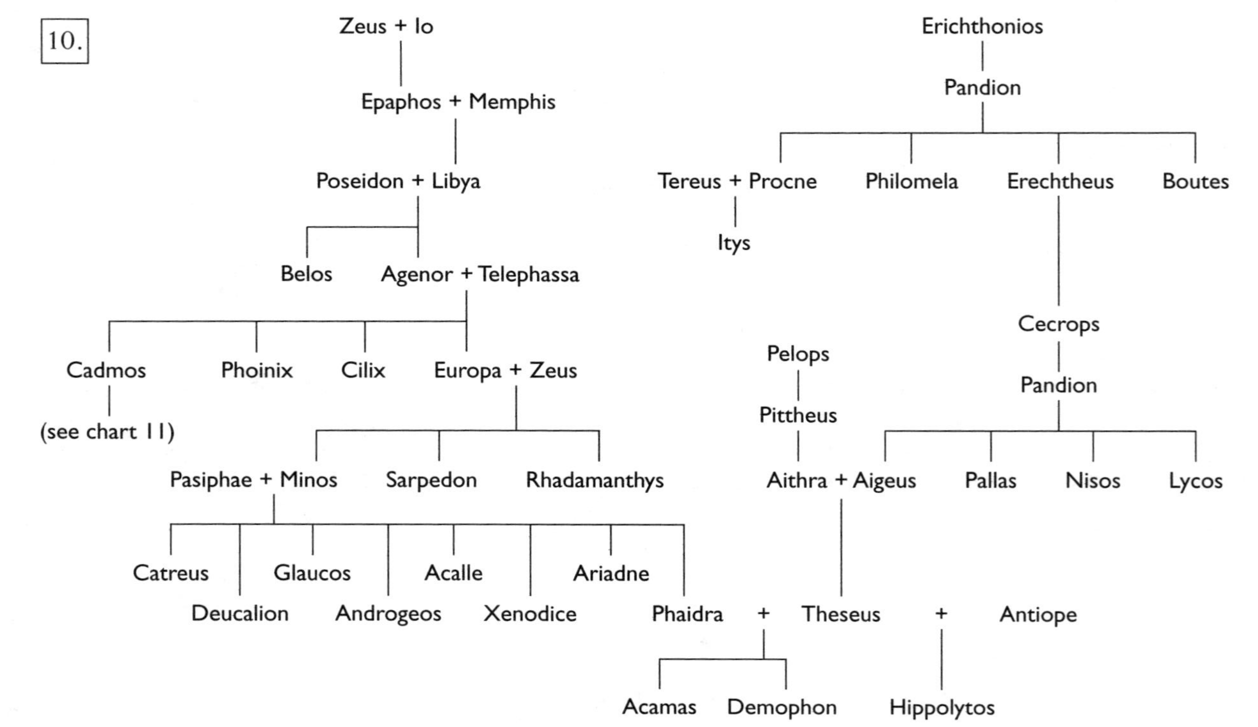
Zeus + Io
Epaphos + Memphis
Poseidon + Libya
Belos
Agenor + Telephassa
Cadmos
(see chart 11)
Phoinix
Cilix
Europa + Zeus
Pasiphae + Minos
Sarpedon
Rhadamanthys
Catreus
Deucalion
Glaucos
Androgeos
Acalle
Xenodice
Ariadne
Phaidra
+
Theseus
+
Antiope
Acamas
Demophon
Hippolytos
Erichthonios
Pandion
Tereus + Procne
Itys
Philomela
Erechtheus
Boutes
Cecrops
Pandion
Pelops
Pittheus
Aithra + Aigeus
Pallas
Nisos
Lycos

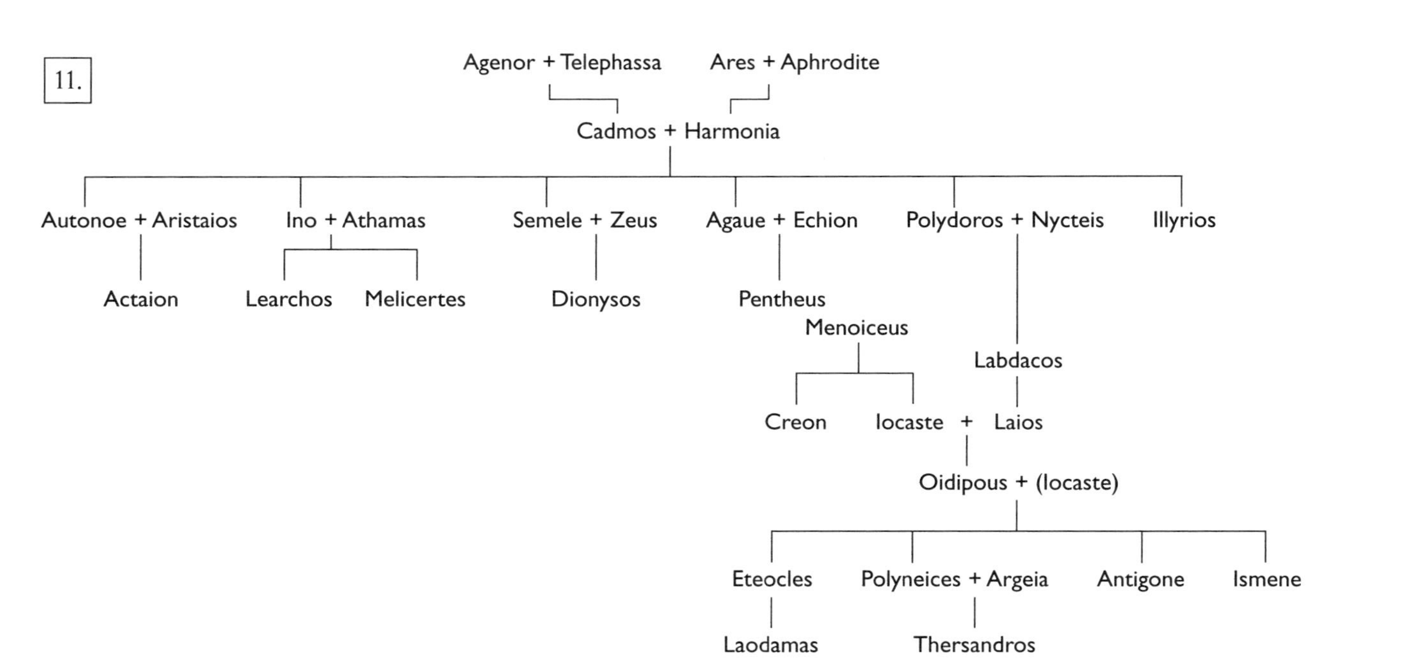
11.
Agenor + Telephassa
Ares + Aphrodite
Cadmos + Harmonia
Autonoe + Aristaios
Ino + Athamas
Semele + Zeus
Agaue + Echion
Polydoros + Nycteis
Illyrios
Actaion
Learchos
Melicertes
Dionysos
Pentheus
Menoiceus
Labdacos
Creon
Iocaste + Laios
Oidipous + (Iocaste)
Eteocles
Polyneices + Argeia
Antigone
Ismene
Laodamas
Thersandros

12.

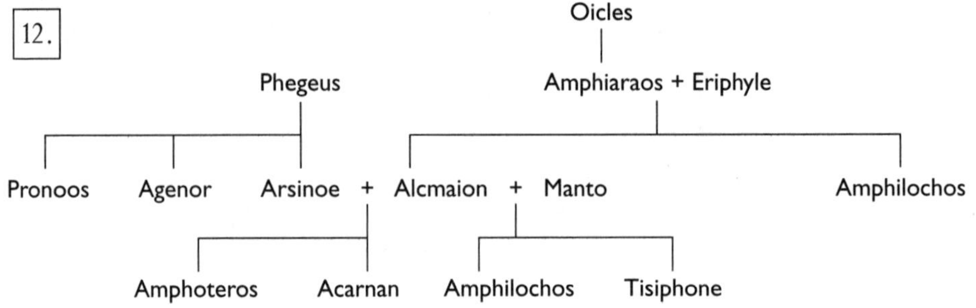

13.

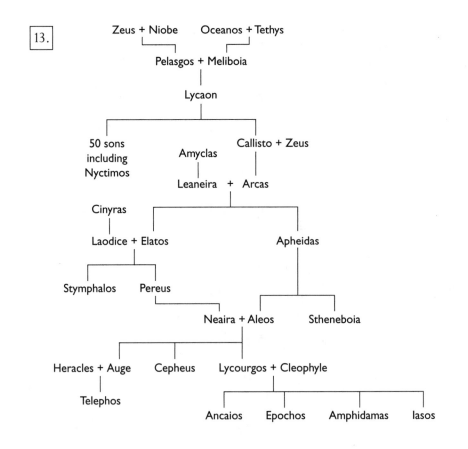

Zeus + Niobe
Oceanos + Tethys
Pelasgos + Meliboia
Lycaon
50 sons including Nyctimos
Callisto + Zeus
Amyclas
Leaneira + Arcas
Cinyras
Laodice + Elatos
Apheidas
Stymphalos
Pereus
Neaira + Aleos
Stheneboia
Heracles + Auge
Cepheus
Lycourgos + Cleophyle
Telephos
Ancaios
Epochos
Amphidamas
Iasos

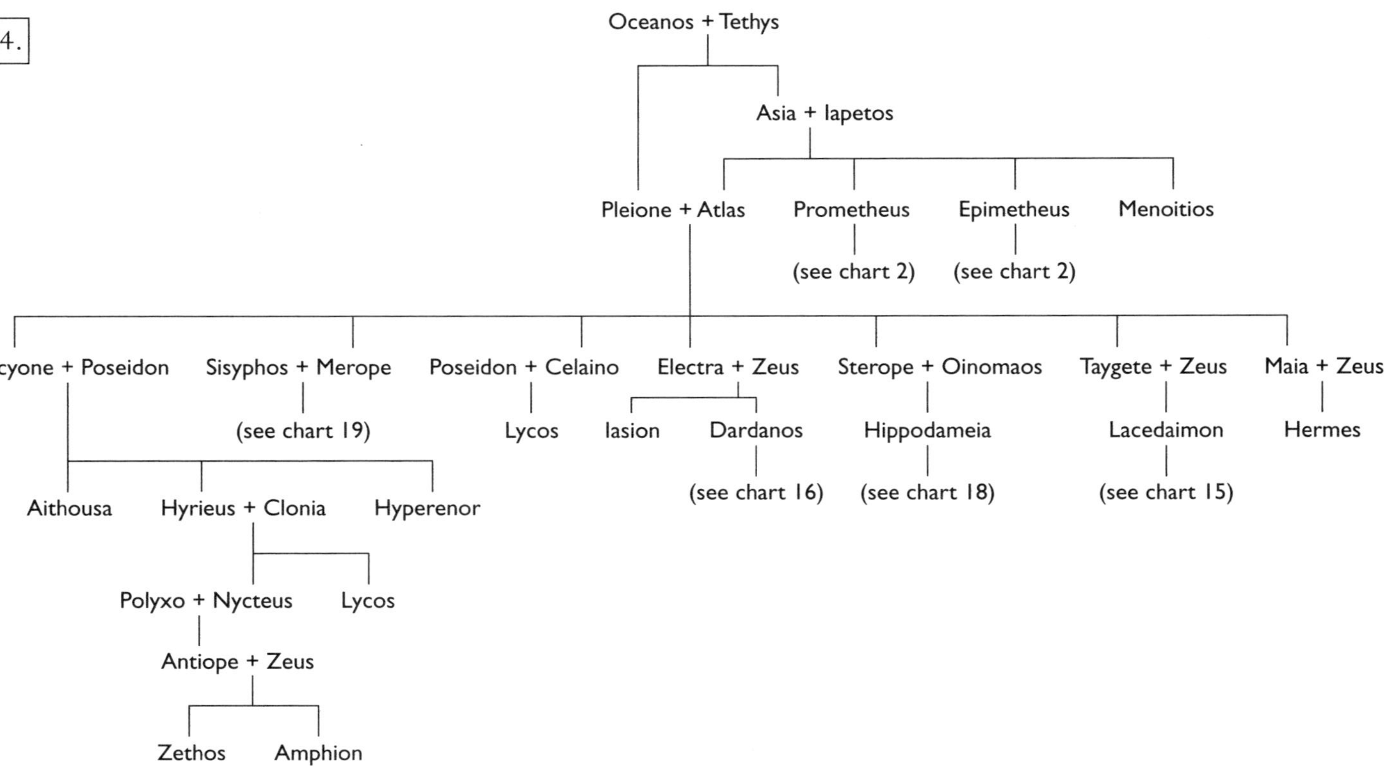
14.
Oceanos + Tethys
Asia + Iapetos
Pleione + Atlas
Prometheus
Epimetheus
Menoitios
(see chart 2)
(see chart 2)
Alcyone + Poseidon
Sisyphos + Merope
Poseidon + Celaino
Electra + Zeus
Sterope + Oinomaos
Taygete + Zeus
Maia + Zeus
(see chart 19)
Lycos
Iasion
Dardanos
Hippodameia
Lacedaimon
Hermes
Aithousa
Hyrieus + Clonia
Hyperenor
(see chart 16)
(see chart 18)
(see chart 15)
Polyxo + Nycteus
Lycos
Antiope + Zeus
Zethos
Amphion

15.

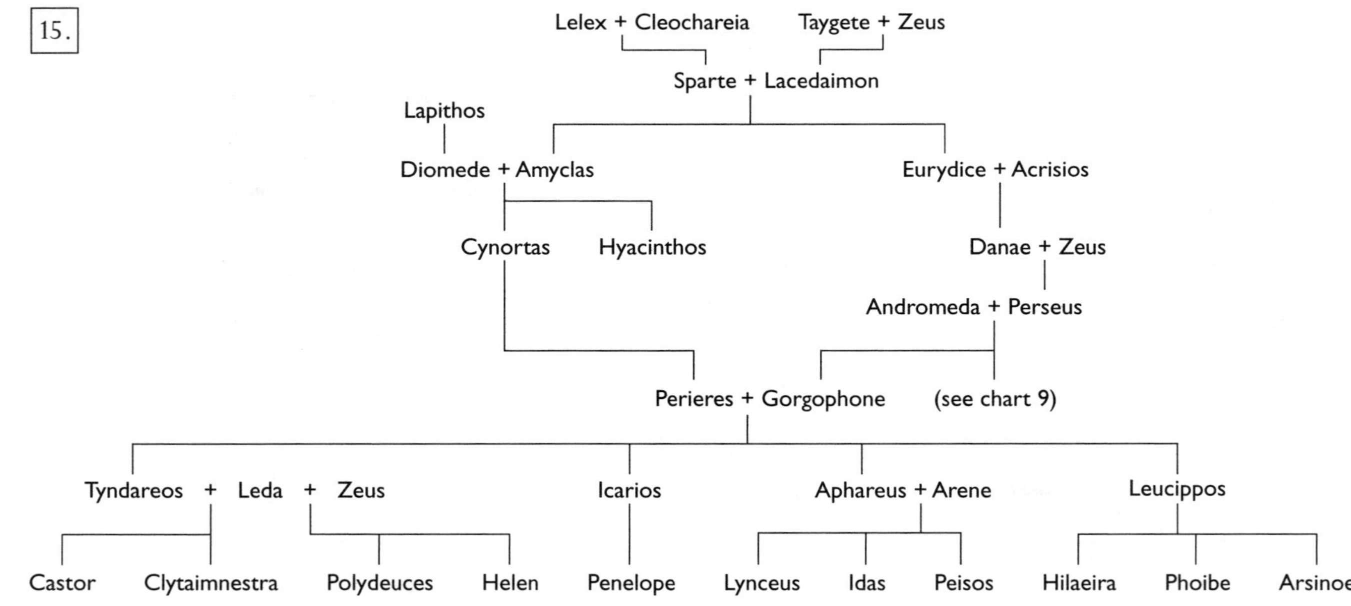
Lelex + Cleochareia
Taygete + Zeus
Sparte + Lacedaimon
Lapithos
Diomede + Amyclas
Eurydice + Acrisios
Cynortas
Hyacinthos
Danae + Zeus
Andromeda + Perseus
Perieres + Gorgophone
(see chart 9)
Tyndareos + Leda + Zeus
Icarios
Aphareus + Arene
Leucippos
Castor
Clytaimnestra
Polydeuces
Helen
Penelope
Lynceus
Idas
Peisos
Hilaeira
Phoibe
Arsinoe

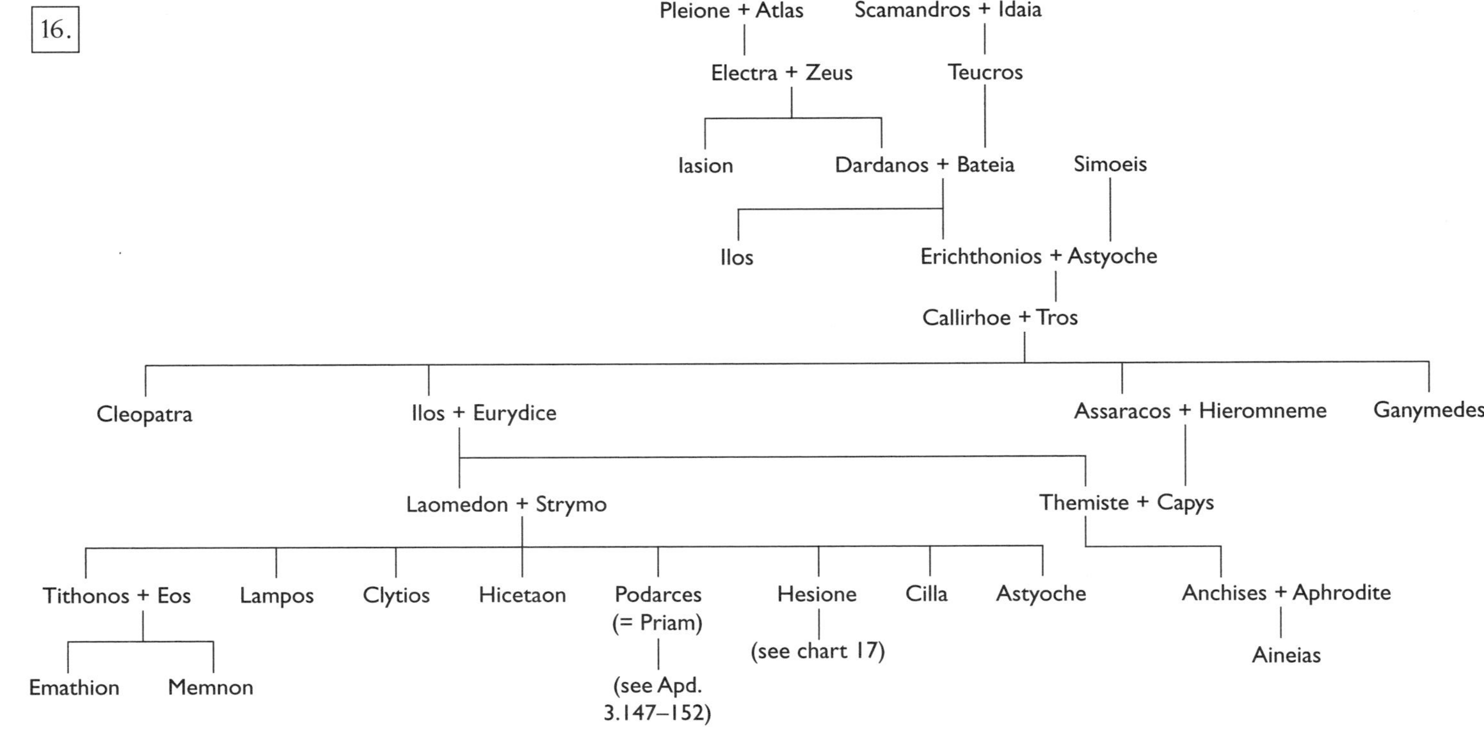
16.
Pleione + Atlas
Scamandros + Idaia
Electra + Zeus
Teucros
Iasion
Dardanos + Bateia
Simoeis
Ilos
Erichthonios + Astyoche
Callirhoe + Tros
Cleopatra
Ilos + Eurydice
Assaracos + Hieromneme
Ganymedes
Laomedon + Strymo
Themiste + Capys
Tithonos + Eos
Lampos
Clytios
Hicetaon
Podarces
(= Priam)
Hesione
Cilla
Astyoche
Anchises + Aphrodite
Emathion
Memnon
(see Apd.
3.147–152)
(see chart 17)
Aineias

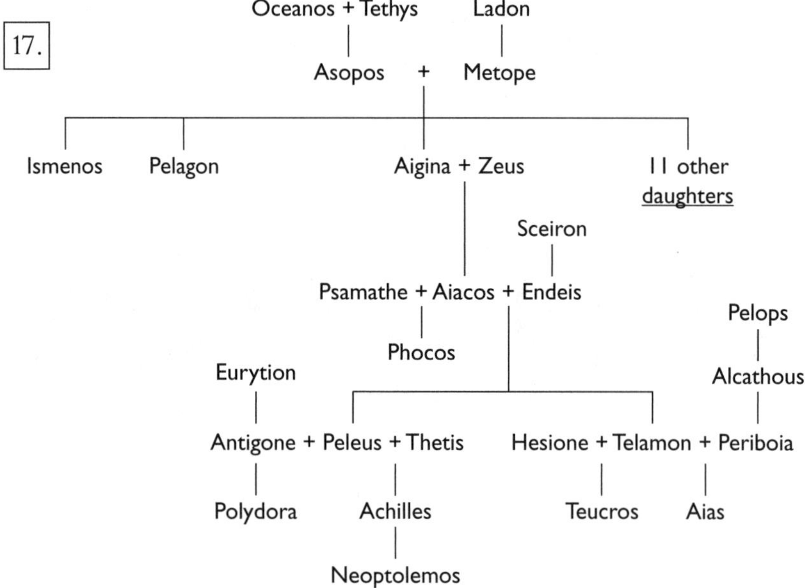
17.
Oceanos + Tethys
Ladon
Asopos + Metope
Ismenos
Pelagon
Aigina + Zeus
11 other daughters
Sceiron
Psamathe + Aiacos + Endeis
Phocos
Pelops
Alcathous
Eurytion
Antigone + Peleus + Thetis
Hesione + Telamon + Periboia
Polydora
Achilles
Teucros
Aias
Neoptolemos

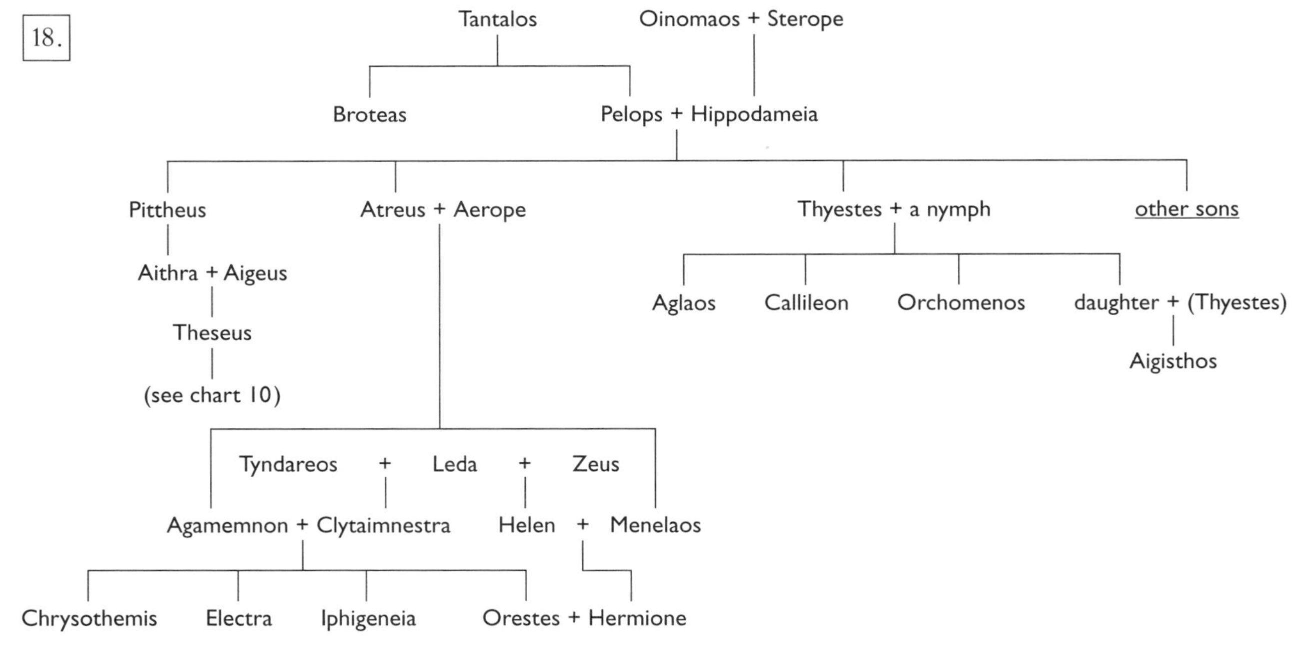
18.
Tantalos
Oinomaos + Sterope
Broteas
Pelops + Hippodameia
Pittheus
Atreus + Aerope
Thyestes + a nymph
other sons
Aithra + Aigeus
Theseus
(see chart 10)
Aglaos
Callileon
Orchomenos
daughter + (Thyestes)
Aigisthos
Tyndareos + Leda + Zeus
Agamemnon + Clytaimnestra
Helen + Menelaos
Chrysothemis
Electra
Iphigeneia
Orestes + Hermione

19.

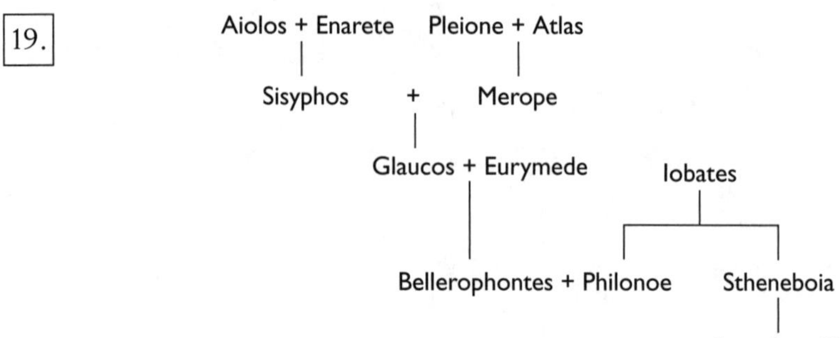
Aiolos + Enarete
Pleione + Atlas
Sisyphos + Merope
Glaucos + Eurymede
Iobates
Bellerophontes + Philonoe
Stheneboia
(see chart 8)

Apollodorus' *Library*

By gathering the coils of time from my learning,
come to know the myths of ancient times.
Look not into the pages of Homer or of elegy,
nor to the tragic Muse or the lyric,
nor seek clamorous verse of Cyclic poets. Look into me
and you will find in me all the cosmos holds.[1]

Book 1
The Gods and the Lineage of Deucalion

Ouranos, Ge, and Their Offspring **1** Ouranos was the first to rule the entire cosmos. [1.1] Having married Ge, he first fathered the ones called Hundred-Handers, namely Briareos, Gyes, and Cottos, who stood unsurpassed in size and power, each with a hundred hands and each with fifty heads. After them Ge bore to him the Cyclopes, namely Arges, Steropes, and Brontes, and each of them had a single eye on his forehead. **2** But Ouranos bound them and threw them into Tartaros (this is a gloomy place in the house of Hades that is as far away from Ge as Ge is from Ouranos). Then he had more children with Ge—sons who were called the Titans, namely Oceanos, Coios, Hyperion, Creios, Iapetos, and, youngest of them all, Cronos; and also daughters, called the Titanesses, namely Tethys, Rhea, Themis, Mnemosyne, Phoibe, Dione, and Theia.

Overthrow of Ouranos; Cronos **3** Ge grew angry at the loss of those of her children who had been thrown into Tartaros. She persuaded the Titans to attack their father and gave an adamantine sickle to Cronos. And, except for Oceanos, they attacked him, and Cronos cut off his father's genitals and threw them into the sea. From the drops of flowing blood the Erinyes were born, Alecto, Tisiphone, and Megaira.

Cronos' Reign; Zeus' Birth Having removed Ouranos from power, the Titans brought up their brothers who had been thrown down into Tartaros and entrusted the kingship to Cronos. **4** But he again bound the Hundred-Handers and Cyclopes and shut them up in Tartaros. He married his sister Rhea, and since Ge and Ouranos told him in a prophecy that he would be deposed from power by his own child, he swallowed his children as they were born. He swallowed the firstborn Hestia, then Demeter and Hera, and after them Plouton and Poseidon. **5** Rhea grew

1. This poem is not in our manuscripts of the *Library* and is perhaps not original to it, but Photios, the learned ninth-century patriarch of Constantinople, reported that it appeared as a preface to the copy he read.

angry at what he had done, and when it happened that her belly was swollen with Zeus, she went to Crete. She gave birth to Zeus in a cave on Mount Dicte and gave him to the Couretes and to the daughters of Melisseus, the nymphs Adrasteia and Ida, to raise. These same nymphs raised the child on the milk of Amaltheia, and the Couretes, wearing armor, stood guard over the infant in the cave and banged their shields with their spears so that Cronos would not hear the sound of his child. Rhea wrapped a stone in swaddling clothes and gave it to Cronos to swallow as if it were their newborn child.

[1.2] **Battle against the Titans (Titanomachy)** **6** When Zeus grew up, he took Metis daughter of Oceanos as his accomplice, and she gave Cronos a drug to swallow. Under its influence he was forced to vomit up first the stone, then the children that he had swallowed. Along with them Zeus fought the war against Cronos and the Titans. They had been fighting for ten years when Ge foretold that Zeus would be victorious if he took as allies those who had been thrown into Tartaros. He killed Campe, who watched over their imprisonment, and released them. **7** And then the Cyclopes gave Zeus thunder, lightning, and the thunderbolt; they gave Hades a helmet; and they gave Poseidon a trident. Armed with these weapons, they defeated the Titans, threw them into Tartaros, and set the Hundred-Handers to guard them. As for themselves, they cast lots for dominion, and Zeus received power in the sky, Poseidon power in the sea, and Plouton power in the house of Hades.

Offspring of the Titans and Other Early Gods **8** The Titans had offspring. Oceanos and Tethys had the Oceanids: Asia, Styx, Electra, Doris, Eurynome, Amphitrite,* and Metis. Coios and Phoibe had Asteria and Leto. Hyperion and Theia had Eos, Helios, and Selene. Creios and Eurybia daughter of Pontos had Astraios, Pallas, and Perses. Iapetos and Asia had Atlas, who holds the sky on his shoulders, Prometheus, Epimetheus, and Menoitios, whom Zeus threw down into Tartaros after striking him with a thunderbolt during the Titanomachy. **9** Cronos and Philyra had Cheiron, a Centaur of double form. Eos and Astraios had the Winds and Stars. Perses and Asteria had Hecate. Pallas and Styx had Nike, Cratos, Zelos, and Bia. And Zeus gave the water of Styx, which flows from a rock in Hades, the power to bind oaths. He gave her this honor as a reward for her joining, along with her children, his fight against the Titans.

10 Pontos and Ge had Phorcos, Thaumas, Nereus, Eurybia, and Ceto. Thaumas and Electra then had Iris and the Harpies (named Aello and Ocypete). Phorcos and Ceto had the Phorcides and the Gorgons, whom we will discuss when we tell the story of Perseus. **11** Nereus and Doris had the Nereids, whose names are Cymothoe, Speio, Glauconome, Nausithoe, Halie, Erato, Sao, Amphitrite, Eunice, Thetis, Eulimene, Agaue, Eudora, Doto, Pherousa, Galateia, Actaia, Pontomedousa, Hippothoe, Lysianassa, **12** Cymo, Eione, Halimede, Plexaura, Eucrante, Proto, Calypso, Panope, Cranto, Neomeris, Hipponoe, Ianeira, Polynome, Autonoe, Melite, Dione, Nesaia, Dero, Euagore, Psamathe, Eumolpe, Ione, Dynamene, Ceto, and Limnoreia.

Divine Offspring of Zeus **13** Zeus married Hera and fathered Hebe, Eilei- [1.3]
thyia, and Ares, but he had intercourse with many mortal and immortal women. By Themis daughter of Ouranos he had daughters, first the Horai, namely Eirene, Eunomia, and Dike, then the Moirai, namely Clotho, Lachesis, and Atropos. By Dione he had Aphrodite. By Eurynome daughter of Oceanos he had the Charites, namely Aglaia, Euphrosyne, and Thaleia. By Styx he had Persephone. By Mnemosyne he had the Muses, first Calliope, then Cleio, Melpomene, Euterpe, Erato, Terpsichore, Ourania, Thaleia, and Polymnia.

Offspring of the Muses **14** Calliope and Oiagros (though really Apollo) had Linos, whom Heracles killed, and Orpheus, who was trained to sing to the cithara and moved stones and trees by his singing. When his wife, Eurydice, died after being bitten by a snake, he went down to the house of Hades, wishing to bring her back, and persuaded Plouton to send her up. **15** Plouton promised to do this if Orpheus would not turn around as he made his way until he arrived at his own house. But Orpheus, in doubt, turned around and looked at his wife, and she returned to the underworld. Orpheus also discovered the mysteries of Dionysos, and he was buried near Pieria after he was torn apart by Mainads.

16 Cleio fell in love with Pieros son of Magnes because of Aphrodite's anger (Cleio had reproached her for loving Adonis). She shared his bed and had a son by him, Hyacinthos. Thamyris, the son of Philammon and the nymph Argiope, came to desire Hyacinthos and was the first to love other men. **17** But Apollo later accidentally killed Hyacinthos, when he was his boyfriend, by hitting him with a discus. Thamyris, on the other hand, who excelled in beauty and singing to the cithara, had a musical contest with the Muses and agreed that if he were found better, he would get to sleep with all of them, but if he lost, he would be deprived of whatever they wished. When the Muses bested him, they deprived him of his sight and his skill at the cithara. **18** Euterpe and the river Strymon had Rhesos, whom Diomedes killed at Troy. According to some he was Calliope's son. Thaleia and Apollo had the Corybantes. Melpomene and Acheloos had the Sirens, of whom we shall speak when we tell the story of Odysseus.

Hephaistos **19** Hera bore Hephaistos without sexual intercourse. According to Homer, however, she had him with Zeus, and Zeus threw him out of heaven for helping Hera when she was in chains. Zeus had hung her from Olympos for sending a storm against Heracles when he was sailing away after capturing Troy. Thetis saved Hephaistos after he fell on Lemnos and became crippled in his legs.

Athena **20** Zeus slept with Metis, who changed into many forms in order not to have sex with him, and when she became pregnant, he swallowed her down quickly because Ge* had said that after having the daughter she was pregnant with she would have a son who would become ruler of heaven. Zeus was afraid of this and swallowed her. When it was time for the birth, Prometheus (although others say it was Hephaistos) struck Zeus' head with an ax, and Athena, dressed for battle, sprang up out of the top of his head near the river Triton.

[1.4] **Daughters of Coios; Apollo and Artemis** **21** As for the daughters of Coios, Asteria changed herself into a quail and threw herself into the sea to avoid intercourse with Zeus, and a city was called Asteria after her in former times, though later it was called Delos. Leto, after sleeping with Zeus, was driven over the whole earth by Hera until she came to Delos. She gave birth first to Artemis, then, with her daughter acting as midwife, she bore Apollo.

22 Artemis spent her time engaged in hunting and remained a virgin. Apollo learned to prophesy from Pan, the son of Zeus and Hubris,* and came to Delphi. At that time Themis gave the oracles. But when the serpent Python, the guardian of the oracle, tried to keep him from passing near the chasm, Apollo killed it and took possession of the oracle. **23** Not much later he also killed Tityos, who was the son of Zeus and Orchomenos' daughter Elare. Out of fear of Hera, Zeus had hidden this woman underground after sleeping with her, though he did bring up into the light her gargantuan son Tityos, with whom she was pregnant. When Leto was coming to Pytho, Tityos saw her and, being filled with desire, tried to drag her off with him. But she called her children, and they shot him down with their bows. Even after death he is punished; vultures eat his heart in the house of Hades.

Marsyas **24** Apollo also killed Marsyas, the son of Olympos, who found a double-flute that Athena had thrown away because it made her face ugly. He entered into a musical contest with Apollo. They agreed that the winner would do whatever he wanted to the loser. When the contest started, Apollo flipped his cithara upside down and competed. He told Marsyas to do the same thing. When he could not, Apollo was declared the winner and, suspending Marsyas from an overhanging pine tree, sliced off his skin and thus killed him.

Orion **25** Artemis killed Orion in Delos. They say he was an *autochthon* and had a gigantic body. Pherecydes says he was the son of Poseidon and Euryale. Poseidon gave him the ability to walk on the sea. He first married Side, whom Hera tossed into the house of Hades because she rivaled her in beauty. Then he went to Chios and sued for the hand of Merope daughter of Oinopion. But Oinopion got him drunk, blinded him after he passed out, and then had him dumped by the shore. **26** Orion went to Hephaistos' forge and picked up a boy. Placing the child on his shoulders, Orion ordered him to guide him to where the sun rises. When he arrived there, he recovered his sight after being completely healed* by the solar brightness and set off quickly after Oinopion. **27** But Poseidon had Hephaistos build a house for Oinopion under the earth, and Eos, who had fallen in love with Orion (Aphrodite made Eos fall in love constantly because she had shared Ares' bed), kidnapped him and brought him to Delos. But Orion, according to others, was killed because he challenged Artemis to a discus contest;* according to some he was shot by Artemis for trying to rape Opis,* one of the virgins who had come from the Hyperboreans. **28** Poseidon married Amphitrite daughter of Oceanos* and fathered Triton and Rhode, the latter of whom Helios married.

Rape of Persephone **29** Plouton fell in love with Persephone and secretly [1.5] kidnapped her with Zeus' help. Demeter wandered over the whole earth in search of her by day and night with torches. When she learned from the people of Hermion that Plouton had kidnapped her, she was angry with the gods and left heaven. She made herself look like a mortal woman and came to Eleusis. **30** First, she sat down upon the rock called Agelastos {"Laughless"} after her, which is located near the well known as Callichoros. Then she went to Celeos, who was at that time the ruler of the Eleusinians. There were women in his house, and they told her to sit with them. An old woman named Iambe joked with the goddess and made her smile. This is why they say women make jokes at the festival of the Thesmophoria.[2]

31 Celeos' wife, Metaneira, had a child, so Demeter took it and nursed it. Wishing to make it immortal, she placed the infant in the fire during the night and stripped away its mortal flesh. By day Demophon (for this was the child's name) grew astoundingly, and so Metaneira* kept watch, and when she found that he had been buried in the fire, she cried out. For this reason the infant was destroyed by the fire, and the goddess revealed herself. **32** She prepared a chariot with winged dragons and gave wheat to Triptolemos, the older of Metaneira's sons. Drawn through the sky in the chariot, he scattered seed over the whole inhabited world. But Panyassis says that Triptolemos was Eleusis' son, for he says that it was to Eleusis' house that Demeter came. Pherecydes says that he was the son of Oceanos and Ge.

33 When Zeus ordered Plouton to send Kore[3] back up, Plouton gave her a pomegranate seed to eat so that she would not remain for a long time by her mother's side. Not foreseeing what would result, she ate it. Ascalaphos, the son of Acheron and Gorgyra, testified against Persephone, and so Demeter placed a heavy rock on top of him in the house of Hades. Persephone was forced to remain for a third of each year with Plouton and the rest of the year with the gods. That is what is told about Demeter.

The Giants **34** But Ge, angry about what happened to the Titans, produced the [1.6] Giants by Ouranos, unsurpassed in bodily size, in power unconquerable. They looked frightful in countenance, with thick hair hanging from their heads and chins, and they had serpent coils for legs. According to some they were born in Phlegrai, but according to others in Pallene. They hurled rocks and flaming trees into heaven. **35** Greatest of them all were Porphyrion and Alcyoneus. Alcyoneus was immortal as long as he fought in the same land where he was born, and he even drove the cattle of Helios out of Erytheia.

It had been prophesied to the gods that none of the Giants could be killed by gods, but that if a certain mortal fought as their ally, the Giants would die. When Ge learned of this, she sought a magic herb to prevent them from being killed even

2. An autumn fertility festival celebrated by women in honor of Demeter, in which ritual insults and dirty jokes played a role.

3. Kore (literally "maiden, daughter") is in Greek frequently used as an alternate name or cult-title for Persephone.

by a mortal, but Zeus forbade Eos, Selene, and Helios to shine. Then he himself cut the herb before Ge could and had Athena call Heracles to help them as an ally. Heracles first shot Alcyoneus, **36** but when he fell onto the earth, he was reinvigorated. At Athena's direction, Heracles dragged him outside of Pallene. That, then, is how he died; but Porphyrion moved against Heracles and Hera in the battle. Zeus put desire for Hera into him. She called for help when the Giant was tearing her clothes in his desire to rape her, and after Zeus hit him with a thunderbolt, Heracles shot and killed him with his bow.

37 As for the other Giants, Apollo shot Ephialtes' left eye out; Heracles shot out the right. Dionysos killed Eurytos with his *thyrsos.* Hecate killed Clytios with torches. Hephaistos killed Mimas* by hitting him with molten metal. Athena threw the island of Sicily onto Encelados as he fled, and she cut the skin off of Pallas and covered her own body with it during the battle. **38** Polybotes was pursued by Poseidon across the sea and came to Cos. Poseidon broke off a piece of the island (called Nisyron) and threw it on him. Hermes, wearing Hades' cap, killed Hippolytos in the fight, while Artemis killed Gration.* The Moirai, fighting with bronze clubs,* killed Agrios and Thoas. Zeus destroyed the rest by hurling his thunderbolts. Heracles shot all of them as they died.

Typhon **39** When the gods had defeated the Giants, Ge became more angry, copulated with Tartaros, and bore Typhon in Cilicia. He had a form that was a mix of man and beast. He bested in size and strength everything that Ge had produced. Down to his thighs he was man-shaped and of such immense size that he was taller than all the mountains, and his head often touched the stars. One of his hands stretched out to the western horizon and one to the eastern, and from them stood out a hundred dragon heads. **40** From the thighs down he had gigantic viper coils that, when stretched out, reached as far as the very top of his head and produced a great hissing. His whole body was covered in wings, hair was blown stiffly out from his head and chin by the wind, and fire flashed from his eyes. Such was Typhon, so great was Typhon when he threw flaming rocks as he moved against heaven itself with hissing and shouting, and he belched a great blast of fire from his mouth.

41 When the gods saw him attacking heaven, they took refuge in Egypt and, being pursued, changed their forms into animals. But Zeus threw thunderbolts when Typhon was far off and struck him with an adamantine sickle when he came close. He doggedly pursued him as he fled all the way to Mount Casios, which looks over Syria. There Zeus saw that Typhon was seriously wounded and engaged him hand-to-hand. **42** But Typhon wrapped his coils around Zeus and got him in a hold. He stripped away the sickle and cut out the sinews of his hands and feet. Lifting Zeus onto his shoulders, he carried him across the sea to Cilicia, and when he arrived, he put him into the Corycian Cave. Likewise, hiding the sinews in a bearskin, he stowed them there. He set the dragoness Delphyne as a guard. This girl was half-beast. But Hermes and Aigipan stole the sinews and put them back in Zeus without being caught.

43 Zeus, having gotten his strength back, suddenly flew down from heaven in a chariot pulled by winged horses and threw thunderbolts at Typhon as he pursued him to the mountain called Nysa, where the Moirai deceived him as he fled, and, persuaded that he would be reinvigorated, he tasted the ephemeral fruits.[4] When the pursuit began again he came to Thrace and, fighting around Mount Haimos, hurled whole mountains. **44** But these were forced back on him by the thunderbolt, and blood {*haima*} gushed out onto the mountain, and they say that it is from this that the mountain is called Haimos. As Typhon tried to flee across the Sicilian Sea, Zeus threw Aitna, a mountain in Sicily, on top of him. This mountain is enormous, and down to this day they say that eruptions of fire from it come from the thunderbolts that were hurled. **45** But enough about that. [1.7]

Prometheus and the Creation of Humans Prometheus fashioned humans from water and earth. He also gave them fire without Zeus' knowledge by hiding it in a fennel stalk. When Zeus discovered this, he ordered Hephaistos to nail his body to Mount Caucasus (this is a mountain in Scythia). Prometheus was nailed to it and bound for many years. Each day an eagle flew down to him and would eat the lobes of his liver, which grew back at night. **46** Prometheus paid this penalty for the stolen fire until Heracles later freed him, as I will explain in the section on Heracles.

Deucalion and the Flood Prometheus had a son, Deucalion. He was king of the area around Phthia and married Pyrrha, the daughter of Epimetheus and Pandora, whom the gods made as the first woman. **47** When Zeus wished to wipe out the bronze race, Deucalion built an ark at Prometheus' direction. He put into it supplies and boarded it with Pyrrha. Zeus poured a great rain from heaven and flooded most of Hellas[5] so that all the people were destroyed except a few who escaped to the nearby high mountains. At that time the mountains in Thessaly split, and everything outside of the Isthmos and the Peloponnesos was flooded. **48** Deucalion was carried in the ark across the sea for nine days and an equal number of nights and landed on Mount Parnassos. There, when the rains stopped, he disembarked and sacrificed to Zeus Phyxios {"God of Escape"}. Zeus sent Hermes to him and bade him choose whatever he wanted. Deucalion chose to have people. At Zeus' direction he picked up rocks and threw them over his head; the ones Deucalion threw became men and the ones Pyrrha threw became women. From this they were also metaphorically called *laoi* {"people"} from the word *laas,* "stone."

Deucalion's Descendants **49** Deucalion had children by Pyrrha: first Hellen, whom some say Zeus fathered; second Amphictyon, who became king of Attica after Cranaos; then a daughter, Protogeneia, by whom Zeus fathered Aethlios. Hellen with the nymph Orseis had Doros, Xouthos, and Aiolos. **50** The people called Greeks he named Hellenes after himself and divided the land among his

4. The Moirai are clearly supposed to have promised that these fruits would heal Typhon, but the story is not told elsewhere in any greater detail.

5. Hellas here, we believe, refers not to Greece generally, but either the northern part of the country generally speaking, or that part of Thessaly known as Hellas.

children. Xouthos got the Peloponnesos, and by Creousa daughter of Erechtheus he fathered Achaios and Ion. The Achaians and the Ionians are named after them. Doros got the land outside the Peloponnesos and named the inhabitants Dorians after himself. **51** Aiolos ruled over the places in Thessaly and called those who dwelled there Aiolians. He married Enarete daughter of Deimachos and fathered seven sons, Cretheus, Sisyphos, Athamas, Salmoneus, Deion, Magnes, and Perieres, and five daughters, Canace, Alcyone, Peisidice, Calyce, and Perimede. **52** Perimede and Acheloos had Hippodamas and Orestes. Peisidice and Myrmidon had Antiphos and Actor.

Heosphoros' son Ceyx married Alcyone. These two died because of their arrogance, for he called his wife Hera and she called her husband Zeus. Zeus turned them into birds; he made her a kingfisher {*alcyon*} and him a gannet {*ceyx*}.

53 Canace bore to Poseidon Hopleus, Nireus, Epopeus, Aloeus, and Triops. Aloeus married Iphimedeia daughter of Triops. She fell in love with Poseidon. Constantly going to the sea, she would scoop up the waves with her hands and pour the water into her lap. Poseidon had sex with her and fathered two sons, Otos and Ephialtes, who were called the Aloadai. **54** They grew a cubit wider and a fathom taller every year. When they were nine years old and were nine cubits wide and nine fathoms high, they decided to fight against the gods. They put Mount Ossa on Mount Olympos, then put Mount Pelion on Ossa. They threatened that they would go up to heaven using these mountains, that they would turn the sea into land by filling it with the mountains, and that they would turn the land into sea. Ephialtes tried to court Hera, and Otos Artemis. **55** They also imprisoned Ares. Then Hermes sneaked him out, and Artemis killed the Aloadai on the island of Naxos with a trick. She made herself look like a deer and jumped between them. In their desire to hit the animal they speared each other.

56 Calyce and Aethlios had a son Endymion, who led the Aiolians from Thessaly and founded Elis. Some say that he was fathered by Zeus. When Selene fell in love with him because of his extraordinary beauty, Zeus allowed him to choose what he wanted. He chose to sleep for all time and to remain immortal and youthful.

57 Endymion and a Naiad nymph (or some say Iphianassa) had Aitolos, who killed Apis son of Phoroneus and went as an exile to the land of the Couretes. He killed his hosts, Doros, Laodocos, and Polypoites, the sons of Phthia and Apollo, and called the land Aitolia after himself.

58 Aitolos and Pronoe daughter of Phorbos had Pleuron and Calydon. The cities in Aitolia were named after them. Pleuron married Xanthippe daughter of Doros and fathered Agenor and three daughters, Sterope, Stratonice, and Laophonte. **59** Calydon and Aiolia daughter of Amythaon had Epicaste and Protogeneia, by whom Ares had Oxylos. Agenor son of Pleuron married Epicaste daughter of Calydon and fathered Porthaon and Demonice, by whom Ares had Euenos, Molos, Pylos, and Thestios.

60 Euenos fathered Marpessa, whom Apollo wished to marry. But Idas son of Aphareus kidnapped her after getting from Poseidon a winged chariot. Pursuing by chariot, Euenos came to the river Lycormas. Because he could not catch him, he slit the throats of his horses and threw himself into the river. The river is named Euenos after him. **61** Idas came to Messene, where Apollo met him and tried to take away the girl. As they fought over who would marry the girl, Zeus broke it up and allowed the maiden herself to choose which of the two she preferred to marry. She feared that Apollo would abandon her when she grew old, so she chose Idas as her husband.

62 Thestios and Eurythemis daughter of Cleoboia had daughters, Althaia, Leda, and Hypermnestra, and sons, Iphiclos, Euippos, Plexippos, and Eurypylos. **63** Porthaon and Euryte daughter of Hippodamas had sons, Oineus, Agrios, Alcathoos, Melas, and Leucopeus, and a daughter, Sterope. They say that Sterope and Acheloos were the parents of the Sirens.

Oineus and His Children; Meleagros and the Calydonian Boar

64 Oineus was king of Calydon and was the first to get a vine plant from Dionysos. [1.8]
He married Althaia daughter of Thestios and fathered Toxeus. When Toxeus jumped over the ditch around the city, Oineus himself killed him. In addition to him, Oineus had Thyreus, Clymenos, a daughter named Gorge, whom Andraimon married, and another daughter, Deianeira, whom they say Althaia had with Dionysos. This daughter drove chariots and trained for war; Heracles wrestled with Acheloos to see who would marry her. **65** Althaia had a son, Meleagros, with Oineus, though they say that he was fathered by Ares. The story goes that when he was seven days old, the Moirai arrived and said that Meleagros would die when the log burning in the fireplace was burned up. When she heard this, Althaia picked up the log and put it into a chest.

Although Meleagros grew to be an invulnerable and powerful man, he died in the following way. **66** When the annual crop had come to the countryside, Oineus sacrificed the first-fruits to all the gods but completely forgot about Artemis. She grew wroth and sent a boar, greater than any other in size and strength, which caused the land to remain fallow and destroyed the livestock and any people who met with it. Oineus called together all the heroes of Hellas to go after this boar and promised to give the hide as a prize of valor to the man who killed the beast.

67 Those who came to hunt the boar were: from Calydon, Meleagros son of Oineus, and Dryas son of Ares; from Messene, Idas and Lynceus, the sons of Aphareus; from Lacedaimon, Castor and Polydeuces, the sons of Zeus and Leda; from Athens, Theseus son of Aigeus; from Pherai, Admetos son of Pheres; from Arcadia, Ancaios and Cepheus, the sons of Lycourgos; from Iolcos, Jason son of Aison; **68** from Thebes, Iphicles son of Amphitryon; from Larissa, Peirithous son of Ixion; from Phthia, Peleus son of Aiacos; from Salamis, Telamon son of Aiacos; from Phthia, Eurytion son of Actor; from Arcadia, Atalante daughter of Schoineus; and from Argos, Amphiaraos son of Oicles. The sons of Thestios also joined them.

69 After they had assembled, Oineus entertained them as his guests for nine days, but on the tenth, Cepheus, Ancaios, and some of the others decided it was beneath them to go out hunting with a woman. Although Meleagros had a wife (Cleopatra, the daughter of Idas and Marpessa), he also wanted to have a child by Atalante. So he forced them to go out hunting with her. **70** When they had surrounded the boar, Hyleus and Ancaios were killed by the beast, and Peleus accidentally killed Eurytion with a javelin. Atalante was the first to shoot the boar with her bow, hitting it in the back. Amphiaraos was the second, hitting it in the eye. But Meleagros killed it with a blow to the flank. When he received the hide, he gave it to Atalante.

71 The sons of Thestios thought it disgraceful that a woman would get the prize for valor when there were men around and took it from her, saying that if Meleagros preferred not to take it, it belonged to them because they were his uncles. Meleagros grew angry, killed the sons of Thestios, and gave the hide to Atalante.

Althaia, out of grief over the death of her brothers, set fire to the log. Meleagros died immediately. **72** But some say that Meleagros did not die in this way, but that when the sons of Thestios laid claim to the skin,* alleging that Iphiclos had struck the first blow, war erupted between the Couretes and the Calydonians. When Meleagros went out and killed some of the sons of Thestios, Althaia called down a curse upon him. He was angry and would not leave his house. **73** But then when the enemy came near the walls of the city and when his fellow citizens, with the olive branches of suppliants in their hands, prayed for him to help, he was with difficulty persuaded by his wife to go out. After he killed the remaining sons of Thestios, he died while fighting. After Meleagros died, Althaia and Cleopatra hanged themselves, and the women who mourned over his corpse were turned into birds.

74 After Althaia died, Oineus married Periboia daughter of Hipponoos. The author of the *Thebaid* says that he took her as a war-prize after the city of Olenos was attacked, but Hesiod says that after she was seduced by Hippostratos son of Amarynceus, her father Hipponoos sent her from Olenos (in Achaia) to Oineus because he lived far away from Elis* and commanded him to kill her. **75** But there are those who say that Hipponoos, upon discovering that his daughter had been seduced by Oineus, sent her off to him carrying his child. Oineus fathered Tydeus with her. Peisandros says that his mother was Gorge because Oineus fell in love with his own daughter in accordance with Zeus' will.

Tydeus **76** After Tydeus had grown into a powerful man, he was driven into exile for murder. Some say he killed Oineus' brother Alcathoos, but the author of the *Alcmaionid* says that he killed the sons of Melas when they were conspiring against Oineus. They were Pheneus, Euryalos, Hyperlaos, Antiochos, Eumedes, Sternops, Xanthippos, and Sthenelaos. Pherecydes, however, says he killed his own brother Olenias. When Agrios had brought him to trial, he went into exile in Argos and came to Adrastos. He married Adrastos' daughter Deipyle and had a son named Diomedes.

77 Then Tydeus marched with Adrastos against the city of Thebes, was wounded by Melanippos, and died. The sons of Agrios (Thersites, Onchestos, Prothoos, Celeutor, Lycopeus, and Melanippos) seized Oineus' kingdom and gave it to their father. What is worse, they put the still-living Oineus in prison and tortured him. **78** Later, Diomedes came secretly from Argos with Alcmaion and killed all the sons of Agrios except Onchestos and Thersites, who ran away to the Peloponnesos before he could catch them. Because Oineus was elderly, Diomedes gave the kingdom to Andraimon, who was married to Oineus' daughter, and took Oineus to the Peloponnesos. **79** The sons of Agrios who got away set an ambush and killed the old man at Telephos' hearth in Arcadia. Diomedes brought his body to Argos and buried him where there is now a city called Oinoe after him. After marrying Aigialeia daughter of Adrastos or, according to some, of Aigialeus, Diomedes marched against Thebes and Troy.

Athamas, His Children, and the Golden Fleece **80** Athamas, one of the sons of Aiolos, ruled Boiotia and fathered by Nephele a son, Phrixos, and a daughter, Helle. He married a second wife, Ino, and had by her Learchos and Melicertes. Ino plotted against the children of Nephele and persuaded the women to parch the wheat. The women got hold of it without their husbands knowing and did just that. The earth, because it was planted with parched wheat, did not yield its annual crop. Because of this Athamas sent to Delphi to ask how to end the famine. **81** Ino convinced the men he sent to tell him that it had been prophesied that the crop failure would end if Phrixos were sacrificed to Zeus. When Athamas heard this, he brought Phrixos to the altar, but only after being forced by the inhabitants of his country to do so. [1.9]

82 Nephele, however, snatched Phrixos up along with her daughter and gave them a ram with a golden fleece that she had gotten from Hermes. Riding it through the sky, they traversed land and sea. When they were over the sea lying between Sigeion and the Chersonesos, Helle slipped off and fell into the deep. Because she died there, the sea is called the Hellespont after her. **83** Phrixos made it to the land of the Colchians, who were ruled by Aietes, the son of Helios and Perseis (and so he was the brother of Circe and Pasiphae, the woman whom Minos married). Aietes welcomed him and gave him one of his daughters, Chalciope. Phrixos sacrificed the golden-fleeced ram to Zeus Phyxios and gave the fleece to Aietes. He in turn nailed it up around an oak in a grove sacred to Ares. Argos, Melas, Phrontis, and Cytisoros were the sons of Phrixos by Chalciope.

84 Because of Hera's wrath Athamas later lost also the children born to him by Ino. He was driven mad and shot Learchos with an arrow, and Ino threw herself and Melicertes into the sea. Driven out of Boiotia, Athamas asked the god where he should make his home. The oracle's response told him to settle in whatever place he was treated as a guest by wild animals. After passing through a lot of territory, he met with some wolves feeding on portions of sheep. But when they caught sight of him, they abandoned the food they were sharing and fled.[6] Athamas settled the area and called the country Athamantia after himself. He married Themisto daughter of Hypseus and fathered Leucon, Erythrios, Schoineus, and Ptoos.

Sisyphos and the Rest of the Sons of Aiolos **85** Sisyphos son of Aiolos founded the city of Ephyra (which is now called Corinth) and married Merope daughter of Atlas. They had a son, Glaucos, who with Eurymede had a son, Bellerophontes, who killed the fire-breathing Chimaira. Sisyphos is punished in Hades' realm by rolling a boulder with his hands and head, wanting to force it over the top. But when the stone is about to be forced over by him, it forces its way back down again. He pays this penalty because of Asopos' daughter Aigina. For, when

6. That is, they provided him with food and so treated him as a guest.

Asopos was looking for her, it is said, Sisyphos revealed to him that Zeus had secretly taken her away.

86 Deion was king of Phocis and married Diomede daughter of Xouthos. He had a daughter, Asterodia, and sons, Ainetos, Actor, Phylacos, and Cephalos, who married Procris daughter of Erechtheus. Later Eos fell in love with him and took him away.

87 Perieres seized the land of Messene and married Gorgophone daughter of Perseus. By her he had sons, Aphareus, Leucippos, Tyndareos, and also Icarios. But many say that Perieres was not the son of Aiolos, but that his father was Cynortas son of Amyclas. For that reason I will explain the stories about the offspring of Perieres in the section on the family of Atlas.

88 Magnes married a Naiad nymph and had sons, Polydectes and Dictys. They colonized Seriphos.

89 Salmoneus first settled in Thessaly, but he later came to Elis and founded a city there. He was punished for his impiety because he was full of hubris and wanted to make himself the equal of Zeus. He said that he actually was Zeus and, stopping offerings to the god, he ordered that sacrifice be made to himself. He used to drag hides tied* along with bronze basins to his chariot and say that he was making thunder.[7] He used to throw burning torches into the air and say that he was making lightning. Zeus struck him with a thunderbolt and obliterated the city he had founded and all of its inhabitants.

Tyro, Pelias, and Neleus **90** Tyro, the daughter of Salmoneus and Alcidice, who was raised by Cretheus (Salmoneus' brother),* fell in love with the river god Enipeus. She would constantly go to his waters and lament over them. Poseidon made himself look like Enipeus and had sex with her. She bore twin sons secretly and exposed them. **91** When the infants were lying exposed, one of the mares of some passing horse herders touched one of them with its hoof and caused a part of his face to be discolored {*pelios*}. The herder took both the children and raised them. He called the one with the mark Pelias and the other Neleus. **92** When they had grown up, they recognized their mother and killed their stepmother, Sidero. They knew that their mother had been wronged by her and attacked her, but she anticipated them by running away to the sanctuary of Hera, but Pelias slaughtered her right on the altars. He continued to dishonor Hera every chance he got.

93 Later, the brothers quarreled with each other. After Neleus was driven out, he came to Messene and founded the city of Pylos. He married Chloris daughter of Amphion, by whom he had a daughter, Pero, and sons, Tauros, Asterios, Pylaon, Deimachos, Eurybios, Epilaos, Phrasios, Eurymenes, Euagoras, Alastor, Nestor, and Periclymenos. Poseidon granted Periclymenos the power to change his shape. When Heracles was plundering Pylos, Periclymenos became a lion during the fight, then a snake, then a bee, but he, along with the other sons of Neleus, was killed by

7. Apollodorus is a bit obscure here, but we believe that the combination of hides and bronze vessels is meant to suggest the *bronteion* or "thunder machine," which was constructed of those materials and used in the Greek theater.

Heracles. **94** Only Nestor was saved since he was being raised in the country of the Gerenians. He married Anaxibia daughter of Cratieus and fathered daughters, Peisidice and Polycaste, and sons, Perseus, Stratios,* Aretos, Echephron, Peisistratos, Antilochos, and Thrasymedes.

95 Pelias settled in Thessaly and married Anaxibia daughter of Bias (though some say he married Phylomache daughter of Amphion). He fathered a son, Acastos, and daughters, Peisidice, Pelopeia, Hippothoe, and Alcestis.

96 Cretheus founded the city of Iolcos and married Tyro daughter of Salmoneus. By her he had sons, Aison, Amythaon, and Pheres. Amythaon lived in Pylos, married Eidomene daughter of Pheres, and had sons, Bias and Melampous.

Bias and Melampous Melampous lived in the country, and in front of his house there was an oak tree in which there was a nest of snakes. After his servants killed the snakes, he gathered firewood and cremated the reptiles, but raised the snakes' young. **97** When they reached maturity, they took up position on either side of his shoulders as he lay sleeping and cleaned out his ears with their tongues. He sprang up, absolutely terrified, but he could understand the voices of the birds that were flying above. He used to learn things from them and then predict the future to mankind. He also gained the power to prophesy by examining sacrificial victims. He had a chance encounter with Apollo near the river Alpheios and for the rest of his life he was a most excellent prophet.

98 Bias asked for the hand of Pero daughter of Neleus in marriage. But there were many suitors for his daughter, and he said that he would give her to the one who would bring him Phylacos'* cows. These were in Phylace and a dog guarded them that no man or animal could approach undetected.* Unable to steal the cows, Bias called upon his brother for assistance. **99** Melampous promised to help. He foretold that he would be caught trying to steal them and that he would get the cows after being imprisoned for a year. After this promise he went off to Phylace and, as he had foretold, he was caught in the act of stealing, imprisoned in a cell, and kept under guard.

With only a little of the year left, he heard the worms in the hidden part of the roof. One was asking what portion of the beam had now been eaten up. The others answered that very little was left. **100** Melampous quickly asked to be transferred to a different cell. This was done, and not much later the first cell collapsed. Phylacos was amazed. Learning that he was an excellent prophet, he released him and invited him to tell how his son Iphiclos might have children. Melampous promised to tell him on the condition that he get the cows. **101** He sacrificed two bulls, cut them into pieces, and called the omen-birds. When a vulture arrived, he learned from it that once, when Phylacos was castrating rams, he had set down his knife next to Iphiclos when it was still bloody. The boy became frightened and ran off. He later stuck the knife in the sacred oak, and the bark grew around the knife and hid it. So Melampous said that, if the knife were found and if he scraped off the rust, and then gave it to Iphiclos to drink for ten days, he would have a child. **102** Learning these things from the vulture, Melampous found the knife, scraped the rust off and gave it to Iphiclos to drink for ten days. So Iphiclos had a son, Podarces. Melampous drove the cows to Pylos, got the daughter of Neleus, and gave her to his brother. For a while he lived in Messene, but when Dionysos drove the women in Argos out of their minds, he healed them in exchange for part of the kingdom and moved there with Bias.

103 Talaos was the son of Bias and Pero. He and Lysimache daughter of Abas (son of Melampous) had Adrastos, Parthenopaios, Pronax, Mecisteus, Aristomachos, and Eriphyle, whom Amphiaraos married. Parthenopaios had Promachos, who marched with the Epigonoi against Thebes. Mecisteus had Euryalos, who went to Troy. Pronax had Lycourgos. Adrastos and Amphithea daughter of Pronax had daughters, Argeia, Deipyle, and Aigialeia, and sons, Aigialeus and Cyanippos.

Admetos and Alcestis **104** Pheres son of Cretheus founded the city of Pherai in Thessaly and fathered Admetos and Lycourgos. Lycourgos then went to live in Nemea, married Eurydice (though some say he married Amphithea), and fathered Opheltes, who was later called Archemoros. **105** When Admetos was king of Pherai, Apollo became his hired hand at the time that Admetos was a suitor for the hand of Pelias' daughter Alcestis. Pelias had promised that he would give his daughter to the one who succeeded in hitching a lion and a boar to a chariot. Apollo hitched them and gave them to Admetos, who brought them to Pelias and got Alcestis. But in making the sacrifice at his wedding, he forgot to sacrifice to Artemis. Because of this, when he opened the door to the bridal chamber, he found it filled with coiled serpents. **106** Apollo told him to appease the goddess and asked the Moirai that Admetos be released from death when he was about to die if someone would willingly choose to die on his behalf. When the day of his death came and neither his father nor his mother was willing to die on his behalf, Alcestis died for him. Kore sent her back up again, but some say that Heracles brought her up to Admetos after fighting with Hades.

Jason and Pelias **107** Jason was the son of Aison son of Cretheus and Polymede daughter of Autolycos. He lived in Iolcos, where Pelias became king after Cretheus. When Pelias consulted an oracle about his kingdom, the god declared that he should beware the one-sandaled man. At first he did not understand the oracle, but later it became clear to him. **108** When he was performing a sacrifice to Poseidon on the shore, he invited many people to it, including Jason. Jason, who lived in the country out of a desire to farm, hurried to the sacrifice. In crossing the Anauros River, he lost a sandal in the stream and so came out the other side "one-sandaled." When Pelias caught sight of him, he connected him with the oracle, approached him, and asked what he would do if he were the ruler and received an oracle saying that he would be killed by one of his citizens. **109** Jason, either because it happened to occur to him or because of the wrath of Hera (so that Medeia would turn out to be Pelias' undoing since he did not honor Hera), said, "I would command him to bring the Golden Fleece." When Pelias heard this, he immediately ordered him to go after the Fleece, which was in a grove of Ares in Colchis, hanging from an oak tree, and guarded by a serpent that never slept.

The Quest for the Golden Fleece **110** Sent in quest of it, Jason summoned Argos son of Phrixos. At Athena's direction Argos built a fifty-oared ship named the *Argo* after its builder. Athena affixed to the prow a piece of wood that could speak from the oak at Dodona. When the ship was built, Jason consulted an oracle, and the god commanded him to set sail after gathering the heroes of Hellas.

The Catalog of Argonauts **111** The ones he gathered were: Tiphys son of Hagnias, who was the ship's helmsman; Orpheus son of Oiagros; Zetes and Calais, the sons of Boreas; Castor and Polydeuces, the sons of Zeus; Telamon and Peleus, the sons of Aiacos; Heracles son of Zeus; Theseus son of Aigeus; Idas and Lynceus, the sons of Aphareus; Amphiaraos son of Oicles; Caineus son of Coronos; **112** Palaimon son of Hephaistos or Aitolos; Cepheus son of Aleos; Laertes son of Arceisios; Autolycos son of Hermes; Atalante daughter of Schoineus; Menoitios son of Actor; Actor son of Hippasos; Admetos son of Pheres; Acastos son of Pelias; Eurytos son of Hermes; Meleagros son of Oineus; Ancaios son of Lycourgos; Euphemos son of Poseidon; Poias son of Thaumacos; Boutes son of Teleon; **113** Phanos and Staphylos, the sons of Dionysos; Erginos son of Poseidon; Periclymenos son of Neleus; Augeias son of Helios; Iphiclos son of Thestios; Argos son of Phrixos; Euryalos son of Mecisteus; Peneleos son of Hippalmos; Leitos son of Alector; Iphitos son of Naubolos; Ascalaphos and Ialmenos, the sons of Ares; Asterios son of Cometes; and Polyphemos son of Elatos.

The Outward Voyage; Lemnos **114** With Jason as captain, these men put to sea and landed on the island of Lemnos. It happened that Lemnos at that time was empty of men and ruled by Hypsipyle daughter of Thoas for the following reason. **115** The Lemnian women did not honor Aphrodite, so she afflicted them with an awful smell. For this reason their husbands took female captives from nearby Thrace and brought them into their beds. Because they were dishonored, the Lemnian women killed their fathers and husbands. Hypsipyle alone hid her father Thoas and saved him. Having landed on Lemnos at that time when it was ruled by women, the Argonauts slept with the women. Hypsipyle took Jason into her bed and had sons, Euneos and Nebrophonos.

Land of the Doliones; King Cyzicos **116** After Lemnos they landed in the land of the Doliones, whose king was Cyzicos. He received them in a very friendly fashion. But when they put to sea from there at night and encountered adverse winds, they landed again among the Doliones without realizing it. The Doliones thought they were a Pelasgian army (they happened to be under constant attack by the Pelasgians) and engaged them in a night battle, the unrealizing attacking the unrealizing. The Argonauts killed many, including Cyzicos. When day came and they realized what had happened, they bitterly lamented, cut off their hair, and gave Cyzicos a lavish burial. After the funeral they sailed off and landed in Mysia.

Loss of Heracles, Polyphemos, and Hylas **117** There they left behind Heracles and Polyphemos. Hylas, the son of Theiodamas, was Heracles' boyfriend.

When he had been sent off to get water, he was abducted by some nymphs because of his beauty. Polyphemos heard him shouting, drew his sword, and chased after him in the belief that the boy was being abducted by pirates. When Heracles met him, he told him about it. While the two of them searched for Hylas, the ship put to sea. Polyphemos founded the city of Cios in Mysia and became its king, while Heracles returned to Argos. **118** But Herodoros says that Heracles at that time did not sail at all, but that he was a slave at the court of Omphale. Pherecydes says that he was left behind at Aphetai in Thessaly after the *Argo* said that it was unable to bear his weight. Demaratos hands down the story that he sailed all the way to Colchis, for Dionysios says that he was in fact the leader of the Argonauts.

Land of the Bebryces; Amycos **119** From Mysia they went off to the land of the Bebryces, ruled by Amycos, the son of Poseidon and the nymph Bithynis. A powerful man, he forced strangers who landed there to box and in that way killed them. Approaching the *Argo* in his usual way, he challenged the best of them to box. Polydeuces took it upon himself to box against him, struck him on the elbow, and killed him. When the Bebryces attacked him, the heroes snatched up their weapons and killed many of them as they tried to flee.

Phineus and the Harpies **120** Setting sail from there, they arrived at Salmydessos in Thrace, where Phineus, a prophet who had lost his sight, lived. Some say he was the son of Agenor; some say he was the son of Poseidon. They say he was blinded by the gods because he foretold the future to mortals; but some say he was blinded by Boreas and the Argonauts because he was persuaded to blind his own children by their stepmother; and some say he was blinded by Poseidon because he told the sons of Phrixos how to sail from Colchis to Hellas. **121** The gods also loosed the Harpies upon him.* They had wings, and when a meal was set out for Phineus, they flew down from the sky. They would snatch up most of it, and what little they left behind was all tainted with a bad odor so that no one could eat it.

When the Argonauts wanted to learn what would happen on their voyage, he said that he would give them advice about it if they would rid him of the Harpies. They set out a table of food for him. The Harpies flew down suddenly with a cry and snatched the food. **122** When Zetes and Calais, the sons of Boreas, saw them, they drew their swords and, being themselves winged, pursued them through the air. It was fated that the Harpies would die at the hands of the sons of Boreas and that the sons of Boreas would die at the time when they would pursue something they could not catch. As the Harpies were pursued, in the Peloponnesos one of them fell into the river Tigres, which is now called the Harpys after her. This one some call Nicothoe, others Aellopous. **123** The other was called Ocypete (or according to some, Ocythoe; Hesiod says she is called Ocypode). She fled across the Propontis until she came to the Echinadian Islands, which are now called the Strophades after her, for she turned around {*strepho*} when she reached them and, coming to the shore, fell from exhaustion, as did the one pursuing her. Apollonios says in his *Argonautica* that they were pursued as far as the Strophades and did not suffer at all after swearing an oath that they would no longer harm Phineus.

The Symplegades; Loss of Idmon and Tiphys **124** Rid of the Harpies, Phineus gave the Argonauts information about their voyage and advised them about the Symplegades in the sea. These were enormous rocks that closed off the passage by sea when they were smashed together by the force of the winds. The fog over them was dense and the clashing loud. It was impossible even for birds to get through them. **125** So Phineus told them to send a pigeon between the rocks. If they saw that it survived, they were to sail through and not worry. But if they saw that it died, they were not to try to press on with sailing. After hearing this they set sail. When they were near the rocks, they released a pigeon from the prow. As it flew, the collision of the rocks cut off the tip of its tail. So they watched for the rocks to retract and then, with earnest rowing and the help of Hera, they passed through, the tip of the ship's stern being clipped off. **126** The Symplegades have stood still since that time, for it was fated that they would stand completely still when a ship passed through them.

The Argonauts came to the Mariandynoi, and their king, Lycos, received them in a very friendly fashion. There Idmon the prophet died after a boar wounded him. Tiphys also died, and Ancaios took over the job of steering the ship.

Arrival in Colchis; Aietes Sets Three Tasks **127** They sailed past the Thermodon River and Mount Caucasus and then came to the Phasis River, which is in Colchis. When the ship came to port, Jason went to Aietes. Explaining what he had been ordered to do by Pelias, he asked Aietes to give him the Fleece. Aietes promised to give it to him if Jason would yoke his bronze-footed bulls by himself. **128** He had two wild bulls of exceptional size that he had received as gifts from Hephaistos. They had bronze feet and breathed fire from their mouths. He ordered Jason to yoke them and then plant teeth from a serpent; he had gotten from Athena the other half of the teeth that Cadmos had planted at Thebes.

Medeia **129** While Jason was at a loss as to how he might be able to yoke the bulls, Medeia fell in love with him. She was the daughter of Aietes and Eidyia daughter of Oceanos. She was a sorceress. Afraid that he would be destroyed by the bulls, she, unbeknownst to her father, promised to help Jason with yoking the bulls and to get the Fleece if he would swear to take her as his wife to Hellas as his companion on the voyage. **130** After Jason swore that he would, she gave him a potion and ordered him to smear it on his shield, spear, and body when he was getting ready to yoke the bulls. She said that when he was smeared with it, he could not be hurt by fire or iron for the space of one day. She explained to him that once the teeth were planted, men were going to rise up fully armed out of the earth and attack him. She told him that when he saw them crowded together, he was to throw some rocks into the middle of them while keeping his distance. When they fought among themselves over this, then he was to kill them.

Jason Completes Three Tasks; Flight from Colchis **131** Jason listened to these instructions and smeared himself with the potion. Going to the temple grove, he searched out the bulls. Though they attacked him with a great deal of fire, he succeeded in yoking them. Jason planted the teeth, and armed men grew up out of the ground. Hidden from view, he threw stones where he saw most of them had gathered. Then he approached them while they fought each other and destroyed them. **132** Although the bulls were yoked, Aietes did not give up the Fleece. He wished to burn the *Argo* and kill its sailors. Medeia anticipated him by leading Jason to the Fleece during the night. She put the guardian serpent to sleep with her potions and then, with the Fleece in hand, went to the *Argo* with Jason. Her brother Apsyrtos also went with her. With them the men set sail at night.

Pursuit by Aietes; Murder of Apsyrtos **133** When Aietes found out what Medeia had dared to do, he set out to pursue the ship. When Medeia saw that he was close, she murdered her brother, dismembered him, and cast the pieces into the sea. Aietes gathered up the pieces of his son and, in doing so, fell behind in the pursuit. For that reason he turned back, buried the recovered pieces of his son, and named the place Tomoi {"Cuts"}. He sent out many Colchians to search for the *Argo,* threatening that they would suffer the punishments he intended for Medeia if they did not bring her to him. They all split up and each made the search in a different place.

134 Angry over the murder of Apsyrtos, Zeus sent a violent storm against the Argonauts when they were just sailing past the Eridanos River and threw them off course. As they sailed past the Apsyrtides Islands, the ship spoke and said that the anger of Zeus would not come to an end unless they went to Ausonia and had the pollution of Apsyrtos' murder cleansed by Circe. After they sailed past the Ligurian and Celtic peoples, crossed the Sardinian Sea, and coasted along Tyrrhenia, they came to Aiaia, where they supplicated Circe and were cleansed.

The Sirens and Other Obstacles **135** When they sailed past the Sirens, Orpheus sang the music to counteract their song and so restrained the Argonauts. Boutes alone swam out to them, but Aphrodite snatched him up and settled him in Lilybaion. **136** After the Sirens, Charybdis awaited the ship, as did Scylla and the Wandering Rocks, over which a lot of fire and smoke was seen rising. But Thetis and the Nereids brought the ship through them at the request of Hera.

Phaiacia; Colchians Search for Medeia **137** They sailed past the island of Thrinacia (which held the cattle of Helios) and came to Corcyra, the island of the Phaiacians ruled by Alcinoos. When the Colchians were unable to find the ship, some of them made new homes in the Ceraunian Mountains, and some went to Illyria and colonized the Apsyrtides Islands. Still others came to the Phaiacians, caught up with the *Argo,* and demanded Medeia from Alcinoos. **138** He said that if she had already had sex with Jason he would give her to him. But if she were still a virgin, he said that he would send her back to her father. Arete, the wife of Alcinoos, anticipated him by having Medeia sleep with Jason. As a result, the Colchians settled with the Phaiacians, and the Argonauts set sail with Medeia.

Anaphe **139** While they were sailing at night, they ran into a strong storm. But Apollo stood on the ridges of Melas and used his bow to shoot a bolt of lightning down into the sea. They saw that an island was nearby and, having anchored at it, called it Anaphe because it had appeared {*anaphaino*} unexpectedly. They dedicated an altar to Apollo Aigletos {"Radiant"}, made sacrifice, and turned their attention to feasting. Twelve female servants given to Medeia by Arete mocked the heroes playfully. As a result, even to this day it is customary for women to make jokes at this sacrifice.

Talos **140** Setting sail from there, they were prevented from landing on Crete by Talos. Some say that he was one of the men of the bronze race, but others say he was given to Minos by Hephaistos and was actually a man made of bronze, though others say he was a bull. He had a single vein stretching down from his neck to his ankles. A bronze nail was set firmly into the end of the vein. **141** This Talos guarded the island by running around it three times a day. Therefore, when he saw the *Argo* sailing in, he threw stones at it in his usual manner. He was tricked and killed by Medeia. According to some, Medeia threw him into a fit of madness with magic. According to others, she promised to make him immortal but pulled out the nail instead, and he died when all his *ichor* flowed out. Still others say that he died after being shot in the ankle with an arrow by Poias.

Aigina and Completion of the Voyage **142** After remaining there for one night, they landed on Aigina because they wanted to get water. A contest arose among them over fetching it. From there they sailed between Euboia and Locris and reached Iolcos. It took them four months to complete the whole voyage.

Situation in Iolcos; Death of Pelias **143** Pelias, who had decided that there was no possibility of the Argonauts' returning, wanted to kill Aison. Aison, however, asked to be allowed to kill himself. While making a sacrifice, he fearlessly drank the bull's blood[8] and died. Jason's mother put a curse on Pelias and hanged herself, leaving behind an infant son named Promachos. Pelias even killed the son she left behind. When Jason returned, he handed over the Fleece and waited for the right moment, wanting to get revenge for the injustices done to him. **144** He sailed then with the heroes to the Isthmos and dedicated the ship to Poseidon. Later, he asked Medeia to look for a way that Pelias might be punished for his crimes against him. She went into the palace of Pelias and by promising to make him young again through magic persuaded his daughters to chop their father up and boil him. To convince them, she butchered a ram and, after boiling it, turned it into a lamb. Believing her, they cut their father up and boiled him. Acastos, with the help of the inhabitants of Iolcos, buried his father and kicked Jason out of Iolcos along with Medeia.

Exile in Corinth; Death of Medeia and Jason's Sons **145** They went to Corinth and lived there prosperously for ten years. Later, when Creon, the king of Corinth, betrothed his daughter Glauce to Jason, Jason decided to divorce

8. An act thought by the ancients to be fatal.

Medeia and marry her. But Medeia called upon the gods by whom Jason had sworn his oaths and criticized Jason's ingratitude over and over again. Then she sent to the bride a dress that had magical potions worked into it. When the girl put it on, she was burned up by vicious fire, as was her father too when he tried to help her. **146** Medeia killed Mermeros and Pheres, the sons she had with Jason. From Helios she got a chariot that was pulled by winged serpents and on it made her escape to Athens. It is also said that when she fled, she left behind her sons, who were still infants, setting them on the altar of Hera Acraia as suppliants. The Corinthians took them out of the sanctuary and wounded them fatally.

Medeia after Jason **147** Medeia went to Athens. There she married Aigeus and bore him a son, Medos. Later, she plotted against Theseus and was driven into exile from Athens with her son. But her son conquered many barbarians and called the whole area under his control Media. He died while campaigning against the Indians. Medeia returned unrecognized to Colchis and discovered that Aietes had been deprived of his kingdom by his brother, Perses. She killed Perses and restored the kingdom to her father.

Book 2
The Lineage of Inachos

[2.1] **Inachos and His Sons, Phoroneus and Aigialeus** **1** Since we have now gone through the family of Deucalion, next let us speak of that of Inachos.

Inachos was the son of Oceanos and Tethys. A river in Argos is named after him. He and Melia daughter of Oceanos had sons, Phoroneus and Aigialeus. Now, Aigialeus died without having children, so his whole land was called Aigialeia. Phoroneus ruled over all the territory that would later be called the Peloponnesos. With the nymph Teledice he had Apis and Niobe. **2** Apis turned his power into tyranny, was a violent dictator, and named the Peloponnesos Apia after himself. Thelxion and Telchis plotted against him and he died childless at their hands. Considered a god, he was called Sarapis.

Argos Argos was the son of Niobe and Zeus (she was the first mortal woman with whom he had intercourse). According to Acousilaos, Pelasgos was also their son and the inhabitants of the Peloponnesos were called Pelasgians after him. But Hesiod says that Pelasgos was an *autochthon.* **3** I will speak of him later. Argos received the kingdom and called the Peloponnesos Argos after himself. He married Euadne, the daughter of Strymon and Neaira, and had Ecbasos, Peiras, Epidauros, and Criasos (the last was the one who inherited the kingdom).

The Second Argos **4** Agenor was Ecbasos' son. He had a son Argos, known as the All-seeing, for he had eyes all over his body. Being extraordinarily strong, he killed the bull that was devastating Arcadia and wore its skin. When Satyros wronged the Arcadians and stole their herds, Argos confronted and killed him. It is said that by waiting for her to fall asleep he killed Echidna, the daughter of Tartaros and Ge, who used to carry off passersby. He also avenged the murder of Apis by killing those guilty of the crime.

Io **5** Argos and Ismene daughter of Asopos had a son, Iasos, who they say was the father of Io. But the chronicler Castor and many of the tragedians say that Io was the daughter of Inachos. Hesiod and Acousilaos say that she was the daughter of Peiren. Zeus seduced her while she was serving as priestess of Hera. When he was caught by Hera, he touched the girl and turned her into a white cow, swearing that he had not had intercourse with her. That is why Hesiod says that oaths made in matters of love do not draw the ire of the gods. **6** Hera got the cow from Zeus and set all-seeing Argos to guard her. Pherecydes says that Argos was the son of Arestor, Asclepiades that he was the son of Inachos, and Cercops that he was the son of Argos and Ismene daughter of Asopos. But Acousilaos says that he was an *autochthon*. Argos tied her to the olive tree that was in the grove of the Mycenaeans. **7** Zeus ordered Hermes to steal the cow. But since Hierax revealed the plan and Hermes could not do so undetected, he killed Argos by throwing a stone at him, and from that he was called Argeiphontes {"Killer of Argos"}.

Io's Journey; the Gadfly; Epaphos Hera sent a gadfly against the cow. First, the cow came to the Ionian Gulf (so called after her), then traveled across Illyria, went over Mount Haimos, and then crossed what at the time was called the Thracian Strait but is now called the Bosporos {"Cow's Crossing"} after her. **8** Going to Scythia and the land of the Cimmerians, she wandered over a great deal of dry land and swam across a lot of sea in both Europe and Asia. Finally, she came to Egypt, where she recovered her old form and by the river Nile bore a son, Epaphos. **9** Hera asked the Couretes to kidnap him, and kidnap him they did. But when Zeus learned of it, he killed the Couretes, and Io went in search of her son. She wandered through all of Syria (it was revealed to her that the wife of the king of Byblos was nursing her son there) and found Epaphos. Coming to Egypt, she married Telegonos, who was then king of the Egyptians. She dedicated a statue of Demeter, whom the Egyptians call Isis. In the same way they also called Io Isis.

Agenor and Belos; Aigyptos and Danaos **10** When Epaphos was king of the Egyptians, he married Memphis, the daughter of Nile, and built a city named Memphis after her. He had a daughter, Libya, after whom the region of Libya was named. Libya and Poseidon had twin sons, Agenor and Belos. Agenor went off to Phoenicia, became king, and became the ancestor of the great lineage there (for that reason we will defer our discussion of him). **11** Belos remained in Egypt, was king of that country, and married Nile's daughter Anchinoe. He had twin sons, Aigyptos and Danaos, and according to Euripides he also had Cepheus and Phineus. Belos sent Danaos off to colonize Libya and Aigyptos to Arabia, but the latter also subdued the land of the Melampodes and called it Egypt after himself.

The Sons of Aigyptos and the Daughters of Danaos **12** With several different women Aigyptos had fifty sons and Danaos had fifty daughters. When they later were at odds over the kingdom, Danaos became afraid of Aigyptos' sons, and, at the direction of Athena, he was the first to build a ship. He put his daughters aboard and fled. **13** Landing at Rhodes, he set up the statue of Lindian Athena.

From there he came to Argos. The king at that time, Gelanor, surrendered his kingdom to Danaos, <who brought the land under his control and called the inhabitants Danaans after himself.>* Now, the land was without water because Poseidon, angry at Inachos for testifying that the country belonged to Hera, had dried up even the springs. So Danaos sent his daughters to fetch water. **14** Searching for water, one of them, Amymone, threw a javelin at a deer and hit a sleeping satyr. He, startled awake, desired to have sex with her. The satyr fled when Poseidon showed up, and Amymone slept with Poseidon, who showed her the springs in Lerna.

15 The sons of Aigyptos came to Argos and called upon Danaos to put aside his hatred and asked to marry his daughters. Danaos both disbelieved their assurances and bore a grudge about his exile, but he agreed to the marriages and apportioned out his daughters. **16** They chose the oldest, Hypermnestra, for Lynceus and Gorgophone for Proteus, for these two were Aigyptos' sons by his wife, Queen Argyphia. As for the rest, Bousiris, Encelados, Lycos, and Daiphron chose lots and got Danaos' daughters by Europe, namely Automate, Amymone, Agaue, and Scaia. Those four had been born to Danaos by a queen, but Gorgophone and Hypermnestra were his daughters by Elephantis. **17** Istros got Hippodameia. Chalcodon got Rhodia. Agenor got Cleopatra. Chaitos got Asteria. Diocorystes got Hippothoe. Alces got Glauce. Alcmenor got Hippomedousa. Hippothoos got Gorge. Euchenor got Iphimedousa. Hippolytos got Rhode. These last ten were Aigyptos' sons by an Arabian woman, and the girls were Danaos' daughters by Hamadryad nymphs, some by Atalanteia, some by Phoibe. **18** Agaptolemos got Peirene. Cercetes got Dorion. Eurydamas got Phartis. Aigios got Mnestra. Argios got Euippe. Archelaos got Anaxibia. Menemachos got Nelo. These seven were Aigyptos' sons by a Phoenician woman, and the girls were Danaos' daughters by an Ethiopian woman.

Aigyptos' sons by Tyria got Danaos' daughters by Memphis. They did not draw lots, but the matches were made because they had similar names. Cleitos got Cleite. Sthenelos got Sthenele. Chrysippos got Chrysippe. **19** Aigyptos' twelve sons by the Naiad nymph Caliadne drew lots for Danaos' daughters by the Naiad nymph Polyxo. So Eurylochos, Phantes, Peristhenes, Hermos, Dryas, Potamon, Cisseus, Lixos, Imbros, Bromios, Polyctor, and Chthonios got Autonoe, Theano, Electra, Cleopatra, Eurydice, Glaucippe, Antheleia, Cleodora, Euippe, Erato, Stygne, and Bryce. **20** Aigyptos' sons by Gorgo drew lots for Danaos' daughters by Pieria. Periphas got Actaia. Oineus got Podarce. Aigyptos got Dioxippe. Menalces got Adite. Lampos got Ocypete. Idmon got Pylarge. The following are the youngest of the sons:* Idas got Hippodice, Daiphron got Adiante (Herse was the mother of these last two girls), Pandion got Callidice, Arbelos got Oime, Hyperbios got Celaino, and Hippocorystes got Hyperippe. These were the sons of Aigyptos by Hephaistine and the daughters of Danaos by Crino.

21 When they had gotten their assigned marriages,* Danaos threw a feast and gave daggers to his daughters. They killed their grooms while they slept, all except Hypermnestra, who spared Lynceus because he had not taken her virginity. On this account Danaos locked her up and set a guard over her. **22** The rest of Danaos' daughters buried the heads of their grooms in Lerna and buried their bodies in front of the city. At Zeus' command Athena and Hermes purified the daughters. Later, Danaos reunited Hypermnestra with Lynceus and gave the rest of his daughters to the victors in athletic games.

Nauplios **23** Amymone and Poseidon had a son, Nauplios, who was long-lived. Sailing over the sea, he lit signal fires that led those who happened upon them to their deaths. Then it happened that he himself died by that death. But before he died,* he married Clymene daughter of Catreus (according to the tragedians), or Philyra (according to the author of the *Nostoi*), or Hesione (according to Cercops), and had Palamedes, Oiax, and Nausimedon.

Acrisios and Proitos **24** Lynceus ruled Argos after Danaos. He had a son, [2.2]
Abas, by Hypermnestra. Abas and Aglaia daughter of Mantineus had twin sons, Acrisios and Proitos. These two were at odds with each other while still in the womb, and when they grew up, they went to war over the kingdom (during this war they were the first to discover shields). Acrisios defeated Proitos and drove him out of Argos. **25** Proitos came to Lycia to the court of Iobates (or, according to some, of Amphianax), whose daughter he married. Her name was Anteia (according to Homer), or Stheneboia (according to the tragedians). His father-in-law with an army of Lycians took him back home, and he captured Tiryns, which the Cyclopes fortified for him. Acrisios and Proitos divided the whole of the Argolid and governed it, with Acrisios ruling Argos and Proitos Tiryns.

26 Acrisios and Eurydice daughter of Lacedaimon had a daughter, Danae.

The Daughters of Proitos Proitos and Stheneboia had Lysippe, Iphinoe, and Iphianassa. These daughters, after they grew up, went mad because (according to Hesiod) they did not accept the rites of Dionysos or because (according to Acousilaos) they ridiculed the wooden statue of Hera. **27** After they went mad, they wandered across the whole Argolid. Then, making their way through Arcadia and the Peloponnesos,* they ran through the wilderness with complete abandon. But Melampous, the son of Amythaon and Eidomene daughter of Abas, being a prophet and the first to discover healing through medicines and purgings, promised to heal the young women if he got one-third of the kingdom. **28** But when Proitos was unwilling to have them cured at such a price, the women raved all the more, and, even worse, all of the other women raved with them. They abandoned their homes, killed their own children, and frequented the wilderness.

When the misfortune had gotten as bad as it could get, Proitos tried to pay the requested price, but Melampous promised to cure them when his brother Bias also got the same amount of the land. Proitos was concerned that if he put off the cure, even more would be demanded, so he assented to the cure on these conditions. **29** Melampous took the strongest young men and pursued the women from the mountains to Sicyon with shouting and a sort of inspired dancing. During the chase the oldest of Proitos' daughters, Iphinoe, perished, but the others received purification and regained their senses in the end. Proitos gave them to Melampous and Bias as wives, and he later fathered a son, Megapenthes.

[2.3] **Bellerophontes, the Chimaira, and Pegasos** **30** Bellerophontes son of Glaucos (Sisyphos' son) came to Proitos and was purified after accidentally killing his brother Deliades (or, according to some, Peiren, or, according to others, Alcimenes). Stheneboia fell in love with him and sent him a message about getting together. He rejected her advances, so she told Proitos that Bellerophontes had sent her a message to seduce her. Proitos believed her and gave Bellerophontes a letter to take to Iobates. In the letter he had written, "Kill Bellerophontes." **31** When Iobates read the letter, he ordered Bellerophontes to kill the Chimaira in the belief that he would be destroyed by the beast, for she could not easily be taken by many men, much less by a single man, for her one body had the power of three beasts* since she had the head of a lion and that of a serpent as a tail, and a third, that of a goat, in the middle. She breathed fire through the last. She was ravaging the land and devastating the livestock. It is said that this Chimaira had been raised by Amisodaros (as Homer too says) and that she was the offspring of Typhon and Echidna (which is Hesiod's account). **32** Bellerophontes got onto Pegasos (this was his winged horse, the child of Medousa and Poseidon) and, carried aloft, shot down Chimaira from its back.

After this task Iobates ordered him to battle the Solymoi. When he had accomplished that too, he ordered him to fight the Amazons. **33** When Bellerophontes had killed them too, Iobates selected those with a reputation among the Lycians for excellence in might* and ordered them to ambush and kill him. But when he killed all these men too, Iobates was astounded at his power, showed him the letter, and asked him to remain at his court. He gave him his daughter Philonoe to marry, and when he lay on his deathbed, he passed the kingdom on to him.

[2.4] **Acrisios, Danae, and Perseus** **34** When Acrisios consulted an oracle about fathering male children, the god told him that from his daughter a son would be born who would kill him. In fear of this, he had a bronze chamber constructed under the earth and put Danae under guard. According to some, Proitos seduced her, and that is how the wrangling started between Proitos and Acrisios, but others say that Zeus transformed himself into gold, flowed down through the ceiling into Danae's lap, and had intercourse with her. **35** When Acrisios later learned that she had given birth to Perseus, he refused to believe that she had been seduced by Zeus and so put his daughter and her child into a chest and cast it into the sea.

Dictys, Polydectes, and the Quest for the Gorgon's Head When the chest landed on the island of Seriphos, Dictys took Perseus and raised him. **36** Dictys' brother Polydectes, who was king of Seriphos, fell in love with Danae, but since Perseus had in the meantime grown to manhood, he was unable to sleep with her. So he called his friends together—and Perseus too—and told them that he was trying to collect contributions so that he could marry Hippodameia daughter of Oinomaos. Perseus said that he would not refuse even to give the head of the Gorgon, so Polydectes asked for and got horses from everybody else. He did not, however, accept the horses from Perseus but ordered him to bring the Gorgon's head.

The Daughters of Phorcos, the Nymphs, and Perseus' Equipment

37 With Hermes and Athena guiding him on his way, he came to the daughters of Phorcos, namely Enyo, Pephredo, and Deino (they were the children of Ceto and Phorcos and so the sisters of the Gorgons). They had been old women from birth. The three had a single eye and a single tooth that they took turns passing between them. Perseus gained possession of the eye and tooth, and when they asked for them back, he said that he would hand them over if they told him the way that led to the nymphs. **38** These nymphs had winged sandals and the *kibisis,* which they say was a pouch. They also had Hades' cap. [Pindar and Hesiod in the *Shield* say about Perseus: "The head of the terrible monster, the Gorgon, covered his whole back, and the *kibisis* surrounded it." It is called that from the fact that clothes and food are put {*keisthai*} there.][1]

Medousa and the Other Gorgons

39 After the Phorcides told him the way, he gave them back their tooth and eye, went to the nymphs, and got what he was searching so earnestly for. He put on the *kibisis,* tied the sandals to his ankles, and put the cap on his head. While he was wearing the cap, he could see whom he wanted, but he could not be seen by others. He got an adamantine sickle from Hermes, flew all the way to Oceanos, and caught the Gorgons while they slept. Their names were Stheno, Euryale, and Medousa. **40** Only Medousa was mortal, and this was the reason that Perseus had been sent for her head. The Gorgons had heads with serpents' coils spiraling around them, large tusks like boars', bronze arms, and gold wings with which they could fly. **41** They turned whoever saw them into stone, so Perseus came to them as they slept. While Athena guided his hand, he turned away, looked into a bronze shield by which he could see the Gorgon's image, and decapitated her. **42** When her head was cut off, the winged horse Pegasos leapt out of the Gorgon, as did Chrysaor, the father of Geryones. Poseidon was the father of both of them. Then Perseus put the head of Medousa into the *kibisis* and went back the way he came. The Gorgons flew from their bed and set off in pursuit of Perseus, but they were unable to see him because of the cap, for he was concealed by it.

Cassiepeia and Andromeda

43 Arriving in Ethiopia, where Cepheus was king, he found the king's daughter, Andromeda, set out as food for a sea monster.

1. The poetic citation and surrounding context, including the unhelpful etymology, was almost certainly added by someone other than Apollodorus. The lexicon known as the *Etymologicum Magnum* has a similarly worded entry (including the Hesiodic citation) that is slightly clearer on the etymology: "It is called that from the fact that food {*bosis*} is put {*keisthai*} there."

Cassiepeia, the wife of Cepheus, had vied with the Nereids over beauty, boasting that she was superior to all of them. Because of this the Nereids were enraged. Since Poseidon shared their anger, he sent a flood and a sea monster against the land. The oracle of Ammon said that the disaster would end if Cassiepeia's daughter, Andromeda, were set out as food for the monster. Forced by the Ethiopians, Cepheus did just that, chaining his daughter to a rock. **44** Perseus saw her and fell in love. He promised Cepheus that he would destroy the monster if he would give him the girl to marry after she had been rescued. Oaths were sworn on these terms, and then Perseus faced the monster, killed it, and freed Andromeda. Phineus, who was Cepheus' brother and had been Andromeda's original fiancé, began to plot against Perseus. When Perseus discovered the plot, he showed him the Gorgon and instantly turned him and his fellow conspirators to stone.

Return to Seriphos **45** When he came to Seriphos and found that his mother had taken refuge with Dictys at the altars because of Polydectes' violence, he went into the palace. After Polydectes had summoned his friends, Perseus turned away and showed them the Gorgon's head. When they looked upon it, each was turned to stone in the position he happened to be in. **46** After installing Dictys as king of Seriphos, Perseus returned the sandals, *kibisis,* and cap to Hermes and gave the Gorgon's head to Athena. Hermes then gave the aforementioned items back to the nymphs, and Athena put the Gorgon's head in the middle of her shield. Some say that Medousa had her head cut off because of Athena; they say that the Gorgon wanted to compare her own beauty to that of the goddess.

Death of Acrisios **47** Perseus hurried with Danae and Andromeda to Argos to see Acrisios. When Acrisios learned of this, he grew fearful of the oracle, left Argos, and went to the land of the Pelasgians. King Teutamides of Larissa was holding athletic games in honor of his father, who had passed away, and Perseus came because he wanted to compete. While competing in the pentathlon, he killed Acrisios instantly by hitting him on the foot with the discus. **48** Understanding that the prophecy had been fulfilled, he buried Acrisios outside the city. But he was ashamed to return to Argos to inherit the kingdom of the man who had died because of him, so he went to Tiryns, traded kingdoms with Proitos' son, Megapenthes, and handed Argos over to him. Megapenthes became king of the Argives, and Perseus became king of Tiryns, fortifying Mideia and Mycenae as well.

Children of Perseus and Andromeda; Their Descendants

49 Perseus had children with Andromeda. Before returning to Hellas he had Perses, whom he left behind with Cepheus (it is said that the kings of the Persians are his descendants). In Mycenae he had Alcaios, Sthenelos, Heleios, Mestor, and Electryon. He also had a daughter, Gorgophone, whom Perieres married. **50** Alcaios had a son, Amphitryon, and a daughter, Anaxo, with Astydameia daughter of Pelops (though some say he had them with Laonome daughter of Gouneus, and still others with Hipponome daughter of Menoiceus). Mestor and Lysidice daughter of Pelops had Hippothoe, whom Poseidon carried off and brought to the Echinadian Islands, where he slept with her, fathering Taphios, who founded Taphos and called his people Teleboans because he had gone far {*telou ebe*} from his home country. **51** Taphios had a son, Pterelaos, whom Poseidon made immortal by implanting a golden hair on his head. Pterelaos had sons, Chromios, Tyrannos, Antiochos, Chersidamas, Mestor, and Eueres.

52 Electryon married Alcaios' daughter Anaxo and fathered a daughter, Alcmene, and sons, Stratobates, Gorgophonos, Phylonomos, Celaineus, Amphimachos, Lysinomos, Cheirimachos, Anactor, and Archelaos. After these, he also had an illegitimate son, Licymnios, by a Phrygian woman named Mideia.

53 Sthenelos and Nicippe daughter of Pelops had Alcyone and Medousa, and later also a son, Eurystheus, who became king of Mycenae. For when Heracles was about to be born, Zeus said in the presence of the gods that the descendant of Perseus who was about to be born at the time would become the king of Mycenae. Jealous, Hera persuaded the Eileithyiai to hold up Alcmene's delivery and to make Eurystheus son of Sthenelos be born though he was two months premature.

Electryon **54** When Electryon was king of Mycenae, Pterelaos' sons came with Taphios and demanded his maternal grandfather Mestor's kingdom.* Electryon paid no attention to them, so they began to drive off his cattle. When Electryon's sons came out to stop them, they challenged and killed each other. Of Electryon's sons, Licymnios survived because he was still a boy; of Pterelaos' sons, Eueres, the one guarding the ships, survived. **55** The Taphians who escaped took the rustled cattle and sailed off, then gave them to King Polyxenos of Elis for safekeeping. Amphitryon, however, ransomed them from Polyxenos and took them back to Mycenae.

Amphitryon and Alcmene Electryon wanted to avenge the deaths of his sons, so he handed his kingdom and daughter Alcmene over to Amphitryon after making him swear that he would keep her a virgin until his return. His intention was to go to war against the Teleboans, **56** but when he got his cows back, one of them bolted, and Amphitryon threw the club he had in his hand at the cow. The club ricocheted off her horns and hit Electryon in the head, killing him. So Sthenelos seized upon this pretext to banish Amphitryon from all of Argos and seize the rule of Mycenae and Tiryns himself. He sent for Pelops' sons, Atreus and Thyestes, and put them in charge of Mideia.

The Cadmeian Fox **57** Amphitryon arrived in Thebes with Alcmene and Licymnios, where he was purified by Creon, and he gave his sister Perimede to Licymnios. Alcmene said that she would marry Amphitryon when he had avenged the deaths of her brothers, and after promising to do so he went to war against the Teleboans and called upon Creon to aid him. Creon said that he would go to war if Amphitryon first rid the Cadmeia of the fox (a fox, a savage beast, was devastating the Cadmeia). Despite his promise, it was fated that no one would catch the fox.

58 Since the country continued to be ravaged, the Thebans set out one of the citizens' children every month for the fox, which would have carried off many if this had not been done. So Amphitryon left to go to Cephalos son of Deioneus in Athens and persuaded him in exchange for a portion of the plunder from the Teleboans to bring his dog to hunt the beast. Procris had brought this dog from Crete after receiving it from Minos. It was destined to catch anything that it might pursue. **59** When the fox was being chased by the dog, Zeus turned them both into stone.

Amphitryon and the War with the Taphians Amphitryon plundered the islands of the Taphians with the following allies: from Thoricos in Attica, Cephalos; from the Phocians, Panopeus; from Argive Helos, Heleios son of Perseus; and from Thebes, Creon. **60** So long as Pterelaos was alive, Amphitryon was unable to capture Taphos. But when Pterelaos' daughter, Comaitho, fell in love with Amphitryon, she plucked the golden hair from her father's head. After Pterelaos died, Amphitryon conquered all of the islands. He killed Comaitho and sailed off to Thebes with the plunder. He gave the islands to Heleios and Cephalos, who settled there and founded cities named after themselves.

Zeus, Alcmene, and Heracles **61** Before Amphitryon reached Thebes, Zeus came during the night and made the one night as long as three. He made himself look like Amphitryon, slept with Alcmene, and told her what had happened with the Teleboans. When Amphitryon arrived and saw that his wife did not welcome him home, he asked the reason. After she said that he had arrived the night before and slept with her, he learned from Teiresias of the encounter she had had with Zeus. Alcmene bore two sons, Heracles, the older by a night, to Zeus, and Iphicles to Amphitryon.

The Infant Heracles and the Snakes **62** When Heracles was eight months old, Hera sent two enormous serpents into his bed because she wanted to destroy the infant. Alcmene called to Amphitryon for help, but Heracles stood up, throttled them, one in each hand, and killed them. But Pherecydes says that Amphitryon, wishing to know which of the boys was his son, put the serpents into the bed. When Iphicles fled and Heracles confronted them, Amphitryon knew that Iphicles was his.

Heracles' Boyhood and Education; Linos **63** Heracles was taught to drive chariots by Amphitryon, to wrestle by Autolycos, to shoot a bow by Eurytos, to fight in armor by Castor, and to play the lyre by Linos, who was Orpheus' brother. After Linos had come to Thebes and become a Theban, he was slain by Heracles, who hit him with his lyre (Heracles killed him in a fit of rage because Linos had punished him by striking him). **64** When some men prosecuted him for murder, he read out a law of Rhadamanthys that said that any man who defends himself against an instigator of unjust violence is innocent. In this way he was acquitted. Afraid that Heracles would do something like that again, Amphitryon sent him out to tend his herd of cattle. Growing up there, Heracles surpassed everyone in size and strength. It was obvious from his appearance that he was Zeus' son, for his body was four cubits tall, and a fiery radiance shone from his eyes. He also did not miss when he shot a bow or threw a javelin.

The Cithaironian Lion, Thespios, and His Daughters **65** When he was eighteen years old and out with the herd, he killed the Cithaironian lion, which used to rush from Mount Cithairon and ravage the cattle of Amphitryon, as well as those of Thespios. Thespios was king of Thespiai, and when Heracles wanted to kill the lion, he went to this man. **66** Thespios entertained him as a guest for fifty days and had one of his daughters (he had fifty of them by Megamede daughter of Arneos) sleep with him every night before Heracles went out to hunt, for he was eager for all of them to have children with Heracles. Though Heracles thought that he was always sleeping with the same one, he slept with all of them. After overpowering the lion, he wore its skin and used its gaping jaws as a helmet.

Erginos **67** When he was returning from the hunt, he ran into some heralds sent by Erginos to collect the tribute from the Thebans. The Thebans paid tribute to Erginos for the following reason: One of Menoiceus' charioteers, named Perieres, hit Clymenos, king of the Minyans, with a stone and wounded him in the precinct of Poseidon in Onchestos. When Clymenos was brought to Orchomenos, he was barely alive. As he was dying, he directed his son Erginos to avenge his death. **68** Erginos marched against Thebes, and after inflicting many casualties, he made an oath-bound treaty that the Thebans would send him a hundred cows as tribute each year for twenty years. As his heralds were going to Thebes to get this tribute, Heracles met up with them and mutilated them. He cut off their ears, noses, and hands; tied them around their necks with cords; and told them to take that back to Erginos and the Minyans as tribute. **69** Enraged by this, Erginos marched against Thebes. After Heracles got armor and weapons from Athena and became the commander, he killed Erginos, routed the Minyans, and forced them to pay double the tribute to the Thebans. It happened that Amphitryon died fighting bravely in the battle. **70** Heracles received from Creon his oldest daughter, Megara, as a prize for bravery. He had three sons with her, Therimachos, Creontiades, and Deicoon. Creon gave his younger daughter to Iphicles, who had already had a son, Iolaos, with Automedousa daughter of Alcathous.

After the death of Amphitryon, Rhadamanthys, the son of Zeus, married Alcmene and, exiled from his country, settled in Ocaleai in Boiotia. **71** After Heracles got further instruction from him in the art of war,* he got a sword from Hermes, a bow from Apollo, a golden breastplate from Hephaistos, and a robe from Athena; he cut his own club at Nemea.

Heracles' Madness and the Labors **72** After his battle against the Minyans it happened that Heracles was driven mad because of the jealousy of Hera. He threw his own children by Megara into a fire, along with two of Iphicles' sons. For this he condemned himself to exile. He was purified by Thespios, and going to Delphi, he asked the god where he should settle. **73** The Pythia then for the first time called him by the name Heracles; up until then he had been called Alceides. She told him to settle in Tiryns and serve Eurystheus for twelve years. She also told him to accomplish the ten labors imposed upon him and said that when the labors were finished, he would become immortal.

[2.5] **First Labor: Nemean Lion** **74** After Heracles heard this, he went to Tiryns and did Eurystheus' bidding. First, he commanded him to bring back the skin of the Nemean Lion. This animal, Typhon's offspring, was invulnerable. When he was going after the lion, he came to Cleonai and was put up as a guest by Molorchos, a poor man. When Molorchos wanted to sacrifice a victim, Heracles told him to hold off for thirty days: if he returned from his hunt safe and sound, he told Molorchos to make a sacrifice fit for a god to Zeus Soter {"Savior"}; if he died, he told Molorchos to make a sacrifice to himself fit for a hero. **75** When he got to Nemea and tracked down the lion, he first shot it with his bow. When he found that it was invulnerable, he brandished his club and pursued it. When it fled into its two-mouthed cave, Heracles blocked up one entrance and went after the beast through the other. Getting it in a headlock, he held on, squeezing until he choked it. He put it across his shoulders and brought it back to Cleonai. He found Molorchos on the last of the thirty days about to offer the victim to Heracles in the belief that he was dead. Instead, Heracles sacrificed it to Zeus Soter and then took the lion to Mycenae. **76** Terrified by Heracles' demonstration of manly courage, Eurystheus forbade Heracles from entering the city in the future and ordered him to display his labors before the gates of the city. They say that out of fear Eurystheus also had a bronze storage jar installed under the ground for him to hide in, and he sent a herald, Copreus, the son of Pelops the Eleian, to command Heracles to do his labors. This Copreus had killed Iphitos, gone into exile in Mycenae, and settled there after receiving purification from Eurystheus.

Second Labor: Lernaian Hydra **77** The second labor Eurystheus commanded Heracles to perform was to kill the Lernaian Hydra, which had been raised in the swamp of Lerna and was making forays onto the plain and wreaking havoc on both the livestock and the land. The Hydra had an enormous body with nine heads, eight of them mortal and the one in the middle immortal. **78** Heracles mounted a chariot driven by Iolaos and traveled to Lerna. He brought his horses to a halt and found the Hydra on a hill by the Springs of Amymone, where she had her lair. He shot flaming arrows at her and forced her to come out. As she did so, he seized her and put her in a hold, but she wrapped herself around one of his legs and held on tight. **79** Heracles got nowhere by smashing her heads with his club, for when one was smashed, two heads grew back. An enormous crab came to assist the Hydra and pinched Heracles' foot. Because of this, after he killed the crab, he, for his part, called for Iolaos to help. Iolaos set fire to a portion of the nearby forest and with the burning pieces of wood he scorched the stumps of the heads, preventing them from coming back. **80** Having overcome the regenerating heads in this way, Heracles then cut off the immortal one, buried it, and placed a heavy rock over it by the road that leads through Lerna to Elaious. As for the Hydra's body, he cut it open and dipped his arrows in her bile. Eurystheus told Heracles that he should not have to count this labor as one of the ten, for Heracles had not overcome the Hydra by himself, but with the help of Iolaos.

Third Labor: Cerynitian Deer **81** The third labor Eurystheus commanded Heracles to perform was to bring the Cerynitian Deer alive to Mycenae. The deer was in Oinoe, had golden horns, and was sacred to Artemis. Because of this Heracles did not want to kill or wound it, so he pursued it for an entire year. When the beast was wearied by the chase, it fled to a mountain known as Artemisios and then to the Ladon River. When it was about to cross this river, Heracles ambushed* and captured it. Putting it on his shoulders, he hurried through Arcadia. **82** But Artemis, accompanied by Apollo, met up with him and was ready to take the deer away. She reproached him because he was going to kill her sacred animal, but he made the excuse that he was being forced to do it and said that the guilty party was Eurystheus. This soothed the goddess' anger, and Heracles brought the beast alive to Mycenae.

Fourth Labor: Erymanthian Boar **83** The fourth labor Eurystheus commanded Heracles to perform was to bring the Erymanthian Boar alive. This beast was causing destruction in Psophis by making attacks from a mountain they call Erymanthos.

The Centaurs and Cheiron Traveling through Pholoe, Heracles stayed as a guest with the Centaur Pholos, the son of Seilenos and an ash-tree nymph. This Centaur offered Heracles meat that was roasted, but he himself ate his raw. **84** When Heracles asked for wine, Pholos said that he was afraid to open the Centaurs' communal storage jar. Heracles told him not to worry and opened the jar. Not much later the Centaurs scented the odor and came armed with rocks and fir trees to Pholos' cave. Heracles repelled Anchios and Agrios, the first to grow bold enough to enter, by hitting them with burning firewood, and he shot the rest with his bow, pursuing them all the way to Malea. **85** From there they fled to the home of Cheiron, who had settled at Malea after being driven from Mount Pelion by the Lapiths. Heracles shot an arrow from his bow at the Centaurs, who had surrounded Cheiron. The arrow went through Elatos' arm and lodged in Cheiron's knee. Distressed by this, Heracles ran up, pulled out the arrow, and applied a drug that Cheiron gave him. Cheiron, with his wound unable to be cured, left to return to his cave. He wanted to die there but was unable to do so because he was immortal. Prometheus offered himself to Zeus to become immortal in Cheiron's place, and that is how Cheiron died.

86 The rest of the Centaurs fled, each to a different place: some came to Cape Malea; Eurytion went to Pholoe; and Nessos went to the river Euenos. Poseidon took in the rest at Eleusis and concealed them with a mountain. As for Pholos, he pulled an arrow out of a corpse and marveled that the small thing could kill such large foes. The arrow slipped from his hand and fell onto his foot, killing him instantly.

Capture of the Boar **87** When Heracles returned to Pholoe and saw that Pholos was dead, he buried him and went to hunt the boar. He chased it from a thicket by shouting, and when it was tired out, he forced it into deep snow, lassoed it, and brought it to Mycenae.

Fifth Labor: Cattle of Augeias **88** The fifth labor Eurystheus commanded Heracles to perform was to clear out the dung of the Cattle of Augeias in only a single day. Augeias was king of Elis. According to some, he was the son of Helios, according to others, of Poseidon, and according to still others, of Phorbas. He had many herds of cattle. Heracles came to him and, without revealing Eurystheus' command, told him he would clear out their dung in a single day if Augeias would give him one-tenth of the cattle. Not believing that it was possible, Augeias promised he would. **89** Heracles called upon Augeias' son Phyleus to act as witness. Then he made a hole in the foundation of the stable and diverted the Alpheios and Peneios, which flowed nearby, and caused them to flow in after he made an outlet through another opening.

When Augeias learned that this had been accomplished at Eurystheus' command, he would not render payment and went so far as to deny ever having promised to do so in the first place, saying that he was ready to be brought to trial over the issue. **90** When the judges had taken their seats, Phyleus was called by Heracles and testified against his father, saying that he had agreed to make a payment to him. Augeias, enraged, ordered both Phyleus and Heracles to depart from Elis before the vote was cast. **91** So Phyleus went to Doulichion and settled there, and Heracles came to Olenos to the house of Dexamenos and found him on the point of being forced to engage his daughter Mnesimache to the Centaur Eurytion. When Heracles was asked by Dexamenos to help, he killed Eurytion when he came for his bride. Eurystheus did not count this labor among the ten either, because he said that it was done for payment.

Sixth Labor: Stymphalian Birds **92** The sixth labor Eurystheus commanded Heracles to perform was to chase away the Stymphalian Birds. There was in the city of Stymphalos in Arcadia a marsh called the Stymphalian Marsh, which was covered by a thick forest. Countless birds took refuge in it out of fear of being eaten by the wolves. **93** When Heracles was at a loss how to drive the birds from the forest, Athena got bronze castanets from Hephaistos and gave them to him. By rattling these on a mountain situated near the marsh, he startled the birds. They could not stand the racket and took to wing in fright. In this way Heracles shot them.

Seventh Labor: Cretan Bull **94** The seventh labor Eurystheus commanded Heracles to perform was to bring the Cretan Bull. Acousilaos says that this was the bull that carried Europa across the sea for Zeus, but some say that it was the one sent forth from the sea by Poseidon when Minos said that he would sacrifice to Poseidon whatever appeared from the sea. But they say that when he caught sight of the beauty of the bull, he sent it off to his herds and sacrificed another to Poseidon, and that the god, angered by this, made the bull go wild. **95** Heracles went to Crete after this bull, and when he asked for help capturing it, Minos told him to take it himself if he could subdue it. He captured it, carried it back, and showed it to Eurystheus. Afterward, he let it go free, and it wandered to Sparta and all of Arcadia, and, crossing the Isthmos, it came to Marathon in Attica, where it plagued the locals.

Eighth Labor: Mares of Diomedes **96** The eighth labor Eurystheus commanded Heracles to perform was to bring the Mares of Diomedes the Thracian to Mycenae. Diomedes was the son of Ares and Cyrene. He was king of the Bistones, a very warlike Thracian tribe, and owned man-eating mares. So Heracles sailed with his willing followers, overpowered the men in charge of the mares' mangers, and drove them to the sea. **97** When the Bistones came out under arms to rescue them, Heracles handed the mares over to Abderos to guard. Abderos, a son of Hermes, was a Locrian from Opous and Heracles' boyfriend. The mares ripped him apart* and killed him. Heracles fought the Bistones, and by killing Diomedes he forced the rest to flee. He founded a city, Abdera, by the tomb of the slain Abderos, and then took the mares and gave them to Eurystheus. Eurystheus released them, and they went to the mountain called Olympos, where they were destroyed by the wild animals.

Ninth Labor: War-Belt of Hippolyte **98** The ninth labor Eurystheus commanded Heracles to perform was to bring the war-belt of Hippolyte. She was the queen of the Amazons, who used to dwell near the river Thermodon, a tribe great in war. For they cultivated a manly spirit; whenever they had sex and gave birth, they raised the female children. They would constrict their right breasts so that these would not interfere with throwing a javelin, but allowed their left breasts to grow so that they could breastfeed. Hippolyte had Ares' war-belt, a symbol of her preeminence over all the Amazons. **99** Heracles was sent to get this belt because Admete, Eurystheus' daughter, wanted to have it.

War at Paros Assembling some willing allies, he sailed with one ship and landed on the island of Paros, where the sons of Minos dwelled, Eurymedon, Chryses, Nephalion, and Philolaos. It happened that those on the ship disembarked, and two of them were killed by the sons of Minos. Angry over their deaths, Heracles killed the sons of Minos on the spot, blockaded the rest of the population, and besieged them. The siege lasted until they sent ambassadors and appealed to him to take whichever two men he wanted in place of those who were killed. **100** So he ended the siege and took with him Alcaios and Sthenelos, the sons of Androgeos son of Minos.

Lycos and the Bebryces He came to Lycos son of Dascylos in Mysia <and was his guest. When Lycos and the king of the Bebryces fought,>* Heracles aided Lycos and killed many Bebryces, including their king, Mygdon, Amycos' brother. He took away a large portion of the Bebryces' territory and gave it to Lycos, who called the whole territory Heracleia.

The Amazons **101** Heracles sailed to the harbor in Themiscyra, and Hippolyte came to him. After she asked why he had come and promised to give him the war-belt, Hera made herself look like one of the Amazons and went among the populace saying that the strangers who had come were abducting the queen. **102** Under arms they rode on horseback down to the ship. When Heracles saw that they were armed, he thought that this was the result of some treachery. He killed Hippolyte and took the war-belt, and then he fought the rest, sailed away, and landed at Troy.

The Walls of Troy, Laomedon, and Hesione **103** It happened at that time that the city was in difficulties because of the wrath of Apollo and Poseidon. For Apollo and Poseidon, desiring to test the insolence of Laomedon, made themselves look like mortals and promised to build walls around Pergamon for a fee. But after they built the walls, Laomedon would not pay them. For this reason Apollo sent a plague, and Poseidon sent a sea monster that was carried up on shore by a tidal wave and made off with the people in the plain. **104** The oracles said that there would be an end to the misfortunes if Laomedon set out his daughter Hesione as food for the sea monster, so he set her out and fastened her to the cliffs near the sea. When Heracles saw that she had been set out, he promised to save her if he would get from Laomedon the mares that Zeus had given as compensation for the kidnapping of Ganymedes. After Laomedon said that he would give them, Heracles killed the sea monster and saved Hesione. But Laomedon refused to pay up, so Heracles set sail threatening that he would make war against Troy.

Other Stops **105** He landed at Ainos, where he was the guest of Poltys. On the Ainian shore, when he was about to sail off, he shot and killed Sarpedon, Poseidon's son and Poltys' brother, because he was insolent. Coming to Thasos and conquering the Thracians who lived there, he gave the island to the sons of Androgeos to live on. He set out from Thasos to Torone, and after being challenged to wrestle by Polygonos and Telegonos, the sons of Proteus son of Poseidon, he killed them in the course of the match. He brought the war-belt to Mycenae and gave it to Eurystheus.

Tenth Labor: Cattle of Geryones **106** The tenth labor Eurystheus commanded Heracles to perform was to bring back the Cattle of Geryones from Erytheia. Erytheia (now called Gadeira) was an island lying near Oceanos. Geryones, the son of Chrysaor and Callirhoe daughter of Oceanos, lived here. He had a body that was three men grown together, joined into one at the belly but separated into three below the waist. He had red cattle, which were herded by Eurytion and guarded by Orthos, the dog that was two-headed and born from Echidna and Typhon. **107** So traveling across Europe in quest of the cattle of Geryones, Heracles killed many wild beasts before arriving in Libya. Going to Tartessos, he set up as tokens of his journey two facing pillars at the limits of Europe and Libya. When he was made hot by Helios during his journey, he pulled his bow back and took aim at the god. Helios marveled at his courage and gave him a golden cup in which he traveled across Oceanos. **108** Arriving in Erytheia, he camped on Mount Abas. The dog sensed his presence and charged him, but Heracles hit it with his club and killed the cowherd Eurytion when he tried to help the dog. Menoites, who was there pasturing Hades' cattle, reported what had happened to Geryones, who caught up with Heracles as he was driving the cattle along the Anthemous River. He joined battle with Heracles, was shot by an arrow, and died. **109** Heracles put the cattle into the cup and sailed over to Tartessos, where he gave the cup back to Helios.

He went through Abderia and arrived at Ligystine, where Ialebion and Dercynos, the sons of Poseidon, tried to steal the cows. But Heracles killed them and went through Tyrrhenia. **110** One of the bulls broke loose {*rhegnumi*} at Rhegion, swiftly plunged into the sea, and swam across to Sicily. Traveling through the nearby territory known as Italy after it (for the Tyrrhenians call a bull "italos"),* the bull came to the plain of Eryx, who was king of the Elymoi. **111** Eryx, the son of Poseidon, incorporated the bull into his own herds. So Heracles handed the cattle over to Hephaistos and hurried off in search of the bull. He discovered it among the herds of Eryx, who said that he would not give it back unless Heracles wrestled and beat him. Heracles beat him three times and killed him during the match. He took the bull and drove it along with the others to the Ionian Sea.

112 When he reached the furthest reaches of the sea, Hera sent a gadfly against the cattle, and they were scattered throughout the foothills of Thrace. Heracles chased after them; he captured some and took them to the Hellespont, but others were left behind and afterward were wild. Because he had such a hard time collecting the cows, he blamed the Strymon River, and, whereas in the old days its stream used to be navigable, he filled it with rocks and rendered it unnavigable. He brought the cows and gave them to Eurystheus, who sacrificed them to Hera.

Eleventh Labor: Golden Apples of the Hesperides **113** Although the labors were finished in eight years and one month, Eurystheus, who would not count the Cattle of Augeias or the Hydra, ordered Heracles as an eleventh labor to bring back the Golden Apples from the Hesperides. These apples were not in Libya, as some have said, but on Mount Atlas in the land of the Hyperboreans. Ge had given them as a gift to Zeus when he married Hera. They were guarded by an immortal serpent, the offspring of Typhon and Echidna, which had a hundred heads and used to make all sorts of various sounds. **114** Alongside the serpent the Hesperides, named Aigle, Erytheia, and Hesperethousa,* stood guard.

Cycnos, Nereus, and Antaios So Heracles traveled to the Echedoros River. Cycnos,* the son of Ares and Pyrene, challenged him to single combat. When Ares tried to avenge Cycnos and met Heracles in a duel, a thunderbolt was thrown in between the two and broke up the fight. Traveling through Illyria and hurrying to the Eridanos River, Heracles came to some nymphs, daughters of Zeus and Themis. These nymphs told him about Nereus. **115** Taking hold of him as he slept, Heracles tied Nereus up though he turned into all sorts of shapes. He did not release him until he learned where the apples and the Hesperides were. After he got this information, he passed through Libya. Poseidon's son Antaios, who used to kill strangers by forcing them to wrestle, was king of this land. When Heracles was forced to wrestle with him, he lifted him off the ground in a bear hug, broke his back, and killed him. He did this because it happened that Antaios grew stronger when he touched the earth. This is why some said that he was a son of Ge.

Bousiris **116** He passed through Egypt after Libya. Bousiris, the son of Poseidon and Lysianassa daughter of Epaphos, was king there. He used to sacrifice foreigners on an altar of Zeus in accordance with a prophecy. For nine years barrenness befell Egypt when Phrasios, a seer by profession, arrived from Cyprus and said that the barrenness would end if a foreigner were sacrificed every year to Zeus. **117** Bousiris sacrificed that seer first and then went on to sacrifice those foreigners who landed on his shores. Heracles too was seized and brought to the altars. He broke the chains and killed both Bousiris and his son, Amphidamas.

Further Travels; Prometheus Freed **118** Passing through Asia, he came to Thermydrai, the harbor of the Lindians. He loosed one of the bulls from a cart-driver's wagon, sacrificed it, and feasted. The driver was unable to protect himself, so he stood on a certain mountain and called down curses. For this reason even today when they sacrifice to Heracles, they do so with curses.

119 Skirting Arabia, he killed Tithonos' son Emathion, and, traveling across Libya to the outer sea, he received* the cup from Helios. Crossing over to the continent on the other side, on Mount Caucasus he shot down the eagle that ate Prometheus' liver and that was the offspring of Echidna and Typhon. He freed Prometheus after taking the bond of the olive for himself, and to Zeus he offered up Cheiron, who was willing to die in Prometheus' place despite being immortal.*

Atlas Prometheus told Heracles not to go after the apples himself, but to take over holding up the sky from Atlas and send him instead. **120** So when he came to Atlas in the land of the Hyperboreans, Heracles followed this advice and took over holding up the sky. After picking three apples from the Hesperides, Atlas came back to Heracles. Atlas, not wanting to hold the sky, <said that he would himself carry the apples to Eurystheus and bade Heracles to hold up the sky in his stead. Heracles promised to do so but succeeded by craft in putting it on Atlas instead. For at the advice of Prometheus he told Atlas to hold up the sky because he>[2] wanted to put a pad on his head. When he heard this, Atlas put the apples down on the ground and took over holding up the sky, so Heracles picked them up and left. **121** But some say that he did not get them from Atlas, but that he himself picked the apples after killing the guardian serpent. He brought the apples and gave them to Eurystheus. After he got them, he gave them to Heracles as a gift. Athena received them from him and took them back, for it was not holy for them to be put just anywhere.

Twelfth Labor: Cerberos **122** The bringing back of Cerberos from the house of Hades was ordered as a twelfth labor. Cerberos had three dog heads, the

2. The missing material is restored from Pherecydes *fr.* 17 Fowler = Sch. L + Ap. Rhod. 4.1396–9b.

tail of a serpent, and along his back, the heads of all sorts of snakes. When Heracles was about to go off to get him, he went to Eumolpos in Eleusis because he wanted to be initiated into the mysteries. But it was not permitted at that time for foreigners to be initiated, so he became the adopted son of Pylios and went and tried to be initiated.* But he was unable to see the mysteries because he had not been purified of the killing of the Centaurs, so Eumolpos purified him and then initiated him.

123 He came to Tainaron in Laconia, where the cave that leads down to the house of Hades is located. He made his descent through it.* When the souls saw him, they all fled except for Meleagros and Medousa the Gorgon. He drew his sword against the Gorgon in the belief that she was still alive, but he learned from Hermes that she was just an empty phantom. **124** When he went near the gates of the house of Hades, he found Theseus together with Peirithous, the man who tried to win Persephone's hand in marriage and for that reason was in bonds. When they caught sight of Heracles, they stretched forth their arms so that they could rise up by means of Heracles' might. He took hold of Theseus by the hand and lifted him up, but when he wanted to raise up Peirithous, the earth shook and he let go. He also rolled Ascalaphos' rock off. **125** He wanted to provide some blood for the souls, so he slaughtered one of the cows of Hades. Their herder, Menoites son of Ceuthonymos, challenged Heracles to wrestle. Heracles grabbed him around the middle and broke his ribs. Menoites was saved when Persephone begged for mercy for him.

When Heracles asked Plouton for Cerberos, Plouton told him to take him if he could defeat him without any of the weapons he carried. **126** Heracles found Cerberos by the gates of Acheron, and, encased by his breastplate and covered entirely by the lion's skin, he threw his arms around Cerberos' head and did not stop holding on and choking the beast until he prevailed, even though he was being bitten by the serpent that served as his tail. So he took Cerberos and returned, making his ascent through Troizen. Demeter turned Ascalaphos into an owl; Heracles showed Cerberos to Eurystheus and then returned him to the house of Hades.

Eurytos, Iole, and Iphitos **127** After the labors Heracles came to Thebes [2.6]
and gave Megara to Iolaos. When he himself wanted to get married, he learned that Eurytos, ruler of Oichalia, had made marriage to his daughter, Iole, the prize for whoever beat him and his sons in an archery contest. **128** So Heracles went to Oichalia and beat them in archery, but he was not allowed the marriage. Although Iphitos, the eldest of Eurytos' sons, said that Iole ought to be given to Heracles, Eurytos and the rest of his sons went back on their word and said that they were afraid that Heracles might once again kill any children he might happen to father.

129 Not long afterward, some cattle were stolen from Euboia by Autolycos. Eurytos thought that this had been done by Heracles, but Iphitos did not believe it and went to Heracles. He met him leaving Pherai, where Heracles had saved the dying Alcestis for Admetos, and invited him to join in the search for the cattle. Heracles promised that he would and treated Iphitos as his guest, but he went crazy once more and threw him from the walls of Tiryns.

130 Wishing to be purified of the killing, he went to Neleus, who was the ruler of the Pylians. After Neleus turned him down because of his friendship with Eurytos,

Heracles went to Amyclai and was purified by Deiphobos son of Hippolytos. But he was afflicted with an awful disease because of the killing of Iphitos and so went to Delphi to find out how to stop the disease.

Delphi and the Quarrel with Apollo When the Pythia would not chant a prophecy for him, he wanted to rob the temple, carry off the tripod, and establish his own oracle. As Apollo fought him, Zeus sent a thunderbolt between them. **131** When they had been separated in that way, Heracles received a prophecy that said there would be an end to his disease when he had been sold, served three years, and given the purchase price as blood money to Eurytos for the killing.

Omphale After the oracle was given, Hermes put Heracles up for sale, and Omphale daughter of Iardanes bought him. She was the queen of the Lydians, for her husband, Tmolos, had bequeathed her the rulership on his death. **132** Eurytos did not accept the compensation when it was brought to him. While Heracles was serving Omphale, he captured and bound the Cercopes near Ephesos, and he killed Syleus at Aulis. Syleus used to force passing strangers to dig, but Heracles burned his vines, roots and all, and killed him along with his daughter Xenodoce. Landing on the island of Doliche, he saw the body of Icaros washed up on the shore, buried it, and named the island Icaria instead of Doliche. **133** In return for this Daidalos made a statue in Pisa in the likeness of Heracles. One night Heracles, not recognizing what it was and thinking it was alive, threw a stone at it and hit it. During the time he served at Omphale's court, it is said that the voyage to Colchis took place, as did the hunt for the Calydonian boar, and that Theseus cleared out the Isthmos as he came from Troizen.

War against Troy **134** After his period of servitude Heracles was rid of his disease and sailed against Ilion with eighteen fifty-oared ships after gathering an army of heroes who volunteered to fight of their own accord. When he landed at Ilion, he left the security of the ships in Oicles' hands and set out for the city with the other heroes. But although Laomedon came against the ships with the main part of his army and killed Oicles in the battle, he was driven off by the troops that were with Heracles and was besieged.

Telamon and the Capture of Troy; Priam **135** Once the siege was under way, Telamon broke through the wall and was the first to enter the city, with Heracles behind him. When Heracles saw that Telamon had been the first to enter, he drew his sword and charged him because he did not want anyone else to be considered greater than himself. When Telamon realized this, he started gathering together stones that were lying nearby. Heracles asked him what he was doing, and he said that he was building an altar to Heracles Callinicos {"Noble Victor"}. **136** Heracles commended him, and when he took the city and shot and killed Laomedon and all of his sons except Podarces, he gave Laomedon's daughter Hesione to Telamon as the prize for bravery and agreed to allow her to take with her whichever of the prisoners she wanted. When she chose her brother Podarces, Heracles said that

Podarces had to become a slave first, and then Hesione could get him, but only after giving something—anything—in exchange. So when he was being sold, she took the veil from her head and paid for him with it. This is why Podarces was called Priam.[3]

137 As Heracles sailed from Troy, Hera sent harsh storms. Zeus grew angry at [2.7]
this and hung her from Olympos. Heracles tried to sail to Cos, but the Coans thought he was leading a fleet of pirates and threw stones to stop him from sailing in. **138** But Heracles took the island* by force and killed King Eurypylos, the son of Astypalaia and Poseidon. Heracles was wounded by Chalcodon during the fight, but he suffered no real injury because Zeus whisked him away. After plundering Cos, he came to Phlegra at Athena's request and alongside the gods defeated the Giants.

War against Augeias **139** Not long afterward, he gathered an army from Arcadia, took on some willing heroes from Hellas, and set out on campaign against Augeias. When Augeias heard about the war being prepared by Heracles, he appointed as generals of the Eleians Eurytos and Cteatos, conjoined twins who surpassed in might all other mortals of the time. They were the sons of Molione and Actor, but they were said to be Poseidon's sons. Actor was Augeias' brother. **140** It happened that Heracles grew ill during the campaign, and for this reason he actually made a treaty with the Molionidai. But when they later discovered that he was ill, they made an attack on his army and killed many. So at that time Heracles withdrew. But later, when the third Isthmian festival was being held and the Eleians sent the Molionidai to take part in the sacrifice as their representatives, Heracles ambushed and killed them in Cleonai, then marched against Elis and took the city. **141** After he killed Augeias and his sons, he brought Phyleus back from exile and gave him the kingdom. He also founded the Olympic Games, established an altar to Pelops, and built six altars to twelve gods.

War against Pylos **142** After the sack of Elis, he marched against Pylos, and after capturing the city, he killed Periclymenos, the mightiest of Neleus' sons, who changed shapes as he fought. Heracles killed Neleus and all his sons except Nestor, for he was young and was being raised in the land of the Gerenians. During the battle, Heracles also wounded Hades, who was helping the Pylians.

War against the Sons of Hippocoon **143** After capturing Pylos, he marched against Lacedaimon out of a desire to punish Hippocoon's sons. He was angry with them because they had fought alongside Neleus, but he was even angrier because they had killed the son of Licymnios. While this man was admiring the palace of Hippocoon, one of the Molossian hounds ran out and made for him. So he threw a rock and hit the dog, and the Hippocoontidai sallied forth and beat him to death with their clubs. **144** To avenge this man's death Heracles gathered an army against the Lacedaimonians. When he came to Arcadia, he asked Cepheus to join him as an ally along with his sons (he had twenty). But Cepheus was afraid that if he

3. Apollodorus follows a common etymology of Priam's name from "to buy" (*priamai*).

left Tegea, the Argives would attack, so he declined to go on the campaign. But Heracles received from Athena a lock of the Gorgon's hair in a bronze urn, and he gave it to Cepheus' daughter, Sterope, telling her that if an army attacked, she should stand on the walls and raise the lock into the air three times, and, so long as she did not look at it, the enemy would be routed. **145** After this Cepheus went on the campaign with his sons. He and his sons all died in the battle, as did Heracles' brother, Iphicles. After Heracles killed Hippocoon and his sons and conquered the city, he brought Tyndareos back from exile and handed the kingdom over to him.

Auge and Telephos **146** As he passed by Tegea, Heracles forced himself on Auge without realizing that she was Aleos' daughter. She gave birth to the baby in secret and set him down in the sanctuary of Athena. But Aleos entered the sanctuary because the land was being devastated by a plague and discovered after a search that his daughter had had a child. So he exposed the baby on Mount Parthenios, but by the gods' providence it was saved. **147** For a deer {*elaphos*} that had just given birth offered her teat {*thele*} to the baby, and some shepherds took him up and named him Telephos {as if somehow from *thele* + *elaphos*}. Aleos gave Auge to Nauplios son of Poseidon to sell into slavery in a foreign land. Nauplios gave her to Teuthras, the ruler of Teuthrania, and he made her his wife.

Deianeira **148** When Heracles came to Calydon, he became a suitor for Deianeira, Oineus' daughter. For her hand in marriage he wrestled with Acheloos, and he broke off one of his horns when he changed himself into a bull. He married Deianeira, and Acheloos got his horn back by trading it for the horn of Amaltheia. Amaltheia was Haimonios' daughter, and she had a bull's horn. This horn, according to Pherecydes, had such great power that it could provide meat or drink aplenty—whatever one might ask for.

Astyoche and Tlepolemos **149** Heracles marched alongside the Calydonians against the Thesprotians. After capturing the city of Ephyra, where King Phylas ruled, he slept with the king's daughter, Astyoche, and became the father of Tlepolemos. While he was living with them, he sent a message to Thespios and told him to keep seven of his sons, to send three off to Thebes, and to send the remaining forty to the island of Sardinia to found a colony.

Death of Eunomos; Exile Again **150** After this happened, during a feast at Oineus' house, with a blow from his fist Heracles killed Architeles' son, Eunomos, while the boy was pouring water over his hands. (The boy was related to Oineus.) But since the event had been an accident, the boy's father pardoned Heracles. Heracles, however, wanted to undergo exile in accordance with the law and decided to leave for the house of Ceyx in Trachis.

Nessos **151** Taking Deianeira, he came to the Euenos River, where Nessos the Centaur stationed himself and ferried passersby across for a fee, saying that he had been set up as ferryman by the gods because of his righteousness. Now, Heracles crossed the river by himself, but he was asked for the fee and entrusted Deianeira to Nessos to carry across. But while Nessos was ferrying her across, he tried to rape her. **152** When Heracles heard her crying out, he shot Nessos through the heart as he was coming out of the river. Just before he died, Nessos called Deianeira over and told her to mix the seed that he had discharged onto the ground with the blood that was flowing from the arrow wound in case she ever wanted a love potion to use on Heracles. She did this and always kept it nearby.

153 As Heracles passed through the land of the Dryopes and ran out of food, he encountered Theiodamas, who was driving a cart. He sacrificed one of the bulls and feasted. When he came to Ceyx's house in Trachis, he was hosted by him and defeated the Dryopes.

Lapiths and Centaurs **154** Later, when he set out from there, he fought as an ally of Aigimios, the king of the Dorians. The Lapiths, with Coronos as their general, were fighting with him over territorial boundaries. He was under siege when he called Heracles to help him in exchange for a portion of the territory. Heracles helped him and killed Coronos and others, but he handed the entire piece of territory over to Aigimios with no strings attached.

155 He also killed Laogoras, the king of the Dryopes, along with his children, as he feasted in the sanctuary of Apollo, for he was insolent and an ally of the Lapiths. As Heracles was passing Itonos, Cycnos, the son of Ares and Pelopia, challenged him to single combat. Heracles fought and killed him. When he came to Ormenion, King Amyntor took up arms and would not allow him to go through his territory. Unable to proceed, Heracles killed him too.

War against Oichalia; Iole Taken Captive **156** Arriving in Trachis, he raised an army against Oichalia out of a desire to punish Eurytos. With the Arcadians, the Melians from Trachis, and the Epicnemidian Locrians as his allies, he killed Eurytos and his sons and took the city. He buried those who had fallen while fighting on his side, Hippasos son of Ceyx, and Argeios and Melas, the sons of Licymnios. He then sacked the city and took Iole captive.

Heracles' Death and Its Aftermath **157** When he anchored his ships at Cenaion in Euboia, he built an altar on a promontory to Cenaian Zeus. Intending to make a sacrifice, he sent his herald Lichas to Trachis to get some splendid clothes. From this man Deianeira learned of the situation with Iole, and, afraid that Heracles might love Iole more than her and thinking that Nessos' spilled blood really was a love potion, she anointed the tunic with it. **158** Heracles put it on and began to make sacrifice, but when the tunic grew warm, the Hydra's poison ate away his flesh. He picked up Lichas by the feet and hurled him off the promontory.* Then he tried to tear off the tunic, but his flesh was torn off with it because it was sticking to his body. Afflicted by such a terrible misfortune, he was brought to Trachis on a ship.

159 When Deianeira learned what had happened, she hanged herself. Heracles ordered Hyllos, who was his oldest child by Deianeira, to marry Iole when he grew to manhood, and then went to Mount Oita (this is in Trachis). He built a pyre there, climbed atop, and gave the command to light it. **160** No one was willing to do this, but Poias, who was passing by looking for his sheep, did light it, and Heracles gave him his bow as a gift. As the pyre burned, they say that a cloud settled under Heracles and with a clap of thunder sent him up to heaven. There he received immortality, was reconciled with Hera, and married her daughter Hebe. He had sons by her, Alexiares and Anicetos.

The Sons of Heracles **161** He had sons by the daughters of Thespios: Antileon and Hippeus by Procris (for the eldest had twins), Threpsippas by Panope, Eumedes by Lyse, Creon by < . . . >, Astyanax by Epilais, Iobes by Certhe, Polylaos by Eurybia, Archemachos by Patro, Laomedon by Meline, **162** Eurycapys by Clytippe, Eurypylos by Eubote, Antiades by Aglaia, Onesippos by Chryseis, Laomenes by Oreia, Teles by Lysidice, Entelides by Menippis, Hippodromos by Anthippe, Teleutagoras by Eury< . . . >, Capylos by Hippo,[*] Olympos by Euboia, Nicodromos by Nike, Cleolaos by Argele, Erythras by Exole, Homolippos by Xanthis, **163** Atromos by Stratonice, Celeustanor by Iphis, Antiphos by Laothoe, Alopios by Antiope, Claametidos by Astybia, Tigasis by Phyleis, Leucones by Aischreis, < . . . > by Antheia, Archedicos by Eurypyle, Dynastes by Erato, Mentor by Asopis, Amestrios by Eone, Lyncaios by Tiphyse, **164** Halocrates by Olympouse, Phalias by Heliconis, Oistrobles by Hesycheia, Terpsicrates by Euryope, Bouleus by Elacheia, Antimachos by Nicippe, Patroclos by Pyrippe, Nephos by Praxithea, Erasippos by Lysippe, Lycourgos by Toxicrate, Boucolos by Marse, Leucippos by Eurytele, and Hippozygos by Hippocrate. **165** Those were with Thespios' daughters.

By other women he had: Hyllos, Ctesippos, Glenos, and Oneites by Deianeira daughter of Oineus. Therimachos, Deiocoon,[*] and Creontiades by Megara daughter of Creon. Agelaos by Omphale (Croisos' lineage comes from him). **166** Thettalos by Chalciope daughter of Eurypylos. Thestalos by Epicaste daughter of Augeias. Eueres by Parthenope daughter of Stymphalos. Telephos by Auge daughter of Aleos. Tlepolemos by Astyoche daughter of Phylas. Ctesippos by Astydameia daughter of Amyntor. And Palaimon by Autonoe daughter of Peireus.

[2.8] **The Heracleidai** **167** After Heracles had been removed to the gods, his children escaped from Eurystheus and went to Ceyx. When Eurystheus told him to give them up and threatened to make war, they grew afraid, left Trachis, and fled through Hellas. In the pursuit they came to Athens, sat themselves at the altar of Pity, and asked for help. **168** The Athenians would not give them up and faced Eurystheus in war. They killed his sons, Alexandros, Iphimedon, Eurybios, Mentor, and Perimedes, and when Eurystheus fled in a chariot, Hyllos chased and killed him just as he was driving past the Sceironian Cliffs. He cut off his head and presented it to Alcmene, and she gouged out his eyes with pins.

Withdrawal from the Peloponnesos **169** After Eurystheus' death the Heracleidai came to the Peloponnesos and captured all the cities. After a year had passed since their return, a pestilence afflicted the entire Peloponnesos. An oracle revealed that this happened because of the Heracleidai, for they had returned before they were supposed to. For this reason they left the Peloponnesos, withdrew to Marathon, and settled there. **170** Now, Tlepolemos accidentally killed Licymnios (he was beating a servant with his cane when Licymnios ran under it) before they left the Peloponnesos, so he went into exile with many followers, came to Rhodes, and settled there. Hyllos married Iole in accordance with his father's instructions and sought to bring about the return for the Heracleidai. **171** So he went to Delphi and asked how they might return. The god told them wait for the third crop and then return.

First and Second Attempts to Return In the belief that "third crop" meant a period of three years, Hyllos waited that long and went back with his army < . . . >[4] of Heracles to the Peloponnesos when Tisamenos son of Orestes was king of the Peloponnesians. A second battle occurred, and the Peloponnesians were victorious, and Aristomachos died.

Third Attempt to Return **172** When Aristomachos'* sons had grown into men, they asked the oracle about returning. Since the god told them the same thing he had before, Temenos criticized the oracle, saying that they had followed it before and met with disaster. The god responded that they were responsible for the disaster, for they had not interpreted the oracle correctly; he did not mean the third crop of the earth, but the third crop in terms of human generations, and by "narrow" he had meant the broad-bellied sea to the right of the Isthmos.[5] **173** Hearing this, Temenos readied his army and built ships in Locris where the place is now called Naupactos {*naus* "ship" + *pactos* "built"} from that event. While the army was there, Aristodemos was struck by a thunderbolt and died, leaving twin sons by Argeia daughter of Autesion, Eurysthenes and Procles.

174 It happened that a misfortune also befell the army at Naupactos, for a seer appeared to them, speaking oracles in a state of inspiration. They thought that he was an enchanter sent by the Peloponnesians to ruin the army, and Hippotes son of Phylas (who was the son of Antiochos son of Heracles) threw a javelin at this man, and hit and killed him. And so after this happened, the naval force was wiped out when the ships were destroyed, and the land force suffered the misfortune of famine,* and the expedition dissolved.

175 Temenos asked the oracle about the misfortune; the god said that these things had happened because of the seer and ordered them to banish the killer for ten years and take the "Three-Eyed One" as their leader. So they banished Hippotes and began searching for the "Three-Eyed One." By chance they encountered Oxylos son of Andraimon, who was sitting on a horse with one eye* (its other eye had been shot

4. There is a major gap in the text here, covering the rest of Hyllos' invasion, his death, and perhaps the death of his son Cleodaios, as well as the beginning of the next invasion led by Aristomachos.

5. Presumably part of the original oracle that Apollodorus fails to mention above, though it might have come in the lacuna. The "broad-bellied sea" is the Gulf of Corinth, west of the Isthmos (i.e., to the right, from the perspective of someone in mainland Hellas north of the Peloponnesos). The gulf is wide from east to west, but narrow from north to south.

out by an arrow). He had gone into exile in Elis for murder and was returning from there to Aitolia after a year had passed. **176** So they figured out the oracle and made him their leader. They joined battle with their enemies, gained the upper hand with both their land and sea forces, and killed Tisamenos son of Orestes. Pamphylos and Dymas, the sons of Aigimios, who were fighting as the allies of the Heracleidai, died.

Division of the Peloponnesos **177** Now that they had control of the Peloponnesos, they established three altars to Zeus Patroos {"ancestral"}, made sacrifice on them, and cast lots for the cities. The first allotment was Argos, the second Lacedaimon, and the third Messene. They brought a jug of water and decided that each[6] would cast a pebble in. Now, Temenos and the sons of Aristodemos, namely Procles and Eurysthenes, put in stones. Cresphontes, on the other hand, wanted to be assigned Messene, so he put in a lump of dirt, since after it dissolved, the two other lots were bound to appear. **178** Temenos' lot was drawn first, and that of Aristodemos' sons was drawn second, and Cresphontes did receive Messene. They found signs lying on the altars on which they had sacrificed: those who had been allotted Argos found a toad; those who had been allotted Lacedaimon found a serpent; and those who had been allotted Messene found a fox. About these signs, the seers said that it would be better for those who received the toad to stay in the city (for their animal has no power when moving), that those who got the serpent would be dangerous when attacking, and that those who got the fox would be crafty.

179 Now, Temenos disowned his sons, Agelaos, Eurypylos, and Callias, and was devoted only to his daughter, Hyrnetho, and her husband, Deiphontes, so his sons persuaded some men to murder their father for a price. Although they murdered him, the army thought it right that Hyrnetho and Deiphontes have the kingdom. **180** Cresphontes had been king of Messene only a short time when he and two of his sons were murdered. So Polyphontes (himself* one of the Heracleidai) became king and took the wife of the murdered man, Merope, though she was unwilling. But he too was killed, for Merope had a third son, named Aipytos, and she had given him to her father to raise. This son grew to manhood, secretly returned, killed Polyphontes, and took back his father's kingdom.

Book 3
The Lineage of Agenor

[3.1] **Agenor and Europa** **1** Now that we have gone through the lineage of Inachos and explained it from Belos down to the Heracleidai, let us tell the story of Agenor next. As we have said, Libya had with Poseidon two sons, Belos and Agenor. **2** Now, Belos was king of the Egyptians and had the sons discussed before. Agenor went to Phoenicia and married Telephassa. They had a daughter, Europa, and sons,

6. Each of the contingents of the expedition that were originally headed by the three sons of Aristomachos—though after Aristodemos' death, his sons stand in his place.

Cadmos, Phoinix, and Cilix. Some say that Europa was not Agenor's daughter, but Phoinix's. Zeus fell in love with her, turned himself into a tame bull breathing forth the scent of roses,* got her to climb up on his back, and brought her across the sea to Crete. **3** Zeus shared her bed there, and she gave birth to Minos, Sarpedon, and Rhadamanthys. According to Homer, however, Sarpedon was the son of Zeus and Laodameia daughter of Bellerophontes.

After Europa's disappearance her father Agenor sent out his sons in search of her, telling them not to return until they had discovered Europa's whereabouts. Her mother, Telephassa, and Thasos son of Poseidon (or son of Cilix, according to Pherecydes) joined them in the search. **4** When they had made a thorough search, they were unable to find her and gave up hope of returning home. They each settled in a different place: Phoinix settled in Phoenicia; Cilix settled near Phoenicia, and the whole territory that was adjacent to the Pyramos River he called Cilicia after himself; Cadmos and Telephassa settled in Thrace. Likewise, Thasos founded the city of Thasos in Thrace and settled there.

Europa's Sons **5** Asterios, the ruler of the Cretans, married Europa and raised her sons. But when they came of age, they quarreled with each other because they all loved a boy named Miletos, who was the son of Apollo and Areia daughter of Cleochos. Since the boy showed greater affection for Sarpedon, Minos went to war against them and prevailed. **6** They fled; Miletos landed in Caria and founded the city of Miletos that is named for himself, and Sarpedon became an ally of Cilix, who was at war with the Lycians, in exchange for a part of his territory and became king of Lycia. Zeus granted that he live for three generations. But some say that they were in love with Atymnios, the son of Zeus and Cassiepeia, and their quarrel was over him. As for Rhadamanthys, he was a lawgiver to the islanders and later went into exile in Boiotia, where he married Alcmene. Since his death he has been acting as a judge with Minos in the realm of Hades. **7** Minos lived in Crete and wrote laws. He married Pasiphae, the daughter of Helios and Perseis, though according to Asclepiades he married Asterios' daughter, Crete. He had sons, namely Catreus, Deucalion, Glaucos, and Androgeos, and daughters, namely Acalle, Xenodice, Ariadne, and Phaidra. With the nymph Pareia he had Eurymedon, Nephalion, Chryses, and Philolaos. With Dexithea he had Euxanthios.

Minos, the Bull, and the Minotaur **8** After Asterios died childless, Minos wanted to be king of Crete, but there was opposition. He claimed that he had received the kingship from the gods, and to prove it he said that whatever he prayed for would happen. He made a sacrifice to Poseidon and prayed for a bull to appear from the depths, promising to sacrifice the one that appeared. Poseidon sent a magnificent bull up for him, and he received the kingdom, but he sent the bull to his herds and sacrificed another. **9** The first to gain control over the sea, he ruled over nearly all the islands.

Poseidon grew angry at Minos because he did not sacrifice the bull. So he made it savage and made Pasiphae lust after the bull. When she had fallen in love with the bull, she took as her accomplice Daidalos, who was an architect exiled from Athens for murder. **10** He constructed a wooden cow, put it on wheels,* and hollowed it out. Stripping the skin from a cow, he sewed it around the wooden one. He placed it in the meadow where the bull usually grazed and put Pasiphae inside. The bull came and mated with it as if it were a real cow. **11** Pasiphae gave birth to Asterios, known as the Minotaur. He had the face of a bull {*tauros*}, but the rest of his body was that of a man. Minos shut him in the labyrinth in accordance with certain prophecies and kept him under guard. The labyrinth, which Daidalos built, was a cell "that confused its exit with tangled twistings."[1] **12** I will give the account of the Minotaur, Androgeos, Phaidra, and Ariadne later in the section on Theseus.

Catreus and Deucalion Catreus son of Minos had Aerope, Clymene, and
[3.2] Apemosyne, and a son, Althaimenes. When Catreus consulted an oracle about the end of his life, the god said that he would be killed by one of his children. **13** Now, Catreus tried to keep the oracle secret, but Althaimenes heard it, and, afraid that he would turn out to be the murderer of his father, he set out from Crete with his sister Apemosyne and came to a certain spot on Rhodes. He settled the place and called it Cretinia. Climbing up onto the mountain called Atabyrion, he surveyed the surrounding islands. Catching sight of Crete as well and remembering his ancestral gods, he set up an altar of Atabyrian Zeus.

14 Not much later he became the murderer of his sister. Hermes loved her, but she ran away, and he could not catch her (for she was faster than him at running). So he spread freshly stripped hides along her path, and when she was coming back from the spring, she slipped on them and was raped. She told her brother what happened, but he thought the god was just a cover story, so he kicked her to death.

15 Catreus gave Aerope and Clymene to Nauplios to sell in foreign lands. Of these, Pleisthenes married Aerope and had sons, Agamemnon and Menelaos. Nauplios married Clymene and fathered sons, Oiax and Palamedes. Later, when Catreus was overcome by old age, he desired to pass the kingdom on to his son, Althaimenes, and because of this went to Rhodes. **16** Disembarking from the ship with his fellow Cretans* in a uninhabited place on the island, he was driven off by the cowherds, who thought pirates had invaded and could not hear him explaining the truth because of the barking of their dogs. While they were throwing things at him, Althaimenes arrived and killed Catreus with a javelin without recognizing him. Later, after learning what happened, he made a prayer and was swallowed by a chasm.

[3.3] **17** Deucalion had Idomeneus and Crete, and an illegitimate son, Molos.

Glaucos and Polyidos When Glaucos was still an infant, he fell into a vat of honey while chasing a mouse and died. When he disappeared, Minos made a great search for him and consulted an oracle about finding him. **18** The Couretes told him that he had a tricolored cow in his herds and that the man best able to provide an analogy for its color would restore his son—alive. When the seers were called together,

1. Apollodorus seems to be quoting a line from an unknown tragedy.

Polyidos son of Coiranos compared the cow's color to a blackberry.[2] He was forced to look for the child and found him through some method of divination.

19 But Minos said that he was supposed to have him back *alive,* and Polyidos was locked up with the corpse. Completely uncertain what to do, he saw a serpent approaching the corpse. He killed it by hitting it with a rock, afraid that he would himself be killed if something happened to the corpse.* Another serpent came, but after seeing the first snake dead it went away. Then it returned carrying an herb and applied it all over the other snake's body. When the herb was applied, the snake came back to life. **20** Seeing this and marveling, Polyidos applied the same herb to the body of Glaucos and resurrected him. Though Minos had gotten his son back, even so he would not allow Polyidos to go back to Argos until he taught the art of prophecy to Glaucos. Under compulsion, Polyidos taught him, and when he was about to sail off, he ordered Glaucos to spit into his mouth. When Glaucos did this, he forgot the art of prophecy. **21** Now, let this be as far as my account of Europa's descendants goes.

Cadmos and the Spartoi After Telephassa died and Cadmos buried her, he [3.4]
was treated as a guest by the Thracians and went to Delphi to inquire about Europa. The god told him not to pursue the matter of Europa, but to make a cow his guide and found a city wherever she collapsed from exhaustion. **22** After receiving this oracle, he traveled through Phocis and then came across a cow among the herds of Pelagon and followed behind her. While she was passing through Boiotia, she lay down where the city of Thebes is now.*

Wishing to sacrifice the cow to Athena, Cadmos sent some of his companions to get water from Ares' Spring. Guarding the spring was a serpent (some say it was Ares' offspring), and it destroyed most of those who had been sent. **23** Cadmos became angry and killed the serpent. On the advice of Athena he sowed the dragon's teeth like seeds. When these were sown {*sparentes*}, there grew up from the earth some armed men whom they called the Spartoi {"Sown Men"}. They killed each other, some more than happy* to enter the fray, some not realizing what was going on. **24** Pherecydes says that when Cadmos saw armed men sprouting up from the earth, he threw rocks at them, and they thought they were being hit by each other and fell to fighting. Five of them survived: Echion, Oudaios, Chthonios, Hyperenor, and Peloros.

In return for those he killed, Cadmos was in Ares' service for an "eternal" year—in those days a year was eight years long. **25** After his service Athena arranged for him to have the kingdom, and Zeus gave him as wife Harmonia, the daughter of Aphrodite and Ares. All the gods left heaven and celebrated the marriage feast in the Cadmeia with much singing. Cadmos gave Harmonia a dress and the necklace made by Hephaistos. Some say it was given as a gift to Cadmos by Hephaistos, but Pherecydes says it was given by Europa, who had gotten it from Zeus.

2. For a clearer account of this episode see Hyginus 136.

Cadmos' Daughters; Semele and Dionysos **26** Cadmos had daughters, Autonoe, Ino, Semele, and Agaue, and a son, Polydoros. Athamas married Ino, Aristaios married Autonoe, and Echion married Agaue. Zeus fell in love with Semele and shared her bed without Hera's knowledge. But Semele was tricked by Hera. Zeus had agreed to do what she asked, and Semele asked him to come to her as he had come to Hera when he courted her. **27** Zeus was unable to refuse and came to her chamber on a chariot with lightning and thunder and hurled a thunderbolt. Semele died from fright,* but Zeus snatched from the fire their child, who was miscarried at six months of age, and stitched him into his thigh.

After Semele's death, the remaining daughters of Cadmos spread a story that Semele had been sleeping with some mortal man and had faked her affair with Zeus, and that that was why she was struck by a thunderbolt. **28** When the proper time came, Zeus gave birth to Dionysos by undoing his stitches. He gave him to Hermes, who brought him to Ino and Athamas and convinced them to raise him as a girl. Hera was enraged and cast madness upon them. Athamas hunted down and killed their oldest son, Learchos, thinking that he was a deer. Ino threw Melicertes into a boiling cauldron, then took him and jumped into the deep with her son's corpse. **29** She is called Leucothea, and her son is called Palaimon, having been given these names by sailors, for the two of them help those caught in storms. The Isthmian Games were founded in Melicertes' honor, and Sisyphos is the one who founded them. Zeus changed Dionysos into a baby goat and thwarted Hera's anger. Hermes took and carried him to some nymphs who lived in Nysa in Asia. Later, Zeus turned them into stars and named them the Hyades.

Actaion **30** Autonoe and Aristaios had a son, Actaion, who was raised by Cheiron and trained to be a hunter, and then later was devoured by his own dogs on Mount Cithairon. He died in this way, according to Acousilaos, when Zeus grew wrathful because Actaion courted Semele. But most say it was because Actaion saw Artemis as she bathed. **31** They say that the goddess changed his shape instantly into that of a deer and sent madness upon the fifty dogs that followed him, and he was eaten by them because they did not recognize him. After Actaion's death his dogs searched for their master and howled terribly. When they came in their search to Cheiron's cave, he made a statue of Actaion, and this put an end to their grieving. **32** [The names of Actaion's dogs from the *<name of a poem missing>* are:

So then
his mighty dogs stood round his beautiful body
as if it were an animal's and they ripped it apart, Arcena first, close by,
< . . . > after her her stout offspring
Lynceus, swift-footed Balios, and Amarynthos.

And those he cataloged by name without interruption:

< . . . > then they killed Actaion at the urging of Zeus.
First to drink the dark blood of their master were
Spartos and Omargos and swift-speeding Bores.

These were the first to devour Actaion and lap up his blood.
After them all the rest rushed in eager excitement.
< . . . >
to be a remedy for mortals' grievous pains.][3].

Dionysos' Travels **33** Dionysos was the one who discovered the grapevine. [3.5]
When Hera cast madness upon him, he wandered through Egypt and Syria. At first Proteus, the king of the Egyptians, was his host, but later he went to Cybela in Phrygia and was purified there by Rhea, learned her rites, and adopted her accoutrements. He pushed on through Thrace on his way to fight the Indians.*

Lycourgos Resists Dionysos **34** Dryas' son Lycourgos, the king of the Edonoi, who dwell along the Strymon River, was the first to treat Dionysos insolently and reject him. Dionysos fled for protection to the sea to Thetis daughter of Nereus, but his Bacchai and the throng of Satyrs that accompanied him were taken captive. **35** Then the Bacchai were suddenly set free, and Dionysos made Lycourgos go mad. In his raving he struck his son Dryas with an ax and killed him, thinking that he was chopping the branch of a vine. After dismembering him, he regained his senses. When the land remained infertile, the god gave a prophecy that it would bear crops if Lycourgos were put to death. When the Edonoi heard this, they led him to Mount Pangaion and tied him up. There, in accordance with the will of Dionysos, Lycourgos was destroyed* by horses and died.

Dionysos Returns to Thebes **36** After going through Thrace and all of India (where he set up pillars),* he came to Thebes and made the women leave their houses and celebrate Bacchic rites on Mount Cithairon. Pentheus, whom Agaue bore to Echion, had inherited the kingdom from Cadmos and tried to keep this from happening. When he came to Cithairon to spy on the Bacchai, he was dismembered by his mother Agaue in a fit of madness, for she thought he was a beast.

Dionysos in Argos; the Tyrrhenian Pirates **37** Having proved to the Thebans that he was a god, he came to Argos, where once again they did not honor him, so he drove the women out of their minds. They had their still-nursing children with them in the mountains and ate their flesh. Then Dionysos wanted to cross from Icaria to Naxos, so he hired a pirate ship manned by Tyrrhenians. **38** They took him aboard, but they sailed past Naxos and made for Asia to sell him into slavery. He turned the mast and the oars into snakes and filled the ship with ivy and the sound of flutes. The pirates went mad, escaped by jumping into the sea, and were turned into dolphins. In this way mortals learned that he was a god and honored him. He brought his mother up from the realm of Hades, gave her the name Thyone, and went with her up to heaven.

3. The material between the square brackets is usually (in our opinion, rightly) deleted as a later insertion. It also suffers from numerous textual corruptions.

Cadmos and Harmonia in Illyria **39** Cadmos left Thebes with Harmonia and went to the Encheleans. These people were being attacked by the Illyrians, and the god delivered an oracle that they would defeat the Illyrians if they took Cadmos and Harmonia as their leaders. So they followed the oracle by making these two their leaders against the Illyrians and were victorious. Cadmos ruled as king of the Illyrians and had a son, Illyrios. Later, Cadmos and Harmonia were changed into serpents and were sent off to the Elysian Fields by Zeus.

Successors of Cadmos in Thebes **40** When Polydoros became king of Thebes, he married Nycteis, the daughter of Nycteus son of Chthonios, and had a son, Labdacos, who was killed after Pentheus for holding similar beliefs. Labdacos left behind a one-year-old son, Laios, and while he was still a child, Nycteus' brother Lycos took power for himself. **41** Both Lycos and Nycteus had gone into exile from Euboia* after killing Phlegyas, the son of Ares and Dotis the Boiotian. There they settled in Hyria, and <after going from there to Thebes,>* they were made citizens because of their relationship with Pentheus. Lycos was chosen by the Thebans as war-leader and exercised the power of a ruler.

Zethos and Amphion After Lycos was king for eighteen years,* he died at the hands of Zethos and Amphion for the following reason. **42** Antiope was Nycteus' daughter, and Zeus slept with her. When she became pregnant, her father threatened her, so she escaped to Epopeus in Sicyon and became his wife. In despair Nycteus killed himself after giving instructions to Lycos to punish both Epopeus and Antiope. Lycos went on a campaign against Sicyon and conquered it. He killed Epopeus, but he brought Antiope back as a prisoner. **43** As she was being brought back, she gave birth to two sons at Eleutherai in Boiotia. They were exposed, but a cowherd discovered them, raised them, and named one of them Zethos and the other Amphion.

Zethos took care of herds of cattle, and Amphion practiced playing the lyre (Hermes had given him a lyre). Lycos and his wife, Dirce, locked Antiope up and tormented her. But her bonds came off of their own accord after a while, and she made her way unnoticed to the cottage of her sons, wanting to be taken in by them. **44** They recognized their mother, killed Lycos, and after tying Dirce to a bull, they threw her dead body into the spring that is now named Dirce after her. Succeeding to the kingdom, they built walls around the city (the stones followed Amphion's lyre) and banished Laios. He lived in the Peloponnesos as the guest of Pelops, and when he was teaching his host's son Chrysippos to drive a chariot, he fell in love with him and kidnapped him.

Niobe **45** Zethos married Thebe, after whom the city is called Thebes, and Amphion married Niobe daughter of Tantalos, who bore seven sons, Sipylos, Eupinytos, Ismenos, Damasichthon, Agenor, Phaidimos, and Tantalos, and the same number of daughters, Ethodaia (or Neaira according to some), Cleodoxa, Astyoche, Phthia, Pelopia, Astycrateia, and Ogygia. But Hesiod says that she had ten sons and ten daughters, Herodoros that she had four* male and three female children, and

Homer that she had six sons and six daughters. **46** Because she was so blessed with children, Niobe said that she was more blessed with children than Leto. Leto was enraged and provoked Artemis and Apollo against them. Artemis shot down the females in their house, and Apollo killed all the males together on Mount Cithairon while they were out hunting. But of the males Amphion was saved, and of the females so was Chloris, the eldest, whom Neleus married. **47** But according to Telesilla, Amyclas and Meliboia were the ones saved, and Amphion was shot down by Artemis and Apollo. Niobe herself left Thebes and came to her father Tantalos in Sipylos. There she made prayer to Zeus and turned into stone, and tears flow from the stone both night and day.

Laios and Iocaste; Oidipous **48** After the death of Amphion, Laios succeeded to the kingdom. He married Menoiceus' daughter, whom some call Iocaste and others Epicaste. They received an oracle not to have children (for their offspring would be a patricide), but Laios got drunk and slept with his wife. After boring through its ankles with pins, Laios gave the child to a shepherd to expose. **49** But although the shepherd exposed it on Mount Cithairon, some herders of Polybos, the king of the Corinthians, found the infant and brought it to the king's wife, Periboia. She adopted it and passed it off as her own. After treating its ankles, she called it Oidipous, giving this name because its feet {*pous*} had swollen {*oideo*}.

50 When the boy grew up, he surpassed his peers in strength. Out of jealousy they mocked him for not really being his parents' son. He asked Periboia, but was not able to find out the truth. So he went to Delphi and inquired about his own parents. The god told him not to travel to his country, for he would kill his father and have sex with his mother. **51** When he heard this, he left Corinth behind, believing that he had been born from those who were said to be his parents. While riding in a chariot through Phocis on a certain narrow stretch of road he ran into Laios driving in a chariot. Polyphontes, who was Laios' herald, ordered Oidipous to get out of the way and killed one of his horses because of the holdup caused by his refusal to do so. So Oidipous became enraged and killed both Polyphontes and Laios. Then he arrived in Thebes.

The Sphinx; Oidipous Becomes King **52** Now, Damasistratos, king of the Plataians, buried Laios, and Creon son of Menoiceus succeeded to the throne of Thebes. While he was king, a great misfortune befell the city; Hera sent the Sphinx, whose mother was Echidna and whose father was Typhon. She had the face of a woman; the chest, feet, and tail of a lion; and the wings of a bird. She had learned a riddle from the Muses, set herself up on Mount Phicion, and proposed it to the Thebans. **53** This was the riddle: What is four-footed and two-footed and three-footed though it has but one voice?[4] The Thebans had at that time an oracle that they would be rid of the Sphinx when they solved her riddle. So they gathered together often to search for what the answer was. And when they did not find it, she would

4. The riddle is given in the Vatican Epitome (and in other sources as well) with the variation "though it has but one form."

snatch and devour one of them. **54** After many had died, and last of all Creon's son Haimon, Creon proclaimed that he would give both the kingdom and Laios' wife to the man who solved the riddle. When Oidipous heard this, he solved it, saying that the answer to the riddle spoken by the Sphinx was a human being, because a person is four-footed as an infant carried on four limbs, two-footed when grown up, and in old age takes a staff as a third foot. **55** Then the Sphinx threw herself off of the acropolis, and Oidipous both received the kingdom and unwittingly married his mother. With her he had sons, Polyneices and Eteocles, and daughters, Ismene and Antigone, though there are some who say that the children's mother was Euryganeia daughter of Hyperphas.

Death of Iocaste and Oidipous **56** When what was hidden was later revealed, Iocaste hanged herself in a noose, and Oidipous put out his eyes and was driven out of Thebes. He laid curses on his sons because they watched him being banished from the city and did not come to his aid. He came with Antigone to Colonos in Attica, where the sanctuary of the Eumenides is, and sat down as a suppliant. He was received as a guest by Theseus and died not long afterward.

[3.6] **Eteocles and Polyneices; Tydeus** **57** Eteocles and Polyneices came to an agreement with each other concerning the kingdom, resolving that they would each rule for one year at a time. Some say that Polyneices ruled first and handed the kingdom over to Eteocles after a year, but others say that Eteocles ruled first and refused to hand over the kingdom. **58** So Polyneices went into exile from Thebes and came to Argos, taking the necklace and dress.[5] Adrastos son of Talaos was king of Argos, and Polyneices approached his palace at night and got into a fight with Tydeus son of Oineus, who was an exile from Calydon. **59** At the sudden noise Adrastos appeared and separated them. Recalling a certain seer telling him to yoke his daughters to a boar and a lion, he chose these two as their husbands, for one had on his shield the forequarters of a boar and the other had those of a lion.[6] Tydeus married Deipyle, and Polyneices married Argeia, and Adrastos promised to restore them both to their homelands. He was eager to march against Thebes first and assembled the nobles.

60 Amphiaraos son of Oicles was a seer and foresaw that all those who undertook the campaign were bound to die except Adrastos. So he himself shrank from campaigning and tried to dissuade the others. But Polyneices came to Iphis son of Alector and asked to learn how Amphiaraos could be forced to go to war. Iphis said that he could be forced if Eriphyle got the necklace. **61** Now, Amphiaraos had forbidden Eriphyle to accept any gifts from Polyneices, but Polyneices gave her the necklace and asked her to persuade Amphiaraos to undertake the campaign. It was in her power, for Amphiaraos had once quarreled with Adrastos,* and after settling it swore to let Eriphyle settle any further dispute he might have with Adrastos. **62** So when it was time to march against Thebes and Adrastos encouraged it and

5. The necklace and dress Harmonia received at her wedding (see 3.25 above). These will be referred to in several places in the subsequent narrative of Thebes.

6. See Hyginus 69 for the relevance of the lion and boar to these heroes.

Amphiaraos discouraged it, Eriphyle took the necklace and persuaded him to campaign with Adrastos. Amphiaraos was compelled to go to war, but he gave his sons instructions to kill their mother and go to war against Thebes when they grew up.

The Seven against Thebes **63** After Adrastos assembled an army with seven leaders, he hurried to make war on Thebes. The leaders were the following: Adrastos son of Talaos, Amphiaraos son of Oicles, Capaneus son of Hipponoos, and Hippomedon son of Aristomachos (some say he was son of Talaos), all from Argos; and Polyneices son of Oidipous from Thebes, Tydeus son of Oineus from Aitolia, and Parthenopaios son of Melanion from Arcadia. But some do not count Tydeus and Polyneices and include in the seven Eteoclos son of Iphis, and Mecisteus.

64 When they arrived in Nemea, where Lycourgos was king, they went looking for water. Hypsipyle showed them the way to a spring, leaving behind Opheltes, an infant that she was nursing, the son of Eurydice and Lycourgos. **65** She was doing so because when the Lemnian women had found out later that she had saved Thoas, they killed him and sold Hypsipyle into slavery. So she was bought and served in the home of Lycourgos. While she was showing them the spring, the child she left behind was killed by a serpent. Adrastos and his men then showed up, killed the serpent, and buried the boy. **66** But Amphiaraos told them that it was a sign that foretold the future, and they called the boy Archemoros {"Beginner of Doom"}. They held in his honor the first Nemean Games. Adrastos was the victor in the horse race, Eteoclos in running, Tydeus in boxing, Amphiaraos in jumping and discus, Laodocos in the javelin, Polyneices in wrestling, and Parthenopaios in archery.

67 When they came to Mount Cithairon, they sent Tydeus ahead to tell Eteocles to yield the kingdom to Polyneices, as they had agreed. Eteocles paid no attention, so Tydeus made a test of the Thebans by challenging them one at a time and defeating them all. The Thebans armed fifty men and had them ambush Tydeus as he departed, but he killed all of them except Maion and then returned to his camp.

68 The Argives took up arms and advanced to the walls. There were seven sets of gates. Adrastos stood at the Homoloidian Gates, Capaneus at the Ogygian, Amphiaraos at the Proitidian, Hippomedon at the Oncaidian, Polyneices at the Hypsistan, Parthenopaios at the Electran, and Tydeus at the Crenidian. **69** Eteocles also armed the Thebans and appointed commanders equal in number to those on the other side and matched them one against the other. He then consulted seers as to how they might defeat their enemies.

Teiresias There was in Thebes a seer who was blind, Teiresias, the son of Eueres and the nymph Chariclo, a descendant of Oudaios, one of the Spartoi. They tell varying accounts of his blindness and his prophetic art. **70** Some say that he was blinded by the gods because he used to reveal to mortals what the gods wished to hide. But Pherecydes says that he was blinded by Athena, for although Chariclo was dearly loved by Athena, < . . . Teiresias>[7] saw Athena completely naked, and she covered

7. Teiresias was clearly in the small gap in the text, though we do not know what else has over time been omitted.

his eyes with her hands and made him blind. Although Chariclo asked her to restore his sight, Athena was unable to do so, but she cleaned out his ears and rendered him capable of understanding every utterance of the birds, and she gave him a cornel-wood staff as a gift, and when he carried this, he could walk around like those who can see. **71** But Hesiod says that near Mount Cyllene he once saw some snakes mating, and when he injured them, he changed from a man to a woman. Then, when he observed the same snakes mating a second time, he changed back into a man. Because of this experience, Hera and Zeus asked him to settle their dispute when they were arguing whether it happens that women or men take more pleasure in the sexual act. **72** Teiresias said that if you divide sexual pleasure into ten portions, men enjoy one of these and women nine. So Hera blinded him, but Zeus granted him the power of prophecy. [What was told by Teiresias to Zeus and Hera: "A man enjoys but a single portion of the ten, but a woman enjoys in her heart all ten."][8] He also lived to an advanced age.

The Battle for Thebes **73** The Thebans consulted Teiresias, and he told them they would be victorious if Menoiceus son of Creon gave himself freely to Ares as a sacrificial offering. When Menoiceus son of Creon heard this, he cut his own throat before the gates. When the battle occurred, the Cadmeians were pushed back all the way to the walls, and Capaneus picked up a ladder and started to climb onto the walls with it, but Zeus struck him with a thunderbolt.

74 After this happened, the Argives were routed. Since many died, both armies made a decision, and Eteocles and Polyneices fought a duel for the kingdom, killing each other. There was another mighty battle, and the sons of Astacos displayed great bravery: Ismaros killed Hippomedon, Leades killed Eteoclos, and Amphidicos killed Parthenopaios. **75** According to Euripides, however, Poseidon's son Periclymenos killed Parthenopaios. Melanippos, the last of Astacos' sons, wounded Tydeus in the stomach. As he lay half-dead, Athena begged Zeus for a drug and brought it with the intention of making him immortal with it. **76** But when Amphiaraos perceived this, in his hatred for Tydeus because he had persuaded the Argives to go on campaign against Amphiaraos' judgment, he cut off Melanippos' head and gave it to Tydeus (Tydeus, though wounded, had killed him). He broke the head open and gulped down the brain. When Athena saw this, she was revolted and withheld the bounty, denying it to Tydeus.

77 As for Amphiaraos, while he was fleeing along the Ismenos River, before he could be wounded in the back by Periclymenos, Zeus split open the earth by casting a thunderbolt. Amphiaraos disappeared along with his chariot and his charioteer Baton (Elaton according to some), and Zeus made him immortal. Adrastos alone was saved by his horse Areion. Demeter bore this horse after having sex in the guise of an Erinys with Poseidon.

[3.7] **Creon and Antigone** **78** Creon, after taking over the kingdom of the Thebans, cast the Argives' corpses out unburied, made a proclamation that no one was

8. This is almost certainly a later addition to the text.

to bury them, and set guards. But Antigone, one of Oidipous' daughters, secretly stole the body of Polyneices and buried it. Caught by Creon, she was buried alive in his tomb.[9] **79** Adrastos came to Athens and fled to the altar of Pity for refuge. After placing an olive branch on it, he asked that they bury the bodies. The Athenians marched with Theseus, captured Thebes, and gave the bodies to their relatives for burial. When the pyre of Capaneus was burning, Euadne, Capaneus' wife and Iphis' daughter, threw herself onto it and was cremated with him.

The Epigonoi **80** Ten years later the dead men's sons, known as the Epigonoi, proposed to march on Thebes, desiring to avenge the deaths of their fathers. When they sought oracles, the god prophesied victory, provided Alcmaion was their leader. **81** Alcmaion did not want to lead the army until he punished his mother, but he went on the campaign anyway, for Eriphyle got the dress from Thersandros son of Polyneices and helped him convince her sons to go on the campaign also. The Epigonoi chose Alcmaion leader and made war on Thebes. **82** Those who went on the campaign were: Amphiaraos' sons Alcmaion and Amphilochos, Aigialeus son of Adrastos, Diomedes son of Tydeus, Promachos son of Parthenopaios, Sthenelos son of Capaneus, Thersandros son of Polyneices, and Euryalos son of Mecisteus. **83** They first plundered the surrounding villages; then when the Thebans, led by Laodamas son of Eteocles, attacked them, they fought mightily. Laodamas killed Aigialeus, but Alcmaion killed Laodamas. After his death the Thebans took refuge within the walls. **84** Teiresias told them to send a herald to the Argives to discuss ending the war while the rest of them fled. So they sent a herald to the enemy while they themselves loaded the women and children onto their wagons and fled from the city. Arriving by night at the spring known as Tilphoussa, Teiresias drank from it and brought his life to a close. **85** After traveling for a long time, the Thebans founded the city of Hestiaia and settled there.

Later, when the Argives discovered the Thebans' getaway, they entered the city of Thebes, collected the plunder, and took down the walls. They sent a portion of the plunder to Apollo in Delphi, including Teiresias' daughter Manto; for they had vowed to dedicate to the god the finest of the plunder if they captured Thebes.

Alcmaion in Exile; His Children **86** After the capture of Thebes Alcmaion grew angrier when he learned that his mother Eriphyle in return for gifts had sold him out too, and when Apollo told him to do so in an oracle, he killed her. Some say that he killed Eriphyle with his brother Amphilochos' help, but others say that he did it by himself. **87** An Erinys from his mother's murder vengefully pursued Alcmaion; crazed, he first went to Oicles' home in Arcadia, and from there he went to Phegeus' in Psophis. Purified by him, he married his daughter Arsinoe and gave her the necklace and dress. **88** Later, the land became barren on account of him, and the god commanded him in an oracle to go off to Acheloos and again <*uncertain text*>.[10] First, he went to Oineus in Calydon and was taken in as a guest by him, then he

9. The text could also be translated "Caught by Creon himself, she was buried alive in the tomb."

10. The text is corrupt here, and we do not think any suggestion to date is likely to be correct. It is clear enough what Alcmaion gets from Acheloos in the following portion of the narrative, and other

came to the Thesprotians but was driven out of their land. Finally, he reached the springs of Acheloos and was purified by him and married his daughter Callirhoe. He established his new home in the place that Acheloos built up with silt.

89 Later, Callirhoe wanted to have the necklace and dress and said that she would not stay married to him unless she got them, so Alcmaion went to Psophis and told Phegeus that an end to his madness had been prophesied to him when he brought the necklace and the dress to Delphi and dedicated them. **90** Phegeus believed him and gave them to him. A servant revealed that now that he had them, he was taking them to Callirhoe, so on Phegeus' orders Alcmaion was ambushed and killed by Phegeus' sons. The sons of Phegeus put Arsinoe into a chest when she condemned their actions and took her to Tegea and gave her as a slave to Agapenor, falsely alleging that she had murdered Alcmaion.

91 Callirhoe learned of the killing of Alcmaion, and when Zeus was trying to sleep with her, she requested that the sons she had had with Alcmaion become fully grown so that they might take revenge for their father's murder. Her sons instantly grew up and set out to avenge their father. **92** Phegeus's sons, Pronoos and Agenor, who were bringing the necklace and dress to dedicate in Delphi, were lodging at Agapenor's at the same time as Alcmaion's sons, Amphoteros and Acarnan. After the latter two killed their father's murderers, they went to Psophis, entered the palace, and killed both Phegeus and his wife. **93** They were pursued all the way to Tegea, where they were saved when the Tegeans and some Argives came to their aid and put the Psophidians to flight. After telling their mother about this, they went to Delphi and dedicated the necklace and dress at Acheloos' command. Traveling to Epeiros, they gathered settlers and founded Acarnania.

94 Euripides says that Alcmaion had two children by Manto daughter of Teiresias during the period of his madness—Amphilochos and a daughter, Tisiphone—and he brought the infants to Corinth and gave them to Creon, the king of the Corinthians, to raise. Tisiphone, he says, because she was extraordinarily beautiful, was sold as a slave by Creon's wife, since she was afraid that Creon would make her his wife. **95** Alcmaion bought her and kept her as a servant, not realizing she was his daughter, and when he came to Corinth to get his children back, he also recovered his son. Following Apollo's oracles, Amphilochos settled Amphilochian Argos.

[3.8] **Pelasgos, Lycaon, and Lycaon's Sons** **96** Let us return now to Pelasgos, whom Acousilaos says was the son of Zeus and Niobe (just as we assumed), but Hesiod says he was an *autochthon.* Pelasgos and Meliboia, the daughter of Oceanos (or, as others say, the nymph Cyllene) had a son Lycaon, who was king of the Arcadians and had by many women fifty sons: Melaineus, Thesprotos, Helix, Nyctimos, Peucetios, Caucon, Mecisteus, Hopleus, Macareus, Macednos, **97** Horos, Polichos, Acontes, Euaimon, Ancyor, Archebates, Carteron, Aigaion, Pallas, Eumon, Canethos, Prothoos, Linos, Corethon, Mainalos, Teleboas, Physios, Phassos, Phthios, Lycios,

---

accounts indicate that Alcmaion is to find a land that the sun did not shine on when he committed his crime.

Halipheros, Genetor, Boucolion, Socleus, Phineus, Eumetes, Harpaleus, Portheus, Platon, Haimon, Cynaithos, Leon, Harpalycos, Heraieus, Titanas, Mantineus, Cleitor, Stymphalos, Orchomenos, and <*fiftieth name missing*>.

98 These surpassed all mortals in arrogance and impiety. Zeus, desiring to test their impiety, visited them disguised as a manual laborer. They invited him in to eat with them; they slaughtered one of the sons of the locals, mixed his innards with those of the sacrificial animal, and set them before him. The eldest brother, Mainalos, was behind this plan. **99** Revolted, Zeus overturned the table {*trapeza*} (in the place that is now called Trapezous) and struck Lycaon and his sons with thunderbolts, all except the youngest, Nyctimos. For before Zeus could strike him, Ge checked his anger by laying hold of his right hand.

But after Nyctimos succeeded to the kingdom, there occurred the flood that happened in the age of Deucalion. Some have said that it occurred because of the ungodliness of Lycaon's sons.

Callisto and Arcas **100** Eumelos and some others say that Lycaon also had a daughter, Callisto. Hesiod says that she was one of the nymphs, Asios says she was Nycteus' daughter, and Pherecydes that she was Ceteus'. She was Artemis' hunting companion, even adopting the same style of dress as her, and swore to her that she would remain a virgin. But Zeus fell in love with her, and, although she was unwilling, he shared her bed after making himself look like Artemis, according to some, but like Apollo, according to others. **101** Desiring to hide this from Hera, Zeus transformed Callisto into a bear. But Hera convinced Artemis to shoot her down like a wild beast. But there are those who say that Artemis shot her down because she did not preserve her virginity. When Callisto died, Zeus snatched her infant and gave him to Maia in Arcadia to raise, giving him the name Arcas. As for Callisto, he turned her into a constellation and called it the Bear.

102 Arcas had two sons, Elatos and Apheidas, with Leaneira daughter of Amy- [3.9]
clas, or with Meganeira daughter of Crocon, or, according to Eumelos, with the nymph Chrysopeleia. These sons divided the land between them, but Elatos had all the power. He had Stymphalos and Pereus with Laodice daughter of Cinyras. Apheidas had Aleos and Stheneboia, whom Proitos married. Aleos and Neaira daughter of Pereus had a daughter, Auge, and sons, Cepheus and Lycourgos.

Auge and Telephos **103** After Auge was raped by Heracles, she concealed her baby in the sanctuary of Athena, whose priestess she was. But the land remained barren, and the oracles revealed that there was some ungodly thing in the sanctuary of Athena, so Auge was found out by her father, and he handed her over to Nauplios to be put to death. Teuthras, the ruler of the Mysians, received her from Nauplios and married her. **104** Her baby was exposed on Mount Parthenios, and he was called Telephos because a deer {*elaphos*} gave him her teat {*thele*}. He was raised by Corythos' herders, and, in searching for his parents, he came to Delphi. After finding out from the god who they were, he went to Mysia and became Teuthras' adopted son. When Teuthras died, Telephos became his successor in power.

Atalante and Melanion **105** Either with Cleophyle or Eurynome, Lycourgos had Ancaios, Epochos, Amphidamas, and Iasos. Amphidamas had Melanion and a daughter, Antimache, whom Eurystheus married. Iasos and Clymene daughter of Minyas had Atalante, whom her father exposed because he wanted male children. But a bear continually came and gave her her teat until some hunters found and raised her among themselves.

106 When she was grown up, Atalante kept herself a virgin and spent her time armed, hunting in the wilderness. The Centaurs Rhoicos and Hylaios tried to rape her, but they were shot down by her and died. She also accompanied the heroes to hunt the Calydonian boar, and, at the games held in Pelias' honor, she wrestled Peleus and beat him. **107** Later on, she found her parents. But when her father urged her to marry, she went off to a place where races were held and stuck a three-cubit-high stake into the ground at the halfway point. She would give her suitors a head start from this point, and she herself would run wearing armor. Any man she caught up to earned his death right there; the man she did not catch earned marriage.

108 Many men had already died when Melanion fell in love with her and came to race, bringing golden apples he had gotten from Aphrodite. As she chased him, he would throw these. Because she picked up what he threw, she lost the race. So Melanion married her, and it is said that once when they were out hunting, they went into the sanctuary of Zeus, and because they had sex there, they were turned into lions. **109** Hesiod and some others say that Atalante was not Iasos' daughter, but Schoineus', but Euripides says that she was Mainalos' and that Melanion was not the one who married her, but Hippomenes. With either Melanion or Ares, Atalante had Parthenopaios, who marched against Thebes.

[3.10] **Atlas and His Daughters** **110** In Cyllene in Arcadia, Atlas and Pleione daughter of Oceanos had seven daughters, the so-called Pleiades, Alcyone, Merope, Celaino, Electra, Sterope, Taygete, and Maia. Of these, Oinomaos married Sterope, and Sisyphos Merope. **111** Poseidon slept with two, first Celaino, from whom Lycos was born, whom Poseidon settled in the Isles of the Blessed, and second Alcyone, who gave birth to a daughter, Aithousa (who bore Eleuther to Apollo), and sons, Hyrieus and Hyperenor. Hyrieus and the nymph Clonia had Nycteus and Lycos, and Nycteus and Polyxo had Antiope, and Antiope and Zeus had Zethos and Amphion.

Hermes Zeus slept with the remaining Atlantids. **112** Maia, the eldest, after sleeping with Zeus, bore Hermes in a cave in Cyllene. Though he was laid in his first set of swaddling-clothes on the winnowing-fan, he slipped out and went to Pieria and stole some cows that Apollo was herding. So that he would not be caught because of their tracks, he put shoes on their feet and brought them to Pylos. He hid the rest of them in a cave, but he sacrificed two, fastened their skins to rocks, then ate some of their flesh after boiling it and burned up the rest. **113** He quickly went off to Cyllene and found a tortoise grazing before his cave. He cleaned it out and over the hollow shell stretched strings made from the cows he had sacrificed. Having produced a lyre, he also invented the plectrum.

In his search for the cows, Apollo arrived in Pylos and questioned the inhabitants. They said that they had seen a boy driving them, but they could not tell him where they had been driven because it was not possible to find a track. **114** Learning the identity of the thief by his prophetic power, he went to Maia in Cyllene and accused Hermes. She pointed him out in his swaddling-clothes. Apollo took him to Zeus and demanded his cows back. When Zeus commanded Hermes to return them, he denied everything. But when he could not fool him, Hermes took Apollo to Pylos and gave him back his cows. When Apollo heard the lyre, he exchanged the cows for it. **115** As Hermes herded them, he fashioned a syrinx as a replacement and played it. Apollo wanted to have this also, so he offered his golden wand, which he held while herding cows. But Hermes wanted to get this and also to gain the power of prophecy in exchange for the syrinx. Apollo gave it and taught him how to prophesy with the pebbles.[11] Zeus made him his own herald and the herald of the underworld gods.

Lacedaimon and His Descendants; Spartan Genealogies **116** Taygete and Zeus had Lacedaimon, the one after whom the country is called Lacedaimon. Lacedaimon and Sparte daughter of Eurotas, who was the son of Lelex the *autochthon* and the Naiad nymph Cleochareia, had Amyclas and Eurydice, whom Acrisios married. Amyclas and Diomede daughter of Lapithos had Cynortas and Hyacinthos. The latter, they say, was a boyfriend of Apollo who was killed by him accidentally when he hit him with a discus. **117** Cynortas had Perieres, who married Gorgophone daughter of Perseus, as Stesichoros says, and fathered Tyndareos, Icarios, Aphareus, and Leucippos. Aphareus and Arene daughter of Oibalos had Lynceus and Idas, and also Peisos. According to many, though, Idas is said to be Poseidon's son. Lynceus had such extraordinarily sharp sight that he could even see what was underground. Leucippos had daughters, Hilaeira and Phoibe, whom the Dioscouroi kidnapped and married. **118** In addition to them, he also had Arsinoe. Apollo slept with her, and she had Asclepios.

Asclepios Some say that Asclepios was not the son of Arsinoe daughter of Leucippos, but of Coronis daughter of Phlegyas in Thessaly. They say that Apollo fell in love with her and immediately slept with her, but she chose to marry Ischys, the brother of Caineus, against her father's will. **119** Apollo cursed the crow that reported the news and he made it black when it had up until then been white, and he killed Coronis. As she was being burned, Apollo snatched her infant from the fire and brought him to Cheiron the Centaur. Raised by him, the child learned both medicine and hunting. **120** He proved to be a skilled surgeon and practiced his craft so well that he not only kept some people from dying, but he even raised people who had died. For he had gotten from Athena the blood that flowed from the veins of the Gorgon: the blood that flowed from the veins on the left side he used to people's detriment; that from the right side he used for their safety, and that is how he raised the dead.

11. A reference to Hermes' connection with the Thriai, a trio of female spirits that divined by casting pebbles (the word *thriai* itself means "pebbles"). Apollo grants Hermes access to and control over this minor form of divination in the *Homeric Hymn to Hermes* 550–568.

121 [I have found some said to have been raised by him: Capaneus and Lycourgos, according to Stesichoros in the *Eriphyle;* Hippolytos, according to the writer of the *Naupactica;* Tyndareos, according to Panyassis; Hymenaios, according to the Orphics; and Glaucos son of Minos, according to Melesagoras.][12]

122 Zeus became afraid that mortals would learn healing from him and so be able to treat each other, so he struck him with a thunderbolt. Apollo became angry at this and killed the Cyclopes that had made the thunderbolt for Zeus. Zeus was going to cast Apollo into Tartaros, but after Leto begged him, he ordered him to serve a mortal man for a year. He went to Pherai to Admetos son of Pheres, tended his herds, and made all the cows produce twins.

Further Spartan Genealogies **123** There are those who say that Aphareus and Leucippos were sons of Perieres son of Aiolos, and that Perieres was son of Cynortas, that Oibalos was son of Perieres, and that Oibalos and the Naiad nymph Bateia had Tyndareos, Hippocoon, and Icarios.[13]

124 Hippocoon had sons, Dorycleus, Scaios, Enarophoros, Euteiches, Boucolos, Lycaithos, Tebros, Hippothoos, Eurytos, Hippocorystes, Alcinous, and Alcon. With these sons Hippocoon drove out Icarios and Tyndareos from Lacedaimon. **125** They went as exiles to Thestios and were his allies in the war he waged against his neighbors. Tyndareos married Thestios' daughter, Leda, but then, when Heracles killed Hippocoon and his sons, they returned from exile and Tyndareos succeeded to the kingship.

126 Icarios and the Naiad nymph Periboia had Thoas, Damasippos, Imeusimos, Aletes, Perileos, and a daughter, Penelope, whom Odysseus married.

Tyndareos, Leda, and Their Children Tyndareos and Leda had Timandra, whom Echemos married, and Clytaimnestra, whom Agamemnon married, and also Phylonoe, whom Artemis made immortal. Zeus, in the form of a swan, slept with Leda, and on the same night Tyndareos also slept with her. Zeus fathered Polydeuces and Helen; Tyndareos fathered Castor.* **127** But some say that Helen was the daughter of Nemesis and Zeus, for when Nemesis was trying to avoid intercourse with Zeus, she changed her form into that of a goose, and he turned himself into a swan and slept with her. From their intercourse she laid an egg, which some shepherd discovered in the marshes* and gave to Leda, who put it into a chest and kept it. When the time came and Helen was born, she raised her as her own daughter.

128 After Helen grew to be strikingly beautiful, Theseus kidnapped her and brought her to Aphidnai. But when Theseus was in the house of Hades, Polydeuces

12. This passage is likely a later addition, and Wagner prints it in square brackets accordingly.

13. This variant is difficult to unpack because of the phrasing. The gist is this: Some say there were two men named Perieres. One, the son of Aiolos, had Aphareus and Leucippos. The other was the son of Cynortas and had Oibalos, who in turn had Tyndareos, Hippocoon, and Icarios. The point of bringing in this alternative genealogy is to tie in Hippocoon, for in the version presented earlier in this book, there was only one Perieres, the son of Cynortas, and he fathered Tyndareos, Icarios, Aphareus, and Leucippos, but not Hippocoon.

and Castor marched against and captured the city and recovered her, taking Theseus' mother, Aithra, prisoner.

Suitors of Helen **129** The kings of Hellas came to Sparta seeking to marry Helen, and these were the suitors: Odysseus son of Laertes; Diomedes son of Tydeus; Antilochos son of Nestor; Agapenor son of Ancaios; Sthenelos son of Capaneus; Amphimachos son of Cteatos; Thalpios son of Eurytos; Meges son of Phyleus; Amphilochos son of Amphiaraos; Menestheus son of Peteos; **130** Schedios and Epistrophos, the sons of Iphitos; Polyxenos son of Agasthenes; Peneleos son of Hippalcimos; Leitos son of Alector; Aias son of Oileus; Ascalaphos and Ialmenos, the sons of Ares; Elephenor son of Chalcodon; Eumelos son of Admetos; Polypoites son of Peirithous; Leonteus son of Coronos; **131** Podaleirios and Machaon, the sons of Asclepios; Philoctetes son of Poias; Eurypylos son of Euaimon; Protesilaos son of Iphiclos; Menelaos son of Atreus; Aias and Teucros, the sons of Telamon; and Patroclos son of Menoitios.

The Oath of Tyndareos; Helen and Menelaos When Tyndareos saw how many there were, he was afraid that if one were chosen, the others would cause trouble. **132** But Odysseus promised that if he helped him marry Penelope, he would suggest a way whereby there would be no quarrel. When Tyndareos promised to help him, he told him to make all the suitors swear that they would come to the aid of the chosen husband if he were to be treated unjustly by anyone else with respect to the marriage. When Tyndareos heard this, he made the suitors swear the oath, then he chose Menelaos as her husband and arranged with Icarios that Odysseus marry Penelope.

133 With Helen, Menelaos had Hermione, and, according to some, he had [3.11]
Nicostratos. With his slave Pieris, an Aitolian woman, or, as Acousilaos says, with Tereis, he had Megapenthes. According to Eumelos, he had Xenodamos with the nymph Cnossia.

Castor and Polydeuces (the Dioscouroi) **134** Of the sons that Leda had, Castor trained in the art of war and Polydeuces in boxing, and on account of their manly vigor the two of them were called the Dioscouroi. Wanting to marry the daughters of Leucippos, they kidnapped them from Messene and married them. Polydeuces and Phoibe had Mnesileos, and Castor and Hilaeira had Anogon. **135** Along with the sons of Aphareus, Idas and Lynceus, they drove off some cows as plunder from Arcadia and put Idas in charge of dividing them up. He cut a cow into four parts and said that the first one to eat his portion would get half the booty and the second would get the rest. Before they could do anything, Idas ate his own portion first and then his brother's portion. Along with his brother he drove the plunder into Messene.

136 The Dioscouroi marched against Messene and drove off those cows as well as a lot of other plunder, and set an ambush for Idas and Lynceus. But Lynceus spotted Castor and told Idas, and he killed him. Polydeuces chased them and killed Lynceus with a cast of his spear, but in his pursuit of Idas he was hit by him in the head with a stone, blacked out, and fell. **137** Zeus hit Idas with a thunderbolt and brought Polydeuces to heaven. But Polydeuces would not accept immortality while his brother was dead, so Zeus granted that on alternating days the two of them would be among the gods and among the mortals. When the Dioscouroi had been removed to the gods, Tyndareos sent for Menelaos to come to Sparta and handed over the kingdom to him.

[3.12] **Early Trojan Genealogies** **138** Electra daughter of Atlas and Zeus had Iasion and Dardanos. Iasion fell in love with Demeter and was hit by a thunderbolt for wanting to disgrace the goddess. Dardanos, aggrieved at the death of his brother, left Samothrace and came to the mainland on the opposite side of the sea. **139** This land was ruled by Teucros, the son of the river Scamandros and the nymph Idaia, and the inhabitants of the land were called Teucrians after him. Taken in by the king and getting a portion of the land and his daughter Bateia, he founded the city of Dardanos, and after Teucros' death he called the whole country Dardania.

140 He had sons, Ilos and Erichthonios. Ilos died without children, and Erichthonios took over the kingship, married Astyoche daughter of Simoeis, and had Tros. When he got the kingdom, he called the country Troy after himself. He married Callirhoe daughter of Scamandros and had a daughter, Cleopatra, and sons, Ilos, Assaracos, and Ganymedes. **141** On account of Ganymedes' beauty, Zeus used an eagle to kidnap him and made him the wine-bearer of the gods in heaven. Assaracos and Hieromneme daughter of Simoeis had Capys, and he and Themiste daughter of Ilos had Anchises. Aphrodite slept with him out of sexual desire and had Aineias and Lyros, the latter of whom died without children.

142 Ilos went off to Phrygia, where he found that games were being held by the king and won in wrestling. He got as a prize fifty young men and the same number of young women, and the king, following an oracle, also gave him a multicolored cow and told him to found a city in whatever spot she lay down. So he followed the cow. **143** When she came to the place called the Hill of Phrygian Ate, she lay down, and Ilos founded a city there. He called it Ilion and prayed to Zeus to send him a sign, and at daybreak he saw that the heaven-sent Palladion was lying in front of his tent. It was three cubits high, its feet were together, and in its right hand it was holding a raised spear and in the other a distaff and spindle.

144 [The story about the Palladion is as follows: they say that after her birth Athena was raised by Triton, who had a daughter, Pallas. Both of them trained in the art of war and at some point they fell to quarreling. When Pallas was about to strike Athena, Zeus was frightened and stretched forth the aegis, and she looked up to avoid it and so fell, wounded by Athena. **145** Athena was distraught over her and had a *xoanon* made in her likeness. She put a goatskin {*aigis*}, the thing that had frightened her, around its chest and paid it honor after setting it up at Zeus' side. Later, when Electra was about to be raped, she fled to it for refuge, and Zeus hurled both her and the Palladion down to the land of Ilion. Ilos paid honor to it after building a temple. And that is what is said about the Palladion.][14]

14. The material in brackets (chapters 144 and 145) was added to Apollodorus from another source.

146 Ilos married Eurydice daughter of Adrastos and had Laomedon, who married Strymo daughter of Scamandros, or, according to some, Placia daughter of Otreus, or, according to others, Leucippe. He had sons, Tithonos, Lampos, Clytios, Hicetaon, and Podarces, and daughters, Hesione, Cilla, and Astyoche. With the nymph Calybe he had Boucolion.

Eos and Tithonos **147** Eos abducted Tithonos out of love and brought him to Ethiopia, and there she slept with him and had sons, Emathion and Memnon. After the capture of Ilion by Heracles, as I mentioned a little before, Podarces, the one called Priam, became king.

Priam and His Children Priam first married Arisbe daughter of Merops, and with her he had a son, Aisacos, who married Asterope, the daughter of Cebren, and when she died Aisacos was turned into a bird as he grieved. **148** Priam gave Arisbe to Hyrtacos and got married for a second time to Hecabe daughter of Dymas or, according to some, daughter of Cisseus or, according to others, of the river Sangarios and Metope. Hector was her firstborn.

Paris/Alexander When Hecabe was about to have her second child, she had a vision in her sleep that she had given birth to a fiery torch and that it was spreading through and burning the whole city. **149** When Priam learned of the dream from Hecabe, he summoned his son Aisacos, for he was a dream-interpreter who had been taught by his maternal grandfather, Merops. He said that their son would prove to be the destruction of his homeland and urged that the infant be exposed. When the baby was born, Priam gave it to a slave to take to Mount Ida and expose. The slave was named Agelaos. **150** The infant exposed by him was nourished for five days by a bear. Finding it still alive, Agelaos picked it up, took it, and raised it on his farm as his own son, naming him Paris. Paris grew into a young man who was both more beautiful and stronger than most, and he received the second name Alexander because he kept away bandits and defended {*alexo*} the herds. Not much later he found his parents.

More Children of Priam **151** After him Hecabe had daughters, Creousa, Laodice, Polyxene, and Cassandra. Because Apollo wanted to sleep with the last, he promised to teach her to prophesy. Although she learned how, she did not sleep with him, so Apollo took away the power to be convincing from her prophecy. Then Hecabe had sons, Deiphobos, Helenos, Pammon, Polites, Antiphos, Hipponoos, Polydoros, and Troilos (she is said to have had Troilos with Apollo).

152 With other women Priam had sons: Melanippos, Gorgythion, Philaimon, Hippothoos, Glaucos, Agathon, Chersidamas, Euagoras, Hippodamas, Mestor, Atas, Doryclos, Lycaon, Dryops, Bias, Chromios, Astygonos, Telestas, Euandros, Cebriones, **153** Mylios, Archemachos, Laodocos, Echephron, Idomeneus, Hyperion, Ascanios, Democoon, Aretos, Deiopites, Clonios, Echemmon, Hypeirochos, Aigeoneus, Lysithoos, and Polymedon; and daughters: Medousa, Medesicaste, Lysimache, and Aristodeme.

Hector and Andromache **154** Hector married Andromache daughter of Eetion, and Alexander married Oinone, the daughter of the river Cebren. This woman learned from Rhea the prophetic art and foretold to Alexander that he should not sail after Helen. She failed to convince him but told him that when he was wounded he should come to her, for she alone could heal him. **155** After he abducted Helen from Sparta and war was being waged against Troy, he was shot by Philoctetes with Heracles' bow and returned to Oinone on Mount Ida. But out of resentment she refused to heal him. Alexander then died as he was being carried to Troy. Oinone changed her mind and brought the drugs to heal him, but found him dead and hanged herself.

Aigina and Aiacos; Peleus and Telamon **156** The river Asopos was the son of Oceanos and Tethys or, according to Acousilaos, of Pero and Poseidon or, according to some, of Zeus and Eurynome. Metope (she was the daughter of the river Ladon) married him and bore two sons, Ismenos and Pelagon, and twelve* daughters, one of whom, Aigina, Zeus abducted. **157** Asopos searched for her and came to Corinth and found out from Sisyphos that Zeus was the kidnapper. As Asopos pursued him, Zeus sent him back to his own streams by blasting him with a thunderbolt (that is why even now pieces of coal can be taken out of this river's streams) and brought Aigina to the island that was then named Oinone but is now called Aigina after her. He slept with her and fathered a son by her, Aiacos. **158** Since Aiacos was the only one on the island, Zeus turned the ants into people. Aiacos married Endeis daughter of Sceiron and had sons by her, Peleus and Telamon. Pherecydes says that Telamon was not Peleus' brother, but a friend, the son of Actaios and Glauce daughter of Cychreus. Later, Aiacos slept with Psamathe daughter of Nereus, who had changed herself into a seal {*phoke*} because she did not want to have sex with him, and he had a son, Phocos.

159 Aiacos was the most pious man of all. So when Hellas was gripped by barrenness—because Pelops, waging war against Stymphalos, the king of the Arcadians, and being unable to capture Arcadia, made a false offer of friendship and then killed him, dismembered him, and scattered his body parts—oracles from the gods said that Hellas would be rid of its current evils if Aiacos made prayers on its behalf. And when Aiacos prayed, Hellas was rid of its unfruitfulness. Since his death, Aiacos has been honored also in Plouton's realm and guards the keys of Hades.

The Exile of Peleus and Telamon; Telamonian Aias **160** Because Phocos was better than his brothers Peleus and Telamon in athletics, they plotted against him. Telamon was chosen by lot, so he killed Phocos by throwing a discus at his head while they were practicing together. He took the body with Peleus' help and hid it in a thicket. **161** But the murder was discovered and they were driven as exiles away from Aigina by Aiacos. Telamon went to Salamis to Cychreus son of Poseidon and Salamis daughter of Asopos. Cychreus had killed a serpent that was ravaging the island and so became king of it.* As he lay dying and without children, he handed over the kingdom to Telamon. **162** Telamon married Periboia daughter of Alcathous son of Pelops. He named his son Aias because Heracles had prayed for him to have a male child, and an eagle {*aietos*} appeared after his prayers. Telamon joined Heracles' campaign against Troy and received as a war-prize Hesione, the daughter of Laomedon, and he had a son, Teucros, by her.

163 Peleus went into exile in Phthia to Eurytion son of Actor and was purified [3.13] by him. He got from him his daughter, Antigone, and a third of his land. He had a daughter, Polydora, whom Boros son of Perieres married. Then when he came with Eurytion to hunt the Calydonian boar, he threw his javelin at the boar but accidentally hit Eurytion and killed him. **164** So he went into exile once more from Phthia and came to Acastos in Iolcos and was purified by him. He also competed in the games held for Pelias, wrestling against Atalante. Acastos' wife, Astydameia, fell in love with Peleus and sent a message to him suggesting a liaison. **165** But when she could not persuade him, she sent a message to his wife and said that he was about to marry Sterope, the daughter of Acastos. The woman hanged herself with a noose when she heard this. Astydameia falsely accused Peleus to Acastos and said that she had been propositioned by him.

When Acastos heard this, he did not want to kill a man he had purified, but he took him to Mount Pelion to go hunting. **166** They had a hunting contest there. Peleus cut out the tongues of the animals he caught and put them in a bag. As Acastos and his friends caught game, they laughed at Peleus, thinking that he had brought down nothing. He showed them all the tongues he had and told them that he had brought down that many animals. **167** After Peleus fell asleep on Mount Pelion, Acastos went back home, abandoning him and hiding his sword in the dung of the cows. When he woke up and was looking for his sword, he was captured by the Centaurs. He was about to be killed, but then was saved by Cheiron, who also located his sword and gave it to him.

Marriage of Peleus and Thetis **168** Peleus married Polydora daughter of Perieres, with whom he supposedly had Menesthios, who was really the son of the river Spercheios.[15] He later married Thetis daughter of Nereus. Zeus and Poseidon were rivals for her hand, but when Themis prophesied that the son born from her would be greater than his father, they gave up. **169** Some say, however, that when Zeus was on his way to sleep with her, Prometheus told him that the son born to him from her would become king of heaven. And some say that Thetis did not want to sleep with Zeus because she had been raised by Hera, so Zeus got angry and wanted to marry her off to a mortal. **170** Cheiron advised Peleus to grab her and hold on tight to her as she changed shapes. Peleus lay in wait for her, grabbed her, and held on. She turned into fire, then water, then a wild animal, but he did not let go until he saw that she had regained her original form. He married her on Mount

15. The content of this sentence is odd. Just above, Polydora is correctly identified as Peleus' own daughter who married Perieres' son Boros, who by all other accounts was the mother of Menesthios by Boros or Spercheios. So Apollodorus made a serious error here or was conflating two traditions, or the text has been garbled in transmission. We lean toward the last explanation and feel that it might have arisen from a little known variant (*scholia* to *Iliad* 16.176) of the story in which a giant named Pelor (perhaps at some point corrupted to Peleus) fathers Menesthios.

Pelion, where the gods celebrated the marriage with songs as they feasted. Cheiron gave Peleus an ash spear, and Poseidon gave him horses, Balios and Xanthos. These were immortal.

Achilles **171** When Thetis had Peleus' baby, she wanted to make it immortal. So unbeknownst to Peleus, at night she would hide it in the fire and destroy the mortal part that came from his father. By day she would rub ambrosia on him. When Peleus spied on her and saw his son squirming in the fire, he gave a shout. Prevented from carrying out her plan, Thetis went off to the Nereids, abandoning her son in his infancy. **172** Peleus brought his son to Cheiron, who accepted him and raised him on the innards of lions and wild boars and the marrow of bears. He named him Achilles (before that, his name had been Ligyron) because he had never put his lips {*cheilos*} to a breast.

173 After that, Peleus sacked Iolcos with the help of Jason and the Dioscouroi and killed Astydameia, Acastos' wife. He cut her in two pieces, limb from limb, and marched the army between them into the city.

174 When Achilles was nine years old, Calchas said that Troy could not be captured without him. Thetis foresaw that he was bound to die if he went to the war, so she disguised him with women's clothes and entrusted him to Lycomedes as if he were a young woman. While he was growing up there, he slept with Lycomedes' daughter Deidameia and had a son, Pyrrhos, who was later called Neoptolemos. When Achilles' location was betrayed, Odysseus sought him at the court of Lycomedes and found him by using a war-trumpet.[16] In that way he went to Troy.

175 Phoinix son of Amyntor accompanied him. He was blinded by his father when his father's concubine, Phthia, made a false accusation that he had forced himself on her. Peleus took him to Cheiron and, after his eyes had been healed by him, made him king of the Dolopians.

176 Patroclos, the son of Menoitios and Sthenele daughter of Acastos (or Periopis daughter of Pheres, or, according to Philocrates, Polymele daughter of Peleus), also accompanied him. In Opous he had had an argument about dice while playing a game and had killed Cleitonymos son of Amphidamas. He went into exile with his father, settled at the court of Peleus, and became Achilles' boyfriend. < . . . >[17]

[3.14] **Cecrops I and Early Athenian Genealogies** **177** Cecrops, an *autochthon,* had a body part man, part serpent. He became the first king of Attica and named the land, which had previously been called Acte, Cecropia after himself. **178** During his reign, they say, the gods decided to take for themselves cities in which each of them would be especially worshiped. Now, Poseidon was the first to come to Attica, and he produced a saltwater pool by striking a blow with his trident in the middle of the Acropolis. They now call it the Erechtheis. Athena came after him, had Cecrops witness her making her claim to the city, and planted an olive tree, which they now show in the shrine of Pandrosos. **179** When a quarrel over the land arose

16. Hyginus 96 gives the details of how he used the war-trumpet.

17. Heyne suggested a lacuna here, but it is difficult to know exactly how much or what is missing.

between the two, Zeus ended it and appointed judges—not Cecrops and Cranaos, as some say, nor Erysichthon, but the twelve gods. With these as the judges, the land was awarded to Athena after Cecrops testified that she planted the olive tree first. So Athena called the city Athens after herself, but Poseidon, angered in his heart, flooded the Thriasian Plain and caused Attica to be beneath the sea.

The Children of Cecrops **180** Cecrops married Actaios' daughter, Agraulis,* and had a son, Erysichthon, who died without children, and daughters, Agraulos, Herse, and Pandrosos. Agraulos and Ares had Alcippe. When she was raped by Halirrhothios, the son of Poseidon and the nymph Euryte, he was caught and killed by Ares. Poseidon brought Ares to trial on the Areiopagos {"Hill of Ares"}. He was tried and acquitted, with the twelve gods acting as judges.

181 Herse and Hermes had Cephalos. Eos fell in love with him, abducted him, and slept with him in Syria. She had Tithonos, who had a son, Phaethon. He in turn had Astynoos, who had Sandocos, who went from Syria to Cilicia, founded the city of Celenderis, married Pharnace daughter of Megassares, king of the Hyrians, and had Cinyras. **182** Cinyras founded Paphos in Cyprus, where he had gone with a group of people. There he married Metharme, the daughter of Pygmalion, king of the Cyprians, and had Oxyporos and Adonis, and, in addition, daughters, Orsedice, Laogora, and Braisia. These girls slept with strangers because of Aphrodite's wrath and died in Egypt.

Adonis **183** Adonis, while still a boy, was struck by a boar while hunting and died because of Artemis' anger. But Hesiod says that he was the son of Phoinix and Alphesiboia, and Panyassis says that he was the son of Theias, king of the Assyrians, who had a daughter, Smyrna. She fell in love with her father through the wrath of Aphrodite (because she did not honor her). Taking her nurse as an accomplice, she slept with her father for twelve nights without him knowing it. **184** When he found out, he drew his sword and chased her. When she was about to be caught, she prayed for the gods to do away with her. The gods took pity on her and transformed her into a tree, which they call *smyrna* {"myrrh"}. Nine months later, the tree split open and the one named Adonis was born. On account of his beauty, unbeknownst to the gods Aphrodite hid him in a chest while he was still an infant and gave him to Persephone for safekeeping. **185** When she got a look at him, she would not give him back. The decision came before Zeus, and the year was divided into three parts: he commanded that Adonis stay by himself for one part, with Persephone for one part, and with Aphrodite for the other. But Adonis added his own portion to Aphrodite's. Later, Adonis was wounded by a boar while hunting and died.

Cecrops' Successors **186** After Cecrops died, Cranaos, who was an *autochthon,* became king. In his reign the flood of Deucalion is said to have taken place. He married Pedias daughter of Mynes, who was from Lacedaimon, and had Cranae, Cranaichme, and Atthis. When Atthis died still a young maiden, Cranaos called the land Atthis. **187** Amphictyon deposed Cranaos and became king. Some say that he was a son of Deucalion, others that he was an *autochthon.*

Erichthonios After Amphictyon had been king for twelve years, Erichthonios deposed him. Some say that this man was the son of Hephaistos and Cranaos' daughter Atthis, but others, giving the following account, say that he was the son of Hepaistos and Athena: **188** Athena went to Hephaistos wanting to have some armor made. He had been jilted by Aphrodite, so he was gripped by lust for Athena and began to chase after her, but she fled. When he came near her after a great deal of trouble (he was lame), he tried to have sex with her. But, being an abstinent virgin, she did not let him, and he spilled his seed on the goddess's leg. Disgusted, she wiped off his semen with some wool and threw it onto the ground. Although she got away and the semen fell on the ground, Erichthonios was born.[18]

189 Athena raised him without the other gods' knowing about it and wanted to make him immortal. She put him in a chest and entrusted it to Pandrosos daughter of Cecrops, forbidding her to open the chest. But Pandrosos' sisters opened it out of curiosity and saw a serpent coiled around the baby. According to some, they were killed by the serpent, but according to others they went crazy because Athena was angry and threw themselves down off the Acropolis. **190** Erichthonios was brought up by Athena herself in her sanctuary. After he deposed Amphictyon, he became king of the Athenians, set up the *xoanon* of Athena that is on the Acropolis, and established the Panathenaic Festival. He married the Naiad nymph Praxithea and with her had a son, Pandion.

Pandion I; Icarios and Erigone **191** After Erichthonios died and was buried in the same precinct of Athena, Pandion became king. In his reign Demeter and Dionysos came to Attica, but Celeos hosted Demeter, and Icarios hosted Dionysos. Icarios got from him a cutting of a grapevine and learned about making wine. **192** Wanting to bestow the god's boons on his fellow men, he went to some shepherds. They tasted the drink, and it was so pleasant that they guzzled it without water. Thinking they had been poisoned, they killed him. By the light of day they realized what had happened and buried him. But his daughter, Erigone, went looking for her father, and Icarios' pet dog named Maira, which used to go around with him, showed her where the body was. In her grief for her father, she hanged herself.

Procne and Philomela **193** Pandion married Zeuxippe, his mother's sister, and had daughters, Procne and Philomela, and twin sons, Erechtheus and Boutes. When war broke out against Labdacos over the boundaries of the land, he called in Tereus son of Ares from Thrace to help. Having won the war with Tereus' aid, he gave him his daughter Procne to marry. **194** Tereus had a son, Itys, with her, but he fell in love with Philomela and forced himself on her,* keeping her hidden on his farm. He cut out her tongue,* but she wove letters into a dress and through them revealed her misfortunes to Procne. **195** After Procne found out where her sister

18. Apollodorus' phrasing is awkward here, and it is difficult to know precisely his intention. He is probably etymologizing the name of Erichthonios, as if from *eris* "struggle" + *chthon* "earth," for which there are many parallels, including Hyginus 166. But the underlying Greek says merely and literally, "Athena fleeing and the semen having fallen to the ground, Erichthonios was born."

was, she killed her son, Itys, boiled him, and served him for dinner to Tereus, who had no idea. With her sister she swiftly fled, but when Tereus figured out what was going on, he picked up an ax and chased after them. When they were about to be overtaken in Daulia in Phocis, they prayed to the gods to be turned into birds. Procne became a nightingale and Philomela a swallow. Tereus, too, was turned into a bird and became a hoopoe.

Erechtheus and Boutes; Cephalos and Procris **196** After Pandion's [3.15]
death, his sons divided their inheritance. Erechtheus got the kingship, and Boutes got the priesthood of Athena and Poseidon Erechtheus.[19] Erechtheus married Praxithea, the daughter of Phrasimos and Diogeneia daughter of Cephisos, and had sons, Cecrops, Pandoros, and Metion, and daughters, Procris, Creousa, Chthonia, and Oreithyia. Boreas abducted the last one. **197** Boutes married Chthonia, Xouthos married Creousa, and Cephalos son of Deion married Procris, who slept with Pteleon after accepting a golden crown. When she was caught by Cephalos, she fled to the court of Minos. He loved her and tried to get her to sleep with him, but if a woman slept with Minos, it was impossible for her to survive. Pasiphae had given Minos a drug because he slept with many women. And whenever he slept with another woman, he ejaculated poisonous creatures into her genitalia, and that is how they died. **198** Now, Minos had a swift dog and a javelin that flew true, and in exchange for these she slept with him after giving him the Circaian root to drink so that he would not harm her at all. But later, afraid of Minos' wife, she came to Athens. After getting back together with Cephalos, she went with him on a hunt, for she liked hunting. As she was chasing something in the brush, Cephalos, not knowing what it was, threw his javelin, and hit and killed Procris. After being tried on the Areiopagos, he was condemned to exile for life.

Oreithyia; Zetes and Calais **199** As Oreithyia played on the banks of the river Ilissos, Boreas abducted her and had sex with her. She had daughters, Cleopatra and Chione, and sons, Zetes and Calais, who were winged. They sailed with Jason and died while pursuing the Harpies, though according to Acousilaos, they were killed by Heracles near Tenos. **200** Phineus married Cleopatra and with her had sons, Plexippos and Pandion. When he had these sons by Cleopatra, he married Idaia daughter of Dardanos, who made the false accusation to Phineus that her stepsons had forced themselves on her. Phineus believed her and blinded them both. The Argonauts punished him when they sailed by with Boreas.

Eumolpos; Cecrops II **201** Chione slept with Poseidon and, unbeknownst to her father, had Eumolpos. So that she would not be found out, she threw the child into the sea. Poseidon picked him up, took him to Ethiopia, and gave him to Benthesicyme, his and Amphitrite's daughter, to raise. When he grew up, Benthesicyme's husband, Endios,* gave him one of his two daughters. **202** Eumolpos, however,

19. Erechtheus is an attested cult-title of Poseidon at Athens (it is Heyne's correction of Erichthonios here).

also tried to rape the sister of the one he married, so along with his son, Ismaros, he was exiled and came to Tegyrios, the king of the Thracians, who married his daughter to Eumolpos' son. Subsequently, it was found out that he was plotting against Tegyrios, and he fled to the Eleusinians and established a friendship with them. Later, after Ismaros' death, he was sent for by Tegyrios and went. He settled their earlier conflict and took over the kingship.

203 When war broke out between the Eleusinians and Athenians, he was called in by the Eleusinians and fought as their ally with a large force of Thracians. When Erechtheus inquired at an oracle about an Athenian victory, the god responded that he would win the war if he slaughtered one of his daughters as a sacrifice. After sacrificing the youngest, the rest of them also sacrificed themselves, for, according to some, they had made a pact to die together. **204** After the sacrifice, battle was joined and Erechtheus killed Eumolpos. But Poseidon destroyed both Erechtheus and his house, so Cecrops, the oldest of Erechtheus' children, became king. He married Metiadousa daughter of Eupalamos and had a son, Pandion. **205** He ruled after Cecrops but was deposed by the sons of Metion in a civil war. He went to Pylas' court in Megara and married his daughter, Pylia. Later, he was also made king of the city, for Pylas killed his father's brother, Bias, and gave Pandion the kingdom while he himself went with part of the population to the Peloponnesos, where he founded the city of Pylos.

Pandion II and His Sons **206** While Pandion was in Megara, he had sons, Aigeus, Pallas, Nisos, and Lycos. However, some say that Aigeus was Scyrios' son and that Pandion just passed him off as his own. After Pandion's death, his sons marched against Athens and cast out the sons of Metion. They divided the leadership four ways, but Aigeus had all the power. **207** He married Meta daughter of Hoples first and then Chalciope daughter of Rhexenor second, but when he did not have a child, he was afraid of his brothers and went to Pytho and consulted the oracle about having children. The god prophesied to him:

> The projecting mouth of the wineskin,[20] O best of men,
> Loose not until you come to the Athenians' peak.

Aithra and Theseus **208** At a loss about the oracle, he set off to return to Athens. As he traveled through Troizen, he stayed with Pittheus son of Pelops, who understood the oracle, got Aigeus drunk, and put him into bed with his daughter, Aithra. That same night Poseidon also had intercourse with her. Aigeus instructed Aithra if she had a boy to raise him but not to tell who the father was. He left under a certain rock a sword and a pair of sandals and told her to send their son to him with the objects when he could roll aside the rock and retrieve them.

Minos, Nisos, and Scylla **209** Aigeus returned to Athens and held the Panathenaic Games, where Minos' son Androgeos defeated everyone. Aigeus sent him

20. A riddling way of referring to his sexual organs.

against the Marathonian bull, and he was killed by it. But some say that while he was traveling to Thebes to attend the funeral games of Laios, he was ambushed and killed by his competitors out of jealousy. **210** When his death was reported to Minos as he was sacrificing to the Charites on Paros, he threw his garland from his head and stopped the flute, but he still finished the sacrifice. For this reason even to the present day they sacrifice on Paros to the Charites without flutes or garlands. Soon thereafter, he attacked Athens with a fleet (he controlled the sea) and captured Megara, a city then ruled by King Nisos, the son of Pandion. He killed Megareus son of Hippomenes, who had come from Onchestos to help Nisos. Through the treachery of his daughter, Nisos also died. **211** He had a purple hair in the middle of his head, and an oracle said that he would die when this was plucked out. His daughter, Scylla, fell in love with Minos and pulled out the hair. After Minos conquered Megara, he tied the girl by the feet to the stern of his ship and drowned her.

212 The war dragged on as he was unable to capture Athens, so he prayed to Zeus to punish the Athenians. When a famine and epidemic broke out in the city, the Athenians, following an ancient oracle, first sacrificed the daughters of Hyacinthos, namely Antheis, Aigleis, Lytaia, and Orthaia, on the tomb of Geraistos the Cyclops. Their father, Hyacinthos, had come from Lacedaimon and settled in Athens.

The Labyrinth, the Minotaur, and Daidalos **213** When that had accomplished nothing, they consulted an oracle about how to rid themselves of their trouble. The god ordained that they pay Minos whatever penalty he might choose. Minos ordered them to send seven young men and the same number of young women, all unarmed, as food for the Minotaur, who had been shut up in a labyrinth, which was impossible for someone who entered to get out of, for it closed off its secret exit with complex twists and turns.

214 Daidalos, the son of Eupalamos (who was the son of Metion) and Alcippe, built the labyrinth. He was the finest architect and the first sculptor of statues. He had gone into exile from Athens for throwing his sister Perdix's* son, Talos, who was his student, off the Acropolis, because he was afraid of being surpassed by him in talent—Talos found the jawbone of a snake and sawed through a thin piece of wood with it. **215** But Talos' body was discovered, and after Daidalos stood trial in the Areiopagos and was condemned, he went to Minos' court in exile. And there, when Pasiphae fell in love with Poseidon's bull, he helped her by building a wooden cow, and he built the labyrinth, into which every year the Athenians sent seven young men and the same number of young women as food for the Minotaur.*

Theseus' Exploits on the Road to Athens **216** Theseus was Aigeus' son [3.16]
by Aithra, and when he grew up he pushed aside the rock, picked up the sandals and sword, and hurried to Athens on foot. He cleared the road of the evildoers who had taken control of it. **217** First, in Epidauros he killed Periphetes, the son of Hephaistos and Anticleia, also known as Corynetes {"Clubber"} because of the club he carried; since he had weak legs, he used to carry an iron club, and with it he would kill passing travelers. Theseus took the club away from him and carried it around with him. **218** Second, he killed Sinis, the son of Polypemon and Sylea daughter of

Corinthos. Sinis was also known as Pityocamptes {"Pine-bender"} because he lived on the Isthmos of Corinth and forced passing travelers to bend down pine trees and hold them. Since they were not strong enough, they could not do so, and when they were catapulted by the trees, they would be utterly destroyed. This is how Theseus also killed Sinis.

Epitome[1]
Events and Genealogies from Theseus to the End of the Trojan War

Theseus' Exploits Continued **1.1** Third, he killed in Crommyon the sow known as Phaia, after the old woman who raised it. Some say it was the offspring of Echidna and Typhon. **1.2** Fourth, he killed Sceiron the Corinthian, who was the son of Pelops or, according to some, Poseidon. He occupied the cliffs in the Megarid called the Sceironian Cliffs after him and used to force passing travelers to wash his feet. As they washed them, he would cast them into the deep as food for an enormous turtle. **1.3** But Theseus grabbed him by the feet and cast him into the sea. Fifth, in Eleusis he killed Cercyon, the son of Branchos and the nymph Argiope. He used to force passing travelers to wrestle and would kill them when they did. Theseus lifted him up high and then slammed him to the ground. **1.4** Sixth, he killed Damastes, whom some call Polypemon. He had his house by the side of the road and had two beds, one short, the other long, and would invite passing travelers to be his guests. He would make short travelers lie in the large bed and beat them with hammers so that they would be the same size as the bed. He would put tall travelers into the short bed and then saw off the parts of the body that hung over the end.

Theseus in Athens; Medeia After clearing the road, Theseus arrived in Athens. **1.5** But Medeia, who at that time was married to Aigeus, plotted against him. She persuaded Aigeus to be on guard, alleging that Theseus was plotting against him. Aigeus did not recognize his own son and in fear sent him against the Marathonian bull. **1.6** When he destroyed it, Aigeus got a poison from Medeia that same day and gave it to him. When Theseus was about to drink the poison, he presented his sword to his father as a gift. When Aigeus recognized it, he knocked the cup from his hands. After being recognized by his father and learning of the plot against him, Theseus drove Medeia out of the country.

Theseus, Ariadne, and the Minotaur in Crete **1.7** Theseus was chosen for the third group sent as tribute to the Minotaur, though some say he volunteered

1. The manuscripts of Apollodorus end at this point and do not preserve the following material, which is available to us only in the much abbreviated form of the Vatican and Sabbaitic Epitomes. From here on we translate the compound text of both epitomes produced by Frazer and note our deviations from it in the endnotes.

to go. The ship had a black sail, but Aigeus instructed his son that if he came back alive he should rig the ship with white sails. **1.8** When he arrived in Crete, Minos' daughter Ariadne fell in love with him and offered to help him if he promised to take her back to Athens and make her his wife. After Theseus promised and swore oaths on it, she asked Daidalos to reveal the way out of the labyrinth. **1.9** At his suggestion she gave a thread to Theseus as he entered. Theseus tied this to the door and went in dragging it behind. He found the Minotaur in the innermost part of the labyrinth and beat him to death with his fists. He got out by following the thread back.

Ariadne and Dionysos; Death of Aigeus During the night he arrived on Naxos with Ariadne and the children. There Dionysos fell in love with Ariadne and carried her off. He brought her to Lemnos and slept with her, fathering Thoas, Staphylos, Oinopion, and Peparethos. **1.10** Grieving for Ariadne, Theseus forgot to rig the ship with white sails as he put into port. From the Acropolis Aigeus saw that the ship had a black sail and thought that Theseus was dead, so he jumped off and died. **1.11** Theseus succeeded to the rule of the Athenians and killed the sons of Pallas, fifty in all. Likewise, any who thought to oppose him were killed by him, and so he alone came to hold all the power.

Daidalos and Icaros **1.12** Minos, learning of the escape of Theseus and his companions, held Daidalos responsible and imprisoned him in the labyrinth along with his son Icaros, whom he had with Naucrate, one of Minos' slaves. But Daidalos made wings for himself and his son, and told his son not to fly too high when he was aloft or else the glue would be melted by the sun and the wings would fall apart, and not to fly near the sea or else the wings would fall apart from the moisture. **1.13** But Icaros, lost in delight, paid no attention to his father's instructions and went ever higher. When the glue melted, he plunged into the sea that is named the Icarian Sea after him and died. Daidalos made it safely to Camicos in Sicily.

Death of Minos **1.14** But Minos pursued Daidalos, and as he searched each land, he brought with him a murex shell, promising to give a great reward to anyone who could pass a thread through the spiral shell. He was sure that he would find Daidalos by this means. When he came to the court of Cocalos in Camicos in Sicily, where Daidalos was being hidden, he presented the shell. Cocalos took it, promised to thread it, and gave it to Daidalos. **1.15** He attached a thread to an ant, bored a hole in the shell, and let the ant pass through it. When Minos found out that the thread had been passed through the shell, he understood that Daidalos was with Cocalos and demanded him back immediately. Cocalos promised to give him back and invited Minos to be his guest. But after Minos took a bath, he was killed by Cocalos' daughters, though others say that he died when he had boiling water poured over him.

The Amazons; Hippolytos; Phaidra **1.16** Theseus joined Heracles' campaign against the Amazons and carried off Antiope, though others say Melanippe, and Simonides says Hippolyte. So the Amazons marched against Athens. They set up their camp around the Areiopagos, but Theseus and the Athenians defeated them. **1.17** He had a son Hippolytos with the Amazon woman, but from Deucalion he later got Minos' daughter Phaidra, and when his wedding to her was being celebrated, his Amazon ex-wife showed up dressed for battle with her Amazonian companions and intended to kill the guests. But they quickly shut the doors and killed her. But some say that she was killed by Theseus in battle.

1.18 After Phaidra bore two sons, Acamas and Demophon, to Theseus, she fell in love with the son he had with the Amazon and begged him to sleep with her. He hated all women and shrank from sleeping with her. Phaidra, afraid that he would tell his father, broke open the doors to her bedroom, ripped open her clothes, and made up a story that Hippolytos raped her. **1.19** Theseus believed her and prayed to Poseidon that Hippolytos be destroyed. As Hippolytos rode on his chariot and was driving next to the sea, Poseidon sent forth a bull from the waves. The horses were spooked, and the chariot was smashed to pieces. Hippolytos, tangled in the reins, was dragged to death. Phaidra hanged herself when her love became public knowledge.

Ixion and Nephele **1.20** Ixion fell in love with Hera and tried to rape her. Hera denounced him, and Zeus wanted to know if it had really happened that way, so he made a cloud {*nephele*} in the image of Hera and put it into bed with Ixion. When he bragged that he had slept with Hera, Zeus bound him to a wheel on which he pays this penalty: he is carried on it by the winds through the sky. Nephele gave birth to Centauros by Ixion.

The Lapiths and Centaurs **1.21** <Theseus was Peirithous' ally when he engaged in battle against the Centaurs. For when Peirithous was betrothed to Hippodameia, he invited the Centaurs to the feasts since they were his relatives.* But being unaccustomed to wine, they guzzled it freely, got drunk, and tried to rape the bride when she was led in. Peirithous, with Theseus at his side, armed himself and joined battle. Theseus killed many of them.>[2]

1.22 Caineus was a woman first. After Poseidon slept with her, she obtained the favor of becoming an invulnerable man. This is why in the battle against the Centaurs he thought nothing of wounds and killed many Centaurs, but the rest surrounded him and buried him in the earth by pounding on him with fir trees.

Theseus and Helen; Peirithous and Persephone **1.23** Theseus made an agreement with Peirithous that they would marry daughters of Zeus. With his help he abducted Helen, who was twelve years old, from Sparta for himself. In an attempt to win for Peirithous a marriage with Persephone, he went down to the house of Hades. The Dioscouroi, with the aid of the Lacedaimonians and the Arcadians, captured Athens. They brought back Helen, and, along with her, they took Aithra daughter of Pittheus as a prisoner, though Demophon and Acamas escaped. They also brought back Menestheus from exile and gave him the kingship over the

2. This material is taken from Zenobius, who probably took it from Apollodorus, though it is not found in the epitomes.

Athenians. **1.24** Theseus came with Peirithous to the house of Hades but was duped; Hades told them first to sit in the chair of Lethe, as if they were going to receive his hospitality. But they stuck to it and were held by serpents' coils. Peirithous remained bound forever, but Heracles brought Theseus back up and sent him to Athens. Driven away from there by Menestheus, he went to Lycomedes, who killed him by throwing him into a chasm.

Tantalos and His Sons **2.1** Tantalos is punished in the house of Hades with a rock that hangs threateningly over him. He resides forever in a lake and can see on either side of his shoulders trees with fruit that are growing next to the lake. The water touches his lower jaw, and when he wants to suck some of it into his mouth, it dries up. And whenever he wants to get some of the fruit, the trees with their fruit are lifted by winds into the sky as high as clouds. Some say he is punished this way because he divulged the mysteries of the gods to mortals and because he tried to share ambrosia with his buddies.

2.2 Broteas was a hunter who did not honor Artemis and used to say that he could not be hurt, even by fire. So he went crazy and threw himself into a fire.

Pelops and Hippodameia **2.3** After Pelops was slaughtered and was boiled at the banquet for the gods, he became even more beautiful when he was restored to life. Because of his extraordinary beauty, he became the boyfriend of Poseidon, who gave him a winged chariot. This could even drive across the sea without getting its axles wet.

2.4 Oinomaos, the king of Pisa, had a daughter, Hippodameia. Either because he loved her, according to some, or because he had an oracle that said he would die at the hands of whoever married her, no one got her as wife. For her father could not persuade her to sleep with him, and her suitors were killed by him. **2.5** He had arms and horses from Ares, and he made the marriage the prize for the suitors. The suitor had to pick up Hippodameia on his own chariot and flee as far as the Isthmos of Corinth. Oinomaos would put on his armor and immediately pursue and kill him if he caught him. The man who was not caught would have Hippodameia as wife. In this way he killed many suitors, some say twelve of them. He cut off the suitors' heads and nailed them to his house.

2.6 Now, Pelops too came to ask for her hand. When Hippodameia caught sight of his beauty, she fell in love with him and persuaded Myrtilos, the son of Hermes, to help him. Myrtilos was Oinomaos' charioteer. **2.7** So Myrtilos, who was in love with her and wanted to oblige her, did not put the pins in the axle-socket of the wheels and made Oinomaos lose in the running of the race and be dragged to death when he became entangled in the reins. But according to some, Oinomaos was killed by Pelops. As he died, realizing Myrtilos' treachery, he called down a curse upon him that he die at Pelops' hand.

2.8 When Pelops took Hippodameia and had reached a particular spot on the journey in the company of Myrtilos, he went a little ways away to bring his wife some water because she was thirsty. At that moment Myrtilos tried to rape her, and when Pelops learned about the incident from her, he threw Myrtilos into the sea that is now named the Myrtoan Sea after him, near Cape Geraistos. As he was being thrown, he laid down a curse on Pelops' family.

2.9 After Pelops went to Oceanos and was purified by Hephaistos, he returned to Pisa in Elis and received the kingdom of Oinomaos after subjugating the land formerly known as Apia and Pelasgiotis, which he then called Peloponnesos {"Pelops' Island"} after himself.

The Sons of Pelops; Atreus and Thyestes **2.10** The sons of Pelops were Pittheus, Atreus, Thyestes, and others. Aerope daughter of Catreus was Atreus' wife, but she loved Thyestes. Atreus once made a vow to sacrifice whichever sheep in his herd was the finest. They say that a golden lamb appeared, but he ignored his vow. **2.11** He choked the lamb, put it in a box, and kept it there. Aerope gave it to Thyestes when he got her to cheat on her husband. The Mycenaeans had gotten an oracle that they should choose as their king a son of Pelops, so they sent for Atreus and Thyestes. There was a debate over the kingdom, and Thyestes declared to the populace that the one who had the golden lamb should have the kingdom. When Atreus agreed, Thyestes showed them the lamb and became king.

2.12 But Zeus sent Hermes to Atreus and told him to get Thyestes to agree that Atreus would become king if the sun traveled backward. Thyestes agreed and the sun set in the east. With the god having thereby testified to Thyestes' ill-gotten kingship, Atreus took over the kingdom and banished Thyestes. **2.13** When Atreus later learned of his wife's infidelity, he sent a herald to Thyestes and invited him to reconcile their differences. He pretended to be friendly, and when Thyestes came, he slaughtered the sons he had had with a Naiad nymph, Aglaos, Callileon, and Orchomenos, despite the fact that they had sat as suppliants at Zeus' altar. He cut them up, boiled them, and set them out as a meal for Thyestes—everything but their extremities. After Thyestes had had his fill of them, Atreus showed him their extremities and cast him out of the land.

2.14 Looking for any way to pay Atreus back, Thyestes inquired at an oracle about this and received a response that it would happen if he produced a son by sleeping with his daughter. So he did this and by his daughter had Aigisthos. When he became a man, he learned that he was Thyestes' son, killed Atreus, and returned the kingdom to Thyestes.

Agamemnon and Menelaos **2.15** <A nurse took Agamemnon and Menelaos to Polypheides, ruler of Sicyon, who sent them on to Oineus the Aitolian. Not much later Tyndareos brought them back again. They drove Thyestes to live in Cytheria after making him swear an oath at an altar of Hera where he found refuge. They became Tyndareos' in-laws through his daughters: Agamemnon took Clytaimnestra as wife after killing her husband, Tantalos son of Thyestes, and their brand-new baby; Menelaos took Helen.>[3]

3. This material is not in the epitomes, but it comes from Tzetzes, *Chiliades* 1.456–465, who is presumably using Apollodorus as his source here, since the end of this passage coincides with what follows in the Sabbaitic Epitome.

2.16 Agamemnon became king of the Mycenaeans and married Tyndareos' daughter, Clytaimnestra, after killing her first husband Tantalos son of Thyestes along with his son. He had a son, Orestes, and daughters, Chrysothemis, Electra, and Iphigeneia. Menelaos married Helen and became king of Sparta after Tyndareos gave him the kingship.

3.1 Later, Alexander abducted Helen, some say by Zeus' will so that Europe and Asia would go to war and his daughter would become famous, or, as others have said, so that the race of demigods might be ended.*

Judgment of Paris; Origins of the Trojan War **3.2** For one of these reasons, then, Eris threw in an apple as a beauty prize* for Hera, Athena, and Aphrodite. Zeus ordered Hermes to take them to Alexander on Mount Ida so that they could be judged by him. The goddesses promised to give Alexander gifts: Hera, if she were chosen the most beautiful of all, promised him kingship over everyone; Athena promised victory in war; and Aphrodite promised marriage to Helen. He chose Aphrodite and sailed off to Sparta after Phereclos built him ships.

Paris and Helen **3.3** For nine days he was hosted at the court of Menelaos. On the tenth, when Menelaos left on a trip to Crete to bury his maternal grandfather, Catreus, Alexander persuaded Helen to go away with him. She abandoned her nine-year-old daughter Hermione, loaded most of their possessions onto the ships, and set sail with him during the night.

3.4 Hera sent a powerful storm against them, and they were forced by it to land at Sidon. Fearing that he would be pursued, he spent a great deal of time in Phoenicia and Cyprus. But when he was confident pursuit was out of the question, he came to Troy with Helen. **3.5** Some, however, say that in accordance with Zeus' will Helen was taken to Egypt by Hermes and given to Proteus, the king of the Egyptians, to guard, and that Alexander arrived at Troy with a duplicate of Helen fashioned from clouds.

Pre–Trojan War Events **3.6** When Menelaos found out about the abduction, he went to Agamemnon in Mycenae and asked him to gather an expedition against Troy and mobilize Hellas. Agamemnon sent a herald to each of the kings and reminded them of the oaths they had sworn and advised each to make secure arrangements for his own wife, telling them that the contempt shown to Hellas was shared equally. Many were eager to go to war; they also went to Odysseus on Ithaca.

3.7 Odysseus did not want to go on the campaign, so he feigned insanity. Palamedes son of Nauplios proved that his insanity was feigned, following him around as he pretended to be crazy. Taking Telemachos from Penelope's lap, he drew his sword as if to kill him. Odysseus, afraid for his son, came clean about his feigned insanity and went to war.

3.8 Odysseus took a Phrygian prisoner and forced him to write a treasonous letter as if it were from Priam to Palamedes. He buried gold in his tents and dropped the letter in the camp. After Agamemnon read the letter and discovered the gold, he handed Palamedes over to his allies to be stoned as a traitor.

3.9 Menelaos, along with Odysseus and Talthybios, went to Cinyras on Cyprus and urged him to join their cause. Cinyras gave some breastplates as a gift to Agamemnon, even though he was not present, and promised to send fifty ships. He sent one, which <*name missing*> son of Mygdalion captained, and made the rest of them out of earth and launched them onto the sea.

3.10 Elais {"Olive Tree"}, Spermo {"Seed"}, and Oino {"Grapevine"}, the so-called Oinotrophoi, were the daughters of Anios son of Apollo. Dionysos granted them the ability to produce oil, grain, and wine from the earth as a boon.[4]

First Muster at Aulis; Catalog of Greeks **3.11** The army gathered at Aulis. Those who went to war against Troy were: from the Boiotians, ten leaders: they brought forty ships. From the Orchomenians, four: they brought thirty ships. From the Phocians, four leaders: they brought forty ships. From the Locrians, Aias son of Oileus: he brought forty ships. From the Euboians, Elephenor, the son of Chalcodon and Alcyone: he brought forty ships. From the Athenians, Menestheus: he brought fifty ships. From the Salaminians, Telamonian Aias: he brought twelve ships. **3.12** From the Argives, Diomedes son of Tydeus and his group: they brought eighty ships. From the Mycenaeans, Agamemnon, the son of Atreus and Aerope: one hundred ships. From the Lacedaimonians, Menelaos, the son of Atreus and Aerope: sixty ships. From the Pylians, Nestor, the son of Neleus and Chloris: forty ships. From the Arcadians, Agapenor: seven ships. From the Eleians, Amphimachos and his group: forty ships. From the Doulichians, Meges son of Phyleus: forty ships. From the Cephallenians, Odysseus, the son of Laertes and Anticleia: twelve ships. From the Aitolians, Thoas, the son of Andraimon and Gorge: he brought forty ships. **3.13** From the Cretans, Idomeneus son of Deucalion: forty. From the Rhodians, Tlepolemos, the son of Heracles and Astyoche: nine ships. From the Symaians, Nireus son of Charopos: three ships. From the Coans, Pheidippos and Antiphos, the sons of Thessalos: thirty. **3.14** From the Myrmidons, Achilles, the son of Peleus and Thetis: fifty. From Phylace, Protesilaos son of Iphiclos: forty. From the Pheraians, Eumelos son of Admetos: eleven. From the Olizonians, Philoctetes son of Poias: seven ships. From the Ainianians, Gouneus son of Ocytos: twenty-two. From the Triccaians, Podaleirios <and Machaon, the sons of Asclepios>:* thirty. From the Ormenians, Eurypylos <son of Euaimon> forty. From the Gyrtonians, Polypoites son of Peirithous: forty.* From the Magnesians, Prothoos son of Tenthredon: forty. All the ships totaled one thousand and thirteen, the leaders totaled forty-three, and the contingents totaled thirty.

3.15 While the army was in Aulis and a sacrifice was being performed to Apollo, a serpent rushed forth from the altar toward the nearby plane tree. There was a nest in it, and the serpent devoured the eight sparrows in it along with a ninth, their mother, and then turned into stone. Calchas said that this sign had happened for them in accordance with Zeus' will. Making his interpretation from what had occurred, he said that in the tenth year they were certain to capture Troy.

4. Anios' daughters are said in several accounts to provision the Greek army, which explains their presence here.

First Attempt to Sail to Troy; Telephos **3.16** They prepared to sail to Troy. Agamemnon himself was commander of the whole army, but Achilles was the naval commander even though he happened to be fifteen years old. **3.17** Not knowing how to sail to Troy, they landed in Mysia and plundered this land in the belief that it was Troy. Telephos, the king of the Mysians and Heracles' son, saw his land being pillaged, led out the Mysians under arms, and drove the Greeks back to their ships. He killed many, including Thersandros son of Polyneices, who turned to face him. But when Achilles attacked Telephos, he could not stand up to him and was chased off. In his flight he became entangled in the branch of a grapevine and took a spear wound in the thigh.

3.18 The Greeks left Mysia and set sail. A powerful storm came upon them, and they landed in their home countries after being separated from each other. Because the Greeks turned back at that time, it is said that the war lasted twenty years. For it was in the second year after the abduction of Helen that the Greeks went to war after making their preparations. Then eight years after withdrawing from Mysia to Hellas they returned to Argos and went to Aulis.

Second Muster at Aulis **3.19** So they assembled again in Argos after the aforementioned eight-year period, but without a guide who could show them the way to Troy they were entirely ignorant of where to sail. **3.20** But Telephos arrived dressed in rags from Mysia in Argos with his wound unhealed. Apollo had told him that he would be healed when the one who wounded him became his physician, so he came and begged Achilles and promised to show them the route to Troy. He was healed when Achilles scraped the rust off of Peleus' spear. Once healed, he revealed to them the route, and Calchas verified the accuracy of his information through his divination.

Iphigeneia **3.21** But after they sailed from Argos and came to Aulis for the second time, the fleet was detained by a lack of wind. Calchas said that there was no way for them to sail unless the most beautiful of Agamemnon's daughters were presented as a sacrifice to Artemis. The goddess was angry at Agamemnon, he said, both because when he had shot a deer he had said, "Not even Artemis could have done it!" and because Atreus had not sacrificed the golden lamb to her. **3.22** When this oracle was delivered, Agamemnon sent Odysseus and Talthybios to Clytaimnestra and asked for Iphigeneia, explaining that he had promised to give her as wife to Achilles in exchange for his serving in the war. When she sent her, Agamemnon set her at the altar and was about to slaughter her when Artemis snatched her away and made her her priestess among the Taurians, substituting a deer in her place at the altar. Some, however, say that she made her immortal.

Second Attempt to Sail to Troy; Tenedos; Philoctetes **3.23** They set sail from Aulis and landed on Tenedos. Tenes, the son of Cycnos (some say Apollo) and Procleia, was king of this island. He had been sent into exile by his father and settled there. **3.24** For Cycnos had a son, Tenes, and a daughter, Hemithea, from Procleia daughter of Laomedon. But then he had gotten remarried to Philonome daughter of Tragasos. She fell in love with Tenes and, when she failed to seduce him, made a false accusation to Cycnos that he had tried to force himself on her, providing as a witness of this a fluteplayer named Eumolpos. **3.25** Cycnos believed her. He put him into a chest with his sister and launched it into the sea. After the chest washed up on the island of Leucophrys, Tenes emerged and settled it, naming it Tenedos after himself. Later, when Cycnos learned the truth, he had the fluteplayer stoned and buried his wife in the ground while she was still alive.

3.26 Tenes watched as the Greeks were sailing in to Tenedos, and he tried to keep them from landing by throwing stones at them. But he took a sword wound from Achilles in the chest and died even though Thetis had warned Achilles not to kill Tenes because he himself would be killed by Apollo if he killed Tenes.

3.27 As they were making a sacrifice to Apollo, a water snake came from the altar and bit Philoctetes. The wound would not heal and gave off a foul odor, and the army could not bear the reek of it. So on Agamemnon's order, Odysseus marooned him on Lemnos with Heracles' bow, which he owned. Philoctetes fed himself on the desert island by shooting birds.

Failed Diplomacy at Troy; War Begins **3.28** Setting sail from Tenedos, they approached Troy and sent Odysseus and Menelaos to demand back Helen and the possessions. The Trojans held an assembly. But they not only would not give back Helen; they actually intended to kill Odysseus and Menelaos. **3.29** Antenor saved them, but the Greeks, infuriated by the impudence of the barbarians, took up their arms again and sailed to attack them. Thetis had advised Achilles not to be the first to leave the ships because the first to disembark would be the first to die. When the barbarians learned that the fleet was attacking, they hurried to the sea with their weapons and tried to keep them from landing by throwing rocks.

Protesilaos and Laodameia **3.30** Protesilaos was the first of the Greeks to leave his ship. After killing quite a few barbarians he was killed by Hector. His wife, Laodameia, continuing to love him even after his death, made a statue in the image of Protesilaos and interacted with it.[5] The gods took pity on her, and Hermes brought Protesilaos up from the house of Hades. When she saw him, Laodameia thought that he was back from Troy, so she was momentarily happy. But then when he was taken back to the house of Hades, she killed herself.

Siege Begins; Early Stages of War **3.31** With Protesilaos dead, Achilles disembarked with the Myrmidons and killed Cycnos by hitting him in the head with a stone. When the barbarians saw him dead, they fled to the city. The Greeks jumped out of the ships and filled the plain with bodies. Having bottled the Trojans up, they settled in for a siege and drew their ships out of the water.

3.32 As the barbarians' morale sank, Achilles ambushed Troilos in the temple of Thymbraian Apollo and killed him, then approached the city at night and captured

5. The verb translated here, "interact with," can carry connotations of socializing from mere conversation to sexual intercourse. Compare Hyginus 104.

Lycaon. With the help of some of the commanders Achilles pillaged the land and went to Mount Ida to get the cattle of Aineias. Although Aineias escaped, Achilles killed the cowherds and Mestor son of Priam before driving the cattle off.

3.33 He captured Lesbos and Phocaia; then Colophon, Smyrna, Clazomenai, and Cyme; and after them Aigialos and Tenos.* Next, in order, were Adramytion and Side, then Endion, Linaion, and Colone. He also captured Hypoplacian Thebes and Lyrnessos, and also Antandros and many other cities.

Trojan Allies

3.34 After nine years passed, allies arrived to fight for the Trojans from the neighboring cities: Aineias son of Anchises, and with him Archelochos and Acamas, the sons of Antenor and Theano, commanding the Dardanians. Commanding the Thracians, Acamas son of Eusoros. Commanding the Ciconians, Euphemos son of Troizenos. Commanding the Paionians, Pyraichmes. Commanding the Paphlagonians, Pylaimenes son of Bisaltes. **3.35** From Zelia, Pandaros son of Lycaon. From Adrasteia, Adrastos and Amphios, the sons of Merops. From Arisbe, Asios son of Hyrtacos. From Larissa, Hippothoos son of Pelasgos. From Mysia, Chromios and Ennomos, the sons of Arsinoos. Commanding the Alizonians, Odios and Epistrophos, the sons of Mecisteus. Commanding the Phrygians, Phorcys and Ascanios, the sons of Aretaon. Commanding the Maionians, Mesthles and Antiphos, the sons of Talaimenes. Commanding the Carians, Nastes and Amphimachos, the sons of Nomion. Commanding the Lycians, Sarpedon son of Zeus and Glaucos son of Hippolochos.

Withdrawal of Achilles and Its Effects (Summary of the *Iliad*)

4.1 Achilles, full of wrath, did not go out to the battle because of Briseis < . . . of Chryseis,>[6] the daughter of the priest Chryses. Encouraged by this, the barbarians came forth from the city. Alexander fought a duel with Menelaos, but Aphrodite snatched Alexander away when he was losing. Pandaros broke the oaths by shooting Menelaos with an arrow.

4.2 When Diomedes was dominating the battlefield, he wounded Aphrodite when she was helping Aineias. Coming face-to-face with Glaucos, he was reminded of their ancestral ties of friendship and swapped armor with him. When Hector challenged the best warrior to a duel, many wanted* to fight him, but Aias was chosen by lot and fought.* But heralds broke up their fight when night fell.

4.3 The Greeks built a wall and ditch in front of where the ships were beached. A battle was fought in the plain, and the Trojans drove the Greeks inside the wall. The Greeks sent Odysseus, Phoinix, and Aias as envoys to Achilles to beg him to fight for them and to promise him Briseis and other gifts.

6. The text here simply reads "Briseis, the daughter of the priest Chryses," but Briseis is not the daughter of Chryses. The easiest solution is to assume, as editors have, a lacuna after Briseis. Chryseis, the daughter of Chryses, was Agamemnon's captive. When forced to return her to her father, Agamemnon then seized Achilles' prize, Briseis, and a summary of this is presumably the information missing from the gap.

4.4 When night fell, they sent Odysseus and Diomedes as scouts. They killed Dolon son of Eumelos and Rhesos the Thracian. The latter had arrived just one day earlier as a Trojan ally and had not fought yet; he had set up camp rather far from the Trojan forces and apart from Hector. They also killed twelve men sleeping around him and brought his horses to the ships. **4.5** At daybreak a fierce battle broke out. Agamemnon, Diomedes, Odysseus, Eurypylos, and Machaon were wounded, and the Greeks were routed. Hector broke through the wall and went inside, and after Aias retreated, he set fire to the ships.

4.6 When Achilles saw that Protesilaos' ship was on fire, he sent out Patroclos dressed in his own armor along with the Myrmidons and gave him his horses. When the Trojans saw him, they thought it was Achilles, so they turned to flee. He pursued them to the city-walls and killed many, including Sarpedon son of Zeus. He was killed by Hector after being wounded by Euphorbos. **4.7** A fierce battle broke out around his corpse, and Aias barely managed to get the upper hand and recover the body.

Achilles set aside his anger and took Briseis back. A set of armor was brought to him from Hephaistos, and dressed in it he went out to battle. He chased the Trojans to the Scamandros. There he killed many, among them Asteropaios son of Pelegon son of the river Axios. The river[7] rushed at him in a rage. **4.8** Hephaistos, however, dried up his streams after forcing them back with a great fire. Achilles killed Hector in a duel, tied his ankles to his chariot, and dragged him all the way to the ships. He buried Patroclos and held games in his honor. In these games Diomedes won in the chariot race, Epeios in boxing, and Aias and Odysseus in wrestling. After the games Priam came to Achilles, ransomed Hector's body, and buried him.

Penthesileia and Events after the *Iliad* **5.1** Penthesileia, the daughter of Otrera and Ares, accidentally killed Hippolyte and was purified by Priam. There was a battle, and she killed many, including Machaon. Then later she was killed by Achilles, who fell in love with the Amazon after her death and killed Thersites for disparaging him.

5.2 Hippolyte (also called Glauce or Melanippe) was the mother of Hippolytos. When Phaidra's marriage was being celebrated, Hippolyte showed up under arms together with her Amazons and said that she was going to kill Theseus' dinner guests. When battle broke out, she died, either accidentally by her ally Penthesileia, or by Theseus, or because Theseus' men saw the arrival of the Amazons and closed the doors quickly, trapping her inside and killing her.[8]

Memnon; Death of Achilles **5.3** Achilles killed Memnon, the son of Tithonos and Eos, who arrived in Troy with a large force of Ethiopians to fight the Greeks and killed many of them, including Antilochos. Achilles also chased the

7. The Scamandros, that is.

8. Because we are translating Frazer's compound text of the epitomes, some of this material (here from the Vatican Epitome) has already appeared above in E.1.17 (where it comes from the Sabbaitic Epitome).

Trojans, and near the Scaian Gates he was shot in the ankle with an arrow by Alexander and Apollo. **5.4** When a battle broke out around the corpse, Aias killed Glaucos. He gave someone Achilles' armor to take back to the ships, while he picked up the body and carried it through the middle of the enemy while they threw spears at him. Odysseus fought off his attackers.

5.5 With Achilles' death a sense of disaster filled the army. They buried him with Patroclos, mixing together the bones of both. It is said that after his death Achilles was Medeia's husband on the Isles of the Blessed. They held games for him, in which Eumelos won at the chariot, Diomedes at running, Aias at the discus, and Teucros at archery.

Judgment over Arms of Achilles; Telamonian Aias' Madness

5.6 His armor was set as a victory prize for the best warrior, and Aias and Odysseus stepped forward to contend for them. With the Trojans acting as judges (though some say the allies did the judging), Odysseus was chosen. Distraught with grief, Aias plotted against the army at night. Athena afflicted him with madness and turned him aside, sword in hand, toward the sheep. Out of his mind, he killed the sheep along with the herdsmen, thinking they were Achaians. **5.7** When he came back to his senses later, he killed himself too. Agamemnon kept his body from being burned, and Aias is the only one of those who died at Troy who lies in a coffin. His tomb is in Rhoiteion.

Conditions for Greek Victory

5.8 When the war was already in its tenth year, the Greeks grew despondent. Calchas prophesied to them that the only way for Troy to be captured was if they had Heracles' bow fighting on their side. When Odysseus heard this, he went with Diomedes to Philoctetes on Lemnos. After gaining possession of the bow by trickery, he convinced Philoctetes to sail to Troy. After he arrived, he was healed by Podaleirios and shot Alexander.

5.9 After Alexander's death, Helenos and Deiphobos had a quarrel over who would marry Helen. When Deiphobos was chosen the winner, Helenos left Troy and lived on Mount Ida. Calchas said that Helenos knew the oracles that were protecting the city, so Odysseus captured him in an ambush, then brought him to the camp. **5.10** Under compulsion Helenos told them how Ilion could be taken: first, if the bones of Pelops were brought to them; second, if Neoptolemos fought as their ally; third, if the sky-fallen Palladion were stolen, for as long as it was inside the city, it could not be captured.

5.11 Upon hearing this, the Greeks had Pelops' bones brought to them and sent Odysseus and Phoinix to Lycomedes in Scyros. They convinced him to let Neoptolemos go. After arriving at the camp and getting his father's armor from Odysseus, who willingly gave it, Neoptolemos killed many Trojans.

5.12 Later, Eurypylos son of Telephos came leading a large force of Mysians to fight as a Trojan ally. Though he proved his dominance on the battlefield, Neoptolemos killed him.

5.13 Odysseus went by night with Diomedes to the city. He had Diomedes wait there, while he beat himself up, put on the clothes of a poor man, and entered the city incognito in his beggar's disguise. He was recognized by Helen and with her help stole the Palladion. After killing many of the men on guard, he along with Diomedes brought it back to the ships.

The Trojan Horse **5.14** Later, he had the idea of building a wooden horse and gave instructions to Epeios, who was a master builder. Epeios cut timber from Mount Ida and built a horse that was hollow inside and could be opened up on the flanks. Odysseus suggested that the fifty best warriors enter it—thirteen* according to the author of the *Little Iliad*—and that the rest of them burn their tents after nightfall, set sail, anchor in wait off Tenedos, and sail back after the following nightfall.

5.15 They followed his plan and put the best warriors into the horse, appointing Odysseus as their commander and carving on the horse letters that said: "The Greeks dedicate this as an offering to Athena in thanks for their return home." They themselves burned their tents, set sail during the night, leaving behind Sinon, who was to light a beacon for them, and dropped anchor off Tenedos.

5.16 When day came, the Trojans saw that the Greek camp was deserted and thought that they had fled. Overjoyed, they dragged the horse in, set it up next to Priam's palace, and discussed what to do. **5.17** Cassandra said that there was an armed force inside, as did Laocoon the seer, so some decided it was best to burn it, and others to hurl it down a cliff. But most decided to leave it alone since it was an offering to a god. They then turned their attention to sacrifice and feasted. **5.18** Apollo sent them a sign: two serpents swam across the sea from the nearby islands and devoured Laocoon's sons.

5.19 When night fell and sleep held them all in its grip, the men from Tenedos sailed in, and Sinon lit a beacon for them from Achilles' tomb. Helen went around the horse and called to the heroes, imitating the voices of all their wives. Anticlos wanted to answer, but Odysseus held his mouth shut. **5.20** When they judged that the enemy was asleep, they opened up the horse and got out with their weapons. Echion son of Portheus, the first to go, jumped down and died. The rest of them got down by tying themselves with rope, made it to the walls, opened the gates, and let in those who had sailed in from Tenedos.

The Fall of Troy; Crimes of the Greeks **5.21** Advancing into the city with weapons drawn, they went from house to house and killed them as they slept. Neoptolemos killed Priam at the altar of Herceian Zeus, where he was seeking refuge. Odysseus and Menelaos recognized Glaucos son of Antenor as he was fleeing into his house, and they came with their weapons drawn and saved him. Aineias picked up his father, Anchises, and escaped; the Greeks let him go because of his piety.

5.22 Menelaos killed Deiphobos and took Helen to the ships. Demophon and Acamas, the sons of Theseus—they had come to Troy late in the action—also recovered Theseus' mother, Aithra. Locrian Aias saw that Cassandra had embraced the *xoanon* of Athena but raped her anyway. This is the reason, they say, that the *xoanon* looks up at the sky.

5.23 After killing the Trojans, they put the city to the torch and divided the plunder. They sacrificed to all the gods, then threw Astyanax from the ramparts and sacrificed Polyxene on Achilles' tomb. **5.24** Agamemnon got Cassandra as a special prize, Neoptolemos got Andromache, and Odysseus got Hecabe. According to some, Helenos got Hecabe, crossed over to the Chersonesos with her, and buried her at the place now called Dog's Tomb after she turned into a dog. **5.25** As for Laodice, the most beautiful of Priam's daughters, the earth swallowed her up as everyone watched. When they were about to sail off after ravaging Troy, they were held back by Calchas, who explained that Athena was full of wrath at them on account of Aias' impiety. They were about to kill Aias, but they let him live after he took refuge at an altar.

The Returns of the Heroes **6.1** After this, they gathered for an assembly, and Agamemnon and Menelaos quarreled. Menelaos said they should sail; Agamemnon urged them to stay put and sacrifice to Athena. Diomedes, Nestor, and Menelaos set sail together. The first two had a good voyage, but Menelaos ran into a storm and arrived in Egypt with only five ships after losing the rest of them.

6.2 Amphilochos, Calchas, Leonteus, Podaleirios, and Polypoites left their ships at Ilion and made their way on foot to Colophon. There they buried Calchas the seer, for it had been foretold to him that he would die if he encountered a seer more skilled than himself. **6.3** They had been received as guests by Mopsos, a seer who was the son of Apollo and Manto. This Mopsos had a divination contest with Calchas. Calchas asked about a fig tree that was there: "How many figs are on it?" Mopsos said, "Ten thousand and a bushel, plus one fig." They found out he was correct. **6.4** Then Mopsos asked about a pregnant sow: "How many piglets does she have, and when will she give birth?" When Calchas said, "Eight," Mopsos smiled and said, "Calchas is not even close to divining accurately. I, on the other hand, am the son of Apollo and Manto and have a great abundance of the sharp sight of accurate divination. She has not eight, as Calchas says, but nine piglets in her belly.[9] These are all male. She will give birth tomorrow directly upon the sixth hour." When this happened, Calchas grew depressed and died. He was buried in Notion.

6.5 After sacrificing, Agamemnon set sail and landed on Tenedos. Thetis came and persuaded Neoptolemos to remain for two days and make sacrifice, and he remained. The rest put to sea and ran into a storm off Tenos, for Athena had asked Zeus to send a storm against the Greeks. Many ships sank.

6.6 Athena hit Aias' ship with a thunderbolt, but although his ship broke up, he made it safely to a rock and said that he had made it despite the goddess' intention. Poseidon split the rock with a blow from his trident, and Aias fell into the sea and died. When he washed up on Myconos, Thetis buried him.

Nauplios **6.7** The rest of the Greeks were driven at night to Euboia, and Nauplios lit a beacon on Cape Caphereus. The Greeks thought that it was from those

9. The accounts vary slightly in the two epitomes, and we as usual follow Frazer, who prints that of the Sabbaitic Epitome. The Vatican Epitome has Calchas give no response, and Mopsos' reply is reported indirectly: "that she had ten piglets, one of them male, and that she would give birth the next day."

who had made it safely to shore, so they sailed toward it, their ships smashed into the Capherean Rocks, and many perished.

6.8 This happened because Palamedes, the son of Nauplios and Clymene daughter of Catreus, had been stoned to death because of Odysseus' intrigues. When Nauplios found out about this, he sailed to the Greeks and demanded justice for the death of his son. **6.9** But he returned home without getting it because everyone was eager to stay on the good side of Agamemnon, who had helped Odysseus kill Palamedes. So he sailed around to the Greek lands and orchestrated the infidelity of the wives of the Greeks: Clytaimnestra with Aigisthos, Aigialeia with Cometes son of Sthenelos, and Idomeneus' wife Meda with Leucos. **6.10** Leucos also killed Meda, together with her daughter Cleisithyra, who took refuge in the temple. He caused ten cities in Crete to revolt and became tyrant of them. After the Trojan war, he also drove Idomeneus out when he had returned to Crete.

6.11 That had been the first part of Nauplios' plans. Later, when he learned that the Greeks were en route home, he lit the beacon on Cape Caphereus, the one now called Xylophagos {"Wood-eater"}. Steering their ships toward it in the belief that it was a harbor, the Greeks perished.

6.12 Neoptolemos followed Thetis' advice and stayed for two days on Tenedos. Then he went off on foot with Helenos to the Molossians, burying Phoinix when he died on the journey. After he defeated the Molossians in battle, he became king and fathered Molossos by Andromache. **6.13** Helenos founded a city in Molossia and settled there. Neoptolemos gave him his mother, Deidameia, as wife. When Peleus was driven from Phthia by the sons of Acastos and died, Neoptolemos took over his father's kingdom.

6.14 When Orestes went mad, Neoptolemos abducted his wife, Hermione, who had originally been betrothed to him at Troy. For this reason he was killed by Orestes in Delphi, but some say that Neoptolemos came to Delphi to demand that Apollo pay for his father's death, stole the offerings, and set fire to the temple, and he was for that reason killed by Machaireus the Phocian.

6.15 The Greeks in their wandering came to and settled in various locations. Some came to Libya, some to Italy, others to Sicily, some to the islands near Iberia, and others to the Sangarios River. There are those that also settled in Cyprus. Of those whose ships wrecked at Caphereus, each was carried in a different direction. Gouneus went to Libya; Antiphos son of Thessalos to the Pelasgians, whose land he took over and called Thessaly; and Philoctetes to the Campanians in Italy. Pheidippos settled in Andros with the Coans, Agapenor in Cyprus, and others elsewhere.

<**6.15a**[10] Apollodorus and the rest say this: Gouneus, after leaving his own ships, came to Libya to the Cinyps River and settled there. Meges and Prothoos perished with many others near Caphereus in Euboia . . . and after Prothoos was shipwrecked near Caphereus, the Magnesians with him washed up in Crete and settled there.[11]>

10. The following sections, 6.15a–c, are taken from Tzetzes' scholia to Lycophron, which seem to preserve information Tzetzes took from an unepitomized text of Apollodorus. They thus present some repetition of material from the surviving epitomes.

11. The ellipsis in this sentence represents material omitted here because it duplicates information from 6.12 above.

<**6.15b** After the sack of Ilion, Menestheus, Pheidippos, Antiphos, Elephenor's men, and Philoctetes sailed together as far as Mimas. Then Menestheus went to Melos and became king after Polyanax, the king there, died. Antiphos son of Thessalos went to the Pelasgians, took over their land, and named it Thessaly. Pheidippos was driven off course with the Coans to Andros, then to Cyprus, and he settled there. Elephenor's men (he had died at Troy) were driven away to the Ionian Gulf and settled Apollonia in Epeiros. Tlepolemos' men landed on Crete, then were driven off course by the winds and colonized the Iberian islands . . . Protesilaos' men were washed up in Pallene near the Canastron Plain.[12] Philoctetes was driven off course to the Campanians in Italy; he fought the Leucanians and settled Crimissa near Croton and Thourion. Done with his wandering {*ale*}, he built a temple to Apollo Alaios, to whom, according to Euphorion, he dedicated his bow.>

<**6.15c** Nauaithos is a river in Italy, so called, according to Apollodorus and the rest, because after the capture of Ilion the daughters of Laomedon (Priam's sisters), Aithylla, Astyoche, and Medesicaste, came to that part of Italy with the rest of the female captives. Afraid of the slavery that awaited them in Hellas, they set fire to the ships, and so the river was called Nauaithos {"Ship-burn"} and the women the Nauprestides {"Ship-lighters"}. The Greeks with them settled there after losing their ships.>

6.16 Demophon landed with a few ships among the Thracian Bisaltai. Phyllis, the daughter of the king, fell in love with and was married to him by her father, the dowry being the kingdom. But Demophon wanted to return to his country. After much begging and taking an oath to return, he left. Phyllis escorted him as far as the so-called Nine Roads, and gave him a chest. She told him there was a sacred object of Mother Rhea in it, and he should not open it until an occasion arose in which he did not think he would return to her.

6.17 Demophon went to Cyprus and settled there. When the agreed-upon time passed, Phyllis placed curses on Demophon and killed herself. Demophon opened the chest and, gripped by fear, got up on his horse. He rode it wildly, and died, for the horse threw him and he tumbled down and landed on his sword. The men with him settled in Cyprus.

6.18 Podaleirios came to Delphi and asked the oracle where he should settle. An oracle was given that he should live in a city where nothing would happen to him if the sky above fell, so he settled the place in the Carian Chersonesos that is encircled entirely by mountains.

6.19 Amphilochos son of Alcmaion, who, according to some, came to Troy later, was driven off course by a storm to Mopsos. Some say they fought a duel for the kingdom and killed each other.

6.20 The Locrians managed to regain their land, and three years later, when pestilence gripped Locris, they received an oracle telling them to appease Athena in Ilion by sending two virgins for a thousand years as suppliants. Periboia and Cleopatra were the first to be chosen by lot. **6.21** When they arrived in Troy, they were chased

12. The ellipsis in this sentence represents materials omitted here because Tzetzes specifically says that it did not come from Apollodorus.

by the local inhabitants but made it into the temple. They did not go near the goddess, but they did sweep out the temple and sprinkle it with water. They did not go outside the temple, and they cut their hair short, and each wore only one garment and no sandals. **6.22** When the first women died, they sent more. They would go into the city at night so that they would not be seen outside of the sanctuary and be killed. Afterward, they sent babies with their nurses. They stopped sending suppliants after the Phocian War when a thousand years had passed.

Agamemnon's Homecoming and Its Aftermath

6.23 When Agamemnon returned to Mycenae with Cassandra, he was killed by Aigisthos and Clytaimnestra. She gave him a tunic with no holes for the arms and head, and while he was trying to put it on, he was killed. Aigisthos became king of Mycenae. They also killed Cassandra.

6.24 Electra, one of Agamemnon's daughters, secretly took her brother, Orestes, and gave him to Strophios, a Phocian, to raise. He raised him with his own son, Pylades. When Orestes grew up, he went to Delphi and asked the god whether to take vengeance on his father's murderers. **6.25** The god commanded him to do this, so he went in secret to Mycenae with Pylades and killed his mother and Aigisthos.

Not much later, he was seized by madness, and, pursued by the Erinyes, he arrived in Athens and was put on trial on the Areiopagos. According to some, he was prosecuted by the Erinyes, according to others, by Tyndareos, and according to others, by Erigone, the daughter of Aigisthos and Clytaimnestra. When the trial was over, he was acquitted when the votes were equally split. **6.26** When he asked how he might get rid of his illness, the god said that he would do so if he brought back the *xoanon* that was in the land of the Taurians. The Taurians are a branch of the Scythians who murder foreigners and throw them into the sacred fire. That fire was in the sanctuary, brought up from the house of Hades through a certain rock.

6.27 When Orestes made it to the Taurians with Pylades, he was found out, taken prisoner, and brought in shackles to King Thoas. Thoas sent them both off to the priestess. Orestes was recognized by his sister,[13] who was the priestess among the Taurians, and fled with her after taking the *xoanon*. It was taken to Athens and is now called the *xoanon* of Tauropolos. But some say that he was driven off course in a storm to the island of Rhodes < . . . > and that it was set up as a dedication in a wall in accordance with an oracle.[14] **6.28** When he came to Mycenae, Orestes married his sister Electra to Pylades, and he himself married Hermione or, according to some, Erigone. He fathered Tisamenos and died after being bitten by a snake in Oresteion in Arcadia.

Menelaos' Homecoming

6.29 Menelaos arrived in Cape Sounion in Attica with a total of five ships. Forced away from there to Crete again by winds, he was driven far off course. As he wandered through Libya, Phoenicia, Cyprus, and Egypt, he gathered much wealth. **6.30** According to some, he discovered Helen at the court

13. Iphigeneia (see 3.22).

14. The text and sense of the last part of this sentence is obscure.

of Proteus, the king of the Egyptians—up until then Menelaos had only had a duplicate Helen made out of clouds. After wandering for eight years, he sailed to Mycenae and upon his arrival there found Orestes, who had avenged his father's murder. Going to Sparta, he gained possession of his own kingdom and went to the Elysian Field with Helen after being made immortal by Hera.

Odysseus' Wanderings (Summary of the *Odyssey*) **7.1** Odysseus wandered, so some say, in Libya, though some say in Sicily, and others say near Oceanos or in the Tyrrhenian Sea. **7.2** After launching from Ilion, he put in at Ismaros, the city of the Ciconians. He captured it in battle and plundered it, sparing only Maron, who was the priest of Apollo. When the Ciconians who lived on the mainland learned of this, they came under arms to attack him, and he put to sea and got away with a loss of six men from each ship.

7.3 He arrived in the land of the Lotus-eaters and sent some of his men to find out about the inhabitants. These men tasted the lotus and stayed there, for in the land a sweet fruit grew that made anyone who tasted it forget everything. When Odysseus learned of this, he kept the rest of his men back and drove the ones who had tasted the lotus back by force to the ships. After sailing away* he approached the land of the Cyclopes.

7.4 He left the rest of his ships at a nearby island, sailed in with one ship to the land of the Cyclopes, and disembarked with twelve companions. There was a cave near the shore, and he went into it, taking the skin of wine that Maron had given to him. It was the cave of Polyphemos, who was the son of Poseidon and the nymph Thoosa, an enormous man, savage and man-eating, with a single eye on his forehead.

7.5 They lit a fire, sacrificed some of the kid goats, and feasted. The Cyclops came and drove his flock into the cave, then set an enormous boulder across the entrance. He spotted them and ate some.

7.6 Odysseus, however, gave him some of Maron's wine to drink, and once he drank, he asked for more. Upon taking his second drink, he asked Odysseus' name. He said that his name was Outis {"Nobody"}, and the Cyclops promised to devour him last after eating the others first, and that was the gift of hospitality he promised to give him. Overtaken by drunkenness, he fell asleep.

7.7 Odysseus found a club lying around, and with the help of four of his companions he sharpened it, hardened it in the fire, and blinded the Cyclops. Polyphemos shouted for help to the Cyclopes nearby, and they came and asked him who was hurting him. When he said "Outis!" they thought he was saying that he was being hurt by "nobody," so they went away. **7.8** When his sheep wanted to go out for their usual feeding, he unblocked the entrance and stood there. Stretching out his hands, he searched the sheep by touch. But Odysseus tied three rams together < . . . >[15] and he got under the lead ram, hid beneath its belly, and went out with the sheep. He untied his companions from the sheep, then drove the animals to the ships. As

15. As is clear from Homer's *Odyssey*, he ties one man under each set of three sheep.

he was sailing away, he shouted to the Cyclops that he was Odysseus and that he had escaped his clutches.

7.9 The Cyclops had been given a prophecy by a seer that he would be blinded by Odysseus. When he found out his name, he pulled up boulders and hurled them into the sea, and the ship barely made it safely through the boulders. From that time forward, Poseidon directed his wrath at Odysseus.

7.10 Setting sail with all his ships, he came to the island of Aiolia, the king of which was Aiolos. He was put by Zeus in charge of both stopping the winds and making them blow. He offered Odysseus hospitality and gave him a cowhide bag in which he had tied up the winds. He then showed him which winds he needed to use while he was sailing and secured the bag on the ship. Odysseus used the proper winds and had a good voyage. When he was close to Ithaca and had already caught sight of the smoke rising from the city, he fell asleep. **7.11** His companions, believing that he was bringing back gold in the bag, untied it and released the winds. Taken by the winds, they went back the way they came. Odysseus went to Aiolos and asked to get a favorable wind, but Aiolos drove him from the island and said that he could not get him safely home because the gods were opposed to it.

7.12 As he sailed, he put in at the land of the Laistrygonians, and* he docked his own ship furthest out. The Laistrygonians were cannibals, and Antiphates was their king. Now, Odysseus wanted to find out about the inhabitants, so he sent some men to make inquiries. The daughter of the king ran into them and brought them to her father. **7.13** He grabbed one of them and ate him, then, shouting and summoning the other Laistrygonians, he chased the rest of the men as they ran. The Laistrygonians came to the sea and broke the ships up by hitting them with rocks and ate the men. Odysseus cut the anchor cable of his ship and put out to sea, but the rest of the ships were lost with their crews.

7.14 With one ship he landed on the island of Aiaia, where Circe lived. She was the daughter of Helios and Perse and the sister of Aietes, and she was an expert in all kinds of magic. Odysseus split up his companions. After picking lots, he himself stayed by the ship, while Eurylochos went to Circe with companions, twenty-two in number. **7.15** She invited them in, and they all went except for Eurylochos. She gave to each of them a drink filled with cheese, honey, barley-groats, and wine after mixing in a magical drug. After they drank it, she touched them with a wand and changed their forms. Some she turned into wolves, some into pigs, some into donkeys, and some into lions.

7.16 Eurylochos saw this and reported it to Odysseus, who got *moly* from Hermes and went to Circe. He threw the *moly* into the magic potion and was the only one not to be affected by drinking it. Drawing his sword, he was about to kill Circe, but she calmed him down and changed his companions back. Odysseus slept with her after extracting oaths from her that he would not be harmed, and he had a son, Telegonos.

7.17 He remained there a year, then sailed to Oceanos.* There he slaughtered victims for the souls, asked Teiresias for a prophecy as Circe had suggested, and viewed the souls of the heroes and heroines. He also saw his mother, Anticleia, and Elpenor, who had fallen at Circe's house and died.

7.18 After making his way to Circe, he put out to sea with a send-off from her and sailed past the island of the Sirens. The Sirens were the daughters of Acheloos and Melpomene, one of the Muses. Their names were Peisinoe, Aglaope, and Thelxiepeia. One played the cithara, one sang, and one played the flute, and that is how they got those who sailed past to stay there. **7.19** From the thighs down they had the forms of birds.

As he sailed past them, Odysseus wanted to listen to their song, so at Circe's suggestion he blocked the ears of his companions with wax and gave orders that he be tied to the mast. As was being induced by the Sirens to remain, he begged to be untied, but his men tied him tighter, and that is how he sailed past. As for the Sirens, they had a prophecy that they would die if a ship made it past them, so they died.

7.20 Next he came to a choice of routes. On one side were the Planctai {"Wandering"} Rocks; on the other were two huge promontories. Scylla was in one. She was the daughter of Crataiis and Trienos or Phorcos, and had the face and torso of a woman, but from the flanks down she had six dog heads and twelve dog feet.

7.21 Charybdis was in the other promontory. She sucked up the water and then sent it forth again three times a day. At Circe's suggestion he avoided the route past the Planctai, and as he was sailing along the route by Scylla, he stood armed on the stern. When Scylla appeared, she snatched up six of his companions and devoured them.

7.22 From there they came to the island of Thrinacia, which belongs to Helios, where some cattle were being pastured. Held up by a lack of wind, Odysseus remained there. When his companions slaughtered and feasted on some of the cows because they had no food, Helios lodged a complaint with Zeus. When Odysseus set sail, Zeus threw a thunderbolt at him.

7.23 His ship broke up, but Odysseus held on to the mast and reached Charybdis. When Charybdis swallowed down the mast, he caught hold of a fig tree growing overhead and waited. When he saw that the mast had come back up, he threw himself at it and was carried to the island of Ogygia.

7.24 There Calypso, the daughter of Atlas, welcomed him and, after sleeping with him, gave birth to a son, Latinos. Odysseus remained with her for five years, then built a raft and sailed away. The raft was broken apart at sea because Poseidon was angry, and Odysseus washed ashore without any clothes in the land of the Phaiacians.

7.25 Nausicaa, the daughter of Alcinoos, the king, was washing her clothes when he supplicated her. She took him to Alcinoos, who made him his guest and sent him on to his homeland with an escort after giving him gifts. Poseidon, raging at the Phaiacians, turned their ship to stone and enclosed their city in a mountain.

Homecoming of Odysseus; the Suitors and Penelope **7.26** Odysseus arrived in his own country and discovered his home had been completely ruined, for there were suitors for Penelope's hand because they thought he had died. From Doulichion there were fifty-seven:[16]

16. As often, lists of names and numbers are easily corrupted, and they will not always match. Here there are fifty-three names given. Below in E.7.29 there are only forty-one names, not forty-four.

7.27 Amphinomos, Thoas, Demoptolemos, Amphimachos, Euryalos, Paralos, Euenorides, Clytios, Agenor, Eurypylos, Pylaimenes, Acamas, Thersilochos, Hagios, Clymenos, Philodemos, Meneptolemos, Damastor, Bias, Telmios, Polyidos, Astylochos, Schedios, Antigonos, Marpsios, Iphidamas, Argeios, Glaucos, Calydoneus, Echion, Lamas, Andraimon, Agerochos, Medon, Agrios, Promos, Ctesios, Acarnan, Cycnos, Pseras, Hellanicos, Periphron, Megasthenes, Thrasymedes, Ormenios, Diopithes, Mecisteus, Antimachos, Ptolemaios, Lestorides, Nicomachos, Polypoites, and Ceraos. **7.28** From Same there were twenty-three: Agelaos, Peisandros, Elatos, Ctesippos, Hippodochos, Eurystratos, Archemolos, Ithacos, Peisenor, Hyperenor, Pheroites, Antisthenes, Cerberos, Perimedes, Cynnos, Thriasos, Eteoneus, Clytios, Prothoos, Lycaithos, Eumelos, Itanos, and Lyammos. **7.29** From Zacynthos there were forty-four: Eurylochos, Laomedes, Molebos, Phrenios, Indios, Minis, Leiocritos, Pronomos, Nisas, Daemon, Archestratos, Hippo[machos, Euryalos, Periallos, Euenorides, Clytios, Agenor,][17] Polybos, Polydoros, Thadytios, Stratios, [Phrenios, Indios,] Daisenor, Laomedon, Laodicos, Halios, Magnes, Oloitrochos, Barthas, Theophron, Nissaios, Alcarops, Periclymenos, Antenor, Pellas, Celtos, Periphas, Ormenos, Polybos, and Andromedes. **7.30** The twelve suitors from Ithaca itself were Antinoos, Pronoos, Leiodes, Eurynomos, Amphimachos, Amphialos, Promachos, Amphimedon, Aristratos, Helenos, Doulichieus, and Ctesippos.

7.31 These men made their way to the palace and feasted, consuming Odysseus' herds. Penelope was forced to promise that she would get married when the burial-shroud for Laertes was finished. She wove it for three years, weaving by day and undoing it at night. The suitors were fooled by Penelope until she was found out.

7.32 When Odysseus learned what the situation was in his house, he went disguised as a beggar to his slave Eumaios. He revealed himself to Telemachos and went into the city. Melanthios, his slave who kept the goats, ran into them and insulted him. Arriving at the palace, Odysseus begged the suitors for some food. Finding a beggar named Iros, he wrestled him. He revealed who he was to Eumaios and Philoitios, and with the help of them and Telemachos, he plotted against the suitors.

7.33 Penelope presented to the suitors Odysseus' bow, which he had gotten once from Iphitos, and she said that she would marry the one who could draw it. None of them were able to draw it, but Odysseus took it and shot down the suitors with the help of Eumaios, Philoitios, and Telemachos. He also killed Melanthios and the maidservants who were sleeping with the suitors, and revealed himself to his wife and father.

Odysseus Wanders Again (Events after the *Odyssey*) **7.34** After making a sacrifice to Hades, Persephone, and Teiresias, he traveled on foot through Epeiros and came to the land of the Thesprotians. He appeased Poseidon by sacrificing in accordance with Teiresias' prophecies. Callidice, who was then queen of the Thesprotians, begged him to stay and gave him the kingdom.

7.35 He slept with her and fathered Polypoites. He married Callidice, became king of the Thesprotians, and defeated in battle the neighboring peoples who attacked.

17. The names in brackets here and just after are repeated from earlier in the list.

When Callidice died, he handed over the kingdom to their son and went to Ithaca. He discovered that Poliporthes had been born to him by Penelope.

7.36 Telegonos learned from Circe that he was Odysseus' son, so he sailed forth to search for him. Arriving in Ithaca, Telegonos rustled some of the cattle and with the spear in his hands, which was tipped with a stingray spine, he wounded Odysseus when he tried to stop him. Odysseus died.

7.37 When Telegonos realized who he was, he lamented much and took Odysseus' body and Penelope to Circe. There he married Penelope. Circe sent them both off to the Isles of the Blessed.

7.38 But some say that Penelope was seduced by Antinoos and was sent away by Odysseus to her father, Icarios, and that when she arrived in Mantineia in Arcadia she gave birth to Pan by Hermes. **7.39** Others, however, say that she died at the hands of Odysseus himself because of Amphinomos, for they say she had been seduced by this man. **7.40** There are those who say that when Odysseus was being accused about the dead men by their relatives, he accepted as judge Neoptolemos, who was king of the islands lying near Epeiros. Neoptolemos, they say, thought that with Odysseus out of the way he would gain possession of Cephallenia, so he condemned him to exile, and Odysseus went to Thoas son of Andraimon in Aitolia and married his daughter. He died an old man, leaving behind a son, Leontophonos, by this woman.

Hyginus' *Fabulae*

Theogony [1] From Mist came Chaos. From Chaos and Mist came Night, Day, Darkness, and Ether. From Night and Darkness came Fate, Old Age, Death, Destruction, Strife,* Sleep (i.e., the Body Relaxer*), Dreams, Thoughtfulness, Hedymeles, Porphyrion, Epaphus, Discord, Misery, Petulance, Nemesis, Cheerfulness, Friendship, Pity, and Styx; also the three Parcae, namely Clotho, Lachesis, Atropos, and the three Hesperides (Aegle, Hesperia, Erythea*).

[2] From Ether and Day came Earth, Sky, and Sea.

[3] From Ether and Earth came Pain, Deception, Anger, Mourning, Lying, Oath, Vengeance, Self-indulgence, Quarreling, Forgetfulness, Sloth, Fear, Arrogance, Incest, Fighting, Ocean, Themis, Tartarus, and Pontus; and the Titans, Briareus, Gyges, Steropes, Atlas, Hyperion and Polus, Saturn, Ops, Moneta, Dione, and the three Furies (Alecto, Megaera, Tisiphone).

[4] From Earth and Tartarus came the Giants: Enceladus, Coeus, *<unintelligible>*, Ophion,* Astraeus, Pelorus, Pallas, Emphytus, Rhoecus, Ienios, Agrius, Palaemon,* Ephialtes, Eurytus, *<unintelligible>*, Theomises, Theodamas, Otos, Typhon, Polybotes, Menephiarus, Abseus, Colophomus, and Iapetus.

[5] From Pontus and the Sea came the species of fish.

[6] From Ocean and Tethys came the Oceanids: Hestyaea, Melite, Ianthe, Admete, Stilbo, Pasiphae, Polyxo, Eurynome, Euagoreis, Rhodope, Lyris, Clytia, *<unintelligible>*, Clitemneste, Mentis, Menippe, Argia. From the same seed came also the Rivers: Strymon, Nilus, Euphrates, Tanais, Indus, Cephisus, Ismenus, Axius,* Achelous, Simois, Inachus, Alpheus, Thermodon, Scamandrus, Tigris, Maeander, and Orontes.

[7] From Pontus and Earth came Thaumas, Ceto, Nereus, and Phorcus.

[8] From Nereus and Doris came the fifty Nereids: Glauce, Thalia, Cymodoce, Nesaea, Spio, Thoe, Cymothoe, Actaea, Limnoria, Melite, Iaera, Amphithoe, Agave, Doto, Proto, Pherusa, Dynamene, Dexamene, Amphinome, Callianassa, Doris, Panope, Galatea, Nemertes, Apseudes, Clymene, Ianira, Panopaea, Ianassa, Maera, Orithyia, Amathia, Drymo, Xantho, Ligea, Phyllodoce, Cydippe, Lycorias, Cleio, Beroe, Ephyra, Opis, Asia, Deiopea, Arethusa, Clymene, Creneis, Eurydice, and Leucothoe.[1]

[9] From Phorcus and Ceto came the Phorcides, namely Pemphredo, Enyo, and Persis (others replace the last with Dino). From Gorgon and Ceto came Sthenno, Euryale, and Medusa.

[10] From Polus and Phoebe came Latona, Asteria, Aphirape, Perses, and Pallas.

[11] From Iapetus and Clymene came Atlas, Epimetheus, and Prometheus.

1. Only forty-nine names are given here in the text.

[12] From Hyperion and Aethra came the Sun, Moon, and Aurora.

[13] From Saturn and Ops came Vesta, Ceres, Juno, Jupiter, Pluto, and Neptune.

[14] From Saturn and Philyra came Chiron and Dolops.

[15] From Astraeus and Aurora came Zephyrus, Boreas, Notus, and Favonius.

[16] From Atlas and Pleione came Maia, Calypso,* Alcyone, Merope,* Electra, and Celaeno.

[17] From the Giant Pallas and Styx came Scylla, Violence, Envy, Power, Victory, Springs, and Lakes.

[18] From Neptune and Amphitrite came Triton.

[19] From Dione and Jupiter came Venus.

[20] From Jupiter and Juno came Mars.

[21] From the head of Jupiter came Minerva.

[22] From Juno without a father came Vulcan.

[23] From Jupiter and Eurynome came the Graces.

[24] From Jupiter, again with Juno, came Youth and Freedom.

[25] From Jupiter and Themis came the Seasons.

[26] From Jupiter and Ceres came Proserpina.

[27] From Jupiter and Moneta came the Muses.

[28] From Jupiter and the Moon came Pandia.

[29] From Venus and Mars came Harmonia and Terror.

[30] From Achelous and Melpomene came the Sirens, namely Thelxiepia, Molpe, and Pisinoe.

[31] From Jupiter and Clymene came Mnemosyne.

[32] From Jupiter and Maia came Mercury.

[33] From Jupiter and Latona came Apollo and Diana.

[34] From Earth came Python, a prophetic serpent.

[35] From Thaumas and Electra came Iris and the Harpies, namely Celaeno, Ocypete, and Podarce.

[36] From the Sun and Perse came Circe, Pasiphae, Aeetes, and Perses.

[37] From Aeetes and Clytia came Medea.

[38] From the Sun and Clymene came Phaethon and the Phaethontides, namely Merope, Helia, Aetheria, and Dioxippe.

[39] From Typhon and Echidna came Gorgon; Cerberus, the snake that guarded the Golden Fleece at Colchis; Scylla (who had a woman's body above the waist, but a dog's below; she was killed by Hercules); the Chimaera; the Sphinx, who lived in Boeotia; the serpent Hydra, who had nine heads and was killed by Hercules; and the serpent of the Hesperides.

[40] From Neptune and Medusa came Chrysaor and the horse Pegasus.

[41] From Chrysaor and Callirhoe came three-bodied Geryon.

1 Themisto Athamas son of Aeolus had by his wife, Nebula, a son, Phrixus, and a daughter, Helle. By Themisto daughter of Hypseus he had two sons, Sphincius and Orchomenus. And by Ino daughter of Cadmus he had two sons, Learchus and Melicertes. Themisto wanted to kill Ino's sons because Ino had ruined her marriage. And so she hid secretly in the palace, and when the occasion presented itself, she killed her own children without realizing it. She thought that she was killing those of her rival, but she was misled by the fact that the children's nurse had dressed them in the wrong clothing. When Themisto realized what she had done, she committed suicide.

2 Ino Ino, the daughter of Cadmus and Harmonia, wanted to kill Phrixus and Helle, Athamas' children by Nebula. So she formed a plan involving the women of the entire country and made them all swear that they would parch the grain they were going to supply for sowing, so that it would not sprout. Thus it happened that because of the crop failure and the shortage of grain, the entire population was dying off, some because of starvation, some because of disease. Athamas sent one of his aides to Delphi to inquire about the matter, but Ino ordered him to report a false oracle: if Athamas were to sacrifice Phrixus to Jupiter, there would be an end to the blight. When Athamas refused to do this, Phrixus willingly came forward of his own accord and declared that he would free the state from its plight. When he had been led to the altar dressed in the sacrificial headdress and his father was about to invoke Jupiter, out of pity for the boy Athamas' aide revealed Ino's scheme to Athamas.

When the king learned of the crime, he handed his wife, Ino, and her son, Melicertes, over to Phrixus for execution. As Phrixus led them to their punishment, Father Liber enveloped him in a mist and rescued Ino because she had raised him. Later, Athamas was driven mad by Juno and killed his son Learchus. As for Ino, she threw herself and her son Melicertes into the sea. Liber ordained that she be called Leucothea (we call her Mater Matuta) and that Melicertes be called the god Palaemon (we call him Portunus). In his honor every four years athletic games are held, which are called Isthmian.

3 Phrixus Phrixus and Helle were driven mad by Liber. When they were wandering in the forest in this state, the story goes that their mother, Nebula, went there and brought them a golden ram, the offspring of Neptune and Theophane. She told her children to get on the ram and travel to the land of the Colchians and their king, Aeetes, the son of the Sun, and once there to sacrifice the ram to Mars. So it is said to have happened; but when they had climbed on and the ram was carrying them over the sea, Helle fell off, and so the sea was named the Hellespont {"Helle's Sea"}.

Phrixus, on the other hand, was carried all the way to Colchis by the ram. Once there, following his mother's orders, he sacrificed the ram and placed its golden fleece in the temple of Mars. (This is the one that Jason, the son of Aeson and Alcimede, went to retrieve, though it was protected by a serpent.) Aeetes welcomed Phrixus kindly and gave his daughter Chalciope to him to be his wife, who later bore him children. But Aeetes feared that they would dethrone him; he had received ominous signs that he should beware of death at the hands of a foreigner, a descendant of Aeolus. So he killed Phrixus. The latter's sons (Argus, Phrontis, Melas, and Cylindrus), however, boarded a raft to cross the sea and rejoin their grandfather, Athamas. They were shipwrecked on the island of Dia but were picked up by Jason while he was on his quest for the Fleece and transported back to their mother, Chalciope. In return for Jason's kind action, she put in a good word for him with her sister, Medea.

4 Euripides' *Ino* King Athamas of Thessaly thought that his wife, Ino, by whom he had fathered two sons, was dead. So he married Themisto, the daughter of a Nymph, and had twin sons by her. Later, he learned that Ino was on Mount Parnassus; she had gone there to celebrate the Bacchic mysteries. He sent men to bring her back, and when they had, he kept her out of view. Themisto learned that they had found a woman but did not know who she was.

Themisto planned to kill Ino's sons and took as her accomplice Ino herself (who, she thought, was just a captive girl), and told her to dress her sons in white and Ino's in black. Ino dressed her own in white clothing and Themisto's in black. Misled in this fashion, Themisto killed her own sons. When she realized her error, she committed suicide. As for Athamas, in a fit of madness he killed his elder son, Learchus, while hunting. Ino threw herself into the sea along with her younger son, Melicertes, and was made a goddess.

5 Athamas Because Semele had slept with Jupiter, Juno was hostile toward her whole family. This is why in a fit of madness Athamas son of Aeolus shot dead his son with arrows while hunting.

6 Cadmus After his children were killed by Mars in retribution for his having slain the serpent that guarded the Castalian Spring,[2] Cadmus, the son of Agenor and Argiope, went to Illyria with his wife, Harmonia, the daughter of Venus and Mars. Both of them were turned into serpents.

7 Antiope Epaphus tricked Antiope daughter of Nycteus into committing adultery with him. Because of the affair her husband, Lycus, threw her out. After her divorce Jupiter came down and ravished her. Lycus married Dirce, who grew suspicious that her husband was secretly sleeping with Antiope. So she ordered her slaves to put her in chains and lock her up in a dungeon. When Antiope was getting close to giving birth, she escaped her chains by the will of Jupiter and fled to Mount Cithaeron. And when birth was imminent, she sought a place to give birth but was compelled by the pain to give birth where the road forks.

Shepherds raised the boys as their own and named one Zethus *because their mother looked for* {Greek *zetein*} *a place,* and the other Amphion *because she bore him at the fork in the road or where the road splits*[3] {Greek *amphi odon*}, that is, because she gave birth where the road forks. When they were reunited with their mother, they killed Dirce by tying her to a wild bull. Because she had been a Bacchant, Liber caused a fountain, which was named Dirce, to be created from her body on Mount Cithaeron.

8 The Same Play of Euripides [Which Ennius Wrote][4] The daughter of King Nycteus of Boeotia was Antiope. Jupiter was attracted to her because of her

2. The Castalian Spring is normally located in Delphi, not in Thebes as Hyginus suggests here.

3. The italicized words are given in Greek, thus explaining the apparent repetition.

4. The words "Which Ennius Wrote" are probably a later addition; the ancient table of contents merely gives "The Same Play of Euripides," and there is no evidence Ennius wrote a play on Antiope.

good looks and got her pregnant. When her father was about to punish her for her fornication and threatened to harm her, Antiope escaped. By chance she came to the same place that Epaphus of Sicyon was staying. He married her, bringing the newly arrived woman into his home. Nycteus took this poorly and on his deathbed made a solemn request of his brother Lycus, the heir to the throne, that he not allow Antiope to go unpunished.

After Nycteus' death Lycus went to Sicyon, killed Epaphus, put Antiope in chains, and brought her to Cithaeron. She gave birth to twins and exposed them. A shepherd raised the twins and named them Zethus and Amphion. Antiope was given to Lycus' wife, Dirce, for her to torture. When the opportunity arose, however, Antiope took to flight and came to her sons, but Zethus did not take her in because he thought she was simply a fugitive slave. It so happened that the frenzied celebration of Liber brought Dirce to the same place. There she found Antiope and began to haul her off to her death, but the young men were informed by the shepherd who had raised them that she was their mother, and they quickly caught up to her and saved her. They killed Dirce by tying her to a bull with her own hair. They were going to kill Lycus, but Mercury stopped them from doing so. Instead, he ordered Lycus to cede the throne to Amphion.

9 Niobe At Apollo's command Amphion and Zethus, the sons of Jupiter and Antiope, enclosed Thebes in a wall that extended as far as Semele's grave, drove Laius son of King Labdacus into exile, and became the rulers there. Amphion took Niobe, the daughter of Tantalus and Dione, in marriage, and they had seven sons and just as many daughters. Niobe threw the fact that she had so many children in Latona's face, spoke insultingly about Apollo and Diana (because she dressed like a man and because of Apollo's long dress and hair), and said that she was better than Latona because she had more children.

Because of this boast Apollo shot her sons dead with arrows while they were hunting in the forest, and Diana killed all her daughters, except Chloris, with arrows inside the palace. As for their mother, they say that she, bereft of her children, turned into a stone from her weeping on Mount Sipylus, and her tears, they say, flow forth even to this day. Amphion was killed by Apollo's arrows since he intended to destroy Apollo's temple.

10 Chloris Chloris was the only one of Niobe's and Amphion's seven daughters who survived. Neleus son of Hippocoon took her as his wife, and they had twelve male children. When Hercules was laying siege to Pylos, he killed Neleus and ten of his sons; the eleventh, Periclymenus, was turned into an eagle by the goodwill of his grandfather, Neptune, and so escaped death. The twelfth, Nestor, was at Ilium,[5] and they say that he lived for three generations through the gift of Apollo, for he added to Nestor's life the years he had stolen from Chloris' brothers.

5. Hyginus implies that the reason Nestor was not killed was because he was fighting at Troy, but that war would not take place for some years. By the usual account, Nestor was being raised in another king's court at the time of the killings.

11 The Children of Niobe Thera,* Tantalus, Ismenus, Eupinus, Phaedimus, Sipylus, Chias, Chloris, Astycratia, Siboe, Sictothius, Eudoxa, Archenor, and Ogygia —these are the sons and daughters of Niobe, Amphion's wife.

12 Pelias Pelias, the son of Cretheus and Tyro, had received a prophecy that should a *monocrepis* man (by which I mean a man with a sandal on only one foot) arrive on the scene while he was making a sacrifice to Neptune, his death was drawing near. While Pelias was making his annual sacrifice to Neptune, his brother Aeson's son, Jason, in his desire to take part in the sacrifice lost a sandal while crossing the Evenus River. He left it there because he was in a hurry to make it to the sacrifice. When Pelias saw this and called to mind the oracle's warning, he ordered him to go to Colchis to get from his enemy, King Aeetes, the Golden Fleece of the ram that Phrixus had consecrated to Mars. Jason called together the leaders of Greece and then set out for Colchis.

13 Juno On the banks of the Evenus River, Juno turned herself into an old woman and stood there in order to test the minds of men, to see if they would transport her across the river. No one was willing to do so except Jason, the son of Aeson and Alcimede, who carried her across. She, angry because Pelias had omitted her in his sacrifices, caused Jason to leave behind a sandal in the mud.

14 The Assembly of the Argonauts [1] Jason, the son of Aeson and Alcimede daughter of Clymene,* leader of the Thessalians.

Orpheus, the son of Oeagrus and the Muse Calliope, a Thracian from the city of Flevia, which is located on Mount Olympus on the river Enipeus. He was a prophet and a *cithara* player.

Asterion, the son of Pyremus and Antigone daughter of Pheres, from the city of Pellene. Some say that he was the son of Hyperasius and hailed from the city of Piresia, located at the foot of Mount Phylleus in Thessaly, where the confluence of two separate flowing rivers, the Apidanus and Enipeus, occurs.

[2] Polyphemus, the son of Elatus and Hippea daughter of Antippus, a Thessalian from the city of Larissa. He was slow in the feet.

Iphiclus, the son of Phylacus and Clymene daughter of Minyas, from Thessaly. He was Jason's maternal uncle.

Admetus, the son of Pheres and Periclymene daughter of Minyas, from Thessaly, specifically Mount Chalcodonius, from which the town and river get their names. They say that Apollo shepherded his flock.

[3] Eurytus and Echion, the sons of Mercury and Antianira daughter of Menetus, from the city of Alope, which is now called Ephesus. Certain authors believe they were Thessalians.

Aethalides, the son of Mercury and Eupolemia daughter of Myrmidon. He was from Larissa.

Coronus son of Caeneus, from the city of Gyrtone, which is in Thessaly. [4] This Caeneus, the son of Elatus, a Magnesian, proved that the Centaurs could in no way wound him with iron, but he was driven into the mud with tree trunks.* Some say Caeneus had been a woman who because she slept with Neptune was granted a wish, and she chose to be turned into a young man who could not be killed by any blow. But this never happened: it is not possible that any mortal could be impervious to being killed by iron or change from a woman to a man.

[5] Mopsus, the son of Ampycus and Chloris. He learned the art of augury from Apollo. He hailed from Oechalia or, as some believe, from the region of the Titaresius.

Eurydamas, the son of Irus and Demonassa. Others say he was son of Ctimenus, who lived in the city of Dolopeis next to Lake Xynius.

Theseus, the son of Aegeus and Aethra daughter of Pittheus, from Troezen. Others say he was from Athens.

[6] Pirithous, the son of Ixion (and so the Centaurs' brother), from Thessaly.

Menoetius, the son of Actor, from Opus.

Eribotes, the son of Teleon, from Eleon.

[7] Eurytion, the son of Irus and Demonassa, from Iton.*

<Canthus, the son of Canethus> from the town of Cerinthus.*

Oileus, the son of Hodoedocus and Agrianome daughter of Perseon, from the city of Narycea.

[8] Clytius and Iphitus, the sons of Eurytus and Antiope daughter of Pylon. They were kings of Oechalia, but others say they came from Euboea. This Eurytus, after learning archery from Apollo, is said to have competed against the bestower of the gift. His son Clytius was killed by Aeetes.

Peleus and Telamon, the sons of Aeacus and Endeis daughter of Chiron, from the island of Aegina. Because they killed their brother Phocus, they left their old home and sought new ones in different places, Peleus in Phthia, Telamon in Salamis, which Apollonius Rhodius calls Atthis.

[9] Butes, the son of Teleon and Zeuxippe daughter of the Eridanus River, from Athens.

Phalerus, the son of Alcon, from Athens.

Tiphys, the son of Phorbas and Hyrmine, from Boeotia. He was helmsman of the ship *Argo*.

[10] Argus, the son of Polybus and Argia. Others say that he was Danaus' son. He was from Argos and wore a bull's hide with black hair on it. He was the builder of the *Argo*.

Phliasus, the son of Father Liber and Ariadne daughter of Minos, from the city of Phlius, which is located in the Peloponnesus. Others say he was from Thebes.

Hercules, the son of Jupiter and Alcmena daughter of Electryon, from Thebes.

[11] Hylas, the son of Theodamas and the Nymph Menodice daughter of Orion. He was a teenager from Oechalia (others say that he was from Argos). He was Hercules' companion.

Nauplius, the son of Neptune and Amymone daughter of Danaus, from Argos.

Idmon, the son of Apollo and Nymph Cyrene, from Argos. Certain authors say he was Abas' son. He was skilled in augury, and although he learned from prophetic birds that he was fated to die, he did not abandon the fateful campaign.

[12] Castor and Pollux, the sons of Jupiter and Leda daughter of Thestius, from Lacedaemon, although some say they were from Sparta. Neither yet wore a beard. It is written[6] that at the same time the stars on their heads fell < . . . >.*

Lynceus and Idas, the sons of Aphareus and Arena daughter of Oebalus, from Messenia in the Peloponnesus. Of these Lynceus is said to have seen everything hidden beneath the earth and no darkness obstructed his sight. [13] Others say that he was the first to see at night by using a lamp.* The reason why this same Lynceus is said to be able to see underground is because he understood gold-mining; when he kept going down and suddenly showing up with gold, the rumor developed that he could see beneath the earth. Idas was relentless and fierce.

[14] Periclymenus, the son of Neleus and Chloris (the daughter of Amphion and Niobe), from Pylos.

Amphidamas and Cepheus, the sons of Aleus and Cleobule, from Arcadia.

Ancaeus, the son (others say grandson) of Lycurgus, from Tegea.

[15] Augeas, the son of the Sun and Nausidame, daughter of Amphidamas, from Elis.

Asterion and Amphion, the sons of Hyperasius (others say Hippasus), from Pellene.

Euphemus, the son of Neptune and Europe daughter of Tityus, from Taenarum. They say that he ran on the top of water without getting his feet wet.

[16] A second Ancaeus, the son of Neptune and Althaea daughter of Thestius, from the island of Imbrasos, which was called Parthenia but is now called Samos.

Erginus, the son of Neptune, from Miletus. Some say that he was Periclymenus' son and hailed from Orchomenus.

Meleager, the son of Oeneus and Althaea daughter of Thestius, from Calydon. Some believe that he was Mars' son.

[17] Laocoon, the son of Porthaon and brother of Oeneus, from Calydon.

A second Iphiclus, the son of Thestius and Leucippe. He was Althaea's brother by the same mother. He came from Calydon,* a swift runner and a spear thrower.*

Iphitus, the son of Naubolus, from Phocis. Others say that he was son of Hippasus and from the Peloponnesus.

[18] Zetes and Calais, the sons of the wind Aquilo and Orithyia daughter of Erechtheus. It is said that they had feathers on their head and feet, had dark blue hair, and flew through the air. They drove the three birds called the Harpies, the daughters of Thaumas and Ozomene (named Aellopous, Celaeno, and Ocypete), away from Phineus son of Agenor at the same time that Jason's crew was heading for Colchis. These birds used to live on the Strophades Islands in the Aegean Sea, which are called the Plotae. It is said that they had young women's heads,* feathers, both wings and human arms, large talons, and chicken's feet, but women's chests

6. This sentence has nothing to do with the voyage of the Argonauts, and we believe that someone later incorporated it into the text. It is in fact a mutilated remnant of a passage in Cicero's *De Divinatione* about an omen involving ornamental golden stars falling off the statues of the two heroes in Delphi. See next endnote.

and bellies.* Zetes and Calais were killed by Hercules' weapons, and the stones put on top of their tombs move under the force of their father's wind-gusts. It is said that they hailed from Thrace.

[19] Phocus and Priasus, the sons of Caeneus, from Magnesia.

Eurymedon, the son of Father Liber and Ariadne daughter of Minos, from Phlius.

Palaemonius, the son of Lernus, from Calydon.

[20] Actor, the son of Hippasus, from the Peloponnesus.

Thersanor,* the son of the Sun and Leucothoe, from Andros.

Hippalcimos, the son of Pelops and Hippodamia daughter of Oenomaus, from Pisa on the Peloponnesus.

[21] Asclepius, the son of Apollo and Coronis, from Tricca.

<Amphiaraus the son of Oecles and Hypermestra>* daughter of Thestius, from Argos.

Neleus, the son of Hippocoon, from Pylos.

[22] Iolaus, the son of Iphiclus, from Argos.

Deucalion, the son of Minos and Pasiphae daughter of the Sun, from Crete.

Philoctetes, the son of Poeas, from Meliboea.

[23] A second Caeneus, the son of Coronus, from Gortyn.

Acastus, the son of Pelias and Anaxibia daughter of Bias, from Iolcus. He wore a two-layered cloak. He joined the Argonauts voluntarily and on his own accord accompanied Jason.

[24] All these were named the Minyans, either because the daughters of Minyas bore a great many of them, or else because Jason's mother was the daughter of Clymene daughter of Minyas. But not all of them made it to Colchis or returned home to their country. [25] Hylas, for instance, was abducted by some Nymphs in Moesia next to Cios and the river Ascanius. In the course of their search for him, Hercules and Polyphemus were left behind when the wind drove the ship from its mooring. Polyphemus in turn was left behind by Hercules. He founded a city in Moesia and died among the Chalybes. [26] Tiphys succumbed to disease among the Mariandyni in the Propontis while staying with King Lycus; in his stead Ancaeus son of Neptune steered the ship to Colchis. Idmon son of Apollo also died while staying with King Lycus. He was gored by a boar after he had gone outside the walls.* Idas son of Aphareus avenged his death by killing the boar. [27] Butes son of Teleon, despite Orpheus' best attempts to divert him by singing and *cithara*-playing, was overcome by the sweetness of the Sirens' song and dove into the sea in an attempt to swim to them. Venus saved him and brought him to shore at Lilybaeum. [28] These are the ones who did not make it to Colchis.

On the return voyage Eribotes* son of Teleon and Canthus son of Canethus* perished. They were killed in Libya by the shepherd Cephalion (Nasamon's brother), the son of the Nymph Tritonis and Amphithemis, whose flock they were plundering like enemies.* [29] Mopsus son of Ampycus also died in Africa from a serpent's bite. He had joined the Argonauts when they were en route after his father, Ampycus, had been killed.* [30] Also joining the Argonauts on the island of Dia were the sons of Phrixus and Chalciope (Medea's sister): Argus, Melas, Phrontides, and

Cylindrus. Others say that they were named Phronius, <*three names lost.*> <Also joining the Argonauts were the sons of Deimachus,> Demoleon, Autolycus, and Phlogius, whom Hercules had summoned to be his companions in his quest for the Belt of the Amazons and subsequently left after they had gotten lost. <Also joining the Argonauts was> Dascylus, the son of Lycus king of the Mariandyni.

[31] When the crew was setting out for Colchis, they wanted to make Hercules their leader. He refused, suggesting instead that Jason be given command since he was the reason they were all setting out. So Jason took command as their leader. [32] The ship-builder was Argus son of Danaus, and the steersman was Tiphys, after whose death Ancaeus son of Neptune steered the ship. Lynceus son of Aphareus stood lookout from the prow since he could see far into the distance. The rowing foremen amidships were Zetes and Calais, the sons of Aquilo, who had feathers on their heads and feet. At the oars near the prow sat Peleus and Telamon; on the middle bench sat Hercules and Idas. The others manned their assigned seats at the oars. Orpheus son of Oeagrus kept time for the rowers. After Hercules was left behind by the Argonauts, Peleus son of Aeacus sat in his place.

[33] This is the ship *Argo* that Minerva elevated into the circle of constellations because she herself had built it. This ship has just been launched onto the sea, appearing in the stars from the rudder to the sail.[7] Its form and appearance Cicero describes in the *Phaenomena* with the following verses:

> At the tail of the Dog-Star the *Argo* glides on,
> sailing with its stern, marked by a luminous star, in front,
> unlike other ships, which are wont to lead with their prows
> on the sea, plowing Neptune's fields with their beaks.
> As when a ship has just reached safe harbor:
> the sailors turn it with its heavy load
> and draw it stern first to the hoped-for shore.
> Just so does the old *Argo* slide backward in heaven.
> From there the rudder stretching from the flying ship
> touches the back feet of the bright Dog.[8]

This ship has four stars on the stern, on the right rudder five, four on the left, all of similar magnitude. Thirteen in all.

15 The Women of Lemnos The women on the island of Lemnos had not made a sacrifice to Venus for some years, and she in her anger made their husbands scorn them and take Thracian women as new wives. The Lemnian women, also goaded on by Venus, conspired and killed every last male on the island. Only Hypsipyle did not take part and secretly put her father, Thoas, on a ship; he was driven by a storm to the Taurian peninsula.

7. As the poem below suggests, the constellation Argo is envisioned as moving in reverse through the heavens, and only the back half of the ship is represented in the constellation.

8. The constellation Canis.

Meanwhile the Argonauts were sailing along and eventually came to Lemnos. The gatekeeper, Iphinoe, saw them and announced their arrival to Queen Hypsipyle. Her aged adviser, Polyxo, recommended that she bind them to their hearth and home. Hypsipyle and Jason had sons, Euneus and Deipylus. There they dallied at some length until Hercules berated them and they left.

As for the Lemnian women, after they learned that Hypsipyle had saved her father, they tried to kill her, but she fled. She was picked up by pirates and taken to Thebes, where she was sold into the service of King Lycurgus.* All the Lemnian women who became pregnant by an Argonaut named their children after the father.

16 Cyzicus Cyzicus, the son of Eusorus, was the king of an island in the Propontis who welcomed the Argonauts with generous hospitality. When they left him and had sailed over the course of one whole day, a storm arose during the night and brought them unawares back to the same island. Thinking that these men were Pelasgians, his people's enemy, Cyzicus engaged them in a night battle on the shore and was killed by Jason. On the next day, when Jason went to the beach and saw that he had killed the king, he laid him to rest and passed Cyzicus' kingdom on to his children.

17 Amycus Amycus was the son of Neptune and Melia and was the king of Bebrycia. He compelled all who came to his kingdom to don boxing gloves and fight him, and he defeated and killed them all. But when he challenged the Argonauts to a boxing match, Pollux fought and killed him.

18 Lycus Lycus, the king of an island in the Propontis, warmly welcomed and honored the Argonauts because they killed Amycus, who had often given Lycus trouble. While the Argonauts were staying at Lycus' palace, they left the walls,* and Idmon son of Apollo was gored and killed by a boar. Tiphys son of Phorbas died because he stood over his grave for an excessive amount of time. Then the Argonauts put Ancaeus son of Neptune in charge of steering the ship *Argo.*

19 Phineus Phineus, the Thracian son of Agenor, had two sons by Cleopatra. They were blinded by their father as a result of their stepmother's accusation.[9] Apollo, the story goes, gave to this Phineus the power of augury. But when he made known the gods' plans, Jupiter blinded him and set upon him the Harpies, which are said to be Jupiter's hounds, to snatch away the food from his mouth.

When the Argonauts landed there and asked him to show them the way to Colchis, he said that he would show them if they freed him from his punishment. Then Zetes and Calais, who, they say, had feathers on their heads and feet (they were the sons of the wind Aquilo and Orithyia), drove the Harpies to the Strophades Islands and freed Phineus from his punishment. So he told them how to pass through the Symplegades: they should send a dove through first, and after these rocks had crashed together, they <should send the ship>* in the space between the rocks

9. For the details of the accusation see Apollodorus 3.200.

<when> they were recoiling. Thus the Argonauts passed through the Symplegades thanks to Phineus' kind assistance.

20 Stymphalian Birds The Argonauts came to the island of Dia and were pelted by birds that used their feathers as arrows. Since they could not withstand the multitude of birds, on the advice of Phineus they took up their shields and spears and, in the style of the Curetes, drove them away with the noise.

21 Phrixus' Sons The Argonauts passed through the Cyanean Rocks (which are also called the Symplegadean Rocks), entered the sea called the Euxine, and got lost. By the will of Juno they landed on the island of Dia. There they discovered the sons of Phrixus and Chalciope (Argus, Phrontis, Melas, and Cylindrus), who were shipwrecked, naked, and helpless.

When Phrixus' sons explained their misfortune, how they were hastening to reach their grandfather, Athamas, but were shipwrecked and washed up there, Jason took them aboard and gave them aid. They guided Jason to Colchis along the Thermodon River, and when they were just about to reach Colchis, they told him to put the ship into a hiding place. They went to their mother, Chalciope, Medea's sister, and told her about Jason's good deed toward them and why he had come.

Then Chalciope told them about Medea, and she and her sons brought her to Jason. When Medea saw Jason, she realized that he was the one she had fallen in love with in a dream sent by Juno, and she promised him everything. They led him to a temple.

22 Aeetes It was foretold to Aeetes son of the Sun that he would hold power so long as the Fleece that Phrixus had dedicated in the sanctuary of Mars remained there. And so Aeetes issued the following challenge to Jason: if he wanted to take away the Golden Fleece, he would have to harness to an adamantine yoke the bronze-footed bulls that breathed fire from their snouts, plow the land, take dragon's teeth from a helmet, and sow them. Immediately, a race of armed men would sprout from these and kill each other.[10]

Juno, however, always wanted to protect Jason for the following reason. When she came to a river, wanting to test men's minds, she took the form of an old woman and asked to be carried across. Though everyone else who crossed just ignored her, Jason carried her across the river. She knew Jason could not complete the tasks enjoined on him without Medea's advice, so because of Jason's good deed she asked Venus to inspire in Medea love for Jason. Goaded on by Venus, Medea fell in love with Jason, and by her help he was delivered from every danger. For after he had plowed the land with the bulls and the armed men were born, he, following Medea's suggestion, threw a rock into the middle of them. They fought among themselves and killed each other. After she put the serpent to sleep with her drugs, Jason took the Fleece from the sanctuary and set out with Medea for home.

10. This last detail was not originally part of Aeetes' plan, but because this is what actually happens, Hyginus incorporates it into Aeetes' speech.

23 Absyrtus When Aeetes learned that Medea had fled with Jason, he ordered a ship to be readied and sent his son Absyrtus with some armed guards to pursue her. He chased after her all the way to Histria in the Adriatic Sea, to the court of King Alcinous. They were about to resort to fighting when Alcinous interposed himself between them to prevent the fight from breaking out. They then made him the judge of their dispute, but he put off making his decision until the following day.

Since Alcinous looked really depressed, his wife, Arete, asked him the reason why. He told her that two separate peoples, the Colchians and the Argives, had made him the judge in their dispute. When Arete asked him what decision he would render, Alcinous responded that if Medea was a virgin, he would return her to her father; if, however, she was a woman, he would give her to her husband. When Arete heard her husband's response, she sent a message to Jason, and that night he deflowered Medea in a cave.

The next day the Colchians and Argives came for Alcinous' decision. When it was discovered that Medea was a woman, she was handed over to her husband. When they had set out, however, Absyrtus, afraid of not fulfilling his father's orders, pursued them to the island of Minerva. There he came upon Jason as he was making a sacrifice to Minerva and was killed by him. Medea buried his body, and they left the island. The Colchians who had come with Absyrtus remained there out of fear of Aeetes and founded a city, which they called Absoris after Absyrtus. This island is situated in Histria facing Pola and is joined to the island of Canta.

24 Jason and the Daughters of Pelias Because he had been forced by Pelias, his father's brother, to undergo so many dangers, Jason began to consider how he might kill his uncle without drawing suspicion. Medea promised to do it. And so, when they were not far from Iolcus,* she ordered the ship to be concealed and went herself to Pelias' daughters after assuming the identity of a priestess of Diana. She promised them that she would make their old father, Pelias, young again, but the eldest daughter, Alcestis, said that it was impossible. In order to bend them more easily to her will, Medea cast a haze over their minds and with her magic produced many miracles that seemed to be real. She put an aged ram into a bronze cauldron, and they saw a beautiful young lamb spring out of it. In this fashion Pelias' daughters (Alcestis, Pelopia, Medusa, Pisidice, and Hippothoe) at Medea's insistence killed their father and cooked him in a bronze cauldron. When they realized that they had been tricked, they fled from their land. Jason, when he received the signal from Medea, took control of the palace and handed over his father's kingdom to Acastus son of Pelias (and so the brother of the Peliades) because he had gone to Colchis with him. Jason set out with Medea for Corinth.

25 Medea Medea (Aeetes and Idyia's daughter) and Jason had two sons, Mermerus and Pheres, and they lived in perfect harmony. But Jason was the object of constant ridicule; for although he was such a brave, handsome, and noble man, he had taken a foreign wife, and a witch at that. Creon, the son of Menoeceus and king of Corinth,[11] gave his youngest daughter, Glauce, to him to be his wife. When Medea saw that she, though she had done Jason a good turn, had been slapped with such an insult, she made a poisoned golden crown and ordered her sons to give it to their stepmother as a gift. Creusa accepted the gift and was consumed by fire along with Jason and Creon.[12] When Medea saw the palace in flames, she killed Mermerus and Pheres, her sons by Jason, and escaped from Corinth.

26 Medea in Exile Exiled from Corinth, Medea came to Aegeus son of Pandion in Athens. He brought her into his house, married her, and had by her a son, Medus. Later, the priestess of Diana denounced Medea and told the king that she could not conduct ritually pure sacrifices because there was a woman in the state who was a witch and a criminal. She was then banished for a second time.

Medea, however, yoked her dragons and returned from Athens to Colchis. On her way she came to Absoris, where her brother Absyrtus was buried. There the citizens of Absoris were being overwhelmed by a swarm of serpents. At their request Medea collected the snakes and threw them into her brother's grave. These still remain there to this day; any that leaves the grave pays its debt to nature.

27 Medus It was prophesied to Perses, Aeetes' brother (and son of the Sun), to beware of death at the hands of one of Aeetes' descendants. Medus, while he was searching for his mother, was driven by a storm to Colchis, King Perses' land. His guards arrested him and took him to the king. When Medus, the son of Aegeus and Medea, saw that he had fallen into the hands of the enemy, he lied and said that he was Hippotes, Creon's son. The king interrogated him carefully and ordered that he be thrown into prison.

The area, they say, was experiencing a crop failure and a shortage of grain. When Medea arrived in a chariot hitched to dragons, she concealed her identity, telling the king that she was Diana's priestess and could end the famine with expiatory rites. She heard from the king that Hippotes, Creon's son, was being held in prison. She thought that he was there to avenge the wrong done to his father, and so she unintentionally betrayed her own son's identity by convincing the king that his captive was not Hippotes, but in fact Aegeus' son, Medus, who had been sent by his mother to kill him. She asked him to hand the captive over so that she could kill him, all the while believing that he really was Hippotes.

So when Medus was led forth to be put to death as punishment for his falsehood, and when Medea saw that the situation was not as she thought, she asked to speak privately with him. She handed him a sword and ordered him to avenge the wrong done to his grandfather. After he heard this, Medus killed Perses and took possession of his grandfather's kingdom. He named the country Media after himself.

11. The king of Corinth is Creon, but not Creon son of Menoeceus, who is a member of the royal family of Thebes.

12. In the usual account Jason is not killed by Medea.

28 Otos and Ephialtes Otos and Ephialtes, the sons of Aloeus and Iphimede (Neptune's daughter), are said to have been extraordinarily huge. Each of them grew by nine inches every month. When they were nine years old, they tried to ascend into heaven. They made their approach like this: they placed Ossa on top of Pelion (this is the reason Mount Ossa is also called Pelion) and then heaped still other mountains on top of that. They met with Apollo and were killed by him.

Other authors, however, say that they were invulnerable sons of Neptune and Iphimede. They wanted to ravish Diana, and when she was unable to resist their brute strength, Apollo sent a deer between them. They burned with a desire to kill it with their spears, and during their attempt they ended up killing each other instead. They are said to suffer the following punishment among the dead. They are bound, facing away from each other, to a pillar by snakes; there is an owl between them, sitting on the pillar to which they have been bound.

29 Alcmena When Amphitryon was away fighting in the siege of Oechalia, Alcmena welcomed Jupiter into her chamber in the belief that he was her husband. He came in and reported what he had done in Oechalia, and so she believed that he was her husband and slept with him. And so happy was he to sleep with her that he took away one day and joined together two nights; Alcmena was amazed to find the night so long. When later it was announced to her that her victorious husband was home, she did not particularly care because she thought she had already seen him. When Amphitryon entered the palace and saw that she was rather blasé about the whole thing, he was shocked and complained that she had not greeted him on his arrival home. Alcmena answered him, "You came home a long time ago, slept with me, and told me all about your deeds in Oechalia."

Based on what she said, Amphitryon realized that some heavenly power had taken his place and from that day forward did not sleep with her. She gave birth to Hercules, the child she had conceived with Jupiter.

30 The Twelve Labors Imposed on Hercules by Eurystheus [1] When Hercules was an infant, he strangled the two snakes sent by Juno, one in each hand, and from this act it was realized that Hercules was the firstborn.[13]

[2] He killed the invulnerable Nemean Lion, which the Moon raised in a cave with two openings, and he used its skin as a protective covering.

[3] He killed the nine-headed Lernaean Hydra, Typhon's daughter, at the Spring of Lerna. This beast had such powerful venom that she killed men just by breathing, and if someone happened to pass by her while she was sleeping, she would breathe on his feet and he would die an excruciating death. Under Minerva's guidance, Hercules killed the Hydra, gutted her, and dipped his arrows in the venom. And so whatever he shot with his arrows thereafter did not escape death. This would also be the cause of his own death in Phrygia later on.

[4] He killed the Erymanthian Boar.

13. This first episode is not part of his twelve labors.

[5] In Arcadia he captured alive the wild stag with golden horns and led it before King Eurystheus.

[6] On the Island of Mars[14] he shot and killed the Stymphalian Birds, which fired off their own feathers as arrows.

[7] In a single day he cleaned out all of King Augeas' cow dung, the greater part with the help of Jupiter. He washed out all of the dung by diverting a river into the barn.

[8] He brought back alive the bull with which Pasiphae slept from the island of Crete to Mycenae.

[9] Along with his servant Abderus he killed Diomedes, the king of Thrace, and his four horses that fed on human flesh. The names of the horses were Podargus, Lampon, Xanthus, and Dinus.

[10] He killed the Amazon Hippolyte, the daughter of Mars and Queen Otrera. He stripped the belt of the Amazon queen off of her; then he gave his prisoner, Antiope, to Theseus.

[11] He killed three-bodied Geryon, the son of Chrysaor, with a single spear.

[12] He killed the monstrous serpent (Typhon's offspring) whose task it was to guard the golden apples of the Hesperides at Mount Atlas, and he brought the apples to King Eurystheus.

[13] He brought the dog Cerberus (also born of Typhon) back from the underworld and brought it to the king.

31 Hercules' Side-Labors [1] In Libya he killed Antaeus son of Earth, who compelled all visitors to wrestle with him, wore them down, and killed them. Hercules wrestled him and killed him.

[2] In Egypt he killed Busiris, who regularly sacrificed foreigners. When Hercules heard Busiris' decree, he allowed himself to be led to the altar dressed in the sacrificial headdress. But when Busiris was about to invoke the gods, Hercules killed both him and his sacrificial attendants with his club.

[3] He overcame Mars' son Cygnus in battle and killed him. When Mars arrived and tried to engage him in a battle over his son, Jupiter sent a thunderbolt between the two and so separated them.

[4] At Troy he killed the sea monster that was about to devour Hesione. He shot dead Hesione's father, Laomedon, with arrows because he refused to hand her over as agreed.

[5] He also shot dead the insatiable eagle that devoured Prometheus' heart.

[6] He killed Lycus son of Neptune because he tried to kill Hercules' wife, Megara daughter of Creon, and his sons, Therimachus and Ophites.

[7] The river Achelous could change himself into any form he wanted, and when he and Hercules were fighting over the right to marry Deianira, he turned himself into a bull. Hercules broke off one of his horns and gave it to the Hesperides (or

14. Hyginus conflates the stories of Hercules' labor in Arcadia and the Argonauts' encounter with the same birds on the Island of Mars (see *Fab.* 20, where the island is called Dia).

Nymphs); these goddesses filled the horn with fruit and called it the Cornucopia {"Horn of Plenty"}.

[8] He killed Neleus son of Hippocoon and ten of his children because he was not willing to cleanse or purify him after he killed his wife, Megara daughter of Creon, and his sons, Therimachus and Ophites.

[9] He killed Eurytus because he wanted to marry his daughter Iole and was rejected by him.

[10] He killed the Centaur Nessus because he tried to rape Deianira.

[11] He killed the Centaur Eurytion because he wanted to marry Deianira, Dexamenus' daughter, who was his fiancée.

32 Megara When Hercules was sent by King Eurystheus to fetch the three-headed dog, Lycus son of Neptune was under the impression that he had died in the attempt. He was getting ready to kill Hercules' wife, Megara daughter of Creon, and his sons, Therimachus and Ophites, and take control of the throne. Hercules arrived on the scene and killed Lycus. Later, Juno threw Hercules into a fit of madness and caused him to kill Megara and his sons, Therimachus and Ophites.

When he came to his senses, he sought an oracle from Apollo about how he could cleanse himself of his crime. Apollo did not wish to give him an oracle, so Hercules grew angry and stole Apollo's tripod from the temple. Jupiter ordered him to return it and told Apollo to deliver a response even though he did not wish to do so. In accordance with the response Hercules was handed over by Mercury to be Queen Omphale's slave.

33 Centaurs When Hercules came and was warmly received by King Dexamenus, he deflowered his daughter Deianira and promised he would take her as his wife. After he left, the Centaur Eurytion, the son of Ixion and Nubis, asked for Deianira's hand in marriage. Her father was afraid that the Centaur would resort to violence and so promised that he would give her to him. On the appointed day the Centaur showed up at the wedding with his brothers. Hercules intervened, killed the Centaur, and led away his fiancée. Likewise, at another wedding, when Pirithous was marrying Hippodamia daughter of Adrastus, drunken Centaurs tried to abduct the wives of the Lapiths. The Centaurs killed many Lapiths, and many Centaurs were killed by the Lapiths.

34 Nessus Deianira asked the Centaur Nessus, the son of Ixion and Nubis, to carry her across the Evenus River. He picked her up and in the middle of the river tried to rape her. When Hercules arrived on the scene and heard Deianira's pleas for help, he riddled Nessus full of arrows. As he lay dying, he collected his own blood and gave it to Deianira (he knew how potent the poison on the arrows dipped in the Lernaean Hydra's venom was), and he said it was a love potion. He directed her, should she ever want to prevent her husband from rejecting her, to smear his garment with it. Deianira believed him, and so she hid it and carefully guarded it.

35 Iole When Hercules sought the hand of Eurytus' daughter, Iole, in marriage and was rejected by him, he sacked Oechalia. In order to make Iole beg for him, Hercules threatened to kill her parents right there in front of her. But she with abiding resolve allowed her parents to be killed before her very eyes. After he killed them all, Hercules took Iole captive and sent her back to Deianira ahead of him.

36 Deianira When Hercules' wife, Deianira daughter of Oeneus, saw that the virgin Iole, a girl of extraordinary beauty, had been brought into her house as a captive, she was afraid that the girl might ruin her marriage. So, remembering Nessus' instructions, she sent one of her servants, Lichas, to bring Hercules a garment smeared with the Centaur's blood. A little later, the drops that had fallen onto the ground were hit by sunlight and burst into flames. When Deianira saw this and realized that it was not as Nessus had said, she sent the same man who had given the garment to get it back, but Hercules had already put it on and immediately burst into flames. He threw himself into a river in an attempt to extinguish the flames, but they only grew stronger. When he tried to take the garment off, the flesh came off along with it. Then Hercules sent Lichas—the one who had brought him the garment—flying like a wheel into the sea. On the very spot he landed a rock arose that bears the name Lichas. Then, the story goes, Philoctetes son of Poeas built a pyre on Mount Oeta for Hercules, who then ascended to immortality. In return for this favor Hercules gave Philoctetes his bow and arrows. As for Deianira, she committed suicide because of what she had done to Hercules.

37 Aethra Neptune and Aegeus son of Pandion both slept with Aethra, Pittheus' daughter, in the temple of Minerva on the same night. Neptune allowed Aegeus to raise the child she would have. When Aegeus was setting out from Troezen to return to Athens, he placed his sword under a stone and instructed Aethra to send his son after him when he was able to lift up the stone and take his father's sword; that would prove his son's identity. When Aethra gave birth to Theseus and he grew into a man, she revealed Aegeus' instructions, showed him the stone so that he could take the sword, and ordered him to go to Aegeus in Athens. He did so and killed all who plagued travelers along the road.

38 The Labors of Theseus [1] He killed Corynetes son of Neptune in armed conflict.

[2] He also killed Pityocamptes, who compelled all passing travelers to help him bend a pine tree to the ground, and when the traveler helped him pull down the tree, Pityocamptes would send the tree flying with his great strength. Thus his victim would crash heavily onto the ground and die.

[3] He killed Procrustes son of Neptune. Whenever someone came to him as a guest, if his visitor were tall, he would offer him a bed too short for him and then lop off whatever part of the body hung over the ends. If his visitor were of small stature, he offered a bed too long for him, placed him on some anvils, and pounded him out until he equaled the length of the bed.

[4] Sciron used to sit on a certain steep point along the sea and compel passersby to wash his feet. In this way he would send them over the cliff into the sea. Theseus hurled him into the sea to his death in the same way, and this is why the rocks there are called Sciron's Rocks.

[5] He killed Cercyon son of Vulcan in armed conflict.

[6] He slew the boar from Cremyon.

[7] He killed the bull in Marathon, the same one Hercules had brought back from Crete to Eurystheus.

[8] He killed the Minotaur in the city of Cnossus.

39 Daedalus Eupalamus' son Daedalus, who, they say, received his skills as a craftsman from Minerva, hurled from the roof of his house his sister's son Perdix out of jealously over his talent because Perdix invented the saw. For this crime he went into exile from Athens to King Minos in Crete.

40 Pasiphae Pasiphae, Minos' wife and the daughter of the Sun, did not perform any sacrifices to the goddess Venus for many years. Because of this, Venus inspired in her heart an unspeakable desire, that she would love a bull.* When Daedalus the exile arrived, she asked him for help. He built for her a wooden cow and covered it with the hide of a real cow. Pasiphae got inside this, slept with the bull, and from this intercourse gave birth to the Minotaur, who had a bull's head but a human body beneath. Then Daedalus built for the Minotaur a labyrinth from which exit was impossible, and he was enclosed in it.

When Minos found out about the whole affair, he cast Daedalus into prison, but Pasiphae freed him from his shackles. He made wings for himself and his son Icarus, put them on, and flew away. Icarus flew too high, and so the wax melted because of the sun's heat, and he plummeted into the sea named Icarian after him. Daedalus flew all the way to King Cocalus on the island of Sicily. Others say that when Theseus killed the Minotaur, he took Daedalus back to his homeland, Athens.

41 Minos Minos, the son of Jupiter and Europa, waged war against the Athenians because his son Androgeus was killed in a fight. After he conquered them, the Athenians fell under his control and were subject to a yearly tax. He ordered them to send seven of their sons for the Minotaur to feast upon every year. When Theseus arrived from Troezen and heard how great a disaster the city was experiencing, he volunteered to be sent to the Minotaur. His father gave him instructions when seeing him off: if he returned victorious, he was to put white sails on the ship since the people sent to the Minotaur sailed on a ship with black sails.

42 Theseus and the Minotaur When Theseus arrived in Crete, Minos' daughter Ariadne fell so hard for him that she betrayed her brother and saved the stranger by showing Theseus the way out of the labyrinth. After Theseus went in and killed the Minotaur, he followed Ariadne's advice and found his way out by rewinding the thread. He carried her away, intending to take her as his wife as he had earlier promised.

43 Ariadne While Theseus was held up on the island of Dia by a storm, he got to thinking that if he brought Ariadne home it would be a disgrace. So he abandoned her on the island while she was asleep. She became the object of Liber's desire, and he took her away and married her. As for Theseus, he forgot to change the black sails when sailing, so his father, Aegeus, assuming that Theseus had been killed by the Minotaur, threw himself off a cliff into the sea named the Aegean after him. Theseus took Ariadne's sister, Phaedra, as his wife.

44 Cocalus Because many of Daedalus' engineering achievements had turned out to be harmful to Minos, he pursued him all the way to Sicily and demanded that King Cocalus hand Daedalus over to him. Cocalus promised he would; when Daedalus found out, he sought help from the king's own daughters. They killed Minos.

45 Philomela Tereus son of Mars was a Thracian and was married to Procne daughter of Pandion. He went to his father-in-law, Pandion, in Athens and asked him to give his other daughter, Philomela, to him in marriage, claiming that Procne had passed away. Pandion pitied him and sent Philomela and some guards along with her. But Tereus threw the guards overboard and raped the unwilling* Philomela on a mountainside.

After he returned to Thrace, he handed Philomela over to King Lynceus. His wife, Lathusa, immediately took her rival to Procne, because she was Procne's friend. When she recognized her sister and realized Tereus' terrible crime, the two of them began to plot how they might repay the king in kind.

Meanwhile, Tereus was receiving ominous signs foretelling that his son Itys would meet his death at the hands of a relative. He thought that this meant his brother Dryas was plotting his son's death, and so he killed his brother Dryas though he was innocent. Procne, however, did kill her and Tereus' son Itys, served him to his father at a banquet, and fled with her sister. When Tereus realized this crime, he pursued the fugitives, but the gods took pity and turned Procne into a swallow and Philomela into a nightingale. They say that Tereus was turned into a hawk.

46 Erechtheus Erechtheus son of Pandion had four daughters who made a pact that if any one of them died, the rest would commit suicide. At the time, Eumolpus son of Neptune came to besiege Athens because he said that the land of Attica belonged to his father. Eumolpus and his army were defeated, and he was put to death by the Athenians. So that Erechtheus would not rejoice over his son's death, Neptune demanded that one of his daughters be sacrificed to him. And so, when his daughter Chthonia was sacrificed, the rest made good on their promise and committed suicide. As for Erechtheus himself, he was struck down by Jupiter's thunderbolt at Neptune's request.

47 Hippolytus Phaedra, the daughter of Minos and wife of Theseus, fell in love with her stepson Hippolytus. When she was unable to win him over to her desire, she wrote and sent a message to her husband that said that she had been raped by Hippolytus. She then committed suicide by hanging. When Theseus heard about the affair, he ordered his son to leave the city and prayed to his father, Neptune, for his son's death. So, when Hippolytus hitched up his horses and was driving his chariot out of town, a bull suddenly appeared out of the sea. Its bellowing spooked the horses, and they dragged him to his death.

48 The Kings of Athens Cecrops son of Earth. Cephalus son of Deion. Aegeus son of Pandion. Pandion son of Erichthonius. Theseus son of Aegeus. Erichthonius son of Vulcan. Erechtheus son of Pandion. Demophon son of Theseus.

49 Asclepius They say that Asclepius son of Apollo resurrected Glaucus son of Minos (some say that it was Hippolytus who was resurrected). Jupiter struck Asclepius down with a thunderbolt because of this. Apollo, because he could not harm Jupiter, instead killed the makers of his thunderbolts, that is, the Cyclopes. In return for what he had done, Apollo was forced to be the slave of King Admetus of Thessaly.

50 Admetus Many men sought to marry Alcestis daughter of Pelias, but after he had rejected a lot of them, he issued a challenge. He would reward the man who yoked wild animals to his chariot: this man could take any woman he wished. So Admetus asked Apollo for help, and because he had treated Apollo kindly when Apollo had been made his slave, Apollo gave him a wild boar and a lion already yoked to a chariot. With these Admetus carried Alcestis away to be his wife.

51 Alcestis Many suitors sought to marry Alcestis, the daughter of Pelias and Anaxibia daughter of Bias. Pelias, unwilling to choose, rejected their offers and issued a challenge: he would allow the man who yoked wild animals to his chariot to carry Alcestis away into wedlock. So Admetus asked Apollo for help, and Apollo, because Admetus had treated him kindly during his period of servitude, gave him a boar and a lion already yoked. With these Admetus carried Alcestis away.

Admetus also received the following gift from Apollo: someone else could voluntarily die in his place. When neither his father nor mother would die willingly in his place, his wife, Alcestis, offered herself up and died for him, substituting her death for his. Later, Hercules brought her back up from the underworld.

52 Aegina Jupiter wanted to ravish Aegina, Asopus' daughter, but was afraid of Juno, so he brought her to the island of Oenone* and got her pregnant. From this, Aeacus was born. When Juno found this out, she sent a serpent into the water there, which poisoned it. All who drank from it paid their debt to nature. Soon Aeacus lost most of his men. When he could no longer hold out because of how few men he had left, he begged Jupiter to give him men for protection while watching some ants. Jupiter turned the ants into men, and these are called Myrmidons because the Greek word for "ants" is *myrmices.* The island took the name Aegina.

53 Asteria Jupiter loved Asteria, Titan's daughter, but she scorned him. So he turned her into an *ortyx* bird (what we call a quail) and threw her into the sea, and from her an island arose called Ortygia. At one time the island used to wander over the sea. Later, Latona was brought here by the North Wind under orders from Jupiter (at the time Python was pursuing her) and there gave birth to Apollo and Diana while clutching an olive tree. This island was thereafter called Delos.

54 Thetis It was fated that a son born from the Nereid Thetis would be greater than his father. No one but Prometheus knew this. When Jupiter was about to sleep with her, Prometheus promised to advise him on the matter if he would free him from his bonds. Jupiter gave his word, and Prometheus warned him not to sleep with Thetis, else someone greater than him would be born and overthrow him just as he had Saturn. So Thetis was given in wedlock to Peleus, Aeacus' son, and Hercules was sent to kill the eagle that kept devouring Prometheus' heart. With the death of the eagle, Prometheus was freed from Mount Caucasus after thirty thousand years.

55 Tityus Because Latona had slept with Jupiter, Juno ordered Earth's enormous son Tityus to assault her. During his attempt to do so, however, Jupiter killed him with a thunderbolt. They say he now lies in the underworld stretched out over six acres and is beset by a serpent that eats out his liver, which grows back with the phases of the moon.

56 Busiris There was a crop failure in Egypt during the reign of King Busiris son of Neptune. Egypt was parched by a drought for nine years, and so Busiris summoned augurs from Greece. Thrasius, the son of Busiris' brother, Pygmalion, indicated to Busiris that rains would come if a foreigner were sacrificed, and he proved that he was right by being sacrificed himself.

57 Stheneboea When the exiled Bellerophon came to stay at King Proetus' palace, the king's wife, Stheneboea, fell in love with him. He refused to sleep with her, so she lied to her husband and made up the story that Bellerophon had propositioned her. When Proetus heard what was going on, he wrote a letter about it and sent Bellerophon to Stheneboea's father, King Iobates. When Iobates read the letter, he did not want to kill such a great man but rather sent him to his death against the Chimaera, who was said to breathe flames from her three mouths. Riding on the back of Pegasus, Bellerophon killed the Chimaera and, they say, fell onto the plain of Aleia and dislocated his hip bones. But King Proetus praised his valor and gave him his other daughter in marriage. When Stheneboea heard this, she committed suicide.

58 Smyrna Smyrna was the daughter of the Assyrian king, Cinyras, and his wife, Cenchreis. Her mother made arrogant boasts, claiming that her daughter was more beautiful than Venus. The goddess, in her desire to punish the mother, inflamed

Smyrna with an unspeakable desire: she made her lust after her own father. She was about to hang herself when the nurse came in and prevented her from going through with it. Through the nurse's agency Smyrna slept with her father, who was not aware of her identity, and conceived a child. Deathly ashamed that this might get out into the open, she went into the forest and hid there. Venus later took pity on her and changed her form into the tree from which myrrh flows. Adonis was born from this tree, the product of Venus' punishment of his mother.

59 Phyllis They say that Theseus' son Demophon came to Thrace and was hospitably received by Phyllis, who then fell in love with him. As he was setting out for home, he promised he would return to her. And when he did not come on the day he was supposed to, they say she ran nine times down to the shore that day. This place is now called Nine Trips in Greek. As for Phyllis, she died pining away for Demophon. When her parents erected a tomb for her, trees grew there that mourn Phyllis' death at a certain time each year when their leaves grow dry and fall off. The Greeks call leaves *phylla* after her.

60 Sisyphus and Salmoneus Sisyphus and Salmoneus, the sons of Aeolus, were bitter enemies. Sisyphus asked Apollo how he could kill his enemy (that is, his brother), and the oracle given was that the children he fathered by sleeping with his brother's daughter, Tyro, would take revenge on his brother. Sisyphus slept with her, and two sons were born. When their mother, Tyro, got wind of the oracle, she killed them. As for Sisyphus, when he learned < . . . >[15] who, because of his ungodly actions, now is said to roll a boulder up a mountain on his shoulders in the underworld only to have it roll back down past him when he reaches the top.

61 Salmoneus Salmoneus, Aeolus' son and Sisyphus' brother, tried to imitate the thunder and lightning of Jupiter by sitting in a chariot and throwing burning torches at the people and the citizens. Because of this he was struck down by Jupiter's thunderbolt.

62 Ixion Ixion son of Leonteus tried to ravish Juno. At Jupiter's behest, she substituted a cloud that to Ixion looked like Juno. Centaurs were born from this cloud. As for Ixion, Jupiter ordered Mercury to take him to the underworld and tie him to a wheel. That wheel, they say, still turns there to this day.

63 Danae Danae was the daughter of Acrisius and Aganippe. She was fated to give birth to a son who would kill Acrisius, who in fear for his life confined her within a stone prison. Jupiter, however, turned himself into golden rain and in this form slept with Danae. From this intercourse Perseus was born. Because of her fornication, her father closed her and Perseus up in a chest and cast it into the sea. By Jupiter's will it was carried to the island of Seriphos, and a fisherman named

15. From the surrounding context and parallel versions of the myth it is clear that Sisyphus took revenge on Tyro, Salmoneus, or both.

Dictys found the chest, opened it, and saw the woman with her child. He took both of them to King Polydectes, who took her as his wife and raised Perseus in Minerva's temple. When Acrisius learned that they were staying with Polydectes, he set out to reclaim them. When he arrived, Polydectes interceded on their behalf, and Perseus promised his grandfather, Acrisius, that he would never kill him.

Acrisius was held up on the island because of a storm, and in the meantime, Polydectes died. They held funeral games for him. When Perseus threw a discus, the wind carried it off course into Acrisius' head, killing him. Thus, what he did not want to do himself was brought to pass by the will of the gods. After the burial Perseus went to Argos and took possession of his ancestral throne.

64 Andromeda Cassiopia claimed that her daughter Andromeda was more beautiful than the Nereids. Because of this Neptune demanded that Andromeda daughter of Cepheus be offered up to a sea monster. When she had been set out for the monster, they say that Perseus swooped in on Mercury's sandals and freed her from the danger. Since he had every intention of leading her away with him, her father, Cepheus, and fiancé, Agenor, secretly plotted to assassinate Perseus. When he uncovered their plot, he showed them the Gorgon's head, and all of them were transformed from their human form into stone. Perseus returned home with Andromeda. When Polydectes saw that Perseus displayed such great prowess, he grew deathly afraid and laid out a snare to kill him. When Perseus discovered his plan, he showed him the Gorgon's head, and he was transformed from his human form into stone.

65 Alcyone When Ceyx, the son of Hesperus (or Lucifer) and Philonis, perished in a shipwreck, his wife, Alcyone, the daughter of Aeolus and Aegiale, hurled herself into the sea out of love for him. The gods pitied both of them and turned them into birds, which are called "halcyons." In wintertime these birds make their nest on the sea, lay their eggs, and give birth to their young, all within seven days' time. During this period the sea is calm; sailors call these the Halcyon Days.

66 Laius Laius son of Labdacus received a prophecy from Apollo warning him to beware death at the hands of his own son. So, when his wife Jocasta, Menoeceus' daughter, gave birth, he ordered the child to be exposed. It just so happened that Periboea, King Polybus' wife, was at the shore washing clothes, found the exposed child, and took it in. When Polybus found out, because they had no children, they raised him as their own, naming him Oedipus because his feet had been pierced.[16]

67 Oedipus [1] When Oedipus, the son of Laius and Jocasta, reached manhood, he was the strongest of all his peers. As they were envious of him, they accused him of not really being Polybus' son because Polybus was so gentle, yet he was so brash. [2] Oedipus felt that their claim had some merit, so he went to Delphi to inquire about <his parentage. Laius>* was experiencing ominous signs that told him that

16. Hyginus here relies on a Greek etymology that he does not explain; see Apollodorus 3.49.

death at his son's hands was near. [3] So he too set out on his way to Delphi, and Oedipus ran into him on the way. The king's guards ordered him to make way for the king. Oedipus refused. The king drove the horses on anyway and ran over Oedipus' foot with the wheel. Oedipus grew angry and threw his father from the chariot, killing him without realizing who he was.

[4] Upon Laius' death, Creon son of Menoeceus took power. Meanwhile, the Sphinx, the daughter of Typhon, was running loose in Boeotia and destroying the Thebans' crops. She issued a challenge to King Creon: if someone solved the riddle she posed, she would leave the area; if, however, the person did not solve the riddle, she would devour him. Under no other circumstances would she leave the territory.

[5] When the king heard these conditions, he made a proclamation throughout Greece. He promised to grant his kingdom and his sister Jocasta in marriage to the man who solved the riddle of the Sphinx. In their desire to be king many came and were devoured by the Sphinx. Oedipus son of Laius came and solved the riddle, upon which the Sphinx threw herself to her death. [6] Oedipus was given his father's kingdom and, not knowing who she was, his mother as wife. By her he fathered Eteocles, Polynices, Antigone, and Ismene.

Meanwhile, Thebes was stricken with a crop failure and a shortage of grain because of Oedipus' crimes. When he asked Tiresias why Thebes was plagued with this, he responded that if a descendant of the Sparti was still alive and died for his country, it would be freed from the plague. Then Menoeceus, Jocasta's father, threw himself from the city walls to his death.

[7] While all of this was going on in Thebes, Polybus died in Corinth. When Oedipus heard this, at first he took it badly because he was under the assumption that it was his father who had died. But Periboea informed him that he was adopted, and at the same time the old man Menoetes (the one who exposed him) recognized from the scars on his feet and ankles that he was Laius' son. [8] When Oedipus heard this and realized that he had committed so many horrible crimes, he removed the brooches from his mother's dress and blinded himself. He then handed his kingdom over to his sons to share in alternate years and went from Thebes into exile with his daughter Antigone as his guide.

68 Polynices After a year had passed, Polynices son of Oedipus sought to reclaim the throne from his brother Eteocles, but he refused to give it up. So Polynices, with the help of King Adrastus, came with seven generals to attack Thebes. There Capaneus was struck down by a thunderbolt while scaling the wall, because he said he would capture Thebes even in opposition to Jupiter's will. Amphiaraus was swallowed whole by the earth. Eteocles and Polynices fought and killed each other. The citizens of Thebes performed funeral sacrifices for them, and although there was a strong wind blowing, the smoke from the altars at no time wafted upward in a single direction but broke off into two separate streams. When the others assaulted Thebes and the Thebans were worried about their chances, the augur Tiresias son of Everes prophesied that the city would be saved from destruction if a descendant of the Sparti died. Menoeceus saw that he alone could secure his city's deliverance and so threw himself off the city walls to his death. The Thebans gained victory.

68A[17] After a year had passed, Polynices son of Oedipus, with the help of Adrastus son of Talaus and seven generals, sought to reclaim the throne from his brother Eteocles, and they attacked Thebes. There Adrastus escaped, thanks to his horse. Capaneus was struck down by Jupiter's thunderbolt while scaling the wall, because he said he would capture Thebes even in opposition to Jupiter's will. Amphiaraus and his chariot were swallowed by the earth. Eteocles and Polynices fought and killed each other. When joint funeral rites were held for them in Thebes, the smoke separated because they had killed one another. The rest perished.

68B After a year had passed, Polynices son of Oedipus <sought to reclaim> his father's <throne from his> bro<ther Eteocles,> but he refu<sed to give it> up. <Polynices> came <to attack Thebes.> There Capaneus was str<uck down by a thunderbolt while scal>ing the wall because he said he would capture <Thebes even> in opposition to <Jupiter's will.> Amphiaraus <was swallowed by the earth. Eteocles and Polynices> fought and killed one another. <In Thebes> they performed funeral sacrifices <for them,> and although there was a strong wind blowing, <the smoke from the altars at no time> wafted upward in a single direction but <broke off into> two different <streams. The others, when> they attacked Thebes, and a Theban < . . . >.

69 Adrastus [1] Adrastus, the son of Talaus and Eurynome, received an oracle from Apollo that foretold he would marry his daughters Argia and Deipyle to a boar and a lion. [2] About the same time, Oedipus' son Polynices, who had been driven into exile by his brother Eteocles, arrived at Adrastus' court, as did Tydeus, the son of Oeneus by his captive slave Periboea, who had been banished by his father because he killed his brother Melanippus on a hunting expedition. [3] When the king's guards announced that two young men had arrived in strange dress—one had on a boar's hide and the other that of a lion—Adrastus remembered the oracle and so ordered them to be brought before him.

He asked them why they had come to his kingdom in such attire. [4] Polynices explained to him that since he had come from Thebes, he put on a lion's skin, for Hercules' origins were in Thebes, and thus he was wearing a symbol of his heritage. Tydeus said that he was Oeneus' son and that his origins were in Calydon, and so he clothed himself in a boar's skin symbolic of the Calydonian boar. [5] The king, mindful of the oracle, gave his older daughter, Argia, to Polynices (Thersander was their son) and the younger daughter, Deipyle, to Tydeus (Diomedes, who fought at Troy, was their son).

17. We have alternate versions of *Fab.* 68–71, which are distinguished by letters after the numbers. The section labeled 68A was originally transmitted in the manuscript after *Fab.* 71, and the other versions have been recovered from an erased copy dating to the fifth century AD.

[6] Polynices asked Adrastus to furnish him with an army to take back his father's kingdom from his brother. Adrastus not only gave him an army, but himself went with six other generals because Thebes was enclosed by seven gates. [7] For when Amphion was putting the wall around Thebes, he constructed seven gates and named them after his daughters. These were Thera, Cleodoxe, Astynome, Astycratia, Chias, Ogygia, and Chloris.

69A Adrastus son of Talaus had <two daughters, Deipyle and Argi>a. He had received an oracle from Apollo foretelling <that he> would give <his daughters to a boar and a lion>. Because Tydeus son of Oeneus <had been driven into exile by his father fo>r <having killed> his brother Melanippus while hunting, he came to Adrastus wearing <a boar's skin>. At the same ti<me Polynices son of Oed>ipus, <who had been expelled> from power by his brother Eteocles, also came, wearing a li<on's skin>. When Adrastus saw them, he remembered the oracle and gave Argia to Polynices <and Deipyle to Tydeus in mar>riage.

70 The Seven Kings Who Set Out against Thebes Adrastus son of Talaus by Eurynome daughter of Iphitus, from Argos.

Polynices son of Oedipus by Jocasta daughter of Menoeceus, from Thebes.

Tydeus son of Oeneus by his captive slave Periboea, from Calydon.

Amphiaraus son of Oecles (or son of Apollo as some authors say) by Hypermestra daughter of Thestius, from Pylos.

Capaneus son of Hipponous by Astynome daughter of Talaus (and so Adrastus' sister), from Argos.

Hippomedon son of Mnesimachus by Metidice daughter of Talaus (and so Adrastus' sister), from Argos.

Parthenopaeus son of Meleager by Atalanta daughter of Iasius, from Mount Parthenius in Arcadia.

All of these generals perished at Thebes except Adrastus son of Talaus. He was saved, thanks to his horse. Later, he armed all their sons and sent them to sack Thebes to gain revenge for the wrongs done to their fathers, who lay unburied by the decree of Creon, Jocasta's brother, who had taken power in Thebes.

70A Adrastus son of Talaus. Capaneus <son of Hip>ponous. <Amphia>raus son of Oecles. Polynices <son of Oedi>pus. <Tydeus> son of <Oen>eus. Parthenopaeus <son> of Atalanta < . . . >.

71 The Seven Epigoni Aegialeus son of Adrastus by Demonassa, from Argos. Of the seven who had set out, he was the only one to die; because his father had survived, he gave up his life in exchange for his father's. The other six returned in victory:

Thersander son of Polynices by Argia daughter of Adrastus, from Argos.

Polydorus son of Hippomedon by Evanippe daughter of Elatus, from Argos.

Alcmaeon son of Amphiaraus by Eriphyle daughter of Talaus, from Argos. Tlesimenes son of Parthenopaeus by the nymph Clymene, from Mysia.

71A Aegialeus son of Adrastus. Polydorus <son of> Hi<ppomedon. Sthe>nelus son of Capaneus. Alcmaeon <son of> Amph<iaraus. Thersander> son of Polynices. Biantes <son of> Parthenopaeus. <Diomedes son of Tydeus.>

72 Antigone Creon son of Menoeceus issued a decree stating that no one was to bury Polynices or any of the others who had accompanied him, since they had come to attack their own country. Polynices' sister Antigone and his wife, Argia, under the cover of night secretly carried off Polynices' body and placed it on the same pyre where Eteocles was cremated. When guards caught them in the act, Argia escaped, but Antigone was led before the king, who handed her over to his son Haemon, who had been her fiancé, to be killed. But Haemon, smitten by love, ignored his father's command and entrusted Antigone to some shepherds and deceitfully told his father that he had killed her. She gave birth to a son, and when he reached manhood, he went to Thebes for some athletic contests. Creon recognized him from the birthmark that all descendants of the Sparti have on their body. Hercules interceded on Haemon's behalf, asking Creon to forgive his son, but he was not successful. Haemon killed both himself and his wife, Antigone. As for Creon, he gave his daughter Megara to Hercules to marry, and she gave birth to Therimachus and Ophites.

73 Amphiaraus, Eriphyle, and Alcmaeon The augur Amphiaraus, the son of Oecles and Hypermestra daughter of Thestius, knew that if he went to attack Thebes, he would not return. He therefore went into hiding. Only his wife, Eriphyle, Talaus' daughter, knew where he was. In order to smoke him out, however, Adrastus made a golden necklace studded with gems and gave it to his sister Eriphyle as a bribe. She wanted the gift, so she betrayed her husband. Amphiaraus gave instructions to his son Alcmaeon that after his death he was to exact punishment from his mother. After Amphiaraus was swallowed whole by the earth at Thebes, Alcmaeon followed his father's orders and killed his mother, Eriphyle. He was later tormented by the Furies.

74 Hypsipyle The seven generals were on their way to attack Thebes when they came to Nemea, where Hypsipyle, Thoas' daughter, was enslaved to King Lycurgus,* whose son Archemorus (or Ophites) she was nursing. She had received an oracle that warned her not to put the boy down on the earth before he could walk. So the seven generals who were going to Thebes came to Hypsipyle in search of water and asked her to show them where they could find some. Afraid to put the boy down on the earth, she placed him instead in a deep patch of parsley that sat next to the spring. While she was drawing the water for them, the serpent that was guarding the spring devoured the boy. Adrastus and the others killed the serpent, appealed to Lycurgus on Hypsipyle's behalf, and established funeral games in the boy's honor. These games still occur every fourth year, and the winners receive a crown of parsley.

75 Tiresias They say that the shepherd Tiresias son of Everes took his staff and struck some snakes on Mount Cyllene while they were copulating; elsewhere it is said that he stepped on them. Because of this he was turned into a woman. Later, when on the advice of an oracle he stepped on some snakes in the same place, he returned to his earlier form. At the same time, a playful dispute arose between Jupiter and Juno as to which sex, male or female, got the most pleasure out of intercourse. They made Tiresias the judge of this dispute because he had expertise on both sides. When his verdict came down in Jupiter's favor, Juno grew angry, backhanded him across the face, and blinded him. But Jupiter in return brought it about that Tiresias lived for seven generations and was the best seer among mortals.

76 The Kings of Thebes Cadmus son of Agenor. Amphion son of Jupiter. Polydorus son of Cadmus. Laius son of Labdacus. Pentheus son of Echion. Creon son of Menoeceus. Oedipus son of Laius. Polynices son of Oedipus. Lycus son of Neptune. Eteocles son of Oedipus. Zethus son of Jupiter. Labdacus son of Polydorus.

77 Leda Jupiter changed his form into a swan and ravished Leda daughter of Thestius by the river Eurotas. By him she gave birth to Pollux and Helen; by Tyndareus, Castor and Clytaemnestra.

78 Tyndareus Oebalus' son Tyndareus fathered Clytaemnestra and Helen by Leda daughter of Thestius. He betrothed Clytaemnestra to Agamemnon son of Atreus. As for Helen, she was wooed by a great host of suitors from different cities because of her outstanding beauty. Tyndareus was afraid that Agamemnon would reject his daughter Clytaemnestra and feared that the whole thing would end in chaos, so he took Ulysses' advice and made them swear an oath,* putting the decision in the hands of Helen herself, who was to place a crown on the head of the man she wanted to marry. She placed it on Menelaus' head, and Tyndareus gave her to him as his wife and on his deathbed bequeathed his kingdom to him.

79 Helen Theseus, the son of Aegeus and Aethra (Pittheus' daughter), and Pirithous son of Ixion kidnapped from Diana's shrine the virgin Helen, the daughter of Tyndareus and Leda, while she was performing a sacrifice, and took her to Athens in the district of Attica. When Jupiter saw that these two men were so bold, willingly risking their lives, he came to them in their dreams and ordered them both to fetch Proserpina from Pluto and make her Pirithous' wife. When they descended into the underworld by way of Cape Taenarum and told Pluto why they had come, they were stretched out on the ground and tortured by the Furies for a long time. When Hercules came to fetch the three-headed dog, they begged him to save them. His negotiations with Pluto were successful, and he led the men out safe and sound. Castor and Pollux, Helen's brothers, went to war to get her back and captured

Aethra, Theseus' mother, and Thisadia,* Pirithous' sister, and gave them to their sister as slaves.

80 Castor Aphareus' sons, Idas and Lynceus from Messenia, were engaged to Leucippus' daughters, Phoebe and Hilaira. They were extraordinarily beautiful virgins, and despite the fact that Phoebe was Minerva's priestess and Hilaira was Diana's, Castor and Pollux were inflamed with desire for them and kidnapped them. Idas and Lynceus took up arms in the hopes of recovering their lost fiancées. Castor killed Lynceus in the fight, and Idas, when he lost his brother, abandoned the war and his fiancée and buried his brother. As he was placing the bones in the memorial pillar, Castor arrived and stopped him from completing the monument, on the grounds that he had defeated his brother as easily as he would have a woman. Offended at this, Idas drew his sword from his side and stabbed Castor in the groin. (Others say that he killed Castor by pushing the whole pillar he had built on top of him.) When Pollux was informed of his brother's death, he rushed over and defeated Idas in single combat. He recovered and cremated his brother's body.

When Pollux was granted a constellation in heaven by Jupiter but his brother was not (because, Jupiter said, Castor and Clytaemnestra were born from the seed of Tyndareus, while Pollux and Helen were Jupiter's children), Pollux begged Jupiter to let him share his gift with his brother. Jupiter agreed to this, and so Castor is said to be "ransomed from death every other day."[18] The Romans also preserve this practice in the performances of the horse-acrobat; when each rider starts out, he has two horses, wears a cap on his head, and jumps from one horse to the other because he is performing not only his part but also that of his brother.

81 Helen's Suitors Antilochus, Ascalaphus, Ajax son of Oileus, Amphimachus, Ancaeus, Ialmenus,* Agapenor, Ajax son of Telamon, Clytius, Cyaneus, Menelaus, Patroclus, Diomedes, Peneleus, Phemius, Nireus, Polypoetes, Elephenor, Eumelus, Sthenelus, Tlepolemus, Protesilaus, Podalirius, Eurypylus, Idomeneus, Leonteus, Thalpius, Polyxenus, Prothous, Menestheus, Machaon, Thoas, Ulysses, Phidippus, Meriones, Meges, Philoctetes. Ancient authors give other names.

82 Tantalus Tantalus, the son of Jupiter and Pluto, fathered Pelops by Dione. Jupiter used to confide his plans to Tantalus and let him come to the gods' feasts. Tantalus told all of this to mankind. Because of this, the story goes, he now stands in water up to his head and is constantly thirsty. When he wants to take a drink of water, the water recedes. Likewise, fruit hangs over his head, and when he wants to take some, the branches are blown out of reach by the wind. Also, a huge boulder hangs over his head, and he is constantly afraid that it will fall down on top of him.

83 Pelops When Pelops, the son of Tantalus and Dione (Atlas' daughter), was chopped up by Tantalus and put out as a feast for the gods, Ceres ate his arm. He

18. A slightly adapted citation of Vergil's *Aeneid* (6.121).

was brought back to life by the will of the gods, but when they were putting all the limbs back together as they had been, because part of his arm was missing, Ceres furnished an ivory one in its place.

84 Oenomaus Oenomaus, the son of Mars and Asterope daughter of Atlas, had as his wife Evarete daughter of Acrisius. They had an exceptionally beautiful young daughter, Hippodamia. Oenomaus refused to allow her to marry anyone because he had received an oracle warning him to beware of death at the hands of his son-in-law. So when many suitors came seeking her hand in marriage, he issued a challenge, saying that he would give her to the man who contended with him in a chariot race and won—he chose this because he had horses faster than the North Wind. Whoever lost, however, would be put to death. Many came and were put to death. Finally, Pelops son of Tantalus came, and when he saw the human heads of Hippodamia's suitors affixed above the double-doors of the palace, he regretted having come, as the king's cruelty struck fear in his heart.

So he won over the king's charioteer, Myrtilus, and promised to give him half of the kingdom in return for his help. Myrtilus gave his word, and when he put together the chariot, he deliberately did not put the linchpins into the wheels. And so, when Oenomaus whipped the horses into a gallop, his chariot broke down, and his horses dragged him to death. Now, when Pelops was returning home victorious with Hippodamia and Myrtilus at his side, he reckoned that Myrtilus would be a source of disgrace for him. So he refused to follow through on his promise and instead threw him into the sea named the Myrtoan Sea after him. He led back Hippodamia to his homeland, which is called the Peloponnesus {"Island of Pelops"}. There he fathered Hippalcus, Atreus, and Thyestes by Hippodamia.

85 Chrysippus At the games held at Nemea, Laius son of Labdacus kidnapped Pelops' illegitimate son, Chrysippus, because of his outstanding beauty. Pelops went to war for his return and got him back. But Atreus and Thyestes killed Chrysippus at the instigation of their mother, Hippodamia. When Pelops accused her, she committed suicide.

86 The Sons of Pelops Thyestes, the son of Pelops and Hippodamia, was driven out of the kingdom by his brother Atreus because he had slept with his wife Aerope. So he sent Atreus' son Plisthenes, whom he had been raising as his own, to kill his father. Atreus, thinking that Plisthenes was his brother's son, unwittingly killed his own.

87 Aegisthus Thyestes, the son of Pelops and Hippodamia, received an oracle predicting that a son he fathered by his own daughter, Pelopia, would take vengeance against his brother. When he heard <this, he slept with his daughter.>[*] A son was born and exposed by Pelopia, but some shepherds found him and placed him under a she-goat to suckle. He was named Aegisthus because in Greek the word for "she-goat" is *aega*.

88 Atreus [1] Atreus, the son of Pelops and Hippodamia, desired to exact justice from his brother Thyestes for the outrages he committed against him. So he reconciled with Thyestes and brought him back into his kingdom. Then he killed Thyestes' infant sons, Tantalus and Plisthenes, and served them to his brother as a meal. [2] While he was eating them, Atreus ordered the hands and heads of the boys to be brought forth. Because of this crime even the Sun turned his chariot away.

[3] When Thyestes learned of the horrific crime, he fled to King Thesprotus' land, where they say Lake Avernus is. From there he went to Sicyon, where his daughter Pelopia had been taken to ensure her safety. While he was there, he by chance came upon a nighttime sacrifice to Minerva and for fear of polluting the sacrifice hid in the woods. [4] Pelopia, who was leading the choral procession, slipped on the sacrificial sheep's blood and soiled her dress. As she was going to the river to wash out the blood, she took off her stained dress. Thyestes covered his face and sprang from the woods. While she was being raped, Pelopia took his sword out of his sheath. Then, returning to the temple, she hid it beneath the pedestal of Minerva's statue. On the following day, Thyestes asked the king to send him to his homeland, Lydia.

[5] Meanwhile, the crops had failed in Mycenae because of Atreus' crime, and the citizens were experiencing a shortage of grain. He received an oracle telling him to bring Thyestes back into the kingdom. [6] When he went to Thesprotus on the assumption that Thyestes was staying there, he caught sight of Pelopia and asked Thesprotus to give her to him in marriage (he thought she was Thesprotus' daughter). He did just that, so as not to raise suspicion, but Pelopia was already pregnant with Aegisthus, her son by her father Thyestes. [7] When she came to Atreus, she gave birth and summarily exposed the baby. But shepherds found the child and placed him under a she-goat to suckle. Atreus ordered him to be sought out, and he raised him as his own.*

[8] Meanwhile, Atreus sent his sons Agamemnon and Menelaus to find Thyestes, and they went to Delphi to inquire into the matter. Thyestes by chance had also come there to consult the oracle about getting revenge on his brother. They arrested Thyestes and led him to Atreus, who ordered him to be thrown into prison. He then called Aegisthus, thinking he was his own son, and sent him to execute Thyestes.

[9] When Thyestes saw Aegisthus and the sword he was carrying, he recognized it as the one he lost during the rape. So he asked Aegisthus where he had gotten it. He responded that his mother, Pelopia, had given it to him and ordered someone to go get her. [10] She said that she had taken it from someone—she did not know who—during a sexual encounter one night, and from that encounter she conceived Aegisthus. Then Pelopia took the sword (pretending to make sure it was the right one) and thrust it into her own chest. [11] Aegisthus took the bloody sword from his mother's chest and took it to Atreus, who was delighted because he thought that meant Thyestes was dead. Aegisthus killed Atreus while he was performing a sacrifice on the shore and returned with his father, Thyestes, to their ancestral throne.

89 Laomedon The story goes that Neptune and Apollo built the wall around Troy. King Laomedon promised to sacrifice to them all the livestock born in his kingdom that year. Laomedon reneged on his promise because of greed. (Others say it was gold that he promised.) Because of this Neptune sent a sea monster to ravage Troy. For this reason the king sent an envoy to consult Apollo, who angrily responded that the plague would end if they bound and offered up young Trojan women to the sea monster.

After a great many had been devoured, Hesione's name was drawn, and she was bound to the rocks. Hercules and Telamon, who were on their way to Colchis with the Argonauts, arrived and killed the sea monster. They returned Hesione to her father on the condition that when they came back, they got to take back home both her and his horses that could walk on top of water and stalks of wheat. Laomedon broke this promise too and refused to hand Hesione over as agreed. So Hercules prepared his ships and came to conquer Troy. He killed Laomedon and handed the throne over to Laomedon's infant son Podarces, who later was named Priam from the fact that he was purchased.[19] Hercules gave the now recovered Hesione to Telamon to marry, and she gave birth to Teucer.

90 The Fifty-Four[20] Children of Priam Hector, Deiphobus, Cebriones, Polydorus, Helenus, Alexander, Hipposidus, Antinous, Agathon, Dius, Mestor, Lyside, Polyxena,* Ascanius, Chirodamas, Evagoras, Dryops, Astynomus, Polymetus, Laodice, Ethionome, Phegea, Henicea, Demnosia, Cassandra, Philomela, Polites, Troilus, Palaemon, Brissonius, Gorgythion, Protodamas, Aretus, Dolon, Chromius, Eresus, Chrysolaus, Demosthea, Doryclus, Hippasus, Hypirochus, Lysianassa, Iliona, Nereis, Evander, Proneus, Archemachus, Hilagus, Axion, Biantes, Hippotrochus, Deiopites, Medusa, Hero, and Creusa.

91 Alexander Paris Laomedon's son Priam had a great many children by sleeping with his wife, Hecuba, the daughter of Cisseus (or of Dymas). Once, while she was pregnant, she envisioned in her sleep that she was giving birth to a burning torch from which a great number of serpents emerged. She reported this vision to every soothsayer, and all of them told her to kill the newborn child to prevent it from bringing destruction to the country. When Hecuba bore Alexander, she handed him over to some of her men to be put to death, but out of pity they only exposed him. Shepherds found the exposed infant, raised him as one of their own, and named him Paris.

When Paris grew into a young man, he had a pet bull. Priam sent some men there to lead back some bull* to be given as a prize at the funeral games being held in Paris' honor, and they started to lead Paris' bull away. He caught up to them and asked where they were taking it. They told him that they were taking the bull to Priam as a prize for the man who was victorious at the funeral games for Alexander. Burning with a desire to get his bull back, Paris went down to the contest and won every event, besting even his own brothers. Deiphobus grew resentful and drew his sword against him, but Paris leaped up to the altar of Jupiter Herceus.

19. The etymology here relies upon the Greek *priamai* ("to buy").

20. The text gives fifty-five names.

When Cassandra divined that he was Deiphobus' brother, Priam acknowledged him and welcomed him into his palace.

92 The Judgment of Paris The story goes that when Thetis was getting married to Peleus, Jupiter summoned all the gods to the feast except for Eris (that is, Discord). When she later arrived at the feast and was not allowed in, she threw an apple from the doorway into the middle of them and said that the most beautiful woman was to take it. Juno, Venus, and Minerva asserted their claim to the title "beautiful," and great discord arose among the three of them. Jupiter ordered Mercury to lead them down to Alexander Paris on Mount Ida and make him be the judge.

Juno promised Alexander Paris, if he judged in her favor, that he would be king of all the lands and surpass everyone else in riches. Minerva promised, if she were to walk away victorious, to make him the bravest mortal of all and skilled at every craft.

Venus, however, promised to give him Helen, Tyndareus' daughter, the most beautiful woman of all, to be his wife. Paris preferred the last gift to the previous two and judged Venus to be most beautiful. Because of this verdict, Juno and Minerva were hostile to the Trojans. Urged on by Venus, Alexander took Helen away from his host, Menelaus, and away from Lacedaemon. He led her back to Troy and made her his wife. He also took her handmaidens, Aethra and Thisadia, whom Castor and Pollux had captured and given to Helen as servants, though once they were queens.

93 Cassandra Cassandra, the daughter of Priam and Hecuba, once fell asleep, they say, in the temple of Apollo after growing weary from play. Apollo wanted to ravish her, but she refused him access to her body. So he made it that no one believed her though she prophesied the truth.

94 Anchises They say that Venus desired Anchises son of Assaracus, slept with him, and gave birth to Aeneas. She instructed Anchises never to reveal this to anyone. One day, however, he drank too much and blurted it out in front of his drinking buddies, and because of this Jupiter struck him down with a thunderbolt. Some say he died of natural causes.

95 Ulysses When Agamemnon and Menelaus, the sons of Atreus, were leading the commanders who were bound by the oath to attack Troy, they came to Ulysses son of Laertes on the island of Ithaca. He had earlier received an oracle warning him that if he went to Troy, he would return home after twenty years, alone, destitute, and having lost his men. And so, when he found out that an embassy was on its way to him, he pretended to be crazy by putting on a felt hat and yoking a horse and a bull together to a plow. When Palamedes saw him, he sensed that he was faking it, so he took Ulysses' son Telemachus from the cradle, put him in front of the plow, and said, "Put aside your trickery and join the others bound by oath." Then Ulysses promised that he would go. From that time on he was hostile to Palamedes.

96 Achilles The Nereid Thetis knew that Achilles, her son by Peleus, would die if he went to sack Troy, so she entrusted him to King Lycomedes on the island Scyros for safekeeping. The king had Achilles dress in women's clothing and kept him in the company of his young daughters under a different name—the young women called him Pyrrha because he had red hair (the Greek word for "red" is *pyrrhos*).

Well, when the Achaeans learned he was being hidden there, they sent an embassy to King Lycomedes with a request that he send Achilles to help the Danaans. The king said Achilles was not there and allowed them access to the palace to conduct a search. Since they could not tell which of the girls was in fact Achilles, Ulysses put in the courtyard gifts suitable for girls, in which he included a shield and spear. He then ordered his trumpeter to sound the call to arms abruptly and his men to produce the clanging and clashing of arms. Achilles thought that the enemy was at hand and so ripped off his womanly clothes and took up the shield and spear. In this way he was identified and promised the Argives his help and that of his soldiers, the Myrmidons.

97 Those Who Went to Capture Troy and How Many Ships They Brought [1] Agamemnon, the son of Atreus and Aerope, from Mycenae, 100 ships.

His brother Menelaus, from Mycenae,[21] 60 ships.

[2] Phoenix son of Amyntor, from Argos, 50 ships.

Achilles, the son of Peleus and Thetis, from the island Scyros, 60 ships.

Automedon, Achilles' charioteer, from Scyros, 10 ships.

Patroclus, the son of Menoetius and Philomela, from Phthia, 10 ships.

[3] Ajax, the son of Telamon and Eriboea, from Salamis, 12 ships.

Teucer, his brother (but his mother was Hesione daughter of Laomedon), 12 ships.

[4] Ulysses, the son of Laertes and Anticlia, from Ithaca, 12 ships.

Diomedes, the son of Tydeus and Deipyle daughter of Adrastus, from Argos, 30 ships.

Sthenelus, the son of Capaneus and Evadne, from Argos, 25 ships.

[5] Ajax, the son of Oileus and the nymph Rhene, from Locris, 20 ships.

Nestor, the son of Neleus and Chloris daughter of Amphion, from Pylos, 90 ships.

Thrasymedes, his brother (but his mother was Eurydice), from Pylos, 15 ships.

Antilochus son of Nestor, from Pylos, 20 ships.

[6] Eurypylus, the son of Evaemon and Opis, from Orchomenus, 40 ships.

Machaon, the son of Asclepius and Coronis, from Tricca, 20 ships.

Podalirius, his brother, 9 ships.

[7] Tlepolemus, the son of Hercules and Astyoche, from Mycenae, 9 ships.

Idomeneus son of Deucalion, from Crete, 40 ships.

Meriones, the son of Molus and Melphis, from Crete, 40 ships.

21. Menelaus is normally from Sparta. Although Menelaus is originally from Mycenae (like his brother Agamemnon), he is usually said to be from Sparta, the city of which he is king.

[8] Eumelus, the son of Admetus and Alcestis daughter of Pelias, from Perrhaebia, 8 ships.

Philoctetes, the son of Poeas and Demonassa, from Meliboea, 7 ships.

Peneleus, the son of Hippalcus and Asterope, from Boeotia, 12 ships.

[9] Leitus, the son of Lacretus and Cleobule, from Boeotia, 12 ships.

Clonius, his brother, from Boeotia, 9 ships.

Arcesilaus, the son of Areilycus and Theobula, from Boeotia, 10 ships.

Prothoenor, his brother, from Thespia, 8 ships.

[10] Ialmenus, the son of Lycus and Pernis, from Argos, 30 ships.

Ascalaphus, his brother, from Argos, 30 ships.

Schedius, the son of Iphitus and Hippolyte, from Argos, 30 ships.

Epistrophus, his brother, likewise from Argos, 10 ships.

Elephenor, the son of Calchodon and Imenarete, from Argos, 30 ships.

[11] <Menestheus, the son of Peteos* and . . . >, from Athens, 50 ships.

Agapenor, the son of Ancaeus and Ios, from Arcadia, 60 ships.

Amphimachus, the son of Cteatus, from Elea, 10 ships.

Eurytus, the son of Pallas and Diomede, from Argos, 15 ships.

Amarynceus son of Onesimachus, from Mycenae, 19 ships.

Polyxenus, the son of Agasthenes and Peloris, from Aetolia, 40 ships.

[12] Meges, the son of Phyleus and Eustyoche, from Dulichium, 60 ships.

Thoas, the son of Andraemon and Gorgis, <from Pleuron, 20 ships.

Protesilaus son of Iphiclus,> from Iton,* 15 ships.

Podarces, his brother, likewise from Iton, 10 ships.

[13] Prothous son of Tenthredon, from Magnesia, 40 ships.

Cygnus, the son of Ocitus and Aurophite, from Argos, 12 ships.

Nireus, the son of Charopus and the nymph Aglaia, from Argos, 16 ships.

[14] Antiphus, the son of Thessalus and Chalciope, from Nisyrus, 20 ships.

Polypoetes, the son of Pirithous and Hippodamia, from Argos, 20 ships.

[15] Leonteus son of Coronus, from Sicyon, 19 ships.

The augur Calchas son of Thestor, from Mycenae; the builder Phocus son of Danaus; the messengers Eurybates and Talthybius; the judge Diaphorus; and Neoptolemus, the son of Achilles and Deidamia, from the island of Scyros (he was also named Pyrrhus by his father,* Pyrrha).[22] The total number of ships was 245.[23]

98 Iphigenia As Agamemnon was on his way to Troy with his brother Menelaus and Achaea's top commanders to fetch back Menelaus' wife, Helen, whom Alexander Paris had carried off, they were detained at Aulis by a storm caused by Diana. She was angry at Agamemnon because he had killed her sacred deer and insulted her. He called a meeting of the seers. Calchas said that Agamemnon could only make atonement by sacrificing his own daughter, Iphigenia. When Agamemnon heard this, he at first refused, but then Ulysses advised him and convinced him to do what was best for everybody.

22. Achilles was called Pyrrha while hiding in girl's clothing at King Lycomedes' court: see *Fab.* 96.

23. This sum given in the text is remarkably low. By our count the number of ships is 1,306.

Ulysses was likewise sent with Diomedes to bring Iphigenia back. When they came to her mother, Clytaemnestra, Ulysses lied to her and said that her daughter was to be married to Achilles. After he had brought her back to Aulis and her father was about to sacrifice her, Diana took pity on the girl, cast a mist around them, and replaced her with a deer. She took Iphigenia through the clouds to the land of the Taurians and there made her priestess of her temple.

99 Auge Auge daughter of Aleus was ravished by Hercules. When the time came, she gave birth on Mount Parthenius and exposed the child right there on the spot. At the same time Iasius' daughter Atalanta exposed her son by Meleager. A deer suckled Hercules' son. Shepherds found both of them, took them in, and raised them. They gave them names: Hercules' son was called Telephus, because a deer had suckled him; Atalanta's son they called Parthenopaeus, because she pretended to be a virgin and exposed the child on Mount Parthenius.[24] As for Auge herself, she, in fear of her father, fled to King Teuthras in Moesia, who regarded her as his own daughter because he was childless.

100 Teuthras Idas son of Aphareus wanted to depose King Teuthras of Moesia. When Hercules' son Telephus arrived in Moesia with his friend Parthenopaeus looking for his mother following the oracle's instructions, Teuthras promised to give him the throne and his daughter Auge in marriage in return for protection from his enemy Idas. Telephus immediately agreed to the king's terms and defeated Idas in a duel with Parthenopaeus' help.

The king made good on his promise, giving Telephus the throne and uniting him in marriage with his unwitting mother, Auge. Since she did not want to have any mortal violate her body, she intended to kill Telephus, not knowing he was her son. And so, when they went into their bridal chamber, Auge picked up a sword to kill Telephus. At that moment, it is said that a serpent of monstrous size came between them by the will of the gods. When Auge saw the serpent, she threw down the sword and told Telephus what she had almost done. When Telephus heard this, he decided to kill her, not realizing that she was his mother. But she invoked the help of Hercules, who had earlier ravished her, and from him Telephus learned she was his mother. So he returned her to her country.

101 Telephus The story goes that Telephus, the son of Hercules and Auge, was struck by Chiron's spear in a battle against Achilles. Since he was in constant excruciating pain from this wound, he consulted the oracle of Apollo as to what might cure him. Apollo's response was that the only thing that could cure him was the very same spear by which he had been wounded. When Telephus heard this, he went to King Agamemnon. At Clytaemnestra's suggestion he kidnapped Agamemnon's

24. These etymologies rely on a knowledge of Greek. For that of Telephus' name, see Apollodorus 2.147 and 3.104. Parthenopaeus is here associated with Mount Parthenius, and *parthenos* in Greek means "virgin."

infant son, Orestes, from his cradle and threatened to kill him if the Achaeans did not heal him.

Now, the Achaeans themselves had earlier received an oracle saying that Troy could not be captured without Telephus' guidance, so they readily reconciled with him and asked Achilles to cure him. Achilles responded that he did not know anything about medicine, but then Ulysses said, "Apollo did not name you but the maker of the wound, the spear." When they shaved the rust off the spear, he was cured.

The Greeks asked Telephus to go with them to sack Troy, but he refused on the grounds that his wife, Laodice, was Priam's daughter. In return for their service (they cured him), however, he led them to Troy and showed them where things were and how to get around. Then he set out for Moesia.

102 Philoctetes When Philoctetes, the son of Poeas and Demonassa, was on the island of Lemnos, a snake bit him on his foot. This snake had been sent by Juno, who was angry at him because he was the only one who had the nerve to build a pyre for Hercules when he discarded his human body and was made immortal. In return for his service, Hercules bequeathed to him his divine arrows. But when the Achaeans could no longer put up with the foul odor that was coming from the wound, on King Agamemnon's orders he was abandoned on Lemnos along with his divine arrows. A shepherd of King Actor named Iphimachus, the son of Dolopion, found him abandoned and took care of him. Later it was revealed to the Greeks that Troy could not be taken without Hercules' arrows. Agamemnon then sent Ulysses and Diomedes to find him. They convinced him to let bygones be bygones and help them sack Troy, and they took him back to Troy with them.

103 Protesilaus The Achaeans received an oracle foretelling that the first one to touch the shores of Troy would die. When they brought their fleet to shore, everyone held back except for Iolaus, the son of Iphiclus and Diomedea, who was the first to leap from his ship and was summarily killed by Hector. All of them called him Protesilaus[25] because he had been the first man to die there. When his wife, Laodamia, Acastus' daughter, heard that her husband was dead, she wept and asked the gods for three hours' time in which to speak with him. They granted her request. Mercury led him back to the world of the living, and she talked with him for three hours. But when Protesilaus died a second time, Laodamia could not endure the pain.

104 Laodamia When Laodamia, Acastus' daughter, had used up the three hours she had received from the gods after the death of her husband, she could not endure the suffering and pain. So she made a waxen* statue in the likeness of her husband Protesilaus, put it in her chamber under the pretense that it was a religious statue, and began to worship it.

25. This depends on a Greek etymology: he was the first (*protos*) of the host (*laos*) to perish.

Early one morning a servant of hers brought her some fruit for her sacrificial offering. He peered through the crack in the door and saw that she was embracing and kissing the statue.* Thinking that she was keeping a lover, he reported it to her father, Acastus. When he arrived and burst into her chamber, he saw the statue of Protesilaus. In order to prevent her from prolonging her torture, he ordered that a pyre be built and that the statue and the sacred objects be burned. Laodamia, unable to endure the pain any longer, threw herself onto the pyre and was consumed by fire.

105 Palamedes Ulysses plotted daily to find some way to kill Palamedes son of Nauplius because he had once foiled his scheme. Finally, he put a plan into motion. He sent one of his men to Agamemnon to report that he had dreamed that the camp had to be moved in a single day. Agamemnon regarded this dream to be true and gave the orders to move the camp in a single day. That night, however, Ulysses secretly buried a great mass of gold at the site where Palamedes' tent had been the day before. In addition, he drew up a letter and gave it to a Phrygian captive to take to Priam; then he sent one of his soldiers ahead to kill the captive just a short distance from the camp.

The next day, when the army was returning to camp, a certain soldier brought Agamemnon the letter that had been written by Ulysses and planted on the Phrygian's dead body. It read, "From Priam to Palamedes," and promised Palamedes, if he betrayed Agamemnon's camp at an agreed-upon time, the exact amount of gold that Ulysses had planted in his tent. So when Palamedes was led before the king and denied having anything to do with the conspiracy, they went to his tent and dug up the gold. When Agamemnon saw the gold, he believed that it really had happened. Thus Palamedes was tricked by Ulysses' scheme and was killed by the whole army though he was innocent.

106 The Ransoming of Hector At the same time Agamemnon returned Chryseis to Chryses, the priest of Apollo Smintheus, he took away from Achilles Briseis, his captive from Moesia and the daughter of the priest Brisa, on account of her exceptional beauty. Enraged at this, Achilles refused to go forth into battle, choosing to spend time in his tent playing the *cithara*. But when Hector was driving the Argives back, Achilles, under harsh criticism from Patroclus, handed over his armor to him. With it Patroclus routed the Trojans, who thought he was Achilles, and killed Sarpedon, the son of Jupiter and Europa. Later, Patroclus himself was killed by Hector, and Achilles' armor was stripped off his dead body.

Achilles reconciled with Agamemnon, who returned Briseis to him. Since he would have gone forth to meet Hector without any armor, his mother, Thetis, got Vulcan to make him armor, which the Nereids carried across the sea. Clad in this armor, he killed Hector, tied him to his chariot, and dragged him around the walls of Troy. Achilles had no intention of handing over the body to his father for burial, so Priam, at Jupiter's behest and with Mercury as his guide, went into the Danaans' camp, where he ransomed his son's body with gold. Then he laid him to rest.

107 The Judgment over Achilles' Armor After Hector was buried, Achilles ranged around the walls of Troy, boasting that he would sack Troy all by himself. Apollo grew angry at this, disguised himself as Alexander Paris, and struck him in the ankle—which they say was mortal—with an arrow, killing him. After Achilles' death and burial, Ajax son of Telamon demanded that the Danaans give him Achilles' armor on the grounds that he was his cousin.

Because of Minerva's anger, however, Agamemnon and Menelaus rejected his claim and awarded the armor instead to Ulysses. Ajax was driven mad, and in a fit of insanity killed first his flock of sheep and then himself, inflicting the wound with the same sword that he had received as a gift from Hector when they fought.

108 The Trojan Horse When the Achaeans were unable to capture Troy after ten years, Epeus, following Minerva's guidance, built a wooden horse of awesome size. Inside it a force was assembled: Menelaus, Ulysses, Diomedes, Thersander, Sthenelus, Acamas, Thoas, Machaon, and Neoptolemus. On the outside of the horse they wrote, "THE DANAANS GIVE THIS OFFERING TO MINERVA," and then transferred their camp to the island of Tenedos. When the Trojans saw this, they concluded that the enemy had gone. Priam ordered the horse to be brought in and placed on the citadel of Minerva. He then proclaimed that there would be a great celebration. The seer Cassandra cried out that there were enemies inside the horse, but not one person believed her. After they had positioned the horse on the citadel and had themselves fallen asleep exhausted by their drunken revelry, the Greeks were let out of the horse by Sinon. They slew the guards at the gates, and when the signal was given, they let in their fellow soldiers and took possession of Troy.

109 Iliona When Polydorus, Priam's son by Hecuba, was born, his parents entrusted him and his upbringing to the care of their daughter Iliona, who was married to Polymnestor, the king of Thrace. She raised him as her own son and raised her son by Polymnestor, Deipylus, in place of her brother Polydorus. She did this so that, if something should happen to one of them, she could make good on her promise to her parents. Now, after Troy was captured, the Achaeans wanted to eradicate Priam's family completely, so they threw Astyanax, the son of Hector and Andromache, from the city's walls. They also sent an embassy to Polymnestor, promising to give him the hand of Agamemnon's daughter Electra in marriage and a hoard of gold if he were to kill Priam's son Polydorus. Polymnestor accepted the embassy's terms and unwittingly killed his own son Deipylus, for he thought he was killing Priam's son Polydorus.

Polydorus meanwhile went to Apollo's oracle to inquire about his parentage. The response was that his homeland had been reduced to ashes, his father had been killed, and his mother was being held in captivity. He left the oracle and returned home. When he saw that the situation there was different than the oracle had said it was (he was still under the impression he was Polymnestor's son), he asked his sister Iliona why the oracle had spoken so inaccurately. She revealed the truth to him and he, following her advice, blinded and killed Polymnestor.

110 Polyxena When the victorious Danaans were boarding their ships to leave Ilium and were getting ready to return, each to his own country with his share of the war-spoils, they say Achilles' voice emanated from his tomb and demanded his share of the spoils. So at his tomb the Danaans sacrificed Priam's daughter Polyxena. She was a most beautiful virgin, and it was on her account (that is, because he wanted to marry her) that Achilles had come to the parley at which he was killed by Alexander and Deiphobus.

111 Hecuba When Ulysses was taking Priam's wife, Hecuba (Hector's mother and daughter of Cisseus, though other sources say of Dymas), home to a life of servitude, she hurled herself into the Hellespont and is said to have turned into a dog.[26] Because of this, part of the sea is also called Cyneum.

112 Challengers and Participants in Fights Menelaus vs. Alexander: Venus rescued Alexander.

Diomedes vs. Aeneas: Venus saved Aeneas.

The same vs. Glaucus: they withdrew after they realized they had ties of hospitality.

The same vs. Pandarus and a different Glaucus: Pandarus and Glaucus were killed.

Ajax vs. Hector: they withdrew, giving gifts to each other. Ajax gave Hector the war-belt by which he was dragged, and Hector gave Ajax the sword with which he committed suicide.

Patroclus vs. Sarpedon: Sarpedon was killed.

Menelaus vs. Euphorbus: Euphorbus was killed but later he became Pythagoras and remembered that his soul had passed into different bodies.[27]

Achilles vs. Asteropaeus: Asteropaeus was killed.

The same vs. Hector: Hector was killed.

The same vs. Aeneas: Aeneas was put to flight.

The same vs. Agenor: Apollo saved Agenor.

The same vs. the Amazon Penthesilea, the daughter of Mars and Otrera: Penthesilea was killed.

Antilochus vs. Memnon: Antilochus was killed.

Achilles vs. Memnon: Memnon was killed.

Philoctetes vs. Alexander: Alexander was killed.

Neoptolemus vs. Eurypylus: Eurypylus was killed.

113 The Deaths of Illustrious Men and Their Killers Apollo in the form of Paris killed Achilles.

Hector killed Protesilaus and Antilochus.

Agenor killed Elephenor and Clonius.

26. Hyginus uses *canis,* the Latin word for "dog," but the etymology depends on the Greek word (*kun-*).

27. Pythagoras, the fifth-century BC Greek philosopher, thought that he was the reincarnated Euphorbus.

Deiphobus killed Ascalaphus and Autonous.
Ajax[28] killed Hippodamus and Chromius.
Agamemnon killed Iphidamas and Glaucus.
Locrian Ajax killed Gargasus and Gavius.
Diomedes killed Dolon and Rhesus.
Eurypylus killed Nireus and Machaon.
Sarpedon killed Tlepolemus and Antiphus.
Achilles killed Troilus.
Menelaus killed Deiphobus.
Achilles killed Astynomus and Pylaemenes.
Neoptolemus killed Priam.

114 How Many Each Achaean Killed Achilles, 72. Antilochus, 2. Protesilaus, 4. Peneleus, 2. Eurypylus, 1. Ajax son of Oileus, 24. Thoas, 2. Leitus, 20. Thrasymedes, 2. Agamemnon, 16. Diomedes, 18. Menelaus, 8. Philoctetes, 3. Meriones, 7. Ulysses, 12. Idomeneus, 13. Leonteus, 5. Ajax son of Telamon, 28. Patroclus, 53. Polypoetes, 1. Teucer, 30. Neoptolemus, 6. The number totals 362.[29]

115 How Many Each Trojan Killed Hector, 31. Alexander, 3. Sarpedon, 2. Panthous, 4. Gargasus, 2. Glaucus, 4. Polydamas, 3. Aeneas, 28. Deiphobus, 4. Clytus, 3. Acamas, 1. Agenor, 2. The number totals 88.[30]

116 Nauplius After Ilium had been taken and the spoils divvied up, the Danaans set out for home. Because the gods were angry at their desecration of the temples and Locrian Ajax's forceful removal of Cassandra from Pallas' icon, a hostile storm with adverse winds arose, and they were shipwrecked on the Capharean Rocks. In the storm Locrian Ajax was struck by lightning from Minerva's hand and dashed against the rocks by the surf; this is where the name Ajax's Rocks comes from.

The rest of them in the dark of night began to beg the gods for deliverance. Nauplius heard them and sensed that the time had come to get his revenge for the wrongs done to his son Palamedes. So, as if he were coming to their aid, he raised a burning torch where the rocks were sharp and the place was most perilous. The Greeks naturally thought that this was an act of human kindness and thus steered their ships in that direction. The result was that a great number of ships broke apart and a great many soldiers were killed in the storm beside their leaders, their limbs and guts smashed against the rocks. All who managed to make it to shore were killed by Nauplius. But the wind drove Ulysses to Maron and Menelaus to Egypt. Agamemnon made it home with Cassandra.

28. The son of Telamon.

29. By our count the number is 329.

30. By our count the number is 87.

117 Clytaemnestra Clytaemnestra, the daughter of Tyndareus and the wife of Agamemnon, heard from Oeax, Palamedes' brother, that Cassandra was being led home to be Agamemnon's mistress. This was a lie that Oeax made up to avenge the wrongs done to his brother. So Clytaemnestra plotted with Thyestes' son, Aegisthus, to kill Agamemnon and Cassandra. They killed them both with an ax while he was performing a sacrifice. Electra, Agamemnon's daughter, took her infant brother, Orestes, and placed him in the care of Strophius, who lived in Phocis and was married to Astyochea, Agamemnon's sister.

118 Proteus It is said that in Egypt there lived Proteus, an old man, a mariner, and a seer, who could at will turn himself into all sorts of forms. Menelaus, acting on the advice of Proteus' daughter Idothea, tied him up in chains to force him to reveal when he would get back home. Proteus informed him that the gods were angry because Troy had been conquered and he should therefore perform the sacrifice that is in Greek called a *hecatomb,* in which a hundred head of cattle are killed. So Menelaus performed a *hecatomb,* and at last, eight years after he left Ilium, he returned home with Helen.

119 Orestes When Orestes, the son of Agamemnon and Clytaemnestra, reached manhood, he made it his mission to avenge his father's death. So he formed a plan with Pylades: he returned to his mother, Clytaemnestra, in Mycenae, said that he was a visitor from Aetolia,* and reported that Orestes—Aegisthus had laid a charge on the general populace to kill him—was dead. Not long afterward, Strophius' son Pylades came to Clytaemnestra carrying an urn he said held Orestes' remains. Aegisthus was overjoyed and welcomed them both into his house. Orestes seized upon the opportunity and with the help of Pylades killed his mother, Clytaemnestra, and Aegisthus during the night. When Tyndareus came to prosecute him, the Myceneans secured Orestes' escape because of their love for his father. Later, his mother's Furies tormented him.

120 Taurian Iphigenia Since the Furies were tormenting Orestes, he set out for Delphi to inquire when he could expect an end to his affliction. The response was this: Orestes was to travel to the land of the Taurians and visit King Thoas (Hypsipyle's father), remove the cult statue of Diana from her temple, and bring it back to Argos; that would bring an end to his miseries. When he heard the response, he boarded a ship with his friend Pylades, Strophius' son, and quickly reached the land of the Taurians.

It was the custom of the Taurians to sacrifice in Diana's temple all foreigners who came to their land. Orestes and Pylades hid themselves in a cave and were waiting for an opportunity, but they were discovered by shepherds and brought before King Thoas. As was customary, he had them put in chains and taken to Diana's temple to be sacrificed. Orestes' sister happened to be the priestess there, and when she figured out who they were and why they had come based on clues and inferences, she cast aside her sacrificial instruments and herself removed Diana's statue from its place. But when the king arrived on the scene and asked her why she was doing that, she lied and said that these wicked men had defiled the statue. She explained that because sinful, wicked men had been led into the temple, the statue had to be carried down to the sea for purification. Then she ordered the king to forbid the citizens to go outside the city walls. The king obeyed the priestess' command. Iphigenia took advantage of the situation: she, Orestes, and Pylades picked up the statue and boarded the ship. They sailed under a favorable wind and were carried to the island Sminthe and came to Apollo's priest Chryses.

121 Chryses When Agamemnon was en route to Troy, Achilles went to Moesia and carried off Chryseis, the daughter of Apollo's priest Chryses, and gave her to Agamemnon to be his wife. Chryses came to Agamemnon and begged him to return his daughter, but he was unsuccessful. Because of Agamemnon's refusal Apollo all but destroyed the army, partly by hunger, partly by disease. So Agamemnon returned to the priest a pregnant Chryseis, who, though she said she had never been touched by him, in due time gave birth to the younger Chryses, claiming that he was Apollo's child.

Later, when Chryses was planning on returning Iphigenia and Orestes to Thoas, Chryseis learned that they were Agamemnon's children, and she revealed the truth to her son Chryses,* that he and they were siblings and that he was Agamemnon's son. When Chryses realized what the truth was, he killed Thoas with his brother Orestes' help and went from there to Mycenae with the statue of Diana unscathed.

122 Aletes Electra, the daughter of Agamemnon and Clytaemnestra and Orestes' sister, received a false report from a messenger that her brother and Pylades had been sacrificed to Diana in the land of the Taurians. When Aegisthus' son, Aletes, learned that there remained no descendant from Atreus' side of the family, he took control of Mycenae. Electra meanwhile set out for Delphi to inquire about her brother's death. She arrived there on the very same day as Iphigenia and Orestes. The same messenger who had told her about Orestes pointed to Iphigenia and said that she was the murderer. When she heard this, she picked up a burning branch from the altar and would have burned Iphigenia's eyes out with it (not knowing she was her sister) if Orestes had not intervened.

After they recognized each other, they went to Mycenae. There, Orestes killed Aletes, Aegisthus' son, and was about to kill Erigone, the daughter of Clytaemnestra and Aegisthus, but Diana stole her away and made her a priestess in Attica. After Neoptolemus' death Orestes brought Menelaus and Helen's daughter, Hermione, home and married her. Pylades married Electra, the daughter of Agamemnon and Clytaemnestra.

123 Neoptolemus Neoptolemus, the son of Achilles and Deidamia, fathered Amphialus by his captive Andromache daughter of Eetion. But when he heard that his fiancée, Hermione, had been given to Orestes in marriage, he went to Lacedaemon and asked Menelaus for his fiancée back. Since Menelaus did not wish to break his promise to Neoptolemus, he took Hermione from Orestes and gave her back to him. Orestes, outraged at this insult, killed Neoptolemus while he was performing a sacrifice at Delphi and recovered Hermione. Neoptolemus' remains were scattered throughout the land of Ambracia in the region of Epirus.

124 The Kings of the Achaeans Phoroneus son of Inachus. Argus son of Jupiter. Peranthus son of Argus. Triops son of Peranthus. Pelasgus son of Agenor. Danaus son of Belus. Tantalus son of Jupiter. Pelops son of Tantalus. Atreus son of Pelops. Temenus son of Aristomachus. Thyestes son of Pelops. Agamemnon son of Atreus. Aegisthus son of Thyestes. Orestes son of Agamemnon. Clytus son of Temenus. Aletes son of Aegisthus. Tisamenus son of Orestes. Alexander son of Eurystheus.

125 The *Odyssey* [1] When Ulysses was on his way home from Ilium to Ithaca, he was driven by a storm to the land of the Cicones. He sacked their city, Ismarus, and divided the plunder among his men. [2] From there they went to the Lotophagi, virtuous men who ate the flower that grows from the leaves of the lotus plant. That food offered such incredible sweetness that whoever ate it forgot about returning home. Two men Ulysses sent to them ate the flowers offered to them and forgot to return to the ships, so Ulysses had to lead them back in chains.

[3] From there they went to the Cyclops Polyphemus, the son of Neptune. Polyphemus had received a prophecy from the augur Telemus son of Eurymus that he should take care lest he be blinded by Ulysses. He had a single eye in the middle of his forehead and dined on human flesh. When he drove his flock back into his cave, he placed a huge mass of rock to block the doorway, [4] shutting Ulysses and his men inside. He began eating his men. When Ulysses saw that he could not oppose Polyphemus' monstrous size and savagery, he got him drunk with the wine he had received from Maron and said that his name was Utis.[31] [5] So when Ulysses scorched his eye with a burning log, he brought all the other Cyclopes together with his screaming and said to them from his closed-off cave, "Utis blinded me!"[32] Believing that this was a joke at their expense, they brushed him off. As for Ulysses, he tied his men to the sheep and himself to a ram, [6] and in this way escaped and came to Aeolus son of Hellen.

Aeolus had been put in charge of the winds by Jupiter. He generously welcomed Ulysses into his home and gave him bags full of the winds as a gift. But when his men, who believed they contained gold and silver, took them, intending to divide up the contents among themselves, they secretly untied the bags and let the winds fly out. Ulysses was carried back to Aeolus, who drove him out because the gods were clearly hostile to him. [7] He came to the Laestrygonians, whose king was Antiphates < . . . > swallowed < . . . >[33] and they destroyed eleven of his twelve ships.

31. Utis is Greek *Outis,* "No One."

32. That is, "No One blinded me!"

33. There is a gap in our text. In Homer's *Odyssey* Antiphates eats one of Ulysses' men, and the rest of the Laestrygonians bombard his ships with boulders.

After his comrades were consumed, Ulysses fled on the one ship that was saved. [8] He came to Circe daughter of the Sun on the island of Aenaria.[34] She used to give men potions and turn them into wild beasts. Ulysses sent Eurylochus out with twenty-two men, and she changed them from their human form. Eurylochus, who had not gone inside out of fear, ran away from there and reported to Ulysses, who went to her by himself. Along the way, Mercury gave him an antidote and showed him how to foil Circe's plan. [9] When he arrived at Circe's house and received the cup from her, he followed Mercury's instructions, added the antidote, drew his sword, and threatened to kill her if she did not restore his men to him. [10] Then Circe realized that this was the work of the gods, and so she promised Ulysses that she would not do the same thing to him, restored his men to their original form, and slept with him, producing two sons, Nausithous and Telegonus.

[11] From there he went to Lake Avernus and went down to the underworld. There he found Elpenor, one of his men, whom he had left at Circe's house, and asked him how he had ended up there. Elpenor responded that he had fallen from a ladder while drunk and had broken his neck. He begged Ulysses to lay his bones to rest when he returned to the world of the living and to put a rudder on his grave mound. [12] There Ulysses also spoke with his mother, Anticlia, about the end of his wanderings. Then he returned to the world of the living, buried Elpenor, and, just as he had been asked, planted a rudder in his grave mound.

[13] Then Ulysses came to the Sirens, the daughters of the Muse Melpomene and the river* Achelous. Above their waist they were women but hens below, and they were fated to live until a mortal who heard them singing sailed past them. Ulysses, following the advice of Circe daughter of the Sun, plugged the ears of his men with wax, ordered them to bind him to the wooden mast, and sailed past them just like that. [14] From there he came to Scylla daughter of Typhon, who was a woman above her groin, a fish below, and had six dogs sprouting from her. She snatched six of Ulysses' men off the ship and devoured them.

[15] He next came to the island of Sicily where the sacred herd of the Sun lived. The animals bellowed when Ulysses' men cooked them in bronze cauldrons. Ulysses had been warned by Tiresias and Circe not to touch the herd, and so he lost many men because of this and was driven all the way to Charybdis, who swallowed the sea three times a day and three times a day vomited it back up. He sailed around it as Tiresias had advised. But the Sun was angry at him because his herd had been violated when he had come to the island of the Sun. Following Tiresias' warning, Ulysses had forbidden his men to touch the herd, but they swooped down and seized the animals while Ulysses slept. While they were cooking, the pieces of meat from the bronze cauldrons bellowed. This is why Jupiter set fire to Ulysses' ship with a thunderbolt. [16] Shipwrecked and having lost all his men, he drifted from these places and waded onto the island of Aeaea.[35]

34. Circe's island is usually said to be Aeaea (even by Hyginus in 127). Aenaria is an island near Naples, Italy.

35. Calypso's island is usually called Ogygia.

On this island lived the Nymph Calypso, the daughter of Atlas, who, smitten with Ulysses' looks, kept him there on the island for a whole year and was unwilling to let him go until Mercury on Jupiter's orders gave notice that she was to let him go. [17] When the raft was built, Calypso gave him everything he needed and sent him off. Neptune destroyed this raft with waves because Ulysses had blinded his son, the Cyclops. While he was being buffeted by the waves, Leucothoe, whom we call Mater Matuta and who lived her life in the sea, gave him a belt so that he could bind himself to her and not sink to the bottom. When he did so, he made it to land.

[18] From there he came to the island of the Phaeacians and, naked, buried himself in a pile of tree leaves. Nausicaa, the daughter of King Alcinous, brought a garment there to be washed in the river. Ulysses crept out of the leaves and asked her to help him. She was moved by pity and covered him with a cloak and brought him to her father, Alcinous. [19] He warmly welcomed Ulysses into his home, gave him gifts, and sent him on to his homeland Ithaca. He was shipwrecked again by Mercury,[36] who was angry. After twenty years, having lost all of his men, he returned to his country alone. No one recognized him. When he reached his house, he saw that it was beset with suitors who were seeking Penelope's hand in marriage, and so he pretended to be a stranger. [20] His nurse, Euryclia, recognized him from a scar while she was washing his feet. Later, he, his son Telemachus, and two servants shot dead the suitors with the help of Minerva.

[Deioneus fathered Cephalus, who fathered Arcesius, who fathered Laertes, who fathered Ulysses. Ulysses fathered Telegonus by Circe, and Telemachus by Penelope. Telegonus fathered Italus by Penelope, Ulysses' wife; he named Italy after himself. From Telemachus was born Latinus, who named the Latin language after his own name.][37]

126 The Recognition of Ulysses [1] After Ulysses had been enriched with gifts and sent off by King Alcinous, Nausicaa's father, he was shipwrecked. He arrived on Ithaca naked and came to a certain hut of his where there lived a *sybotes* (that is, a swineherd) by the name of Eumaeus. Though his dog recognized him and fawned upon him, Eumaeus did not recognize him because Minerva had changed Ulysses' appearance. [2] Eumaeus asked him where he had come from, and Ulysses responded that he had come there because of a shipwreck. When the swineherd asked him if he had seen Ulysses, he said that he was one of his men and said things that would prove this was true. [3] Eumaeus then took him into his house and refreshed him with food and drink.

When some servants came, sent in the usual way to get some pigs, he asked Eumaeus who they were. Eumaeus said, "After Ulysses set out and some time had passed, suitors came seeking Penelope's hand in marriage. [4] She held them off with this condition: 'I will marry when I have finished this weaving.' What she wove

36. The god responsible in Homer's *Odyssey* is Poseidon (Neptune).

37. This genealogical material is likely a later addition. Micyllus, the first editor of Hyginus, remarked that he found the material given in brackets above in the margin of the manuscript.

during the day she unraveled at night and in this way held them off. But now they lie with Ulysses' servant girls and consume his herds."

[5] Then Minerva restored his former appearance. When the swineherd suddenly saw it was Ulysses, he grabbed and embraced him, breaking into tears of joy and marveling at the power that had changed Ulysses' form. Ulysses said to him, "Lead me tomorrow to my palace and Penelope." [6] While he was being led there, Minerva changed his appearance once again, into that of a beggar. When Eumaeus had gotten him through to the suitors, who were reclining with his servant girls, he said to them, "Look, you have a second beggar to amuse you along with Irus." [7] Then Melanthius,[38] one of the suitors, said, "Let them instead wrestle and let the victor receive a sausage, as well as a cane so that he can drive out the loser!" When they wrestled, Ulysses body-slammed Irus and drove him out.

Eumaeus led Ulysses, still in the guise of a beggar, to his nurse, Euryclia, and said that he was one of Ulysses' men. When she was about to < . . . >, Ulysses clamped her mouth shut and gave instructions that she and Penelope were to give his bow and arrows to the suitors and announce that the suitor that drew back the bow would be awarded Penelope as wife. [8] When she did this < . . . > they competed against each other, and no one was able to draw it back. Eumaeus said mockingly, "Let us give < . . . >," but Melanthius would not allow it, as he was < . . . >. Eumaeus handed the bow over to the old man.[39] [9] He shot every suitor with the exception of his servant Melanthius. He secretly to the suitors < . . . > was found out. Ulysses cut off, little by little, his nose, arms, and all the other parts of his body, and he took possession of his house along with his wife. He ordered his servant girls to take their bodies down to the sea. Then, after the slaughter of the suitors, he, at Penelope's request, punished them.

127 Telegonus When Telegonus, the son of Ulysses and Circe, was sent by his mother to find his father, he was driven by a storm to Ithaca. Compelled by hunger, he pillaged the fields. Ulysses and Telemachus came out and met him in a battle not knowing who he was. Ulysses was killed by his son Telegonus, in accordance with the oracle he had once received that warned him to beware death at the hands of his son. When he learned whom he had killed, Telegonus on Minerva's orders returned to his home on the island of Aeaea along with Telemachus and Penelope. They returned Ulysses' dead body to Circe and there laid him to rest. Again on Minerva's orders, Telegonus took Penelope and Telemachus took Circe in marriage. From Circe and Telemachus was born Latinus, who gave his name to the Latin language; from Penelope and Telegonus was born Italus, who gave his name to Italy.

128 Augurs Ampycus son of Elatus. Mopsus son of Ampycus. Amphiaraus son of Oecles (or of Apollo). Tiresias son of Everes. Manto daughter of Tiresias. Polyidus

38. Antinous is the name given at *Odyssey* 18.32ff., and Melanthius is given below as Ulysses' servant (although seemingly still connected with the suitors).

39. The names as well as the details are at odds with *Odyssey* 21.288ff., and there are many gaps in the narrative.

son of Coeranus. Helenus son of Priam. Cassandra daughter of Priam. Calchas son of Thestor. Theoclymenus son of Proteus. Telemus son of Eurymus. Sibyl from Samos (others have said she was from Cumae).

129 Oeneus When Liber came to visit Oeneus son of Porthaon, he fell in love with his wife, Althaea daughter of Thestius. When Oeneus sensed this, he voluntarily left the city under the pretense that he was going to perform a sacrifice. Liber slept with Althaea, and she gave birth to Deianira. In return for Oeneus' generous hospitality, he gave him the gift of the vine, showed him how to plant it, and ordained that its fruit should be called *oenos* {Greek "wine"} after his host.

130 Icarius and Erigone When Father Liber set out to show men the sweetness and pleasantness of his fruits, he found generous hospitality in the home of Icarius and Erigone. In return for their hospitality he gave them a gift, a wineskin full of wine, and told them to spread its cultivation over the rest of the lands. So Icarius loaded up his cart and came with his daughter Erigone and his dog Maera to some shepherds in Attica. He showed them the special nature of the grape's sweetness, but the shepherds drank too much, became drunk, and passed out. Thinking that Icarius had given them some evil drug, they pummeled him to death. His dog, Maera, howled over Icarius' dead body and thus showed Erigone where her father lay unburied. When she arrived, she hanged herself from a tree above her father's body.

Enraged at the Athenians' terrible actions, Father Liber afflicted their daughters with a similar punishment. They went to Apollo to inquire about the problem, and they were told that it was because they had been indifferent to Icarius and Erigone's deaths. So after this reply, they punished the shepherds, instituted the festival of swinging[40] in honor of Erigone to commemorate the rash of hangings, and began offering the first-fruits to Icarius and Erigone during the grape harvest. By the will of the gods they were given a place among the constellations: Erigone became the constellation Virgo, which we call Justice; Icarius is called Arcturus among the constellations, and the dog Maera is called Canicula {"Little Dog"}.

131 Nysus While Liber was leading an army into India, he handed the kingdom of Thebes over to Nysus, the man who raised him, until he could return. When he returned from India, however, Nysus refused to surrender power. Since Liber wanted to avoid a fight with the man who raised him, he allowed him to keep power until an opportunity of retaking control presented itself to him. So three years later he reconciled himself with Nysus and feigned a desire to perform in his kingdom the sacrifices that are called the *trieterica* {"Third-Year Sacrifices"} because he was performing them after the third year. He brought with him soldiers dressed in women's clothing instead of the Bacchae, arrested Nysus, and recovered his kingdom.

40. Hyginus, *De Astronomia* 2.4 describes the festival: participants would swing on planks attached to ropes hanging from a tree—a symbolic "hanging" in memory of Erigone's death.

132 Lycurgus Lycurgus son of Dryas drove Liber from his kingdom. He denied that Liber was a god, so one day, when he drank too much and in his drunken state felt a desire to rape his mother, he tried to uproot the vines completely because, he said, wine was an evil drug that changed men's minds. He was driven insane by Liber and killed his wife and son. As for Lycurgus himself, Liber threw him to his panthers on Rhodope, a mountain in Thrace where Liber held sway. Lycurgus is said to have cut off one of his feet instead of the vines.

133 Hammon When Liber was searching for water in India and could not find any, a ram, they say, suddenly rose out of the sand and led him to some water. So he asked Jupiter to give the ram a place among the constellations; to this day he is called the Ram of the Equinox. On the spot where he found the water Liber built a temple, which is called the temple of Jupiter Hammon.

134 The Tyrrhenians When the Tyrrhenians, who were later called the Etruscans, were making pirate raids, Father Liber boarded their ship in the guise of a young boy and asked them to take him to Naxos. They took him on board and planned to gang up and rape him because of his beauty. The helmsman Acoetes opposed them but himself suffered injury at their hands. When Liber saw that they had no intention of abandoning their plan, he changed the oars into *thyrsi,* the sails into vine tendrils, and the ropes into ivy. Then lions and panthers suddenly sprang forth. When the sailors saw this, they in fear threw themselves overboard into the sea, and he transformed the men into another miracle in the sea: all those who had jumped overboard were changed into the form of a dolphin. This is where dolphins got the name Tyrrheni and the sea got the name Tyrrhenum. There were twelve of them in all,[41] and these are their names: Aethalides, Medon, Lycabas, Libys, Opheltes, Melas, Alcimedon, Epopeus, Dictys, Simon, and Acoetes. The last of these was the helmsman, whom Liber saved because he was merciful.

135 Laocoon Laocoon, the son of Capys, brother of Anchises and priest of Apollo, married and had children against Apollo's will. One day he was chosen by lot to perform a sacrifice to Neptune on the beach. Apollo seized this opportunity and sent two serpents across the sea from Tenedos to kill Laocoon's sons Antiphas and Thymbraeus. When Laocoon was on his way to help them, the serpents also wrapped him in their coils and killed him. The Phrygians thought this happened because Laocoon threw a spear into the Trojan horse.

136 Polyidus [1] Glaucus, the son of Minos and Pasiphae, fell into a big vat full of honey while playing ball. When his parents were looking for him, they asked Apollo about their son. Apollo responded to them, "A supernatural omen has been born unto you; whoever discovers its meaning will restore your son to you." [2] When Minos heard the oracle, he asked his subjects if they knew of any supernatural occurrence. They told him that a calf had just been born that changed its color

41. One of the names has dropped out of the manuscript. Ovid gives Proreus.

three times a day, every four hours: first white, then red, and finally black. [3] Minos called together the augurs to figure out what it meant. All of them were at a loss when Polyidus, Coeranus' son from Byzantium, demonstrated that the omen was similar to a blackberry bush: at first it is white, then it turns red, and finally completely black. [4]Then Minos said to him, "According to Apollo's oracle, you are supposed to restore my son to me." While Polyidus was taking his augury, he saw an owl sitting above the wine cellar keeping the bees away. He interpreted this sign and pulled the dead boy from the vat.

[5]Then Minos said to him, "Now that the body has been found, bring him back to life." When Polyidus said that this was not possible, Minos ordered him to be enclosed in the tomb along with the boy and a sword to be placed within. [6] After they had been shut in, a serpent suddenly came toward the boy's body. Polyidus thought that the serpent was going to devour the boy, so he immediately struck it with the sword and killed it. When a second serpent seeking its mate saw that it had been killed, it came forth and applied an herb. At its touch, the serpent came back to life. [7] Polyidus did the same thing. They called out from inside, and a passerby reported this to Minos. He ordered the tomb to be opened, and when he recovered his son alive and well, he sent Polyidus back home with many gifts.

137 Merope When King Polyphontes of Messenia killed Aristomachus' son Cresphontes, he took possession of his kingdom and his wife, Merope.[42] Merope took her infant son by Cresphontes and secretly handed him over to her friend in Aetolia. Polyphontes went to extraordinary pains to find him and promised gold as a reward for his death. When Merope's son grew into a man, he formed a plan to avenge the death of his father and brothers. He went to King Polyphontes to demand the gold, saying that he had killed Telephontes, the son of Cresphontes and Merope. The king bade him to lodge there for the time being so that he could conduct a more thorough investigation into the matter.

After Telephontes had fallen asleep out of weariness, the old man who was acting as a messenger between mother and son came to Merope in tears and reported that her son was not at her friend's place and had not surfaced anywhere else. Believing that her son's murderer was the man sleeping in the palace, she took up an ax and went to the porch with the intention of killing the man, not knowing he was her son. The old man, however, recognized him and stopped the mother from committing the crime. When Merope saw that an opportunity to take revenge on her enemy had presented itself to her, she reconciled with Polyphontes. When the king, delighted, was performing a sacrifice, his guest pretended that he was going to deliver the blow* to the sacrificial victim, but killed the king and took possession of the throne that had belonged to his father.

42. The text of the beginning of this *Fabula* has suffered severe disruption in transmission, and the following material has been transposed here from the end of *Fab.* 184, where it is clearly out of place. We have omitted a sentence that is obscure due to the joining of the two sections.

138 Philyra, Who Was Changed into a Linden Tree As Saturn was combing the earth looking for Jupiter, he came to Thrace, turned himself into a horse, and slept with Philyra daughter of Ocean. She gave birth to the Centaur Chiron, who is said to have been the first to discover the art of medicine. When she realized that she had given birth to a species never before seen, Philyra asked Jupiter to change her into some other form. She was changed into the *philyra* tree, that is, a linden tree.

139 The Curetes When Opis gave birth to Jupiter by Saturn, Juno asked that he be given to her. Saturn had already cast Orcus beneath Tartarus and Neptune beneath the seas because he knew that if a son was born to him, he would be dethroned by him. So when Saturn told Opis to give him the new child to eat, she offered him a stone wrapped up in swaddling-clothes, which he gobbled down. After he realized what had transpired, Saturn went all over the earth in search of Jupiter. Juno, meanwhile, brought Jupiter down to the island of Crete. Amalthea, the child's nurse, placed him in a cradle hanging in a tree so that he could not be found in the sky, on earth, or on the sea. To prevent the boy's wailing from being heard, she called some young boys together, gave them small bronze shields and spears, and ordered them to create a ruckus around the tree. In Greek they are called the Curetes; others call them Corybantes, but they are also called by the name Lares.

140 Python Python son of Earth was a huge serpent. This serpent gave forth responses from the oracle on Mount Parnassus before the arrival of Apollo. Python was fated to meet his death at the hands of one of Latona's offspring. At that time Jupiter slept with Latona, Polus' daughter. When Juno found out about this, she brought it about that Latona would give birth where the sun's rays did not reach the earth. When Python realized that Latona was pregnant with Jupiter's child, he went in pursuit to kill her, but the North Wind at Jupiter's behest picked her up and carried her to Neptune. He made sure she was safe, but lest he go against Juno's decree, he carried her down to the island of Ortygia and covered it with waves. When Python could not find her, he returned to Mount Parnassus.

Neptune made the island of Ortygia reappear on the surface, and this island would later be called Delos.[43] There Latona, while grasping an olive tree, gave birth to Apollo and Diana. Vulcan gave both of them bows and arrows as a gift. The fourth day after their birth, Apollo gained revenge for the wrongs committed against his mother; he went to Parnassus, slew Python with arrows (this is why Apollo is called Pythian), tossed his bones in a tripod, and put it in his own temple. Then Apollo established funeral games in his honor, which are called the Pythian Games.

141 The Sirens The Sirens were the daughters of the river Achelous and the Muse Melpomene. Wandering about after Proserpina's abduction, they came to the

43. Greek *delos* means "visible."

land of Apollo, where they were turned into flying creatures by the will of Ceres because they had not helped Proserpina. It was foretold to them that they would live so long as no one sailed past them while listening to their song. Ulysses was the man destined to seal their fate; for through a clever ploy he sailed past the cliffs occupied by the Sirens, and they threw themselves into the sea. The place, located between Sicily and Italy, received the nickname Sirenides.

142 Pandora Prometheus son of Iapetus was the first to fashion men out of clay. Later, Jupiter ordered Vulcan to make out of clay the form of a woman, to whom Minerva gave life and the rest of the gods their own personal gift. Because of this they named her Pandora.[44] She was given to Prometheus' brother Epimetheus in marriage, and they had a daughter named Pyrrha, who is said to have been the first mortal begotten by birth.

143 Phoroneus Inachus son of Ocean fathered Phoroneus by his own sister, Argia. He, they say, was the first mortal to be a king. For many generations before Phoroneus, men lived their lives without cities or laws, speaking a single language and under Jupiter's authority. But once Mercury divided up men's languages—this is why a translator is called in Greek a *hermeneutes* (Mercury is called Hermes in Greek; he also divided men into different nations)—discord arose among mortals, and this did not please Jupiter. So he made Phoroneus the first king because he was the first to make a sacrifice to Juno.

144 Prometheus There was once a time when men had to beg the gods for fire and did not know how to preserve it. Then Prometheus carried it down to earth in a fennel stalk and showed men how to preserve it by burying it in ash. Because of his theft, Mercury, on Jupiter's orders, bound him to a rock on Mount Caucasus with iron nails and beset him with an eagle that would eat out his heart. All that the eagle ate during the day would grow back at night. Hercules killed the eagle after 30,000 years and freed him.

145 Niobe (or Io) From Phoroneus and Cinna were born Apis and Niobe. The latter was the first mortal Jupiter slept with. She gave birth to Argus, who gave his name to the city of Argos. Argus and Evadne had three children: Criasus, Piranthus, and Ecbasus. Piranthus and Callirhoe had Argus, Arestorides, and Triopas. He < . . . >[45] from him and Eurisabe came Anthus, Pelasgus, and Agenor. From Triopas and Oreasis came Xanthus and Inachus; from Pelasgus came Larissa; and from Inachus and Argia came Io.

Jupiter desired Io and ravished her. He changed her into the form of a cow to prevent Juno from recognizing her. When Juno did find out, she sent Argus, whose whole body was covered with gleaming eyes, to keep watch over her, but Mercury,

44. In Greek *pan* means "all," and *dora* means "gifts."

45. Marshall prints a lacuna here, but this *Fabula* probably has many other gaps as well.

under orders from Jupiter, killed him. Juno, however, drove terror into Io's heart and forced her, haunted by this constant fear, to throw herself into the sea now called the Ionian Sea. From there she swam across to Scythia, and this is how the area got the name Bosporus {"Cow's Ford"}. Then she went to Egypt, where she gave birth to Epaphus. When Jupiter found out that Io had undergone so many trials because of his own doing, he restored her to her proper form and made her a goddess among the Egyptians, where she is called Isis.

146 Proserpina Pluto asked Jupiter if he could marry Proserpina, his daughter by Ceres. Jupiter said that Ceres would never allow her daughter to reside in the darkness of Tartarus; he told him, however, to abduct her while she was picking flowers on Mount Aetna, which is in Sicily. So, while Proserpina was picking flowers there with Venus, Diana, and Minerva, Pluto came on a chariot and abducted her. Later Jupiter granted Ceres' request that Proserpina spend half of each year with her and the other half with Pluto.

147 Triptolemus When Ceres was searching for her daughter Proserpina, she came to King Eleusinus, whose wife Cothonea had given birth to a boy, Triptolemus. Ceres pretended to be a lactating nurse, and the queen gladly brought her in to nurse her son. Ceres wanted to make this nursling of hers immortal, so by day she nourished him with divine milk and at night secretly buried him in the hearth's fire. Because of her divine attention, he grew more rapidly than mortal infants normally do. The parents were amazed at what was happening, so they spied on her. When Ceres was on the verge of putting the child in the fire, his father let out a cry.* She grew angry at Eleusinus and killed him.

As for her nursling Triptolemus, Ceres gave him an eternal gift: a dragon-drawn chariot with which to spread the cultivation of grain. Transported by this, he sowed the world with grain. When Triptolemus returned home, Celeus ordered him to be put to death because of Ceres' gift. When the plot was discovered, Celeus on Ceres' orders bequeathed his kingdom to Triptolemus, who named it Eleusis after his father and instituted a sacrifice in honor of Ceres, which is called the Thesmophoria in Greek.

148 Vulcan When Vulcan realized that Venus was secretly sleeping with Mars and that he could not oppose his great strength, he forged a chain out of adamantine and set it up around his bed so that he could foil him with cunning. When Mars came around at the appointed time, he and Venus fell so completely into Vulcan's snare that they could not escape it. The Sun reported this to Vulcan, who saw the two of them lying together there naked. He then summoned all the gods and < . . . >[46] they saw. Thereafter shame kept Mars from doing this, but from their union Harmonia was born. Minerva and Vulcan gave her a gift, a dress that was

46. The full account of this scene and the amused reactions of the other gods can be supplied from Homer, *Odyssey* 8.266–366.

imbued with crimes, and this is why Harmonia's descendants were all cursed. Because the Sun snitched on her, Venus was hostile to his descendants ever after.

149 Epaphus Jupiter ordered Epaphus, his son by Io, to found cities in Egypt, fortify them, and rule over the people there. He founded Memphis first and then went on to found many more. By his wife, Cassiopia, he fathered a daughter, Libya, from whom the land got its name.

150 The Titanomachy When Juno saw that Epaphus, Jupiter's son by his mistress, had gained such great power, she took great pains to ensure Epaphus would be killed on a hunt. She also urged the Titans to remove Jupiter from his kingship and restore Saturn to the throne, but when they tried to climb into heaven, Jupiter along with Minerva, Apollo, and Diana cast them headlong into Tartarus. Jupiter made Atlas, who was their leader, place the whole vault of the sky on his shoulders. He, they say, holds up the sky to this very day.

151 The Children of Typhon and Echidna The Giant Typhon and Echidna had the following children: Gorgon; the three-headed dog Cerberus; the serpent that guarded the apples of the Hesperides beyond Ocean; the Hydra that Hercules killed at the Spring of Lerna; the serpent that guarded the ram's fleece in Colchis; Scylla, who was woman above the waist, a fish* below the waist, and had six dogs sprouting from her; the Sphinx, which lived in Boeotia; and the Chimaera in Lycia whose front part had the form of a lion, the rear that of a snake, and the middle that of a goat {Greek *chimaira*} itself.

To Medusa daughter of Gorgon and Neptune were born Chrysaor and the horse Pegasus. Chrysaor and Callirhoe had three-bodied Geryon.

152 Typhon Tartarus and Earth* produced Typhon, a creature of monstrous size and portentous appearance: from his shoulders sprouted a hundred viper heads. He challenged Jupiter to a duel for the right to be king. Jupiter cast a blazing thunderbolt that struck Typhon in the chest and then placed Mount Aetna (which is in Sicily) on top of him as he burned. They say he still sends forth flames from the mountain to this day.

152A Phaethon[47] When Phaethon, the son of the Sun and Clymene, secretly mounted his father's chariot and flew too high in the sky, he panicked and plummeted into the river Eridanus. When Jupiter struck him with his thunderbolt, everything started burning. Now Jupiter, so that he could justify killing the entire race of mortals, acted as if he wanted to put out the flames: he flooded every stream and river, and the entire race of mortals perished except for Pyrrha and Deucalion.

47. This story was originally transmitted as part of 152 but is clearly a separate story, although it is not listed in the table of contents that accompanies the manuscript.

As for Phaethon's sisters, they—because they had hitched the horses of their father's chariot without his permission—were changed into poplar trees.

153 Deucalion And Pyrrha When the *cataclysmus* occurred, which we would call "a deluge" or "a flood," the entire human race perished except for Deucalion and Pyrrha, who took refuge on Mount Aetna, which is said to be the highest mountain on Sicily. When they could no longer bear to live because of loneliness, they asked Jupiter either to give them some more people or to kill them off with a similar catastrophe. Then Jupiter ordered them to toss stones behind them. Jupiter ordered the stones Deucalion threw to become men and those Pyrrha threw to become women. From this comes the word *laos* {Greek "people"}, since the Greek word for "stone" is *laas.*

154 Hesiod's Phaethon Phaethon was the son of Clymenus (son of the Sun) and the Nymph Merope who, as we have been told, was an Oceanid. When Phaethon learned that his grandfather was the Sun from something his father said, he was granted use of the Sun's chariot but grossly mishandled it. For when he flew too close to the ground, everything was burned up by the nearby flame, and he, struck by a thunderbolt, fell into the Po River. This river is called the Eridanus by the Greeks (Pherecydes was the first to call it this).

The Indians turned black because their blood was changed into a dark color by the heat of the nearby flame. Phaethon's sisters turned into poplar trees while they were weeping over their brother's death; their tears, Hesiod tells us, hardened into amber. They are called the Heliades. Their names were Merope, Helia, Aegle, Lampetia, Phoebe, Aetheria, and Dioxippe. Cygnus, the king of Liguria and one of Phaethon's relatives, was turned into a swan {*cygnus*} while he was lamenting over his relative. The swan too, as it dies, sings a mournful dirge.

155 Jupiter's Children Liber by Proserpina; the Titans ripped him apart. Hercules by Alcmena. Liber by Semele, the daughter of Cadmus and Harmonia. Castor and Pollux by Leda daughter of Thestius. Argus by Niobe daughter of Phoroneus. Epaphus by Io daughter of Inachus. Perseus by Danae daughter of Acrisius. Zethus and Amphion by Antiope daughter of Nycteus. Minos, Sarpedon, and Rhadamanthus by Europa daughter of Agenor. Hellen by Pyrrha daughter of Epimetheus. Aethlius by Protogenia daughter of Deucalion. Dardanus by Electra daughter of Atlas. Lacedaemon by Taygete daughter of Atlas. Tantalus by Pluto daughter of Himas. Aeacus by Aegina daughter of Asopus. Aegipan by a she-goat. <*unintelligible*> Arcas by Callisto daughter of Lycaon. Pirithous by Dia daughter of Deioneus.

156 <The Sun's Children> Circe, Pasiphae, <Aeetes, and Perses>* by Persis daughter of Ocean. By Clymene daughter of Ocean: Phaethon, Lampetia, Aegle, Phoebe, <Merope, Helia, Aetheria, and Dioxippe>.*

157 <Neptune's Children>[48] Boeotus and Hellen by Antiope daughter of Aeolus.[49] Agenor and Belus by Libya daughter of Epaphus. Bellerophon by Eurynome daughter of Nysus. Leucon* by Themisto daughter of Hypseus. Hyrieus by Alcyone daughter of Atlas. Abas by Arethusa daughter of Nereus. Epopeus by Alcyone daughter of Atlas.* Dictys by Agamede daughter of Augeas. Evadne by Pitana <daughter of the river Eurotas. Peratus by Calchinia>* daughter of Leucippus. Megareus by Oenope daughter of Epopeus. Cygnus by Calyce daughter of Hecato. Periclymenus[50] and Ancaeus by Astypalaea daughter of Phoenix. Neleus and Pelias by Tyro daughter of Salmoneus. Euphemus, Lycus, and Nycteus by Celaeno daughter of <Atlas>*. Hopleus* < . . . >. <*unintelligible*>. Antaeus < . . . >. Eumolpus by Chione daughter of Aquilo. <Nauplius by> Amymone <daughter of Danaus>.* Also the Cyclops <Polyphemus . . . >. Euphemus < . . . >.* Amycus by Melia daughter of Busiris.

158 <Vulcan's Children> Philammon. Cecrops. Erichthonius. Corynetes. Cercyon. Philottus. Spinther.

159 <Mars' Children> Oenomaus by Sterope. Harmonia by Venus. Leodocus by Pero. Lycus. Thracian Diomedes. Ascalaphus. Ialmenus. Cygnus. Dryas.

160 <Mercury's Children> Priapus. Echion by Antianira. Eurytus. Cephalus by Creusa daughter of Erechtheus. <*unintelligible*>. Libys by Libya daughter of Palamedes.

161 <Apollo's Children> Delphus. Asclepius by Coronis daughter of Phlegyas. Euripides by Cleobula.[51] Ileus son of Urea* daughter of Neptune. Agreus by Euboea daughter of Macareus. Philammon by Leuconoe daughter of the Morning Star. Lycoreus by a nymph. Linus by the Muse Urania. Aristaeus by Cyrene daughter of Peneus.

162 <Hercules' Children> Hyllus by Deianira. Tlepolemus by Astyoche. <*unintelligible*>. Telephus by Auge daughter of Aleus. Leucippus. Therimachus. Creontiades. Archelaus. Ophites. Deicoon. Evenus. Lydus. And the twelve Thespiades, whom he fathered by the daughters of King Thespius.

48. This *Fabula* is extremely corrupt, and there are many mistakes found here. In some cases we have reconstructed lineages based on parallels in mythographic sources elsewhere. In other cases we have let a corrupt text stand.

49. By all accounts the mother of Boeotus (and Aeolus) is Melanippe daughter of Aeolus (see *Fab.* 186). Hellen is normally son of Deucalion and father of Aeolus (Melanippe's father).

50. In *Fab.* 10 Neptune is his grandfather.

51. As the text stands, Hyginus suggests that Euripides the tragedian is Apollo's son. But it also may be that this is merely another variant of Asclepius' parentage, "Euripides [says he was son] of Cleobula."

163 <The Amazons> Ocyale, Dioxippe, Iphinome, Xanthe, Hippothoe, Otrera, Antioche, Laomache, Glauce, Agave, Theseis, Hippolyte, Clymene, Polydora, and Penthesilea.

164 Athens When an argument arose between Neptune and Minerva as to who would be the first to found a city on Attic soil, they made Jupiter judge of their dispute. The judgment fell in Minerva's favor because she planted the first olive tree in that land (which, they say, still stands there). Neptune grew angry over this and began flooding the land with the sea, but Jupiter ordered Mercury to prevent him from doing so. So Minerva founded a city and called it Athens after her own name;[52] this town is said to be the first one built in the land.

165 Marsyas They say that Minerva was the first to fashion a flute out of deerbone. She came to the gods' banquet table to play it, but Juno and Venus made fun of her because she turned blue and puffed out her cheeks. So, because they thought her ugly and ridiculed her for her song, she went to a spring in the forest of Mount Ida. When she played a tune there, she saw herself in the water and realized that there was every reason for them to poke fun at her. So she flung aside the flute right there and placed a curse on it so that whoever found the flute would be afflicted with a grave punishment.

The shepherd Marsyas, Oeagrus' son and a Satyr, found the flute. He practiced it assiduously, so the quality of his sound grew more and more melodious by the day. He got so good that he challenged Apollo to a contest with the *cithara.*

Apollo accepted the challenge, and they made the Muses their jury. Just when Marsyas was about to walk away the winner, Apollo played his *cithara* upside down, and the sound was the same. Marsyas could not do the same with his flute, so Apollo tied the vanquished Marsyas to a tree and handed him over to a Scythian, who removed his skin little by little. Apollo entrusted the rest of his body to his student Olympus to be laid to rest. The river that flows from his blood is called the Marsyas.

166 Erichthonius Vulcan made thrones out of gold and adamant for Jupiter and the rest of the gods. When Juno sat in hers, she was suddenly suspended in midair. When the order reached Vulcan telling him to free his mother, whom he had confined, he, still angry over having been thrown from heaven, said that he did not have a mother. When Father Liber got him drunk and led him back to the assembly of the gods, he could no longer disregard his duty as son. Then Jupiter offered him the choice of whatever he wanted from them. So then Neptune, who was hostile to Minerva, urged Vulcan to ask for Minerva as his wife. This request was granted, but when he came into her chamber, Minerva, under Jupiter's orders, defended her chastity by putting up a fight, and while they were grappling, his semen fell on the ground and a boy was born who was a serpent below the waist. They named him Erichthonius because the Greek words for "struggle" and "earth" are *eris* and *chthon.*

52. Hyginus again assumes a knowledge of Greek: Minerva is the Roman equivalent to the Greek goddess Athena.

Minerva raised him in secret, put him in a small chest, and gave it to Cecrops' daughters, Aglaurus, Pandrosus, and Herse, for safekeeping. When they opened the chest, a crow snitched on them. They were driven mad by Minerva and hurled themselves into the sea.

167 Liber Liber, the son of Jupiter and Proserpina, was ripped apart by the Titans. Jupiter ground up his heart, put it in a potion, and gave it to Semele to drink. When she became pregnant from this, Juno took the form of Beroe, Semele's nurse, and said to her, "Dear child, ask Jupiter to come to you as he comes to Juno, so that you may know how great a pleasure it is to lie with a god." Prodded in this fashion, she asked Jupiter to do so and was struck by a thunderbolt. Jupiter took Liber out of her womb and gave him to Nysus to raise. This is why he is called Dionysus and Twice-mothered.

168 Danaus Danaus son of Belus had fifty daughters by several wives. His brother Aegyptus had just as many sons, and he wanted to kill his brother Danaus and his daughters so that he alone would possess his father's kingdom. He demanded that his brother provide wives for his sons. When Danaus realized what was going on, he fled from Africa to Argos with the help of Minerva, who, they say, built the first two-prowed ship so that Danaus could escape. When Aegyptus found out Danaus had escaped, he sent his sons to pursue his brother and ordered them either to kill him or not to return home. After they reached Argos, they began a siege against their uncle. When Danaus saw he could not hold them off, he promised them his daughters as wives if they ceased their attack. They took the cousins they asked for as wives, but the women following their father's orders killed them after they got married. Hypermestra was the only one to save her husband, Lynceus. They say that the rest of them, because of their crime, pour water into a pot full of holes in the underworld. A shrine was built for Hypermestra and Lynceus.

169 Amymone While Amymone daughter of Danaus was intensely tracking her prey in the forest, she hit a Satyr with her spear. The Satyr wanted to rape her. She prayed to Neptune for help. When Neptune arrived, he drove the Satyr away and slept with Amymone himself. From this union Nauplius was born. At the spot where all of this took place, it is said that Neptune struck the earth with his trident and water flowed out from there. The spring is called Lernaean, and the river Amymonian.

169A Amymone[53] Amymone daughter of Danaus was sent by her father to find some water that he needed to perform a sacrifice. While she was looking for some, she fell asleep out of exhaustion. A Satyr wanted to rape her; she prayed to Neptune for help. When Neptune threw his trident at the Satyr, it planted itself in a rock, and he drove the Satyr off. When he asked the girl what she was doing all by

53. This alternate version of the Amymone myth is clearly separate from the prior one but is not given an entry in the ancient table of contents.

herself in the middle of nowhere, she said that her father had sent her out to look for some water. Neptune slept with her, and in return for this he helped her out. He told her to remove the trident from the rock, and when she did, three waterspouts followed. This spring is called Amymonius after her name, and from their union Nauplius was born. This spring was later called Lernaean.

170 Which Daughter of Danaus Killed Which Husband[54] Midea killed Antimachus. Philomela killed Panthius. Scylla killed Proteus. Amphicomone killed Plexippus. Evippe killed Agenor. Demodice killed Chrysippus. Hyale killed Perius. Trite killed Enceladus. Damone killed Amyntor. Hippothoe killed Obrimus. Myrmidone killed Mineus. Eurydice killed Canthus. Cleo killed Asterius. Arcadia killed Xanthus. Cleopatra killed Metalces. Phila killed Philinus. Hipparete killed Protheon. Chrysothemis killed Asterides. Pyrante killed Athamas. <*unintelligible*> killed <*unintelligible*>. Glaucippe killed Niavius. Demophile killed Pamphilus. Autodice killed Clytus. Polyxena killed Aegyptus. Hecabe killed Dryas. Achamantis killed Ecnominus. Arsalte killed Ephialtes. Monuste killed Eurysthenes. Amymone killed Midamus. Helice killed Evideas. Oeme killed Polydector. Polybe killed Iltonomus. Helicta killed Cassus. Electra killed Hyperantus. Eubule killed Demarchus. Daplidice killed Pugnon. Hero killed Andromachus. Europome killed Athletes. Pyrantis killed Plexippus. Critomedia killed Antipaphus. Pirene killed Dolichus. Eupheme killed Hyperbius. Themistagora killed Podasimus. Celaeno killed Aristonos. Itea killed Antiochus. Erato killed Eudaemon.

Hypermestra saved Lynceus. When Danaus died, Abas was the first one to inform Lynceus of this. As Lynceus looked around the temple to see whether there was something he could give to Abas as a reward, he happened to catch sight of the shield that Danaus had carried in his youth and later dedicated to Juno. He took it off the peg and gave it to Abas, and he established games called the Shield in Argos, which are held every four years. At these games, runners are not given a crown but a shield instead. As for Danaus' daughters, after their father's death they married Argive men; those born from them are called Danaans.

171 Althaea Both Oeneus and Mars slept with Thestius' daughter Althaea on the same night. When Meleager was born to them, the Parcae—namely Clotho, Lachesis, and Atropos—suddenly appeared in the palace and foretold his fate as follows: Clotho said that he would be a man of noble character; Lachesis said that he would be a man of bravery; Atropos caught sight of a log burning on the hearth and said, "He will live until this log is consumed." When his mother, Althaea, heard this, she leaped from her bed, put the log out, and buried the fateful thing in the middle of the palace to prevent it from being consumed by fire.

172 Oeneus When Oeneus, the son of Porthaon and king of Aetolia, had made his annual sacrifice to all of the gods and passed over Diana, she grew angry and sent

54. The list of names in this passage is extremely corrupt. Only forty-seven of the fifty daughters are named here (one unintelligible), and many of the names are corrupt and cannot be relied on.

a boar of monstrous size to lay waste to the fields of Calydon. Then Meleager son of Oeneus promised that he would go out with the finest leaders of Greece to destroy the beast.

173 Those Who Went to Hunt the Calydonian Boar Castor and Pollux, the sons of Jupiter, and Eurytus son of Mercury, from Sparta. Echion son of Mercury, from Thebes. Asclepius son of Apollo. Jason son of Aeson, from Thessaly.* Alcon son of Mars, from Thrace. Euphemus son of Neptune. Iolaus son of Iphiclus. Lynceus and Idas, the sons of Aphareus. Peleus son of Aeacus. Telamon son of Aeacus. Admetus son of Pheres. Laertes son of Arcesius. Deucalion son of Minos. Theseus son of Aegeus. Plexippus, Ideus, and Lynceus, the sons of Thestius and brothers of Althaea. Hippothous son of Cercyon. Caeneus son of Elatus. Mopsus son of Ampycus. Meleager son of Oeneus. Hippasus son of Eurytus. Ancaeus son of Lycurgus. Phoenix son of Amyntor. Dryas son of Lapithus.* Enaesimus, Alcon, and Leucippus, the sons of Hippocoon, from Amyclae. Atalanta daughter of Schoeneus.

<173A>[55] The Cities That Sent Aid to Oeneus Tenedos, Iolcus, Sparta, Pleuron, Messene, Perrhaebia, Phthia, Magnesia, Salamis, Calydon, Thessaly, Oechalia, Ithaca, Tegea, Crete, Dolopea, Athens, and Arcadia.

174 Meleager Althaea daughter of Thestius gave birth to Meleager by Oeneus. The story goes that a burning log appeared there in the palace. The Parcae went there and foretold his destiny, that he would live so long as the log remained intact. Althaea shut this log in a chest and carefully guarded it. Meanwhile, enraged at Oeneus' omission of her in his annual sacrifice, Diana sent a boar of unbelievable size to lay waste to the fields of Calydon. Meleager, along with the finest young men of Greece, killed it, and he gave its hide to the maiden Atalanta because of her courage. Althaea's brothers—Ideus, Plexippus, and Lynceus—wanted to take it away from her, and so she begged Meleager to help her. He intervened and, putting love before kinship, killed his uncles. When his mother Althaea heard about this, that her son had dared such a crime, she, remembering the decree of the Parcae, took the log out of the chest and threw it in the fire. So in her desire to avenge the wrongs done to her brothers she killed her son. As for his sisters, the gods willed all of them except for Gorge and Deianira to be transformed while they wept into birds called *meleagrides* {"guinea hens"}. As for Meleager's wife, Alcyone, she died from mourning and grief.

175 Agrius When Agrius son of Porthaon saw that his brother Oeneus had lost all his children, he drove him destitute from the kingdom and put himself on the throne. Meanwhile, Diomedes, the son of Tydeus and Deipyle, heard after Ilium fell that his grandfather, Oeneus, had been deposed. So he came to Aetolia with Sthenelus son of Capaneus, fought and killed Agrius' son Lycopeus, drove Agrius

55. This passage is not listed in the ancient table of contents but is provided with a separate title in the manuscript.

himself destitute from the kingdom, and restored his grandfather, Oeneus, to power. Agrius committed suicide after he was driven from power.

176 Lycaon They say that Jupiter visited Lycaon son of Pelasgus and ravished his daughter Callisto. From this union Arcas was born, who bestowed his name onto the land. Now, Lycaon's sons got the urge to test Jupiter to see whether he was really a god, so they mixed human flesh with that of other animals and put it in a feast before him. When he realized what was happening, he flung the table over in anger and killed Lycaon's sons with a thunderbolt. On that very spot Arcas later would found the city that is named Trapezos {Greek "Table"}. Jupiter changed their father into a wolf.[56]

177 Callisto They say that Lycaon's daughter Callisto was changed into a bear because of Juno's anger over her affair with Jupiter. Later Jupiter assigned her a place among the stars, and she is called Septentrio.[57] This constellation neither moves from its place nor sets because Tethys, Ocean's wife and Juno's nurse, prevents her from setting into the ocean. This is the great Septentrio that is the subject of these verses in the *Cretica:*

> And you, Arcas, scion of the changed Lycaonian Nymph,
> the Nymph stolen from the icy peak of Nonacrina
> whom Tethys ever keeps from touching Ocean's deep
> because she dared to sleep once in her nursling's stead.

Accordingly, this Bear is called *Helice*[58] by the Greeks. She has seven faint stars on her head, two on each ear, one on her arm, a bright one on her chest, one on the front foot, a bright one on the outermost edge of her haunch, two on the back thigh, two at the tip of her foot, and three on her tail. Twenty stars in all.

178 Europa Europa was the daughter of Argiope and Agenor and lived in Sidon. Jupiter turned himself into a bull, transported her from Sidon to Crete, and fathered by her Minos, Sarpedon, and Rhadamanthus. Her father, Agenor, sent his sons either to bring their sister back or otherwise not to return to his sight. Phoenix set out for Africa and remained there; from his name the Africans are called Phoenicians. Cilix bestowed his name on Cilicia. Cadmus roamed about and came to Delphi. There he received an oracle telling him to buy from some herders a cow that had a mark resembling a moon on its side and drive it before him. He was fated, the oracle continued, to found a city and reign wherever the cow happened to lie down.

56. The Greek word for wolf is *lykos.*

57. This name is derived from *septem,* the Latin word for "seven," referring to the seven major stars of the constellation, which was also known as the Wagon or Great Bear.

58. Greek for "revolving," so named because the constellation revolves around the North Star in a relatively tight circle.

When Cadmus heard his destiny, he did exactly as he was told. He went out in search of water and came to the Castalian Spring, which was guarded by a serpent, the son of Mars. After the serpent killed his men, Cadmus killed it with a stone.

Following Minerva's instructions, Cadmus plowed the land and sowed the teeth, from which the Sparti sprouted. They fought each other, and only five survived: Chthonius, Udaeus, Hyperenor, Pelorus, and Echion. The land was called Boeotia {Greek "Cow-land"} after the cow he followed.

179 Semele Cadmus, the son of Agenor and Argiope, had with Harmonia, the daughter of Mars and Venus, four daughters, Semele, Ino, Agave, and Autonoe, and one son, Polydorus. Jupiter wanted to sleep with Semele. When Juno found out, she changed her appearance into that of Semele's nurse Beroe, came to her, and persuaded her to ask Jupiter to come to her as he came to Juno, "So that you may know," she said, "how great a pleasure it is to lie with a god." So Semele asked Jupiter to come to her as Juno advised, and she got what she asked for. Jupiter came with thunder and lightning and consumed Semele with fire. From her womb was born Liber, who was saved from the fire and given by Mercury to Nysus to be raised. In Greek he is called Dionysus.

180 Actaeon The shepherd Actaeon, the son of Aristaeus and Autonoe, watched Diana as she bathed and wanted to rape her. Diana was enraged at this and made him grow horns on his head and be consumed by his own dogs.

181 Diana When Diana became exhausted from constant hunting in the summer heat, she went to the well-shaded valley called Gargaphia and washed herself in the Spring of the Virgin. Actaeon, Cadmus' grandson and son of Aristaeus and Autonoe, came to the same place to refresh himself and his dogs, which he had pushed hard in pursuit of prey. He unintentionally stumbled into the sight of Diana. To prevent him from saying anything, she changed his form into a deer, and he was torn apart by his dogs who thought he was a deer.

The dogs' names were for the male dogs: Melampus, Ichnobates, Pamphagos, Dorceus, Oribasus, Nebrophonus, Laelaps, Theron, Pterelas, Hylaeus, Nape, Ladon, Poemenis, Therodanapis, Aura, Lacon, Harpyia, Aello, Dromas, Thous, Canache, Cyprius, Sticte, Labros, Arcas, Agriodus, Tigris, Hylactor, Alce, Harpalus, Lycisce, Melaneus, Lachne, and Leucon. Likewise, the three female dogs that consumed him were called Melanchaetes, Agre, Theridamas, and Oresitrophos.[59]

Likewise other authors pass down these names: Acamas, Syrus, Aeon, Stilbon, Agrius, Charops, Aethon, Corus, Boreas, Draco, Eudromus, Dromius, Zephyrus, Lampus, Haemon, Cyllopodes, Harpalicus, Machimus, Ichneumo, Melampus, Ocydromus, Borax, Ocythous, Pachitos, Obrimus; the females were: Argo, Arethusa, Urania, Theriope, Dinomache, Dioxippe, Echione, Gorgo, Cyllo,

59. The first list of names is taken almost entirely from Ovid, *Metamorphoses* 3.206–233, with some differences.

Harpyia, Lynceste, Leaene, Lycaena, Ocypode, Ocydrome, Oxyboe, Orias, Sainon, Theriphone, Hylaeos, and <*unintelligible*>.[60]

182 The Daughters of Ocean Ida, Amalthea, and Adrastea* were the daughters of Ocean. Others say that they were the daughters of Melisseus and were Jupiter's nurses, the ones that are called Dodonian Nymphs (others call them the Naiads). < . . . > whose names are Cisseis, Nysa, Erato, Eriphia, Dromia, Polyhymno. On Mount Nysa their nursling[61] bestowed upon them a gift: he asked Medea to take away their old age and turn them into young women. Later they were given an exalted position among the stars and called the Hyades. Others hand down that they were named Arsinoe, Ambrosia, Bromia, Cisseis, and Coronis.

183 The Names of the Sun's Horses and the Seasons Eous, who turns the heavens. Aethiops, who is like a flame: he ripens the grain with his warmth. These two trace-horses are males. The females, the yoke-horses, are Bronte and Sterope, whom we call Thunder and Lightning. My source for this fact is Eumelus the Corinthian. In like manner Homer hands down the following names: Abraxas, <*unintelligible names*>. Ovid gives us these:[62] Pyrois, Eous, Aethon, and Phlegon.

The names of the Horae, daughters of Jupiter son of Saturn and Themis the Titaness* are as follows: Auxo, Eunomia, Pherusa, Carpo, Dice, Euporia, Irene, Orthosia, and Thallo. Other authors hand down ten with the following names: Auge, Anatole, Musica, Gymnastica, Nymphe, Mesembria, Sponde, <*unintelligible names*> Hesperis, and Dysis.

184 Pentheus and Agave Pentheus, the son of Echion and Agave, said that Liber was not a god, and he was unwilling to accept his mysteries. Because of this his mother, Agave, and her sisters, Ino and Autonoe, tore him apart in a fit of madness brought on by Liber. When Agave regained her senses and saw that she had been driven by Liber to commit such a gruesome crime, she fled from Thebes. In her wandering she eventually came to the land of the Illyrians ruled by King Lycotherses, who took her in.

185 Atalanta They say that Schoeneus had an extraordinarily beautiful virgin daughter, Atalanta, whose natural talent allowed her to run faster than men. She asked her father to keep her unmarried. So when many suitors came to seek her hand in marriage, her father issued a challenge. Whoever wanted to marry her would first have to contend with her in a race. He laid out a course, and the suitor was to run away unarmed while she pursued with a spear. All those she overtook on the course she would kill and put their heads up in the stadium.

She defeated and killed a great number of suitors until she was at last beaten by Hippomenes, the son of Megareus and Merope. Venus had given him three apples

60. Many names in the second list are found in a fragmentary papyrus (*PMed. inv.* 123).

61. The god Liber.

62. From *Metamorphoses* 2.153.

of outstanding beauty and taught him what to do with them. By throwing the apples during the contest itself, he slowed her down. For as she collected the apples and admired the gold, she got sidetracked and handed victory to the young man.

Schoeneus willingly gave him his daughter in marriage as agreed. As Hippomenes was leading her back to his home, he forgot that it was due to Venus' service that he won and did not thank her. Venus grew angry at this, and when he was sacrificing to Jupiter Victor on Mount Parnassus, she inflamed him with desire, and he slept with Atalanta in the temple. Because of this Jupiter turned him into a lion and her into a lioness, and the gods prevented them from engaging in sexual intercourse.[63]

186 Melanippe [1] Neptune slept with Desmontes'[64] exceptionally beautiful daughter Melanippe (other poets say she was Aeolus' daughter) and fathered two sons by her. [2] When Desmontes found out about this, he blinded Melanippe, shut her in a tower, and ordered that she receive only a little food and water and that the infants be exposed to wild animals. [3] After they were exposed, a lactating cow came to the infants and offered her teats to them. Some herdsmen saw the two boys and picked them up with the intention of raising them.

[4] Meanwhile, Metapontus, the king of Icaria, demanded that his wife, Theano, bear him children or leave the kingdom. Afraid, she sent to the shepherds a request that they furnish some infant whom she could secretly substitute as the king's own. They sent her the two infants whom they had found, and she passed them off on King Metapontus as her own. [5] Later Theano did give birth to two sons by Metapontus. Since, however, Metapontus adored the older pair—they were extremely handsome—Theano sought to get rid of them and guarantee the throne for her real sons. [6] So the day came for Metapontus to set out for the temple of Diana Metapontina to perform a sacrifice. Theano seized the opportunity and, telling her real sons that the older pair were not the king's children, said, "And so, when they go out to hunt, murder them with knives." [7] They, following their mother's order, went to the mountains, where a fight broke out between the two pairs. The sons of Neptune were aided by their father and came out on top, killing the others. When their bodies were brought back to the palace, Theano killed herself with a hunting knife.

[8] Then Boeotus and Aeolus, having punished their attackers, sought refuge with the shepherds who had raised them. There Neptune revealed to them that he was their father and that their mother was being held in prison. [9] They went to Desmontes and killed him. They freed their mother from her imprisonment, and Neptune restored her vision. Her sons took her to Icaria, introduced her to King Metapontus, and informed him about Theano's treachery. [10] Then Metapontus

63. In late antiquity the belief arose that lions did not mate with other lions, which may be a misunderstanding of Pliny the Elder, *NH* 8.41-42, which states that in Africa different species frequently mated.

64. Desmontes is a figure invented here because of a misunderstanding of the Greek title of the Euripidean play *Melanippe Desmotis,* or *Melanippe the Captive,* which was somehow taken to mean Melanippe "daughter of Desmo(n)tes."

took Melanippe as wife and adopted them as his children. They later founded cities on the Propontis and bestowed their names on them, Boeotus giving his name to Boeotia, Aeolus his to Aeolia.

187 Alope [1] Neptune slept with Cercyon's daughter Alope because she was extraordinarily beautiful. From their union she gave birth and then without her father's knowledge handed the infant over to her nurse to be exposed. When the infant had been exposed, a mare came and offered the child her milk. [2] A certain shepherd who was following the mare saw the infant and took it home. When he arrived at his cottage carrying a young infant swaddled in royal clothes, another shepherd asked that the child be given over to him. [3] He gave him the child but not the royal clothes, and when a quarrel broke out between the two—the one who had gotten the child demanded the tokens of his noble birth, but the other refused—the arguing pair took their case to King Cercyon and began to argue in front of him. [4] The one who had been given the child demanded the tokens. When the swaddling-clothes in question were brought in as evidence, Cercyon realized that they had been cut from his daughter's dress. Out of fear Alope's nurse confessed to the king that the infant was indeed Alope's child. The king ordered his daughter to be locked up until she died and the infant to be exposed. [5] Once again the mare came and nourished the infant, and once again the shepherds found the child and took him in, sensing that it was the will of the gods that he be nurtured, and they raised him, giving him the name Hippothous.[65]

[6] Theseus killed Cercyon as he passed by there on his way from Troezen. Hippothous approached Theseus and asked to be given his grandfather's throne. Theseus willingly granted his request since he knew that Hippothous was the son of Neptune, from whom he too was born. [7] As for Alope, Neptune turned her body into a spring, which was named after Alope.

188 Theophane Theophane was the extraordinarily beautiful virgin daughter of Bisaltes. Many suitors came to ask her father for her hand in marriage, but Neptune kidnapped her and carried her to the island of Crumissa. When the suitors learned that she was staying there, they readied a ship and sailed for Crumissa. In order to throw them off the trail, Neptune changed Theophane into a beautiful ewe, himself into a ram, and all the citizens of Crumissa into a flock. When the suitors got there and did not find any people, they started killing the flock and eating them as sustenance. When Neptune saw that the men he had turned into the flock were being consumed, he turned the suitors into wolves. He, still a ram, slept with Theophane, who gave birth to a ram with a golden fleece. This is the ram that carried Phrixus to Colchis and whose fleece Aeetes placed in the grove of Mars. The fleece was later carried off by Jason.

189 Procris [1] Procris was the daughter of Pandion and the wife of Cephalus son of Deion. Held fast by their love for one another, they both promised each other

65. *Hippos* is the Greek word for "horse."

that they would not sleep with anyone else. [2] But Cephalus was also devoted to the hunt, and when one morning at dawn he had gone into the mountains, Tithonus' wife, Aurora, fell in love with him and asked to sleep with him. Cephalus refused because he had made a promise to Procris. [3] Then Aurora said, "I do not want you to break your promise unless she has broken hers first." So she changed him into the form of a stranger and gave him many gifts for him to take to Procris. When Cephalus visited Procris in this disguise, he gave her the many gifts and slept with her.

Aurora then took away the stranger's disguise. [4] When Procris saw Cephalus, she realized that she had been deceived by Aurora and fled to the island of Crete, where Diana was hunting. When Diana caught sight of her, she said to her, "Virgins hunt with me. You are not a virgin, so leave our company." [5] Then Procris told her about her misfortunes and how Aurora had deceived her. Diana was touched by pity, so she gave her a spear that never missed its mark and a dog, Laelaps, that no prey could elude. Then Diana ordered her to go and compete with Cephalus. [6] So she, with her hair cut off and wearing men's clothing, went to Cephalus by the will of Diana, challenged him to a hunting contest, and defeated him. When Cephalus saw the great potential of both the dog and the spear, he asked the stranger—not suspecting she was his wife—to sell him the spear and dog. She refused. He promised her a share of the throne. [7] She refused. "But," she said, "if you just have to have it, give me what boys normally give." His desire for the dog and spear was so strong that he promised he would, [8] so they went into the bedroom. Procris lifted up her dress and showed him that she was a female and his wife. Cephalus accepted the gifts Procris offered, and they were reconciled.

[9] Still, fearful of Aurora, she followed him in the morning to keep her eye on him, and she hid in some bushes. When Cephalus saw the bushes move, he threw the spear that did not miss and killed his wife, Procris. [10] Cephalus did have one child by her, a son named Arcesius, who would later become the father of Laertes, the father of Ulysses.

190 Theonoe [1] The seer Thestor had a son, Calchas, and two daughters, Leucippe and Theonoe, the latter of whom pirates kidnapped while she was playing by the sea and carried off to Caria. There, King Icarus purchased her to be his concubine. [2] Thestor, meanwhile, set out to search for his lost daughter and came to the land of Caria because of a shipwreck. He was put in prison in the same location where Theonoe was staying.

[3] Now Leucippe, who had lost both her father and sister, went to Delphi to ask whether a search ought to be conducted for them. Apollo responded, "Travel the earth as my priest, and you will find them." [4] When Leucippe heard the oracle, she cut off her hair and as a young man traveled over the earth to find them. When she came to Caria, Theonoe saw her and, thinking she was a priest, fell in love with her male visitor. She ordered him to be led to her chamber so that she could sleep with him. [5] Leucippe said this was not possible because she was in fact a woman. Enraged, Theonoe ordered the priest to be locked up in a chamber and one of the prisoners to be sent in to execute the priest. [6] The man sent in to kill the priest (but

really to execute his own daughter) was the unwitting old man Thestor. Theonoe did not recognize him, so she gave him a sword and ordered him to kill the priest.

When he had entered the chamber holding the sword, he said that he was called Thestor; that he had lost two daughters, Leucippe and Theonoe; and that his life had come to the point that he was ordered to commit a crime. [7] Then he turned his sword on himself and was about to commit suicide when Leucippe, hearing her father's name, wrenched the sword out of his hand. She called out to her father, Thestor, to help her go and kill the queen. When Theonoe heard her father's name, she revealed that she was his daughter. King Icarus, when the truth became known, presented Thestor with gifts and sent him back to his home.

191 King Midas Midas, the king of Mygdon and the son of the Mother Goddess, was made a judge by Tmolus when Apollo faced off against Marsyas (or Pan) in a piping contest. Though Tmolus gave the victory to Apollo, Midas said that it should have been awarded to Marsyas. Apollo was offended at this and said to Midas, "What heart you had in judging, so too shall be the ears you have." After he said this, he made Midas have the ears of an ass.

At that time Father Liber was leading an army into India. Silenus got himself lost, but Midas generously welcomed him into his home and provided him with a guide to lead him back to Liber's company. Father Liber in return for his kindness gave Midas the opportunity to choose whatever he wanted from him. Midas asked him to have whatever he touched be turned into gold. Liber granted him this wish, and when he returned to the palace, everything he touched became gold. Now when his hunger came to the point of torture, he asked Liber to take away his specious gift. Liber ordered him to wash in the Pactolus River; when his body touched the water, it turned the color of gold. This river is now called the Chrysorrhoas {Greek "Goldenflow"} in Lydia.

192 Hyas Atlas and Pleione (or another Oceanid) had twelve daughters and a son, Hyas, who was killed by either a boar or a lion. His sisters perished from grief as they mourned his death. Of these, the first five who died were raised to the stars and occupy the place between the horns of Taurus: Phaesyla, Ambrosia, Coronis, Eudora, and Polyxo, who are called the Hyades after their brother's name. They call these same stars *Suculae* {"Rainy Ones"} in Latin, but certain authors say that they are called the Hyades from the fact that they are positioned in the shape of the Greek letter Υ.[66] Quite a few say that it is because they bring rain with them when they rise (the Greek for "to rain" is *hyein*). There are also those who think that these women are among the stars because they were Father Liber's nurses, whom Lycurgus had driven from the island of Naxos.

As for the other sisters, who died from grief, they too were later made into a constellation, and because there were more of them, they are called the Pleiades.[67]

66. All Greek words that begin with the letter upsilon (Υ) were pronounced with an *h-* sound at the beginning, so here *hy-*.

67. The Greek word *pleion* means "more."

Some think that they are named this because they are all joined together, that is, they are near {Greek *plesion*} each other. In fact, they are so bunched together that they can barely be counted, nor can anyone with their eyes make out for certain whether they should be considered six or seven stars. These are their names: Electra, Alcyone, Celaeno, Merope, Sterope, Taygete, and Maia. They say that of these, Electra does not appear, because her son Dardanus was lost and Troy was stolen from her. Others think that Merope is too ashamed to be seen, because she married a mortal man while all the rest married gods; because of this she mourns, banished from the chorus of her sisters, and wears her hair unbound, which is called *cometes* {Greek "long-haired"} or *longodes* {Greek "spear-like"}, because it is drawn out lengthwise, or *xiphias* {Greek "sword"}, because it produces the form of a sword's blade. This star[68] predicts mourning.

193 Harpalycus The Thracian Harpalycus, king of the Amymneans, had a daughter, Harpalyce. When she lost her mother, he nursed her on the teats of heifers and mares, and as she grew up, he trained her in warfare, intending to make her the successor of his kingdom eventually.* Nor did the girl fail to meet her father's expectations; she turned out to be such a warrior that she even served as her father's protector. For when Neoptolemus on his way home from Troy defeated Harpalycus and wounded him severely, she made a charge into the onslaught, saved her father from the brink of death, and set the enemy to flight. Later, however, Harpalycus was killed in a mutinous uprising of his people. Harpalyce took this so hard that she withdrew to the woods, and after she had destroyed many stables full of cattle, she was finally killed by a posse of shepherds.

194 Arion [1] The Methymnian Arion was exceptionally talented with the *cithara,* and for that he was esteemed by the Corinthian king Pyranthus. When he had asked the king whether he could display his skill in other cities and had accumulated a great fortune, his slaves conspired with some sailors to kill him. [2] Apollo came to him in his sleep and told him to put on his costume and crown, play his music, and give himself over to those who came to his rescue. So when his slaves and sailors were just about to kill him, he asked them to let him sing first. [3] When the sounds of his *cithara* and voice were heard, dolphins came around the ship, and when Arion saw them, he threw himself into the sea. They buoyed him up and took him back to King Pyranthus in Corinth. But when he reached land, out of a desire to get on his way he did not push a dolphin back into the sea, and the dolphin died there. [4] When Arion told Pyranthus his trials and tribulations, Pyranthus ordered the dolphin to be buried and a memorial be built for it.

After a short while word reached Pyranthus that the ship that had transported Arion had been driven to Corinth by a storm. [5] He ordered the men to be brought before him. When he inquired about Arion, they said that he had died and that they had buried him. The king responded to them, "Tomorrow, you will swear to this at the dolphin's memorial." [6] For this purpose he ordered them to be kept under

68. By "this star" Hyginus refers to a comet.

guard. He told Arion to hide in the dolphin's monument the next morning dressed in the same costume he was wearing when he threw himself overboard. [7] When the king led the men to the memorial and ordered them to swear by the dolphin's ghost that Arion had died, Arion emerged from the memorial. They were rendered speechless, wondering by what divine power he had been rescued. [8] The king ordered them to be crucified at the dolphin's memorial. As for Apollo, he placed among the stars both Arion, because of his skill at the *cithara,* and the dolphin.

195 Orion Jupiter, Neptune, and Mercury all came to Thrace and visited King Hyrieus. He welcomed them into his home and was a generous host, so they allowed him to choose whatever he wanted. He chose to have children. Mercury brought forth the hide of a bull that Hyrieus himself had sacrificed to them. They urinated in it[69] and buried it in the ground, and from this Orion was born. When Orion tried to rape Diana, she killed him. Later, he was raised into the stars by Jupiter, and they call this constellation Orion.

196 Pan When the gods were afraid of Typhon's monstrous brutality in Egypt, Pan told them to turn themselves into wild animals to elude him more easily. Later, Jupiter killed Typhon with a thunderbolt. By the will of the gods Pan was raised into the stars because it was by his command that they escaped Typhon's violence. Because he had turned himself into a goat at that time, he was called Aegoceros, whom we call Capricorn.[70]

197 Venus It is said that an egg of remarkable size once fell from the sky into the Euphrates River and that the fish pushed it out onto the bank. Doves came and alighted upon the egg, and after it grew warm, it hatched. Out came Venus, who afterward was called the Syrian Goddess. Since she was far more just and upright than the rest of the gods, Jupiter gave her a choice, and she had the fish raised into the stars. Because of this the Syrians consider fish and doves to be gods and do not eat them.

198 Nisus They say that Nisus, the son of Mars (others say he was Deion's son) and king of the Megarians, had a purple hair on his head, and an oracle foretold to him that he would rule so long as he kept this hair. When Minos son of Jupiter came to attack him, Venus prompted Nisus' daughter Scylla to fall in love with him. So that he would be victorious, Scylla cut off the fateful hair from her father's head as he slept. And so Nisus was conquered by Minos.

When Minos was returning to Crete, she asked him to take her away with him as he had promised. He replied that Crete was a most sacred place and would never shelter such a crime. She hurled herself into the sea so that her father could not pursue her. But while Nisus was pursuing her, he turned into a *haliaetos* bird (that is, a sea-eagle), while his daughter Scylla turned into the fish that they call a *ciris.* Today,

69. The Latin *urina* ("urine") is used here to etymologize Orion's name.

70. Greek *aig-* and Latin *capr-* mean "goat"; Greek *keros* and Latin *cornu* mean "horn."

whenever this bird sees that fish swimming, it propels itself into the water, grabs it, and tears it apart with its talons.

199 The Other Scylla They say that Scylla, the daughter of the river Crataeis, was a spectacularly beautiful young woman. Glaucus loved her, but Circe daughter of the Sun loved Glaucus. Since it was Scylla's habit to bathe in the sea, Circe daughter of the Sun poisoned the waters out of jealousy. When Scylla went into the water, dogs sprouted from her loins and she became savage. Yet she got her revenge for the injuries done to her: she robbed Ulysses of some of his crew as he sailed by.

200 Chione They say that both Apollo and Mercury slept with Chione (other poets call her Philonis) daughter of Daedalion on the same night. She bore Philammon to Apollo, and Autolycus to Mercury. Later, on a hunt she spoke insultingly about Diana, who shot her dead with arrows. As for her father, Daedalion, while he was weeping over his only daughter, Apollo turned him into a *daedalion* bird, that is, a hawk.

201 Autolycus Mercury endowed Autolycus, his son by Chione, with the gift of being the most thievish of all men and never being caught during a theft. So that he could steal anything, Mercury gave him the power to change into whatever appearance he wished: from white to black or black to white, from having horns to not having them, and back again. He kept raiding Sisyphus's livestock. Sisyphus could not catch him, but he surmised that Autolycus was the thief from the fact that the number of Autolycus' livestock was increasing while his own was shrinking. So he branded the hooves of his livestock in order to catch him. After Autolycus made his usual raid on Sisyphus' livestock, Sisyphus came to him and by the marks on their hooves found the livestock he had raided and carried off. While he was there, Sisyphus slept with Autolycus' daughter Anticlia, who later was given to Laertes in marriage. She gave birth to Ulysses. This is why some authors call Ulysses Sisyphus' son, and that is why Ulysses was clever.

202 Coronis When Apollo had impregnated Coronis, the daughter of Phlegyas, he had a crow watch over her to prevent anyone from violating her. Ischys son of Elatus slept with her. Because of this, he was killed by Jupiter with a thunderbolt, and Apollo struck and killed Coronis though she was pregnant. He cut the child Asclepius out of the womb and raised him. He changed the crow that had kept watch from white to black.

203 Daphne When Apollo was pursuing Daphne, the virgin daughter of the river Peneus, she asked Earth for protection. Earth took her in and turned her into a laurel tree. Apollo broke a sprig off of it and put it on his head.

204 Nyctimene They say that Nyctimene daughter of Epopeus, the king of the Lesbians, was an extremely beautiful young woman. Her father, Epopeus, became inflamed with desire for her and raped her. She hid in the forest out of shame.

Minerva took pity on her and turned her into an owl, which because of shame does not come out into the light but appears at night.

205 Arge They say that when the huntress Arge was chasing a deer, she said to the deer, "Though you may run as far as the sun travels, I will still catch you." Enraged, the Sun changed her into a doe.

206 Harpalyce The Arcadian king, Clymenus son of Schoeneus, was smitten with desire for his daughter Harpalyce and slept with her. When she gave birth, she served their son in a meal to her father, Clymenus. When he found out what had happened, he killed Harpalyce.

207–218 <*are not found in the manuscript*>[71]

219 Archelaus Archelaus son of Temenus was driven into exile by his brothers and went to King Cisseus in Macedonia. Since Cisseus was at that time being attacked by the neighboring peoples, he promised to give Archelaus both the kingdom and his daughter in marriage if he protected him from the enemy, for Archelaus was descended from Hercules (Temenus was Hercules' son). He routed the enemy in a single engagement and asked the king to fulfill his promise.

The king's friends, however, talked the king into breaking his promise and attempting to lure Archelaus to his death. He ordered his men to dig a pit, heap up a pile of coals in it, set them on fire, and place thin branches over top of it so that Archelaus would fall into it when he came. One of the king's slaves revealed the plot to Archelaus, and when he found out about the scheme, he asked for a private conference with the king. When all witnesses were removed from the scene, Archelaus grabbed the king and threw him into the pit, thus killing him. Then he fled, following a goat to Macedonia as he was bidden to do by Apollo's oracle, and there he established a town, naming it Aegeae after the word "goat".[72] Alexander the Great is said to be a descendant of Archelaus.

220 Cura When Cura {"Worry"} was crossing a certain river, she saw muddy clay, picked it up, pondered for a moment, and then molded a human. While she was thinking about just what she had created, Jupiter arrived on the scene. Cura asked him to give breath to the human, and Jupiter readily agreed to do it. But then, when Cura was about to name this creature after herself, Jupiter stopped her and said that it should be named after him. Now, while Cura and Jupiter were debating over the name, Earth rose up as well and said that it should be named after her, seeing how she was the one who had furnished her own body. They took up Saturn as the judge of their case, and it appears that he judged fairly in their case: "Jupiter,

71. According to the table of contents given at the beginning of the manuscript, the entries would have been: 207 Macareus, 208 Rhodos, 209 Cyrene, 210 Hecate, 211 Herse, 212 Endymion, 213 Atys, 214 Narcissus, 215 Hermaphroditus, 216 Eurydice, 217 Maleas, 218 Hyacinthus.

72. Hyginus uses the Latin word *capra* ("goat"), but the etymology depends on the Greek word (*aig-*).

because you gave it breath <you shall reclaim the breath after death; Earth, because you offered up your body,>* you shall reclaim the body. Because Cura first molded it, she shall possess it so long as it lives. But because there is some disagreement about the name, it shall be called "human" {*homo*} because it was clearly created from earth {*humus*}.

221 The Seven Wise Men Pittacus from Mitylene. Periander from Corinth. Thales from Miletus. Solon from Athens. Chilon from Lacedaemon. Cleobulus from Lindus. Bias from Priene. These are their sayings:

Cleobulus, who dwells in Lindus, says, "Moderation is best."
Periander from Ephyra, you teach, "Practice is everything."*
Pittacus, who hails from Mitylene says, "Know the occasion."
The famous Bias from Priene asserts "Most people are bad."
The Milesian Thales warns, "Losses go to the guarantor!"
Chilon, who comes from Sparta, says, "Know yourself."
Cecropian Solon bids, "Nothing in excess."

222 The Seven Lyric Poets <*is not found in the manuscript*>

223 The Seven Wonders [1] The temple of Diana in Ephesus built by the Amazon Otrera, the wife of Mars.

[2] The tomb of King Mausolus made with gleaming Parian marble, 80 feet high[73] and 1,340 feet in circumference.

[3] The bronze statue of the Sun at Rhodes (that is, the Colossus) at a height of 90 feet.

[4] The statue of Olympian Jupiter, which was sculpted by Phidias out of ivory and gold, seated on a throne, 60 feet high.

[5] The house of King Cyrus in Ecbatana built by Memnon out of white and variegated marbles covered with gold.

[6] The wall in Babylonia that Semiramis daughter of Dercetis built out of brick and tar and joined by iron, 25 feet wide, 60 feet high, and 300 stades in circumference.

[7] The pyramids in Egypt, the shadow of which is not seen,[74] 60 feet high.

224 Mortals Who Became Immortal Hercules, the son of Jupiter and Alcmena.

Liber, the son of Jupiter and Semele.

Castor and Pollux, the brothers of Helen and sons of Jupiter and Leda.

Perseus, the son of Jupiter and Danae, who was admitted into the stars.

Arcas, the son of Jupiter and Callisto, who was raised into the stars.

73. The numbers in this *Fabula* are corrupt, so readers should not put any credence in the accuracy of these figures.

74. At noon during the vernal equinox the pyramid of Cheops does not cast a shadow.

Ariadne, the daughter of Minos and Pasiphae, whom Father Liber named Libera.

Callisto daughter of Lycaon, who became the constellation Septentrio.

Cynosura, Jupiter's nurse, who became the other Septentrio.[75]

Asclepius, the son of Apollo and Coronis.

Pan, the son of Mercury and Penelope.

Crotos, the son of Pan and Eupheme, the foster brother of the Muses, who became the constellation Sagittarius.

Icarius and his daughter Erigone became constellations: Icarius became Arcturus, Erigone Virgo.

Ganymedes son of Assaracus became Aquarius of the Zodiac.

Ino daughter of Cadmus became Leucothea, whom we call Mater Matuta.

Melicertes son of Athamas became the god Palaemon.

Myrtilus, the son of Mercury and Theobula, became the constellation the Charioteer.[76]

225 Those Who First Dedicated Temples to the Gods Pelasgus son of Triopas built the first temple to Olympian Jupiter in Arcadia.

Thessalus built the temple of Jupiter Dodonaeus in Macedonia in the land of the Molossians.

Eleuther was the first to set up a statue of Father Liber and show how it should be worshipped.

Phoroneus son of Inachus built the first temple to Juno in Argos.

The Amazon Otrera, the wife of Mars, built the first temple to Diana in Ephesus, which later by King < . . . >[77] they restored.

Lycaon son of Pelasgus built the temple to Cyllenian Mercury in Arcadia.

Pierius < . . . >.

226–237 *<are not found in the manuscript>*[78]

238 Fathers Who Killed Their Daughters Agamemnon son of Atreus: his daughter Iphigenia, but she was saved by Diana.

Likewise Callisthenes < . . . >* of Euboea: his daughter, in order to save his country in accordance with an oracle.[79]

75. Ursa Minor.

76. Hyginus uses the Greek *Heniochos*. The Latin would be *Auriga*.

77. The missing material presumably contains information about the burning of the temple by Herostratus in 356 BC and perhaps something about its restoration.

78. According to the table of contents accompanying the manuscript, the entries would have been: 226 Mortal Women Who Slept with Jupiter, 227 With Apollo, 228 With Neptune, 229 With Mercury, 230 With Liber, 231 With Mars, 232 With Aquilo, 233 Goddesses Who Slept with Mortals, 234 Those Who Killed Their Fathers, 235 Those Who Killed Their Mothers, 236 Those Who Killed Their Brothers, 237 Fathers Who Killed Their Sons.

79. This sentence is obscure in sense and refers to a story otherwise unknown. Some believe that it was added later. See the endnote to this sentence.

Clymenus son of Schoeneus: Harpalyce, because she had served him his own son in a meal.

The Spartan Hyacinthus: his daughter Antheis, to save the Athenians in accordance with an oracle.

Erechtheus son of Pandion: Chthonia, to save the Athenians in accordance with an oracle; the rest of her sisters hurled themselves to their deaths.

Cercyon son of Vulcan: Alope, because of her fornication with Neptune.

Aeolus: Canace, because of her incestuous crime with her brother Macareus.

239 Mothers Who Killed Their Sons Medea daughter of Aeetes: Mermerus and Pheres, her sons by Jason.

Procne daughter of Pandion: Itys, her son by Tereus son of Mars.

Ino daughter of Cadmus: Melicertes, her son by Athamas son of Aeolus, while fleeing Athamas.

Althaea daughter of Thestius: Meleager, her son by Oeneus son of Porthaon, because he had killed his maternal uncles.

Themisto daughter of Hypseus: Sphincius and Orchomenus, her sons by Athamas son of Aeolus, goaded into doing it by Ino daughter of Cadmus.

Tyro daughter of Salmoneus: her two sons by Sisyphus son of Aeolus in accordance with an oracle of Apollo.

Agave daughter of Cadmus: Pentheus son of Echion, goaded on by Father Liber.

Harpalyce daughter of Clymenus: the child she and her father conceived together, because of his impiety (he had forced her to sleep with him against her will).

240 Wives Who Killed Their Husbands Clytaemnestra daughter <of Tyndareus and Leda daughter>* of Thestius: Agamemnon son of Atreus.

Helen, the daughter of Jupiter and Leda: Deiphobus son of Priam.

Agave: Lycotherses in Illyria, so that she could give his kingdom to her father, Cadmus.

Deianira daughter of Oeneus: Hercules, the son of Jupiter and Alcmena, at Nessus' prompting.

Iliona daughter of Priam: Polymnestor, the king of the Thracians.

Semiramis: King Ninus in Babylonia.

241 Husbands Who Killed Their Wives Hercules son of Jupiter: Megara daughter of Creon, in a fit of madness.

Theseus son of Aegeus: the Amazon Antiope daughter of Mars, in accordance with Apollo's oracle.

Cephalus son of Deion (or of Mercury): Procris daughter of Pandion, unintentionally.

242 Men Who Committed Suicide Aegeus son of Neptune threw himself into the sea, and because of this the sea is called the Aegean Sea.

Evenus son of Hercules threw himself into the river Lycormas, which is now called Chrysorrhoas.

Ajax son of Telamon killed himself because of the judgment over who would get Achilles' armor.

Lycurgus son of Dryas was driven insane by Liber and committed suicide.

Macareus son of Aeolus committed suicide over Canace, his sister (i.e., his fiancée).

Agrius son of Porthaon killed himself after being driven from his kingdom by Diomedes.

Caeneus son of Elatus killed himself.

Menoeceus, Jocasta's father, hurled himself from the walls of Thebes because of the plague.

Nisus son of Mars committed suicide when he lost his fateful lock of hair.

Clymenus, the king of Arcadia, the son of Schoeneus, committed suicide because he had slept with his daughter.

Cinyras son of Paphus, the king of the Assyrians, killed himself because he slept with his daughter, Smyrna.

Hercules son of Jupiter threw himself into a fire.

Adrastus and his son Hipponous also threw themselves into a fire in accordance with Apollo's oracle.

Pyramus in Babylonia killed himself out of love for Thisbe.

Oedipus son of Laius, after gouging out his eyes, killed himself because of his mother Jocasta.

243 Women Who Committed Suicide [1] Hecuba daughter of Cisseus (or Dymas) and wife of Priam threw herself into the sea, and this is why the sea is called the Cynean Sea, for Hecuba had changed into a dog.[80]

Ino daughter of Cadmus threw herself into the sea with her son, Melicertes.

Anticlia daughter of Autolycus and mother of Ulysses committed suicide when she received a false report about her son.

[2] Stheneboea daughter of Iobates and wife of Proetus killed herself because of her love for Bellerophon.

Evadne daughter of Phylacus killed herself because of the death of her husband, Capaneus, at Thebes by throwing herself onto his pyre.

Aethra daughter of Pittheus killed herself over her children's deaths.[81]

[3] Deianira daughter of Oeneus committed suicide over Hercules; she, deceived by Nessus, had sent him the garment in which he burned.

Laodamia daughter of Acastus killed herself out of longing for her husband, Protesilaus.

Hippodamia daughter of Oenomaus and wife of Pelops committed suicide because Chrysippus was killed at her urging.

[4] Neaera daughter of Autolycus committed suicide over the death of her son, Hippothous.

80. Hyginus uses *canis,* the Latin word for "dog," but the etymology depends on the Greek word (*kun-*).

81. Theseus is the only recorded son of Aethra. Perhaps Henioche, Pittheus' other daughter, is meant.

Alcestis daughter of Pelias died in her husband Admetus' place.

Iliona daughter of Priam killed herself because of her parents' downfall.

[5] Themisto daughter of Hypseus committed suicide because she killed her own children at Ino's urging.

Erigone daughter of Icarius committed suicide by hanging because of the death of her father.

Phaedra daughter of Minos killed herself by hanging because of her stepson Hippolytus, whom she desired.

[6] Phyllis hanged herself because of Demophon son of Theseus.

Canace daughter of Aeolus committed suicide because of her brother Macareus' love.

Byblis daughter of Miletus killed herself because of her love for her brother Caunus.

[7] Calypso daughter of Atlas committed suicide because of her love for Ulysses.

Dido daughter of Belus killed herself because of her love for Aeneas.

Jocasta daughter of Menoeceus killed herself because of the death of her children and her transgression.

[8] Antigone daughter of Oedipus committed suicide because of the burial of her brother Polynices.

Pelopia daughter of Thyestes killed herself because of her father's crime.

Thisbe in Babylonia committed suicide over Pyramus, because he had himself committed suicide.

Semiramis in Babylonia threw herself onto the pyre after her horse died.[82]

244 Men Who Killed Relatives Theseus son of Aegeus: Pallas < . . . >.

< . . . > son of his brother Neleus.

Amphitryon: Electryon son of Perseus.

Meleager son of Oeneus: his mother's brothers Plexippus and Agenor because of Atalanta daughter of Schoeneus.

Telephus son of Hercules: Hippothous and Cepheus, the sons of his maternal grandmother, Neaera.

Aegisthus: Atreus and his son Agamemnon.

Orestes: Aegisthus son of Thyestes.

Megapenthes son of Proetus: Perseus, son of Jupiter and Danae, in revenge for his father's death.

Abas killed Megapenthes in revenge for his father, Lynceus.

Phegeus son of Alpheus: <*name missing*> the son of his daughter Alphesiboea.*

Amphion son of Tereus: his grandfather's sons.

Atreus son of Pelops: Tantalus and Plisthenes, the infant sons of his brother, Thyestes, and served them to him in a meal.

Hyllus son of Hercules: Sthenelus, the brother of his great-grandfather, Electryon.

82. Pliny the Elder (*NH* 8.156) reports that Semiramis fell in love with and had sexual relations with her horse.

Medus son of Aegeus: Perses, Aeetes' brother and son of the Sun.

Daedalus son of Eupalamus: Perdix, his sister's son, because he was jealous of his creative skills.

245 Men Who Killed Their Fathers-in-Law or Sons-in-Law Jason son of Aeson < . . . >*

< . . . > Phlegyon.

Pelops son of Tantalus: Oenomaus son of Mars.

Those who killed their sons-in-law:

Phegeus son of Alpheus: Alcmaeon son of Amphiaraus; he also killed Eurypylus.

Aeetes son of the Sun: Phrixus son of Athamas.

246 Those Who Ate Their Own Sons at Meals Tereus son of Mars: Itys, his son by Procne.

Thyestes son of Pelops: Tantalus and Plisthenes, his sons by Aerope.

Clymenus son of Schoeneus: his son by his daughter, Harpalyce.

247 Those Who Were Devoured by Dogs Actaeon son of Aristaeus.

On the island of Delos, Thasius son of Apollo's priest Anius; this is why there are no dogs on Delos.

Euripides the writer of tragedies was devoured in a temple.

248 Men Who Died from Boar Attacks Adonis son of Cinyras.

Ancaeus son of Lycurgus, by the Calydonian boar.

Idmon son of Apollo, who had with the Argonauts left the walls* while visiting King Lycus.

Hyas, the son of Atlas and Pleione, was killed by a boar or perhaps a lion.

249 Accursed Torches The torch that Hecuba daughter of Cisseus (or of Dymas) dreamed she gave birth to.

Nauplius' at the Capharean Rocks, when the Achaeans were shipwrecked.

Helen's, which she showed from the walls of Troy and which destroyed the city.

Althaea's, which killed Meleager.

250 Chariots That Brought Death to Their Drivers[83] Phaethon, the son of the Sun by Clymene.

Laomedon, the son of Ilus by Leucippe.

Oenomaus, the son of Mars by Asteria daughter of Atlas.

Diomedes, the son of Mars, also by Asteria.

Hippolytus, the son of Theseus by the Amazon Antiope.

Amphiaraus, the son of Oecles by Hypermestra daughter of Thestius.

The mares of Glaucus son of Sisyphus consumed him during the funeral games in honor of Pelias.

83. The Latin translated as "chariots" here can also mean simply a team of horses.

Iasion, the son of Jupiter and Electra daughter of Atlas.

Salmoneus, who made fake thunderbolts while sitting on his chariot, was struck, along with his chariot, by a thunderbolt.

251 Those Whom the Parcae Allowed to Return from the Underworld Ceres, who was searching for her daughter, Proserpina.

Father Liber descended into the underworld to get his mother, Semele daughter of Cadmus.

Hercules son of Jupiter went to bring out the dog Cerberus.

Asclepius, the son of Apollo and Coronis.

Castor and Pollux, the sons of Jupiter and Leda, return, alternating being dead.

Protesilaus son of Iphiclus came back because of Laodamia daughter of Acastus.

Alcestis daughter of Pelias, who descended because of her husband, Admetus.

Theseus son of Aegeus, who descended because of Pirithous.

Hippolytus son of Theseus by the will of Diana; he was afterwards named Virbius.

Orpheus son of Oeagrus, who descended because of his wife Eurydice.

Adonis, the son of Cinyras and Smyrna, by the will of Venus.

Glaucus son of Minos, who was restored to life by Polyidus son of Coeranus.

Ulysses son of Laertes, who went down to get back to his homeland.

Aeneas son of Anchises, who went down because of his father.

Mercury son of Maia constantly makes the journey.

252 Those Nourished by the Milk of Wild Animals Telephus, the son of Hercules and Auge, by a doe.

Aegisthus, the son of Thyestes and Pelopia, by a she-goat.

Aeolus and Boeotus, the sons of Neptune and Melanippe, by a cow.

Hippothous, the son of Neptune and Alope, by a mare.

Romulus and Remus, the sons of Mars and Ilia, by a she-wolf.

Antilochus son of Nestor, who was exposed on Mount Ida, by a dog.

Harpalyce daughter of Harpalycus, the king of the Amymneans, by a cow and a mare.

Camilla daughter of Metabus, the king of the Volscians, by a mare.

253 Those Who Committed Incest Jocasta with her son Oedipus.

Pelopia with her father Thyestes.

Harpalyce with her father Clymenus.

Hippodamia with her father Oenomaus.

Procris with her father Erechtheus, which union produced Aglaurus.

Nyctimene with her father Epopeus, king of the Lesbians.

Menephron with his daughter Cyllene and his mother Blias in Arcadia.

254 Exceptionally Devoted Women and Men [1] Antigone daughter of Oedipus buried her brother Polynices.

Electra daughter of Agamemnon toward her brother Orestes.

Iliona daughter of Priam toward her brother Polydorus and her parents.

[2] Pelopia daughter of Thyestes toward her father, in that she freed him.

Hypsipyle daughter of Thoas toward her father, in that she allowed him to live.

Chalciope daughter of Aeetes did not abandon her father after he lost his kingship.

Harpalyce daughter of Harpalycus saved her father in war and drove the enemy to flight.

[3] Erigone daughter of Icarius killed herself by hanging after her father died.

Agave daughter of Cadmus killed Lycotherses, the king of Illyria, and gave his kingdom to her father.

Xanthippe offered her breast milk to her father Mycon, who was locked up in prison, to keep him alive.

Tyro daughter of Salmoneus killed her sons to save her father.

[4] As soon as Mount Aetna on Sicily began to spew fire, Damon snatched his mother from the flames. Likewise Phintias[84] saved his father. Similarly, in Ilium Aeneas saved his father, Anchises, from the inferno by carrying him on his shoulders, as well as his son Ascanius.

[5] Cleops and Bitias, the sons of Cydippe, the priestess of Argive Juno: when the oxen Cydippe had sent out to graze were late[*] and did not return at the appointed time when the sacred objects were to be transported to Juno's temple on the mountain and the sacrifices were to be held (if the sacrifices were not performed at the precise time, the priestess was put to death), amid her alarm, [6] Cleops and Bitias took the place of the oxen, put on the wagon's harness, and transported the sacred objects and their mother to the sanctuary in the wagon. When the sacrifice was done, Cydippe prayed that Juno, if she had performed ritually pure sacrifices to her and if her sons had acted dutifully toward her, might bestow upon them whatever is a blessing to mortals. [7] When she finished her prayer, the sons brought back home both the wagon and their mother and, exhausted, fell asleep < . . . >.[85] Cydippe knew well that nothing better could happen to mortals than death, and because of this she met her death willingly.

255 Women Who Acted Wickedly toward Their Family Scylla daughter of Nisus killed her father.

Ariadne daughter of Minos killed her brother.

<Medea daughter of Aeetes killed her brother>[*] and her sons.

Procne daughter of Pandion killed her son.

The daughters of Danaus killed their cousins, whom they had married.

The women of the island Lemnos killed their fathers and sons.

Harpalyce daughter of Clymenus killed the son she had conceived in intercourse with her father.

84. The names normally associated with this story are Amphinomus and Anapius.

85. The sons die in their sleep, as is recorded by Herodotus (where their names are Cleobis and Biton, as usual), but more than that may be missing.

Among the Romans, Tullia drove a chariot over her father's body, and this is how the Wicked District got its name.

256 Exceptionally Faithful Women Penelope daughter of Icarius, Ulysses' wife.

Evadne daughter of Phylax, Capaneus' wife.

Laodamia daughter of Acastus, Protesilaus' wife.

Hecuba daughter of Cisseus, Priam's wife.

Theonoe daughter of Thestor < . . . >.

Alcestis daughter of Pelias, Admetus' wife.

Among the Romans, Lucretia daughter of Lucretius, Collatinus' wife.

257 Close Friends [1] Pylades son of Strophius and Orestes son of Agamemnon.

Pirithous son of Ixion and Theseus son of Aegeus.

Achilles son of Peleus and Patroclus son of Menoetius.

[2] Diomedes son of Tydeus and Sthenelus son of Capaneus.

Peleus son of Aeacus and Phoenix son of Amyntor.

Hercules son of Jupiter and Philoctetes son of Poeas.

Harmodius and Aristogiton were like brothers.

[3] In Sicily, since Dionysius was a remarkably cruel tyrant and used to torture and kill his own citizens, Moerus[86] tried to kill him. When the king's bodyguards caught him with a weapon, they led him to the king, [4] who interrogated him. He responded that he had been planning to kill the king, and the king ordered him to be crucified. Moerus asked him for three days' postponement, so that he could arrange for his sister's wedding, and offered the tyrant his friend and comrade Selinuntius to guarantee that he would show up on the third day. [5] The king granted his request for a postponement so that he could marry off his sister and said to Selinuntius that if Moerus did not return at the agreed-upon time, he would suffer the punishment reserved for Moerus and Moerus would be released.

[6] After he married his sister and was on his return trip, suddenly a storm with heavy rain broke out. The river swelled so much that it was impossible to cross it either by foot or by swimming. Moerus sat down by the river and wept for fear that his friend might die in his stead. [7] When Phalaris ordered Selinuntius to be crucified—because it was now the sixth hour of the third day and Moerus was not coming—Selinuntius responded that the day was not done yet. When it was the ninth hour, the king ordered Selinuntius to be led to the cross, [8] and as he was being led out, Moerus finally got past the river, caught up with the executioner, and cried out from a distance, "Executioner, wait! I am here, the one he is standing in for." They reported what had happened to the king, who commanded that they be brought to him. He requested that they make him their friend and granted Moerus his life.

86. The two characters in this story, Moerus and Selinuntius, are in other accounts named Damon and Phintias.

[9] Harmodius and Aristogiton. In Sicily, when Harmodius[87] was likewise planning on killing this same Phalaris, he—in order to create a false impression—killed a sow that had piglets and then went to his friend Aristogiton with the bloody sword, saying that he had killed his mother[88] and asking him to hide him. [10] He did, and Harmodius later asked him to go out and report back any rumors that had arisen concerning his mother. He reported back that there were no rumors. [11] That night they got into such a quarrel that they kept heaping bigger and bigger insults on each other, but even so Aristogiton was not willing to throw in his face that he had killed his mother. So Harmodius revealed that he had killed a sow that had piglets, and that is what he meant by "mother." He informed him that he was planning on killing the king and asked him to be his accomplice.

[12] When they went to kill the king, they were caught with weapons by his guards. When they were being taken to the king, Aristogiton got away from the guards and escaped, but Harmodius was brought alone before the king. When they asked him who his associate had been, in order not to betray his friend he bit his own tongue off and spit it in the king's face.

[13] Nisus and his friend Euryalus, for whom he too died.

258 Atreus and Thyestes When the brothers Atreus and Thyestes were at odds but could not harm each other, they pretended to reconcile. This gave Thyestes the chance to sleep with his brother's wife; Atreus in turn served Thyestes' son to him as a meal. The Sun, to avoid the pollution, fled the scene. But this is the truth of this story: Atreus was the first among the Myceneans to predict a solar eclipse; jealous of this, his brother left the city.

259 Lyncus Lyncus was the king of Sicily. After he received into his home Triptolemus, who had been sent by Ceres on a mission to show grain to mankind, he decided to kill his guest in order that all the glory would fall to him. Ceres was enraged at such a plot and changed him into a lynx of various colors because he showed himself to be of a devious {*varius*} mind.

260 Eryx Eryx was the son of Venus and Butes and was killed by Hercules. He gave his name to the mountain because he was buried there. Aeneas built a temple to Venus on this mountain, and Anchises is said to be buried there as well, though according to Cato he made it all the way to Italy.

261 Agamemnon Who Unwittingly Killed Diana's Deer After the Danaans came to Aulis from Greece, Agamemnon unwittingly killed Diana's deer. Diana was angry because of this and stopped the winds from blowing. Since they

87. Harmodius and Aristogiton are the famous tyrannicides in Athens and have nothing to do with the following story. Their names are erroneously given.

88. The Latin can mean either "he said that he killed his mother" or simply "a mother." The ambiguity in the language means that Harmodius can test his friend while not really telling a falsehood, since the sow in fact did have piglets.

could not sail and were being overwhelmed by a plague, they consulted the oracle, which told them that only someone of Agamemnon's blood would satisfy Diana. On the pretence of her getting married, Ulysses brought Iphigenia there so that she could be sacrificed. But the goddess pitied her, stole her away, and substituted a deer in her place. She was then transported to the city of the Taurians and given over to King Thoas, who made her a priestess.

While she was conducting human sacrifices to appease the power of Diana Dictynna in accordance with the established custom there, she recognized her brother Orestes. On the instructions of an oracle, he had been headed to Colchis with his friend Pylades to rid himself of his madness. With their help she killed Thoas and took away the image of the goddess, hidden in a bundle of wood and took it to Aricia. This is another reason why the statue is called "fascilis" {*fascis* = "bundle of wood"}, not just because of the torch {*fac-*} with which she is depicted in paintings—which is why it is also called Light-bearer {*lucifer*}.

Later, when the Romans no longer approved of the ritual's cruelty—although slaves were sacrificed—the statue of Diana was moved to Laconia, where the spirit of the ritual was preserved in the whipping of young boys who were given the name *Bomonicae* {from Greek *bomos,* "altar"} because they, stretched out on the altars, contended to see who could endure the most blows. Orestes' bones were transferred from Aricia to Rome and buried in front of the temple of Saturn, which is in front of the Capitoline Hill and next to the temple of Concord.

262–268 <*are not found in the manuscript*>[89]

<269 Enormous Men> < . . . >, the son of Jupiter and Europa.

The other Cygnus, the son of Mars, whom Hercules likewise killed.

270 Especially Handsome Men Iasion son of Corythus; the story goes that Ceres loved him, and this very fact is given credence in the histories.

Cinyras son of Paphus, the Assyrian king.

Anchises son of Assaracus, whom Venus loved.

Alexander Paris, the son of Priam and Hecuba, whom Helen accompanied.

Nireus son of Charops.

Cephalus son of Pandion, whom Aurora loved.

Tithonus, the son of Laomedon, who was Aurora's husband.

Parthenopaeus, the son of Meleager and Atalanta.

Achilles, the son of Peleus and Thetis.

Patroclus son of Menoetius.

Idomeneus, who loved Helen.

Theseus, the son of Aegeus and Aethra, whom Ariadne loved.

89. According to the table of contents given at the beginning of the manuscript, the entries would have been: 262 Noctua; 263 Ceres; 264 Those Killed by a Thunderbolt; 265 Those Killed by Neptune, Merucury, and Minerva; 266 Those Killed by Apollo; 267 Extremely Warlike Women; 268 Exceptionally Brave Heroes.

271 Especially Handsome Teenagers Adonis, the son of Cinyras and Smyrna, whom Venus loved.

Endymion son of Aetolus, whom the Moon loved.

Ganymedes son of Erichthonius, whom Jupiter loved.

Hyacinthus son of Oebalus, whom Apollo loved.

Narcissus son of the river Cephisus, who loved himself.

Atlantius, the son of Mercury and Venus, who is called Hermaphroditus.

Hylas son of Theodamas, whom Hercules loved.

Chrysippus, the son of Pelops, whom Theseus[90] kidnapped at athletic games.

272 Trials of Parricides Who Pleaded Their Cases on the Areopagus <*is not found in the manuscript*>

273 Those Who Established Competitions up to Aeneas, the Fifteenth [1] < . . . >[91] fifth is the competition in singing established by Danaus son of Belus in Argos in honor of his daughters' wedding; this is why it is called the *hymenaeus* {"wedding song"}.

[2] Sixth, also in Argos, is the competition which Lynceus son of Aegyptus held in honor of Argive Juno, called the Shield in Argos. The winner in this competition receives a shield instead of a crown because Abas, the son of Lynceus and Hypermestra, reported to his parents that Danaus had passed away. Lynceus took down from the temple of Argive Juno the shield that Danaus had carried as a youth and had dedicated to Juno, and gave it to his son Abas as a reward. [3] In these games the man who is victorious once and competes again < . . . > so that if he should not come out victor a second time < . . . > often compete.

[4] Seventh are the funeral games Perseus, the son of Jupiter and Danae, gave for Polydectes, the man who raised him on the island of Seriphos. While he was competing in the games he struck his grandfather, Acrisius, and killed him. Thus, what he did not want to do himself was brought to pass by the will of the gods.

[5] Eighth is the athletic contest Hercules in Olympia established for Pelops son of Tantalus, where Hercules himself competed against Achareus in the *pammachion,* which we call the *pancratium.*

[6] Ninth is the competition held in Nemea for Archemorus, the son of Lycurgus* and Eurydice, established by the seven generals who were on their way to sack Thebes. Later, at these games Euneus and Deipylus, the sons of Jason and Hypsipyle, were victorious. [7] Also, at these games the flute player (these played Pythian hymns) had seven robed men who sang vocally, and because of this he later was called a *choraules* {from Greek *chor-* "chorus" + *aul-* "flute"}.

[8] Tenth are the Isthmian Games, which they say Eratocles established—other poets say it was Theseus—in honor of Melicertes, the son of Athamas and Ino.

90. This is clearly a mistake, as Chrysippus is normally abducted by Laius (see *Fab.* 85) at the Nemean Games.

91. The first four competitions described in this *Fabula* are missing along with the previous *Fabula.*

[9] Eleventh is the competition the Argonauts established on the Propontis for King Cyzicus son of Aeneus,[*] whom Jason inadvertently killed at night on the shore. The contests held were jumping, wrestling, and the javelin-toss.

[10] Twelfth is the competition Acastus son of Pelias put on for the Argives. In these games Zetes son of Aquilo won the long-distance race. His brother Calais won the two-lap race. Castor son of Jupiter won the sprint. His brother Pollux won in boxing. Telamon son of Aeacus won the discus. His brother Peleus won wrestling. Hercules son of Jupiter won the *pammachion.* Meleager son of Oeneus won the javelin-toss. [11] Cygnus son of Mars killed in combat Pilus son of Diodotus. Bellerophon was victor in the horse race. In the chariot race Iolaus son of Iphicles defeated Glaucus son of Sisyphus, whose horses tore him apart with their teeth. Eurytus son of Mercury won in archery. Cephalus son of Deion won with the sling. Olympus, the student of Marsyas, won the flute contest. Orpheus son of Oeagrus was victorious with the *cithara.* Linus son of Apollo won the solo singing contest. And Eumolpus son of Neptune won with his song in accompaniment to Olympus' flute.

[12] Thirteenth are the athletic contests that Priam gave in Ilium at the empty tomb of Paris, the child he had ordered to be killed. During these games the following competed in the footrace: Nestor son of Neleus; Helenus, Deiphobus, and Polites, all sons of Priam; Telephus son of Hercules; Cygnus son of Neptune; Sarpedon son of Jupiter; and Paris Alexander, Priam's shepherd and son, although he was not aware of it. Paris won the race and was discovered to be Priam's son.

[13] Fourteenth are the funeral games Achilles gave in honor of Patroclus. Ajax took first in wrestling and received a golden bowl as a prize. Then Menelaus won the javelin-toss and received a golden javelin as a prize. After the spectacle was broken up, Achilles also threw on Patroclus' pyre twelve Phrygian prisoners, a horse, and a dog.

[14] Fifteenth is the competition given by Aeneas, the son of Venus and Anchises, at the court of his host Acestes son of the river Crinisus, in Sicily. There Aeneas prepared his father's funeral and dutifully paid due honor to the dead with an athletic competition. The first event of the games was a boat race. The competit<ors were Cloanthus on the ship *Scylla,*>[*] Menestheus on *Pistris,* Gyas on *Chimera,* and Sergestus on *Centaur.* [15] Cloanthus with the ship *Scylla* took first and received as prizes a talent of silver and a gold-embroidered, purple cloak with an image of Ganymedes woven in. Menestheus received a breastplate. Gyas took away with him bowls and cups with silver inlay, and Sergestus got a captive girl by the name of Pholoe and her two children. [16] The second event was a footrace between Nisus, Euryalus, Diores, Salius, Helymus, and Panopes. Euryalus came in first and received the prize of a horse with fine trappings. To the runner-up, Helymus, went an Amazonian quiver, and to the third place finisher, Diores, went an Argive helmet. Aeneas gave Salius the skin of a lion and Nisus a shield, the work of Didymaon. [17] The third event was the boxing match between Dares and Entellus. Entellus won and received a bull as a prize, and Aeneas bestowed on Dares a helmet and a sword. [18] The fourth event was an archery contest, and Hippocoon, Mnestheus, Acestes, and Eurytion

competed. The last of these received a helmet as a prize, since he, following Jupiter's judgment, had yielded to Acestes because of an omen.* [19] For the fifth event the young men, led by the boy Ascanius, performed a "Troy."[92]

274 Discoverers and Their Discoveries [1] < . . . > a certain man named Cerasus mixed wine with the Achelous river in Aetolia, and this is why "mixing" is called *cerasai* {Greek for "to mix"}. Our distant ancestors had as decoration on the backs of their dining couches the heads of small asses crowned with vine, signifying that it was an ass who discovered the pleasure of wine. They also discovered the art of pruning because the vine that a goat had nibbled on produced more fruit.

[2] Pelethronius invented reins and saddle-blankets for horses.

[3] Belone invented the first needle, which in Greek is called a *belone*.

[4] Cadmus son of Agenor in Thebes was the first to discover how to make bronze. Aeacus son of Jupiter first discovered gold on Mount Tasus in Panchaia. King Indus in Scythia was the first to discover silver, which Erichthonius first brought into Athens.

[5] In Elis, a city in the Peloponnesus, chariot races were first established.

[6] Midas son of Cybele, a Phrygian king, first discovered tin and lead.

[7] The Arcadians were the first to perform rituals to the gods.

[8] Phoroneus son of Inachus was the first to perform sacrifices* to Juno, and because of this he was the first to hold power as king.

[9] The Centaur Chiron son of Saturn discovered how to treat wounds with herbs, Apollo ophthalmology, and his son Asclepius clinical medicine.

[10] The ancients did not have midwives, and because of this many women died from a sense of shame because the Athenians made sure that no slave or woman learned medicine. A certain young girl named Agnodice desired to learn medicine; because of this desire she cut off her hair, put on men's clothing, and became the student of a certain Herophilus for formal instruction. [11] After she was trained, whenever she heard a woman was having trouble below her waist, she went to her. Women did not trust her, thinking that she was a man, so Agnodice would lift up her tunic and prove that she was a woman. In this guise Agnodice would take care of these women.

[12] But when doctors saw that their services were not being called upon by women, they accused Agnodice, asserting that she was an effeminate gigolo and seducing them, and that the women were only pretending to be sick. [13] The Areopagites assembled and found Agnodice guilty. She lifted her tunic and showed them that she was a woman. The doctors then raised stronger accusations against her. Because of this the women leaders converged on the court and said, "You are not our husbands but our enemies, for you have condemned the woman who discovered a means to provide for our well-being." The Athenians then changed the law to allow free-born women to learn medicine.

92. "Troy" was the name given to the performance of cavalry maneuvers conducted by young Roman soldiers.

[14] Perdix, the son of Daedalus' sister, invented both the compass and the saw from the backbone of a fish.

[15] Daedalus son of Eupalamus was the first to make statues of the gods.

[16] Oannes, who is said to have risen out of the sea in Chaldaea, figured out astronomy.

[17] The Lydians in Sardis dyed wool; later they invented spinning.

[18] Pan invented the song of the pan-pipes.

Ceres was the first to discover grain on Sicily.

[19] Tyrrhenus son of Hercules invented the trumpet for the following reason. [20] Since Tyrrhenus' companions seemed to be eating human flesh,* the inhabitants throughout the region fled because of their savagery. Then, because one of his men died, he made a hole in a conch-shell and blew into it, calling the village together, and Tyrrhenus and his men made it clear that they buried the dead man and did not eat him. [21] This is why the trumpet is called the Tyrrhenian song. The Romans continue to preserve this precedent, and when someone dies, they play trumpets and friends of the dead assemble to verify that he did not die from poison or the sword.

Sailors invented the bugle.

[22] At one time the Africans and Egyptians fought with clubs, but later Belus son of Neptune fought using a sword, and this is the origin of the word *bellum* {"war"}.

275 Cities and Their Founders [1] Jupiter founded Thebes in India, naming it after his nurse Thebais; it is also called *Hecatompylae* {Greek "Hundred-gated"} because it has a hundred gates.

[2] Minerva founded Athens in Chalcis, naming it after herself.

Epaphus son of Jupiter founded Memphis in Egypt.

[3] Arcas son of Jupiter founded Trapezos in Arcadia.

Apollo son of Jupiter founded Arnae.

Eleusinus son of Mercury founded Eleusis.

[4] Dardanus son of Jupiter founded Dardania.

Argus son of Agenor founded Argos.

Cadmus son of Agenor founded Thebes called *heptapylae* {Greek "Seven-gated"} because it is said to have seven gates.

[5] Perseus son of Jupiter founded Perseis.

Castor and Pollux, the sons of Jupiter, founded Dioscoris.

Medus, the son of Aegeus and Medea, founded Meda in Ecbatana.

[6] Camirus son of the Sun founded Camira.

Liber founded Hammon in India.

The Nymph Ephyra daughter of Ocean founded Ephyra, which they later named Corinth.

Sardo daughter of Sthenelus founded Sardis.

[7] Cinyras son of Paphus founded Smyrna, naming it after his daughter.

Perseus son of Jupiter founded Mycenae.

Semiramis daughter of Dercetis founded Babylonia in Syria.

276 The Largest Islands Mauritania, located in the far west with a circumference of 76,000[93] stades.

Egypt, located to the south and east, surrounded by the Nile's waters, with a circumference of <*missing number*> stades.

Sicily, in the form of a triangle, with a circumference of 570,000 stades.

Sardinia with a circumference of 250,000 stades.

Crete, in length <*missing dimensions*>, and has a hundred towns on each side, with a circumference of 200,000 stades.

Cyprus, located between Egypt and Asia,* shaped like a Gallic shield, with a circumference of 150,000 stades.

Rhodes, shaped like a circle, with a circumference of 100,000 stades.

Euboea, in the shape of a bow, with a circumference of 200,000 stades.

Corcyra, fertile land, with a circumference of 100,000 stades.

Scyros,* fertile land, with a circumference of 110,000 stades.

Tenedos, the island across from Ilium, with a circumference of 120,000 stades.

Corsica, very infertile land, with a circumference of 1,120 stades.

There are nine Cyclades: Andros, Myconos, Delos, Tenos, Naxos, Seriphos, Gyarus, Paros, and Rhenia.

277 Inventors of Things The Parcae (Clothos, Lachesis, and Atropos) invented seven Greek letters: Α, Β, Η, Τ, Ι, Υ < . . . >. Others say that Mercury invented them from the flight of cranes, which form letters when they fly. Palamedes son of Nauplius likewise invented eleven letters: < . . . >; Simonides four: Ω, Ε, Ζ, Φ; the Sicilian Epicharmus two: Π, Ψ. They say that Mercury first brought these Greek letters to Egypt, Cadmus then imported them from Egypt to Greece, and finally the exile Evander exported them from Arcadia to Italy where his mother Carmenta changed them into Latin characters, fifteen in number.

< . . . >* Apollo added the rest on the *cithara*.

Mercury also was the first to teach mortals wrestling.

Ceres taught men how to domesticate cattle and showed her nursling Triptolemus how to sow grain. When Triptolemus had sown the seed, a *sus* (that is, a hog) dug up what he had sown, so he grabbed the hog, led it to the altar of Ceres, placed some grain on top of its head, and sacrificed it. This is how the practice of putting salted grain on the heads of sacrificial victims originated.

Isis was the first to discover sailing. While she was looking for her son Harpocrates, she set sail on a skiff.

Minerva built the first two-prowed ship for Danaus, and he fled from his brother Aegyptus in it.

93. All the numbers in this *Fabula* are corrupt, but we have translated them nonetheless. Readers should not put any credence in their accuracy.

ENDNOTES TO APOLLODORUS' *LIBRARY*

1.8 Amphitrite: Wagner deletes Amphitrite from the daughters of Oceanos because she reappears below in 1.11 as a daughter of Nereus, her usual lineage. Wagner likewise deletes the words "daughter of Oceanos" after her name in 1.28. Although the duplication is suspicious, it is not impossible that the duplication is original to Apollodorus.

1.20 Ge: Heyne adds Ge here (in Greek the sequence is ΕΛΕΓΕ<ΓΗ>ΓΕΝΝΗΣΕΙΝ) to match the fact that Hesiod has Gaia and Ouranos warn Zeus. If one does not accept the addition, Metis herself makes the prediction to Zeus.

1.22 Hubris: Aegius proposed and Wagner accepted reading Thymbris here instead of Hubris based on the scholiastic hypothesis of Pindar, *Pyth.* 1, which distinguishes Pan the son of Zeus and Thybris (or Thymbris) from Pan the son of Hermes and Penelope.

1.26 healed: We follow Hercher's change of ἐκκαείς ("set alight") to ἐξακεσθείς ("healed completely").

1.27 discus contest: Possibly read οἰστεύειν ("archery contest") with Jacobs since Artemis has nothing elsewhere to do with the discus.

1.27 Opis: Papathomopoulos notes that in one of the manuscripts (R) someone has written OU above the name, indicating we should correct it to Oupis, a form given elsewhere.

1.28 Oceanos: Wagner deletes "daughter of Oceanos" because he deletes Amphitrite from the list of Oceanids in 1.11.

1.31 Metaneira: Here and just below in 1.32 the manuscripts give the name as Praxithea, which editors have corrected.

1.37 Mimas: We accept Mayer's change of μᾶλλον ("rather") to Μίμαντα (the name Mimas).

1.38 Gration: The name is probably corrupt. The true reading and perhaps the instrument (ἄκοντι?) with which Artemis kills the Giant is hidden by the corruption.

1.38 bronze clubs: We accept Heyne's correction (μαχόμεναι) of the manuscript readings (μαχομένους or μαχομένας) so that it is the Moirai who fight with the bronze clubs rather than the two giants and so that the participle is in the proper case. This clearly parallels the rest of the account where the particular weapons and methods described belong to the gods, not the Giants.

1.72 skin: We accept Frazer's δορᾶς ("skin") for the manuscripts' θήρας ("beast").

1.74 Elis: For τῆς Ἑλλάδος we are conjecturing τῆς Ἤλιδος. Elis is the city where Hippostratos and his father Amaryнceus are from, so we believe Hipponoos is trying to send his daughter away from there. Cf. the Hesiodic *Catalog fr.* 12 MW (= schol. on Pind. *Ol.* 10.46): "Hippostratos of the line of Amaryнceus <*verb not present*> her, a scion of Ares | the glorious son of Phyctes, leader of the Epeians" (Epeian = Elean). Note that Apollodorus mistakes Amaryнceides ("descendant of Am.") for a real patronymic ("son of Am."), indicating he was working from a source that cited the first line of the fragment but not the second, which would have clarified Hippostratos' lineage.

1.89 tied: The translation reflects our conjecture of ἐξημμένας ("tied") for ἐξηραμμένας ("dried"). See *Philologus* 149 (2005) 351–354.

1.90 brother: Wagner deletes the words "Salmoneus' brother."

1.94 Stratios: Papathomopoulos confirms that R reads Stratios here, not Stratichos, as Wagner prints.

1.98 Phylacos': Wagner prints Aegius' emendation of Iphiclos for Phylacos following Pherecydes *fr.* 33 (Fowler), which may be correct. Apollodorus, however, does not seem to be following Pherecydes closely, and his source may have given Phylacos, which we leave in our translation.

1.98 undetected: Papathomopoulos says that the correct reading of R is ὃν . . . πελάζον λαθεῖν ("that . . . approach undetected") not οὗ . . . πέλας ἐλθεῖν ("that . . . come near"), which Wagner prints.

1.121 upon him: We suggest ἐπέπεμψαν ("loosed . . . upon") for ἔπεμψαν ("sent . . . to") (SMT).

2.13 himself: There is a gap here in the text. We follow Aegius and Robert in filling the lacuna with material from the Homeric *scholia* to *Il.* 1.42.

2.20 of the sons: The text transmitted, ὀκτὼ δέ εἰσι νεώτατοι, is garbled ("Eight are youngest"), and there are only six sons here. We translate Hercher's suggested οἱ δέ εἰσι νεώτατοι.

2.21 marriages: We deviate from Wagner's text by retaining the plural verb here and assuming the subject is the sons of Aigyptos, not Danaos himself.

2.23 died: We deviate from Wagner's text in this clause and the preceding sentence, sticking more closely to the text of the manuscripts. But we do not pretend to think that it is a correct text, and we believe that this entire paragraph shows extensive textual corruption.

2.27 Peloponnesos: Wagner, following a suggestion of Hercher (though he attributes it to Heyne), omits "and the Peloponnesos." For a defense of these words see M. Huys, "Geographica Apollodorea," *Hermes* 126 (1998) 124–129 at 124–125.

2.31 three beasts: We follow Wagner's suggestion and move "for her one body . . . three beasts" here from after "devastating the livestock" below.

2.33 in might: We hesitantly accept Hercher's γενναιότητι ("in might") for Gale's τότε νεότητι ("in youth at that time"), which Wagner prints.

2.54 Mestor's kingdom: We translate the text as Wagner prints it, but we have our doubts. Heyne prints μετὰ Ταφίων οἱ Πτερελάου παῖδες ἐλθόντες τὴν Μήστορος ἀρχὴν τῷ μητροπάτορι ἀπήτουν ("The sons of Pterelaos came with some Taphians and demanded Mestor's kingdom for their maternal grandfather"). Frazer follows Heyne but deletes the reference to the maternal grandfather as a gloss ("The sons of Pterelaos came with the Taphians and demanded Mestor's kingdom"). Apollodorus may be trying to reconcile two incompatible genealogies (note the great discrepancy in age between the sons of Pterelaos and Electryon, the brother of their great-great-grandfather). To give some idea of the difficulties involved in working this out, we have references to Pterelaos as the son of Hippothoe (Herodorus *fr.* 15 Fowler = Sch. L+ Ap. Rhod. 1.747–51b), as her grandson through Taphios (Apollodorus), as her grandson through Teleboas (Anaximander *fr.* 1 Fowler = Athen. 11.99), and even as her husband (Sch. to Hom. *Il.* 19.116).

2.71 art of war: We hesitantly suggest τακτικήν ("tactics, art of war") here for τοξικήν ("archery"), the reading of the manuscripts. Others keep the manuscripts' reading but alter παρ' αὐτοῦ ("from him") to παρ' Εὐρύτου ("from Eurytos," who taught Heracles archery in 2.63 above) and accept προμαθών ("having first learned," a reading in some, but not all, manuscripts) for προσμαθών ("having learned more").

2.81 ambushed: Instead of the manuscripts' τοξεύσας ("having shot with his bow") we translate here λοχήσας ("having laid an ambush," proposed by RSS). Possible also is ἐνεδρεύσας ("having snared," proposed by SMT). Diodorus Siculus (4.13.1) gives three versions of the way Heracles captured the deer (with nets, waiting until it is asleep, and by tiring it out), but he insists that what distinguished this labor was the lack of violence in capturing it.

2.97 ripped him apart: We translate Frazer's suggested διασπασάμεναι ("ripped apart"; cf. διεσπάσαντο in Hellanicus *fr.* 105 Fowler) instead of the transmitted ἐπισπασάμεναι ("dragged").

2.100 Bebryces fought: The text is that restored by Sommer (Wagner simply prints a lacuna) and gets the gist of what must have been lost here, but it is entirely conjectural in detail.

2.110 "italos": Wagner deletes the words "known as . . . 'italos.'" For a defense of them as original, see M. Huys, "Geographica Apollodorea," *Hermes* 126 (1998) 124–129 at 125–127.

2.114 Hesperethousa: The manuscripts here transmit the last of these names as two, Ἑστία Ἐρέθουσα ("Hestia and Erethousa"), and this has been corrected variously. We follow Steuding's correction Ἑσπερέθουσα, a version of the name attested elsewhere, including in Hesiod's *Theogony.*

2.114 Cycnos: H. Lloyd-Jones ("Lycaon and Cycnos," *Zeitschrift für Papyrologie und Epigraphik* 108 [1995] 38–44) argues that we should read Lycaon here and in the next sentence. We think he is correct that Lycaon is original to this myth, but the error is likely older than Apollodorus (the conflation of Cycnos [Cygnus] and Lycaon occurs also in Hyg. *Fab.* 31.3), and so we cannot justify altering the text here.

2.119 received: We adopt Frazer's παραλαμβάνει ("received") for the manuscripts' καταλαμβάνει ("forcibly took").

2.119 immortal: Wagner deletes ἀθάνατον ("despite being immortal").

2.122 be initiated: Wagner deletes this entire sentence (it is missing in the Vatican Epitome) as a gloss (it is also garbled). We have adopted the text of the *scholia* (L) to Hom. *Il.* 8.368, δι' ὃ γίγνεται Πυλίου θετὸς υἱός, καὶ παραγενόμενος ἐμυεῖτο.

2.123 through it: We translate Heyne's κατῄει ("went down") instead of ἐπῄει ("went after"), the reading of the Vatican Epitome printed by Wagner.

2.138 the island: Reading τὴν νῆσον ("the island," reflecting the *insulam* Papathomopoulos reports in M) instead of the manuscripts' τὴν νύκτα ("through the night") or Wagner's αὐτὴν νυκτός ("it by night").

2.158 promontory: We translate Frazer's suggested ἀπὸ τοῦ ἀκρωτηρίου, in lieu of anything better. The manuscripts transmit a garbled text.

2.162 Hippo: Hippo is the name restored by Hercher.

2.165 Deiocoon: Wagner prints this name as Deicoon on the basis of R, but R according to Papathomopoulos reads Deiocoon with the other manuscripts.

2.172 Aristomachos': We follow Frazer's suggestion, since elsewhere Temenos, Cresphontes, and Aristodemos are Aristomachos' sons. Wagner prints Cleodaios, Gale's correction of the manuscripts' Cleolaos.

2.174 famine: We translate the manuscripts' λιμῷ ("famine"), but this is quite possibly an easy mistake for λοιμῷ ("plague"). The two words would have been pronounced identically in late Greek, and the Latin translation in M has *pestilentia* ("plague").

2.175 one eye: We follow Frazer (who follows Pausanias and the Suda) in assuming the horse, not the rider, has one eye.

2.180 himself: We follow Faber's αὐτός ("himself") rather than the manuscripts' problematic αὐτῶν, which Wagner prints.

3.2 scent of roses: The words "breathing forth the scent of roses" translate Sevinus' ῥόδου ἀποπνέων rather than the corrupt ῥόδου ἀποπλέων of the manuscripts, which Wagner prints.

3.10 put it on wheels: We follow Papathomopoulos' reordering of the manuscripts' words: κατασκευάσας καὶ ταύτην ἐπὶ τροχῶν βαλών.

3.16 Cretans: We translate Bekker's correction of ἥρωσι ("heroes") to Κρησί ("Cretans"), though we are not sure this is the real solution to the corruption.

3.19 corpse: We translate Bekker's εἴ τι τὸ σῶμα πάθοι instead of the manuscripts' εἰ τοῦτο συμπάθῃ or the Vatican Epitome's εἰ τούτῳ συμπάθῃ.

3.22 Thebes is now: We translate the text of the Sabbaitic Epitome. The general sense is clear, but the manuscripts and the Vatican Epitome present slightly different texts.

3.23 more than happy: We accept the Vatican Epitome's ἑκούσιον ("willingly") rather than the manuscripts' ἀκούσιον ("unwillingly"), which is also in the Sabbaitic Epitome.

3.27 from fright: Perhaps read διὰ τὴν φλόγγα ("from the flame," suggested by RSS) rather than διὰ τὸν φόβον ("from fright").

3.33 Indians: Wagner deletes "on his way to fight the Indians." M. Huys, "Geographica Apollodorea," *Hermes* 126 (1998) 124–129 at 127–129, defends these words.

3.35 was destroyed: Perhaps read not διαφθαρείς ("destroyed") but διαφορηθείς ("ripped apart," suggested by SMT).

3.36 pillars: Wagner deletes "and all of India (where he set up pillars)." M. Huys, "Geographica Apollodorea," *Hermes* 126 (1998) 124–129 at 127–129, argues we should retain these words.

3.41 from Euboia: Wagner deletes "from Euboia." For a defense of the phrase as authentic, see C. Brillante, "Apollod. *Bibl.*III 5," *Rivista di cultura classica e medioevale* 21–22 (1979–1980) 195–198.

3.41 Thebes: There is a gap in the text. We translate Heyne's supplement, but it is merely *exempli gratia.*

3.41 eighteen years: Wagner prints "twenty," in the belief that all of the manuscripts had this number. But Papathomopoulos has confirmed that R has "eighteen," which is also in the Vatican Epitome.

3.45 four: Papathomopoulos confirms that R reads "four," not "two," which Wagner prints.

3.61 Adrastos: The text has a slight corruption here, and various scholars have attempted many solutions, most involving a sense like that we have given.

3.126 Castor: Wagner adds "Clytaimnestra" here ("Tyndareos fathered Castor and Clytaimnestra"), following Gale.

3.127 marshes: The manuscripts read ἄλσεσιν ("groves") here. We accept and translate Preller's ἕλεσιν ("marshes"), both because the etymological connection between Ἑλένη and ἕλος is made elsewhere, e.g., in the *Etymologicum Magnum* (s.v. Ἑλένη), and because marshes are a more suitable setting for the waterfowl involved in this myth (compare Hyginus *Fab.* 77, where the bank of the river is the scene of Jupiter and Leda's encounter).

3.156 twelve: Papathomopoulos confirms that R very likely reads "twelve," rather than "twenty," which Wagner prints. Diodorus Siculus 4.72.1 also says that they had twelve daughters. In the same place Diodorus gives Pelasgos as the name of the second son, which may need to be restored here, since Papathomopoulos reads Pelasgon (Πελάσγοντα) in R.

3.161 king of it: We accept Heyne's αὐτῆς for the manuscripts' ἧς αὐτός.

3.180 Agraulis: The manuscripts transmit this name as Agraulos (i.e., the same as her daughter). We alter it to Agraulis on the authority of Porphyry, who (*Abst.* 2.54) gives the name of Cecrops' wife in this form (though he specifies that she was a nymph).

3.194 forced himself on her: The text transmitted (and printed by Wagner) here contains the words "saying that Procne was dead," which we delete with Hercher.

3.194 tongue: Before this clause, the manuscripts contain the words "Later, he married Philomela and slept with her," which we delete with Hercher.

3.201 Endios: Papathomopoulos confirms that M gives the name as Endios. The text in the other manuscripts is corrupt, though Bekker anticipated Papathomopoulos' discovery and conjectured the correct text.

3.214 Perdix's: Wagner deletes the name Perdix here, and he may well be correct, since only here and in Photios is the sister so named (though the latter attributes the information to a lost play of Sophocles). The nephew of Daidalos, on the other hand, is named either Talos (or Kalos!) or Perdix, depending on the source, so it is possible the name crept in here from someone noting the variation of names.

3.215 Minotaur: Heyne (Wagner follows him) deletes everything from "And there" to the end of the paragraph on the grounds that it merely repeats material from 3.9–11.

E.1.21 his relatives: Zenobius here has "her relatives." Whether the Centaurs are her relatives or not is unknown (but unlikely given that in Diodorus Siculus 4.70.3 this Hippodameia seems to be Athenian), but they are certainly Peirithous' relatives (all are sons of Ixion), and there is probably a simple error here of αὐτῇ for αὐτῷ in Zenobius, and we ought to translate this as "his relatives." We also doubt the likelihood of the Centaurs being her relatives, because it strikes us as odd for them to rape their kinswoman.

E.3.1 might be ended: In their translations Frazer and Hard both take this word in the sense "to be exalted/raised to glory," which is possible. But the beginning of the now lost *Cypria,* the epic poem that covered these pre–Trojan War events, refers to Zeus' will to relieve overpopulation by having mortals fight a war (*fr.* 1 Bernabé). The fragmentary remains of the Hesiodic *Catalog* (*fr.* 204.95–128 MW) likewise show Zeus planning to "destroy the souls of the demigods" (using the same word as Apollodorus) by means of the Trojan War.

E.3.2 apple as a beauty prize: The Greek here in the epitome literally means "threw an apple over beauty among Hera, Athena, and Aphrodite," but the phrase "apple over beauty" is as odd sounding in Greek as it is in English. We suspect, as Wagner did when he published the Vatican Epitome, that the word for apple was not originally in the text but later crept in. Wagner at first thought that "apple" had ousted a word like νεῖκος "quarrel," but later accepted it as authentic. But if one compares Proclus' summary of the lost epic, the *Cypria,* which is very close to Apollodorus' account, there is no mention of the apple there, and the oddity of the phrase leads us to believe that Wagner's original position is closer to the truth.

E.3.14 sons of Asclepios: Adopting Wagner's supplements here and in the next sentence.

E.3.14 forty: The number Papathomopoulos says is in the text of the Sabbaitic Epitome here. Wagner mistakenly read "thirty."

E.3.33 Tenos: Kerameus deletes after this name the words "the so-called Hundred Cities," which have presumably crept into the Sabbaitic Epitome because there is another city called Tenos, which is one of the so-called Hundred Cities.

E.4.2 many wanted: Adopting Frazer's suggested θελόντων ("wanting") for the epitomes' ἐλθόντων ("coming").

E.4.2 and fought: Retaining the epitomes' πυκτεύειν (normally "box," but in later Greek also simply "fight") instead of following Frazer's ἀριστεύειν ("do doughty deeds," Frazer's rendering).

E.5.14 thirteen: The epitomes say 3,000 here, but that is absurd; we follow Severyns' correction (also accepted by A. Bernabé in *Poetarum Epicorum Graecorum Testimonia et Fragmenta* [Leipzig 1987], where this passage is *fr.* 8 of the *Iliades Parvae*). In fact, however, there are several reasonable alternatives and corrections (Hyginus *Fab.* 108 gives a list of nine heroes in the horse).

E.7.3 sailing away: We accept Wagner's change of the Sabbaitic Epitome's προσπλεύσας to ἀποπλεύσας.

E.7.12 Laistrygonians, and: We do not accept the lacuna proposed by Wagner here and printed by Frazer.

E.7.17 to Oceanos: We accept Frazer's suggested <εἰς> τὸν Ὠκεανόν.

ENDNOTES TO HYGINUS' *FABULAE*

Th.1 Strife: We accept Muncker's *Contentio* for F's *Continentia.* RSS suggests that possibly *Invidentia* ("Envy") should be read.

Th.1 Body Relaxer: Marshall prints *Somnus, Somnia, <Amor>, id est Lysimeles,* following the suggestion of Schmidt that *Lysimeles* is an epithet attributed to *Amor* ("Love"), but *Lysimeles* is commonly an epithet of sleep as well, and we believe (suggested by SMT) that it is easier simply to move *Somnia* after the epithet.

Th.1 Erythea: We accept *Erythea* (Muncker *Erythia*) for F's *Aerica* (see Hesiod *apud* Servius Auctus *ad* 4.484).

Th.4 Ophion: We accept Muncker's *Ophion* for F's *ophius.*

Th.4 Palaemon: We accept Schmidt's *Palaemon* for F's *Alemone.*

Th.6 Axius: We accept Scheffer's *Axius,* the name of a river, for F's *Axenus,* a name for the Black Sea.

Th.16 Calypso: Calypso is a daughter of Atlas, but not one of the Pleiades. Perhaps the name is a corruption for *Taygeta,* one of the Pleiades listed in *Fab.* 192.

Th.16 Merope: Perhaps we are to read (suggested by SMT) *Merope <Sterope>* by haplography; compare *Fab.* 192.

11 Thera: We accept Muncker's *Thera* for F's *Lerta* (see *Fab.* 69.7).

14.1 Clymene: We have restored the feminine *Clymene* for *Clymenus* following Bunte and Schmidt, because this links Jason with Minyas through his mother; cf. *Fab.* 14.2, 14.24.

14.4 tree trunks: We read (following SMT) *in caenum adactus* [or *adactus est*] ("driven into the mud") for F's *in cuneum adactis* (something like "with trunks of trees sharpened to a point," trans. Grant). This removes an obvious oddity, provides a clean text in line with other versions of the myth, and restores what we think was an attempt at a Latin etymology for the name Caeneus (from *caenum,* "mud").

14.7 from Iton: F reads *Ixition,* which has been taken by some to be a corrupt name, but we think this highly unlikely. All the Argonauts here are assigned a place of residence, and so we believe (proposed by RSS) that *ixition* is a corruption of *ex* and the name of some city in northern Greece. Iton is one possibility, but not the only one. See next note.

14.7 Cerinthus: We read (proposed by RSS): *Eurytion Iri et Demonassae filius, ex <corrupt city. Canthus Canethi filius> ab oppido Cerintho.* In Apollonius Rhodius (1.77–79), Hyginus' ultimate source, Canthus son of Canethus from Cerinthus was sent to join the Argonauts, and later in this *Fabula* (at 14.28) Canthus is mentioned again.

14.12 heads fell: Rose notes *ad loc.* "unde haec, nescio," but the passage is clearly a corrupt reminiscence of Cic., *Div.* 1.75 and 2.68.

14.13 using a lamp: We translate SMT's *alii aiunt lychno eum noctu primum vidisse* for F's *alii aiunt Lynceum noctu nullum vidisse.*

14.17 from Calydon: We emend (suggested by SMT) F's *Lacedaemonius* to *Calydonius.* Iphiclus is Calydonian, a relative of Meleager and Laocoon, both of whom are just above given as Calydonian by Hyginus.

14.17 spear thrower: We correct (suggested by RSS) F's *Arcas* to *alacer.* SMT, however, suggests that the Latin originally reflected the strong balanced phrasing of Apollonius' Greek (1.199–200: εὖ μὲν ἄκοντι | εὖ δὲ καὶ ἐν σταδίῃ) and conjectures *aeque cursor <ac> iaculator* ("as good a runner as a javelin thrower"). In either case, it appears that the word *cursor* ("runner") is a mistaken translation of Apollonius Rhodius' ἐν σταδίῃ.

14.18 women's heads: Translating our correction (suggested by RSS) of *virgineis capitibus* ("young women's heads," from Ver., *Aen.* 3.216) for F's *gallinaceis capitibus* ("chicken heads"). Literary and artistic representations give them human heads. On the basis of Hes. *Theog.* 267 (ἠυκόμους), SMT suggests that perhaps *capillatis capitibus* ("heads full of hair") should be read. The corruption would have been prompted by *gallinaceis* in the description below.

14.18 chests and bellies: We read (proposed by SMT) *pectus alvomque feminae [humana]* ("the chest and abdomen of a woman") for F's *pectus alvom feminaque humana* ("human chests, abdomens, and thighs"). To our knowledge Harpies of the hybrid form are not portrayed in art with human legs.

14.20 Thersanor: The name is a correction of F's *Thersanon.* The form Thersanor appears in an alphabetic list of Argonauts on papyrus (*POxy* 61.4097).

14.21 Hypermestra: Following Perizonius and Rose's supplement (cf. Apollodorus 1.111), where Amphiaraos son of Oicles is listed as an Argonaut.

14.26 walls: The text of F here has *stramentatum* ("to gather straw"), which, if correct, is a verb attested only here in Latin. We have translated (SMT's conjecture) *extra munimenta,* although perhaps *extra tramitem* (SMT) or *ex tramite* (RSS) ("off the path") lies beneath the corruption. Idmon's death is told in two other places in Hyginus (*Fab.* 18, 248), where the original phrase is corrupted differently in each place.

14.28 Eribotes: Standardizing the name (F here has *Eurybates*) to match 14.6.

14.28 Canethus: We accept Micyllus' emendation of F's *Cerionis* to *Canethi.*

14.28 like enemies: Adopting *infeste* ("like enemies," hesitantly suggested by SMT) for the corrupt reading of F's *fuste* ("with a cudgel").

14.29 had been killed: From here to the end of 14.30 we believe that the text has suffered extensive corruption. Our reconstruction assumes that after Mopsus Hyginus originally listed three separate occasions where others joined the original crew of the *Argo:* the four sons of Phrixus, the three sons of Deimachus (in Apollonius Rhodius the name is Deileon instead of Demoleon), and Dascylus son of Lycus. Our supplements are simply *exempli gratia* (we also accept Robert's *errore propulsos* for *terrore perculsos*). Moreover, we believe that the final sentence in 14.29 is also corrupt, as Mopsus is listed by Hyginus himself at 14.5 as part of the original crew. Without our reconstructions and changes, Marshall's text may be translated: "Cylindrus, but others say that they were named Phronius, Demoleon, Autolycus, and Phlogius, and that Hercules, after having taken them as companions in his quest for the belt of the Amazons, left them terror-stricken by Dascylus son of Lycus, the king of the Mariandyni."

15. King Lycurgus: We hesitantly have restored Lycurgus for Lycus in the belief that it is an error of transmission and not a mistake on the part of Hyginus (see Lact. Plac. *ad Stat. Theb.* 5.29 [noted in Marshall] and esp. First Vatican Mythographer 2.31).

18 walls: We translate SMT's *extra munimenta* for F's *extra venatum* ("outside to go hunting") or Muncker's correction to *stramentatum* ("to gather straw"). See our endnote to *Fab.* 14.26.

19 ship: The supplements in this sentence are ours and are *exempli gratia,* suggested by RSS who posits a lacuna after *illi* and not *earum.*

24 Iolcus: Accepting Schmidt's *itaque cum iam <non> longe a Iolco essent* ("and so when they were not far from Iolcos") for the transmitted *itaque cum iam longe a Colchis essent* ("when they were far away from Colchis").

40 love a bull: The text is unclear, and several attempts have been made to correct it. We give the general sense of the text.

45 unwilling: We accept Bunte's *invitam in monte* for Marshall's *inventam in monte* (F gives *in vitam in monten*).

52 Oenone: We conjecture (suggested by RSS) *Oenon<en>* for *Delon.* As Micyllus in the margin of his edition notes, the original name of Aegina was Oenone (see, e.g., Apollodorus 3.157). Once the rare name became corrupted, we think that the erroneous correction to *Delos* was natural because it is a more well-known name, and because Delos appears again at the end of the next *fabula.*

67.2 Laius: Marshall prints a lacuna here. We have adopted Muncker's supplement *exempli gratia.*

74 Lycurgus: We correct F's *Lycus* to *Lycurgus*; see our endnote to *Fab.* 15.

78 swear an oath: We conjecture *iureiurando eos obligavit* ("made them swear an oath," proposed by SMT) for F's *iureiurando se obligavit* ("put himself under oath").

79 Thisadia: We have changed *Phisadie* to *Thisadie* to match the orthography at *Fab.* 92.5. The confusion of *ph-* and *th-* is common in Hyginus.

81 Ialmenus: We follow Muncker's emendation of F's *Blanirus.*

87 daughter: We follow Castiglioni's supplement to provide the general sense.

88.7 as his own: The text reads *iussit . . . pro suo educari* ("he ordered him . . . to be raised as his own"), which we emend (suggested by SMT) to *iussit . . . educavit* ("he ordered him . . . and he raised him as his own").

90 Polyxena: We correct F's *Polymena* to *Polyxena* following Scheffer, although many names that follow are likely corrupt as well, corrected variously by scholars.

91 some bull: The transmitted text *missi a Priamo ut taurum aliquis adduceret venissent* can only mean "when those sent by Priam arrived so that someone could bring back a bull," which reads oddly. Our translation supposes that originally something like *taurum aliquem adducerent* was read (suggested by RSS). See *Fab.* 186.4 for a possible parallel for the phrasing: *illa timens mittit ad pastores ut infantem aliquem explicarent quem regi subderet.*

97.11 Peteos: The name is garbled, and we have followed Micyllus' recovery of Menestheus' name and provided his usual patronymic.

97.12 from Iton: The text is missing a name before "Podarces, his brother," and editors have normally placed the lacuna immediately before *Podarces.* We propose (suggested by RSS) that the lacuna belongs between *filius* and *Tyto* (i.e., Iton) and would thus read: *Thoas . . . filius <ex Pleurone, navibus XX* [city, number *exemplorum gratia*]. *Protesilaus Iphicli filius> ex Itone, navibus XV. Podarces.* Protesilaus is associated with Iton at Homer, *Il.* 2.697.

97.15 father: We have translated the text as transmitted, but *Pyrrha* may be a later gloss to remind us of Achilles' name while disguised (see *Fab.* 96). Or perhaps we are to read *a patris <nomine>*, "from the name of his father" (suggested by SMT).

104 waxen: We accept Scheffer's *cereum* (waxen) for Marshall's *aereum* (bronze).

104 statue: We have omitted in translation the odd Latin phrase *ab amplexu Protesilai,* which would mean perhaps "far from the embrace of Protesilaus." We suspect that the phrase *ab amplexu Protesilai* has been inserted here from Ovid, *Her.* 13.12, *solvor ab amplexu, Protesilae, tuo.*

119 Aetolia: Accepting Bursian's *Aetolium* for F's *Aeolium.*

121 Chryses: Schmidt has pointed the way to fixing this corrupt text, which Marshall marks as a crux, by restoring *Chryseis* for *Chryses* and deleting *senior.* But instead of adding *ut* and deleting *qui,* we would simply change the latter to *quae,* which would have quite naturally been changed to *qui* once the masculine *Chryses* had crept into the text.

125.13 river: We read *Acheloi <fluminis> filias* (suggested by RSS).

137 deliver the blow: We emend (suggested by RSS) F's *percussisse* to *percussurum esse.*

147 let out a cry: We read *exclamavit* for F's *expavit,* comparing several later sources seemingly derived from Hyginus.

151 fish: F reads *canis,* which is not impossible (cf. Th. 39), but the language is almost identical to that of *Fab.* 125.14 (*inferiorem ab inguine piscis et sex canes ex se natos habebat*), and so we restore *piscis* here (suggested by RSS).

152 Earth: Accepting Micyllus' *Terra* for *Tartara* (see Th. 4).

156 Perses: We restore the names based on Th. 36.

156 Dioxippe: We restore the names from *Fab.* 154 and Th. 38.

157 Leucon: Correcting F's *Leuconoe* to *Leucon* (suggested by RSS); see Apollodorus 1.84.

157 Atlas: After the word *Atlas* F has *Belus Actor,* which we do not translate. Those names have likely been reinserted here by a later hand after they dropped out of the first line (see Schmidt's supplement in Marshall).

157 Calchinia: We translate Rose's supplement based on Pausanias 2.5.7.

157 Atlas: We follow Bunte's supplement.

157 Hopleus: F's *Peleus* cannot be right. Hopleus (suggested by RSS) is by no means certain, but he is a son of Neptune and Canace.

157 Danaus: We follow Muncker's supplement.

157 Euphemus < . . . >: We restore Polyphemus, perhaps omitted by haplography due to the name Euphemus.

161 Urea: Marshall places a crux here, and the text may well be irremediable, but it is possible (suggested by SMT) that *Ileus* is *Oileus* (the variation in spelling is unremarkable): see the Hesiodic *Catalog fr.* 235 MW, where Ileus is Apollo's son by an unnamed nymph.

173 Thessaly: We follow Bursian's *Thessalia* for F's *Thebis.*

173 Lapithus: F reads *Iapeti,* which was plausibly corrected by Bursian to *Lapithi.* His conjecture has since been verified by *POxy.* 61.4097 (see M. Huys, *Mnemosyne* 50.2 [1997] 202–205).

182 Adrastea: We read (suggested by RSS) *Ida, Amalthea, Adrastea* for Φ *ideo et* [F *Idothea*] *Althaea, Adrasta* (Marshall prints *Idyia, Althaea, Adrasta*), combining the two daughters of Melisseus (see Apollodorus 1.5) and Amalthea, who is listed as Jupiter's nurse at *Fab.* 139.

183 Titaness: We hesitantly read *Themidis [filiae] Titanidis* for F's *Themidis filiae Titanidis.*

193 eventually: We have translated F's *postmodum* ("eventually"), but RSS suggests that perhaps *post mortem* ("after his death") should be read.

220 body: We translate Rose's supplement.

221 everything: Marshall prints *cuncta emeditanda,* "everything must be thought through" (F *cuncta et meditanda*), but the text is likely corrupt. The verb *emeditor* is not attested except in this context. Since Periander's apothegm μελέτη τὸ πᾶν ("practice is everything") is elsewhere preserved for us and since we believe that something like this underlies the text, we have translated accordingly.

238 Callisthenes < . . . >: We translate *item Callisthenes* < . . . > *Euboeae* (suggested by RSS) for F's *idem Callisthenem Euboeae,* although the text is probably hopelessly corrupt.

240 Leda daughter: F reads *Clytaemnestra Thestii filia* ("Clytaemnestra daughter of Thestius"), which is a lineage nowhere else found, and so we read (suggested by SMT) *Clytaemnestra* <*Tyndarei et Ledae*> *Thestii* <*filiae*> *filia,* comparing the wording of, e.g., *Fab.* 14.16, 73.1.

244 Alphesiboea: We conjecture (suggested by RSS) *Phegeus Alphei filius* <*missing name*> *Alphesiboeae filiae suae filium* (F *filiam*), as there are no others female relatives killed in the list; compare the loss of name ealier in the *fabula.*

245 Aeson: It is possible (suggested by RSS) that this entry belongs at the end of the previous *fabula* (244) and once read "Jason son of Aeson killed his uncle Pelias." Jason's two fathers-in-law, Aeetes and Creon, are not killed by him.

248 walls: Reading *extra munimenta* (suggested by SMT) for F's *extra metam* and Muncker's *stramentatum* (see our endnotes at *Fab.* 14.26 and 18).

254.5 were late: We read (suggested by SMT) *essent morati* for F's *essent mortui* (see Cicero, *Tusculan Disputations* 1.113).

255 brother: Reading *filia fratrem* <*occidit. Medea Aeetae filia fratrem*> *et filios occidit* for Marshall's *filia fratrem* < . . . > *et filios occidit.* This reconstruction (by RSS and SMT) would explain the corruption (haplography of *fratrem*), and the presence of Medea is supported by *Fab.* 239, where Medea's crime is, as here, listed directly before Procne's.

273.6 Lycurgus: As elsewhere (*Fab.* 15, 74), we have corrected F's *Lycus* to *Lycurgus.*

273.9 Aeneus: We accept Schneider's *Aenei* for F's *una cum.*

273.14 Scylla: We accept Muncker's supplement.

273.18 omen: The text is corrupt here, and we translate (suggested by SMT) *iudicio Iovis* for F's *iudicis.*

274.8 sacrifices: Reading *sacra* (proposed by RSS) here for F's *arma,* on the basis of *Fab.* 143: *itaque exordium regnandi tradidit [sc. Zeus] Phoroneo, ob id beneficium quod Iunoni sacra primus fecit.* It may be possible, as SMT suggests, that *sacra* at 143 is a misleading translation of ἱερά, and that a temple is meant both here and there (note *templum* at *Fab.* 225). Both are supported by the scant evidence elsewhere: see Clement, *Protrepticus* 3.44, who states that Phoroneus first set up temples and altars and second sacrifices.

274.20 human flesh: We read (suggested by SMT) *cum . . . vesci viderentur* ("since they seemed to be eating") for F's *cum . . . vescerentur* ("since they were eating") although it is possible that Hyginus' language is simply unclear.

276 Asia: Reading *Asiam* for *Africam.*

276 Scyros: F's *Sicyon* cannot be right, as it is a landlocked region, and we conjecture *Scyros* (suggested by RSS) as a plausible alternative.

277 < . . . >: The transmitted text as Marshall prints it reads *Apollo in cithara ceteras adiecit* directly after *numero* XV ("fifteen in number") without a lacuna. If this is correct, *ceteras* must mean "the rest of the letters," which yields a highly suspicious sense. We propose a lacuna here (suggested by SMT), in which the story about the invention of the lyre/*cithara* originally was told, and we suggest that *ceteras* refers to *chordas,* "strings." Note *idem Mercurius* in the next line, which suggests that Mercury's invention of the lyre may have been contained in the lacuna.

APPENDIX

Excerpt from Pseudo-Dositheus

The material translated below has been taken from a bilingual schoolbook produced by an unknown teacher, probably in the third century AD. At one point the book was attributed to the fourth-century teacher Dositheus, the author of the *Ars Grammatica,* a Latin grammar for Greek speakers, but since the present text belongs to an anonymous composer of an earlier period, we now refer to him by the cumbersome name Pseudo-Dositheus. His schoolbook presents Greek and Latin words, phrases, and short passages side by side in order to facilitate language acquisition. The most interesting aspect of the book is that the author decided to excerpt parts of Hyginus' "world-famous" *Genealogy,* although we cannot tell whether its objective was to help native Greek speakers learn Latin or vice versa, so it adds nothing to the controversy of whether the original language of the *Fabulae* was Greek or Latin.

Ps.-Dositheus transcribed four lists and twenty-eight mythical accounts. Although none of the lists are found in Hyginus, many of the titles that Ps.-Dositheus provides have analogues in the *Fabulae* (we note them in braces {}). Unfortunately, the text of Ps.-Dositheus has suffered damage, and most of the myths he transcribed have been lost. Three, however, are well enough preserved that we can compare them to extant *Fabulae* (Prometheus, *Fab.* 144; Philyra, *Fab.* 138; Ulysses and the Sirens, *Fab.* 141). The accounts, although not exact pairs, are close enough that we can safely say that the copy of Hyginus' *Genealogy* used by Ps.-Dositheus was a relative of our *Fabulae.*

Since the text provides both a Greek and Latin version, we have had to make a choice in our translation. We have decided to use Latinate names so that readers can more easily compare these versions with the ones from the *Fabulae.*

Text

Preface

Three days before the Ides of September during the consulship of Maximus and Aper [September 11 in AD 207], I transcribed the world-famous *Genealogy* of Hyginus. You will find a good many stories in it translated in this book. In the second book we went through the names of the gods and goddesses; in this one you will find detailed accounts of them, if not all, at least as many as I was able to provide as time permitted. In many places paintings bear witness to the value of this work; teachers, too, not only praise the richness of this work but also make use of it; and the stories acted out by the pantomime dancers gain praise from it, and the dancers in their dances bear witness that what is written is true. So that you may easily find them, you may locate each account from the index below.

Index

First, the names of all nine Muses, as well as their arts, children, and their lovers. Then the names of the twelve gods. The seven days of the week. The twelve constellations of the zodiac. Prometheus {144}. Venus and Mars {148}. Minerva and Neptune {164}. Actaeon {180/181}. Daedalus {39/40}. Apollo and Cassandra {93}. Tantalus {82}. Philyra {138}. Ulysses {specifically, his encounter with the Sirens, 141}. The Creation of Humans {220?}. The Great Flood {152/153}. Pentheus {184}. Serpents {6?}. Jupiter and Juno {75}. Ixion {62}. Medea {22–27}. Aeolus. Melanippe {186}. Leda {77}. Alcyon {65}. Anchises {94}. Jupiter's Upbringing {139}. Marsyas {165}. The Minotaur {40?}. The < . . . > of Jupiter. Judgment of Arms {107}. Argos {145?}. Discovery of Arts {274, 277}.

[1] I shall begin my composition with the Muses:
Clio, the *cithara;* to Pierus she bore Hymenaeus.
Euterpe, tragedy; to Strymon she bore Paean.
Thalia, comedy < . . . >.
Melpomene, the lyre; to Achelous she bore the Sirens.
Terpsichore, the flute; to Neptune she bore Eumolpus.
Erato, the *cithara;* to Actaeon she bore Thamyris.
Polyhymnia, the lyre; to Hercules she bore Triptolemus.
Urania, astronomy; to Apollo she bore Linus.
Calliope, poetry; to Oeagrus she bore Orpheus.
[2] The names of the twelve gods: Juno, Vesta, Neptune, Mars, Ceres, Venus, Minerva, Diana, Latona, Mercury, Apollo, Jupiter.
[3] The seven days of the week: one, of Sol {Sun}, two, of Luna {Moon}, three, of Mars, four, of Mercury, five, of Jupiter, six, of Venus, seven, of Saturn.
[4] The names of the twelve zodiac constellations with commentary:[1]
Aries, because he found a source of water for Liber while he was traveling.
Taurus was handed over to Jupiter by Neptune, because it had human intelligence.
The Gemini are representations of Hercules and Theseus, since they performed similar labors.
Cancer, because he helped Hercules kill the Hydra.[2]

1. There are only eleven signs given here because originally the Greek sign Scorpio occupied two parts of the zodiac, which in Roman times was broken into two zones (see Hyginus, *De Astronomia* 2.26), Scorpio proper and Libra (originally the claws of Scorpio).

2. Here Hyginus—or Ps.-Dositheus—uniquely has the crab a helper of Hercules. Normally, the crab is sent by Hera/Juno or comes of its own accord to *attack* Hercules.

The Nemean Lion {Leo}: he was created by Juno's design and killed by Heracles.
Virgo is Erigone, who killed herself after her father was killed.
Libra: at Diana's bidding he {i.e., Scorpio}[3] killed Orion, whom Jupiter wanted to bring back to life.
Sagittarius: he was brought up with the Muses, and he is also named Crotus; he was a genius.
Capricorn: because he killed Typhon.
Aquarius: he was versed in every art and he taught them to mortals.
Pisces: these brought out from the sea a large egg, from which sprang the Syrian goddess, who showed humankind what was honorable.

[5] **The Story of Prometheus** {*Fab.* 144} Prometheus stole fire from heaven, hid it in a narthex plant, brought it down to humans, and showed them how to preserve it in ash. For this reason Jupiter ordered Mercury to bind him on Mount Caucasus and subjected him to an eagle that would by day dine on his innards, which would grow back again at night. Now, this eagle <Hercules killed . . . >.[4]

<*five stories and most of the next missing*>

[11] **<The Story of Tantalus>** {*Fab.* 82} <. . . > the finest of the fruit, such that he can see but cannot touch.

[12] **The Story of Philyra** {*Fab.* 138} Looking everywhere for Jupiter, Saturn changed himself into a horse and got Philyra daughter of Oceanus pregnant, and she gave birth to the Centaur Chiron, who discovered medicine. Philyra was ashamed of her son's unprecedented form. The gods pitied her, and she was changed into a tree bearing her name.

[13] **The Story of Ulysses** {*Fab.* 141} How he was able to get by the Sirens. The Sirens, the daughters of Achelous and the Muse Melpomene, lamenting the abduction of Proserpina, took refuge on the rock of Apollo. There by the will of the gods they were changed into birds, keeping only their human heads. There they held sailors spellbound with their singing. When Ulysses passed them by, they threw themselves into the sea and perished.

<*the rest of the stories not preserved*>

3. Although the entry is "Libra," the myth provided for it actually belongs to Scorpio (see note 1).
4. This reconstruction to complete the basic sense is taken from *Fab.* 144.

GENERAL INDEX

The General Index covers every personal name in both Apollodorus and Hyginus (about 2,000 of them), along with a few other names and terms (*aegis, cithara,* etc.), though place names and the names of ethnic groups are generally found in the Geographic Index, and the names of authors and works cited as authorities by Apollodorus and Hyginus are all found in the Index of Authors and Works Cited. Because Apollodorus wrote in Greek and Hyginus in Latin, the forms of the names used by them often differ. Most of these differences are simple matters of transliteration (Greek *ai* vs. Latin *ae,* Greek *oi* vs. Latin *oe*) that will cause few problems. In general, if the name is found in both authors, the entry will be found under the transliterated Greek spelling, though if it is found only in Hyginus, we have let the Latin form stand. We have provided cross-references where confusion is most likely to occur.

Minimal information accompanies each entry; it was thought that providing more would add unnecessary length and would not have been particularly helpful—following up a few references will generally serve a reader better than a canned index entry would have. We have broken down the more common figures and provided highlights of certain myths to avoid a long string of references. We have also attempted where possible to distinguish between individuals of the same name, marking each with a Roman numeral in boldface. In the interest of saving space the common familial relationships, "mother," "father," "son," and "daughter" have been abbreviated m., f., s., and d. (and, in a few occasions, b. for "brother" and sis. for "sister").

Abas: **I** s. of Lynceus, Apd. 2.24, 2.27 | Hyg. 14.11, 170, 244, 273.2 **II** s. of Neptune, Hyg. 157 **III** s. of Melampous, Apd. 1.103

Abderos: boyfriend of Heracles, Apd. 2.97 | Hyg. 30.9

Abraxas: one of the Sun's horses, Hyg. 183

Abseus: Giant, Hyg. Th.4

Absyrtus: *see* Apsyrtos

Acalle: d. of Minos, Apd. 3.7

Acamas: **I** s. of Theseus, Apd. E.1.18, E.1.23, E.5.22 | Hyg. 108 **II** s. of Eusoros, Trojan ally, Apd. E.3.34 | Hyg. 115 **III** s. of Antenor, Trojan ally, Apd. E.3.34 **IV** suitor of Penelope, Apd. E.7.27 **V** one of Actaeon's dogs, Hyg. 181

Acarnan: **I** s. of Alcmaion, Apd. 3.92 **II** suitor of Penelope E.7.27

Acastos: s. of Pelias, Argonaut, Apd. 1.95, 1.112, 1.144, 3.164–167, 3.173, 3.176, E.6.13 | Hyg. 14.23, 24, 103, 104, 243.3, 251, 256, 273.10

Acestes: king of Sicily, Hyg. 273.14, 273.18

Achaios: eponym of the Achaians, Apd. 1.50

Achamantis: Danaid, Hyg. 170

Achareus: competes with Heracles, Hyg. 273.5

Acheloos: river god, Apd. 1.18, 1.52, 1.63, 1.64, 2.148, 3.88, 3.93, E.7.18 | Hyg. Th.6, Th.30, 31.7, 125.13, 141, 274.1

Acheron: river (god) in underworld, Apd. 1.33, 2.126

Achilles: s. of Peleus & Thetis, greatest Greek warrior at Troy, Apd. 3.171–172, 3.174, 3.176, E.3.14–E.5.5, E.5.19, E.5.23 | Hyg. 96, 97.2, 97.15, 101, 106–107, 110, 112–114, 121, 123, 242, 257.1, 270, 273.13

Acoetes: Tyrrhenian sailor, Hyg. 134

Acontes: s. of Lycaon, Apd. 3.97

Acrisios: s. of Abas, f. of Danae, Apd. 2.24–26, 2.34–35, 2.47–48, 3.116 | Hyg. 63, 84, 155, 273.4

Assaracos: s. of Tros, Apd. 3.140 | Hyg. 94, 224, 270

Astacos: a Theban, Apd. 3.74–75

Asteria: **I** d. of Coios & Phoibe, Apd. 1.8–9, 1.21 | Hyg. Th.10, 53 **II** Danaid, Apd. 2.17 **III** d. of Atlas, Hyg. 250

Asterides: s. of Aegyptus, Hyg. 170

Asterion: **I** Argonaut, s. of Pyremus, Hyg. 14.1 **II** Argonaut, s. of Hyperasius, Hyg. 14.15

Asterios **I** king of Crete, Apd. 3.5, 3.7–8 **II** original name of the Minotaur, 3.11 **III** s. of Cometes, Apd. 1.113 **IV** s. of Neleus, Apd. 1.93 **V** s. of Aegyptus, Hyg. 170

Asterodia: d. of Deion, Apd. 1.86

Asteropaios: s. of Pelegon, Apd. E.4.7 | Hyg. 112

Asterope: **I** d. of Cebren, Apd. 3.147 **II** d. of Atlas, Hyg. 84 **III** m. of Peneleus, Hyg. 97.8

Astraios: s. of Creios & Eurybia, Apd. 1.8–9 | Hyg. Th.4 [here Giant], Th.15

Astyanax: **I** s. of Hector, Apd. E.5.23 | Hyg. 109 **II** s. of Heracles, Apd. 2.161

Astybia: d. of Thespios, Apd. 2.163

Astycrateia: d. of Niobe, Apd. 3.45 | Hyg. 11, 69.7

Astydameia: **I** wife of Acastos, Apd. 3.164–165, 3.173 **II** d. of Pelops, Apd. 2.50 **III** d. of Amyntor, Apd. 2.166

Astygonos: s. of Priam, Apd. 3.152

Astylochos: suitor of Penelope, Apd. E.7.27

Astynome: **I** d. of Amphion, Hyg. 69.7 **II** d. of Talaus, Hyg. 70

Astynomus: s. of Priam, Hyg. 90, 113

Astynoos: s. of Phaethon, Apd. 3.181

Astyoche: **I** d. of Phylas, m. of Tlepolemos, Apd. 2.149, 2.166, E.3.13 | Hyg. 97.7, 162 **II** d. of Niobe, Apd. 3.45 **III** d. of Laomedon, Apd. 3.146, E.6.15c **IV** d. of Simoeis, m. of Tros, Apd. 3.140

Astyochea: sis. of Agamemnon, wife of Strophius, Hyg. 117

Astypalaia: **I** m. of Eurypylos, Apd. 2.138 | **II** d. of Phoenix, Hyg. 157

Atalante: d. of Schoineus or Iasius, Calydonian boar hunter, Argonaut, Apd. 1.68–71, 1.112, 3.105–106, 3.109, 3.164 | Hyg. 70, 99, 173–174, 185, 244, 270

Atalanteia: m. of some Danaids, Apd. 2.17

Atas: s. of Priam, Apd. 3.152

Ate: goddess of recklessness, Apd. 3.143

Athamas: **I** s. of Aiolos, Apd. 1.51, 1.80–81, 1.84, 3.26, 3.28 | Hyg. 1–4, 5, 21, 224, 239, 245, 273.8 **II** s. of Aegyptus, Hyg. 170

Athena, Minerva: d. of Zeus, goddess of war & craft, often referred to as Parthenos (the Virgin), helper of many heroes, Apd. 1.20 birth, 1.24 invents double-flute, 1.35–37 Gigantomachy, 1.110 helps build *Argo,* 1.128, 2.12–13 & Danaos, 2.22 purifies Danaids, 2.37 guides Perseus, 2.41 helps Perseus kill Gorgon, 2.46 gets Gorgon's head, 2.69 gives Heracles arms, 2.71 gives Heracles robe, 2.93 gives Heracles castanets, 2.121 gets golden apples, 2.138, 2.144 gives Heracles Gorgon's hair, 2.146, 3.22–25 & Cadmos, 3.70 blinds Teiresias, 3.75–76 & Tydeus, 3.103, 3.120 gives Asclepios Gorgon's blood, 3.144–145 & the Palladion, 3.178–179 contest with Poseidon over Athens, creates olive tree, 3.187–191 Erichthonios, 3.196, E.3.2 judged by Paris, E.5.6 makes Aias insane, E.5.15 & Trojan Horse, E.5.22 Cassandra at her icon, E.5.25 anger at Greeks, E.6.1, E.6.5–6 sends storm against Greeks, E.6.20 | Hyg. Th.21, 14.33 makes *Argo* a constellation, 23, 30.3 helps Hercules with Hydra, 37, 39 teaches Daedalus, 63, 80, 88.3, 88.4, 92 judged by Paris, 107 arranges that Ulysses gets Achilles' arms, 108 helps with Trojan horse, 116 kills Locrian Ajax, 125.20, 126.1, 126.5–6 helps Ulysses, 127 advises Telegonus to marry Penelope, 142 gives life to first woman, 146 picks flowers with Proserpina, 148 gives Harmonia cursed dress, 150 helps defeat Titans, 164 competes with Neptune over Athens, 165 makes first flute, 166 drives Cecrops' daughters insane, wards off Vulcan, 168 & 277 builds ship for Danaus, 178 gives Cadmus advice, 204 turns Nyctimene into an owl, 275.2 founds Athens in Chalcis

Athletes: s. of Aegyptus, Hyg. 170

Atlantids: daughters of Atlas, Apd. 3.111

Atlantius: *see* Hermaphroditus

Atlas: s. of Iapetos, f. of Pleiades & others, holds up sky as punishment, Apd. 1.85, 1.87, 2.119–2.121, 3.110, 3.138, E.7.24 | Hyg. Th.3, Th.11, Th.16, 83–84, 125.16, 150, 155, 157, 192, 243.7, 248, 250

Brontes: one of the Cyclopes, Apd. 1.1

Broteas: hunter who does not honor Artemis, Apd. E.2.2

Bryce: Danaid, Apd. 2.19

Bu-: *see* Bou-

Byblis: d. of Miletus, Hyg. 243.6

Cadmos: s. of Agenor, king of Thebes, Apd. 1.128, 3.2, 3.4, 3.21–3.27, 3.36, 3.39| Hyg. 1, 2, 6, 76, 155, 178–179, 181, 224, 239–240, 243.1, 251, 254.3, 274.4, 275.4, 277

Cae-: *see* Cai-

Caineus: **I** s. (originally d.) of Coronos, Argonaut, Apd. 1.111, 3.118, E.1.22| Hyg. 14.23, conflated in Hyg. with **II** s. of Elatus, Hyg. 14.3, 173, 242 **III** f. of Phocus & Priasus, Hyg. 14.19

Calais: s. of Boreas, Argonaut, Apd. 1.111, 1.122, 3.199| Hyg. 14.18, 14.32, 19, 273.10

Calchas: s. of Thestor, seer, Apd. 3.174, E.3.15, E.3.20–21, E.5.8–9, E.5.25, E.6.2–4| Hyg. 97.15, 98, 128, 190.1

Calchinia: d. of Leucippus, Hyg. 157

Calchodon: f. of Elephenor, Hyg. 97.10

Caliadne: m. of some of Aigyptos' sons, Apd. 2.19

Callianassa: Nereid, Hyg. Th.8

Callidice: **I** queen of the Thesprotians, Odysseus' lover, Apd. E.7.34–35 **II** Danaid, Apd. 2.20

Callileon: s. of Thyestes, Apd. E.2.13

Calliope: Muse, Apd. 1.13–14, 1.18| Hyg. 14.1

Callirhoe: **I** d. of Acheloos, Apd. 3.88–91 **II** d. of Oceanos, Apd. 2.106 **III** d. of Scamandros, Apd. 3.140 **IV** wife of Chrysaor, m. of Geryon, Hyg. Th.41, 151 **V** wife of Piranthus, Hyg. 145

Callisthenes: killed own daughter, Hyg. 238

Callisto: d. of Lycaon, Apd. 3.100–101 | Hyg. 155, 176–177, 224

Calybe: nymph, Apd. 3.146

Calyce: **I** d. of Aiolos, m. of Endymion, Apd. 1.51, 1.56 **II** m. of Cygnus, Hyg. 157

Calydon: s. of Aitolos, Apd. 1.58–59

Calydoneus: suitor of Penelope, Apd. E.7.27

Calydonian boar: monstrous boar hunted by Meleagros & his companions, Apd. 1.66–71, 2.133, 3.106, 3.163| Hyg. 69.4, 172–173, 248

Calypso: **I** d. of Atlas, Apd. E.7.24| Hyg. Th.16, 125.16–17, 243.7 **II** Nereid, Apd. 1.12

Camilla: d. of Metabus, Hyg. 252

Camirus: s. of the Sun, Hyg. 275.6

Campe: jailer in Tartaros, Apd. 1.6

Canace: d. of Aiolos, incest with brother Macareus, Apd. 1.51, 1.53| Hyg. 238, 242, 243.6

Canache: one of Actaeon's dogs, Hyg. 181

Canethos: **I** s. of Lycaon, Apd. 3.97 **II** f. of Canthus, Hyg. 14.7, 14.28

Canicula: constellation, Hyg. 130

Canthus: **I** Argonaut, Hyg. 14.7, 14.28 **II** s. of Aegyptus, Hyg. 170

Capaneus: one of the Seven against Thebes, Apd. 3.63, 3.68, 3.73, 3.79, 3.82, 3.121, 3.129| Hyg. 68–71A, 97.4, 175, 243.2, 256, 257.2

Capricorn: constellation, Hyg. 196

Capylos: s. of Heracles, Apd. 2.162

Capys: s. of Assaracos, Apd. 3.141 | Hyg. 135

Carmenta: m. of Evander, Hyg. 277

Carpo: one of the Horae, Hyg. 183

Carteron: s. of Lycaon, Apd. 3.97

Cassandra: d. of Priam, a seer never believed, Apd. 3.151, E.5.17, E.5.22, E.5.24, E.6.23| Hyg. 90–91, 93, 108, 116–117, 128

Cassiepeia, Cassiopia: m. of Andromeda, Apd. 2.43, 3.6| Hyg. 64, 149 [here wife of Epaphus]

Cassus: s. of Aegyptus, Hyg. 170

Castor: one of the Dioscouroi, s. of Tyndareos & Leda, Calydonian boar hunter, Argonaut, Apd. 1.67, 1.111, 2.63, 3.126, 3.128, 3.134, 3.136| Hyg. 14.12, 77, 79–80, 92, 155, 173, 224, 251, 273.10, 275.5

Catreus: s. of Minos, Apd. 2.23, 3.7, 3.12–16, E.2.10, E.3.3, E.6.8

Cattle of Augeias: Heracles' fifth labor, Apd. 2.88–91| Hyg. 30.7

Cattle of Geryones: Heracles' tenth labor, Apd. 2.106–112| Hyg. 30.11

Caucon: s. of Lycaon, Apd. 3.96

Caunus: s. of Miletus, brother of Byblis, Hyg. 243.6

Cebren: river god near Troy, Apd. 3.147, 3.154

Cebriones: s. of Priam, Apd. 3.152| Hyg. 90

Cecrops: **I** first king of Athens, Apd. 3.177–180, 3.186, 3.189| Hyg. 48, 158, 166 **II** s. of Erechtheus, Apd. 3.196, 3.204–205

Celaineus: s. of Electryon, Apd. 2.52

Celaino: **I** d. of Atlas, Apd. 3.110–111 | Hyg. Th.16, 157, 192 **II** Danaid, Apd. 2.20| Hyg. 170 **III** a Harpy, Hyg. Th.35, 14.18

Celeos: king of Eleusis, Apd. 1.30–31, 3.191 | Hyg. 147

Celeustanor: s. of Heracles, Apd. 2.163

Celeutor: s. of Agrios, Apd. 1.77

Lapithos, Calydonian boar hunter, Apd. 1.67| Hyg. 159, 173 **IV** s. of Aigyptos, Apd. 2.19| Hyg. 170 **V** brother of Tereus, Hyg. 45
Drymo: Nereid, Hyg. Th.8
Dryops: s. of Priam, Apd. 3.152| Hyg. 90
Dymas: **I** f. of Hecabe, Apd. 3.148| Hyg. 91, 111, 243.1, 249 **II** s. of Aigimios, Apd. 2.176
Dynamene: Nereid, Apd. 1.12| Hyg. Th.8
Dynastes: s. of Heracles, Apd. 2.163
Dysis: one of the Horae, Hyg. 183

Earth: *see* Ge
Ecbasos: s. of Argos, Apd. 2.3–4| Hyg. 145
Echemmon: s. of Priam, Apd. 3.153
Echemos: husband of Timandra, Apd. 3.126
Echephron: **I** s. of Nestor, Apd. 1.94 **II** s. of Priam, Apd. 3.153
Echidna: monstrous serpent, d. of Tartaros & Ge, Apd. 2.4, 2.31, 2.106, 2.113, 2.119, 3.52, E.1.1| Hyg. Th.39, 151
Echion: **I** s. of Mercury, Argonaut, Calydonian boar hunter, Hyg. 14.3, 160, 173 **II** one of the Spartoi, f. of Pentheus, Apd. 3.24, 3.26, 3.36| Hyg. 76, 178, 184, 239 **III** s. of Portheus, Apd. E.5.20 **IV** suitor of Penelope, E.7.27
Echione: one of Actaeon's dogs, Hyg. 181
Ecnominus: s. of Aegyptus, Hyg. 170
Eetion: f. of Andromache, Apd. 3.154| Hyg. 123
Eidomene: wife of Amythaon, Apd. 1.96 (d. of Pheres), 2.27 (d. of Abas)
Eidyia: d. of Oceanos, Apd. 1.129
Eileithyia: d. of Zeus & Hera, Apd. 1.13
Eileithyiai: plural collective version of foregoing, Apd. 2.53
Eione: Nereid, Apd. 1.12
Eirene: one of the Horai, Apd. 1.13| Hyg. 183
Elacheia: d. of Thespios, Apd. 2.164
Elais: d. of Anios, Apd. E.3.10
Elare: m. of Tityos, Apd. 1.23
Elaton: *see* Baton
Elatos: **I** f. of Argonauts, Apd. 1.113| Hyg. 14.2, 173, 242 **II** f. of Ampycus, Hyg. 128 **III** s. of Arcas, f. of Ischys, Apd. 3.102| Hyg. 202 **IV** f. of Evanippe, Hyg. 71 **V** Centaur, Apd. 2.85 **VI** suitor of Penelope, Apd. E.7.28
Electra: **I** d. of Atlas, Apd. 3.110, 3.138, 3.145| Hyg. Th.16, Th.35, 155, 192, 250 **II** d. of Agamemnon, Apd. E.2.16, E.6.24, E.6.28| Hyg. 109, 117, 122, 254.1 **III** Danaid, Apd. 2.19| Hyg. 170 **IV** Oceanid, Apd. 1.8, 1.10
Electryon: s. of Perseus, Apd. 2.49, 2.52–56| Hyg. 14.10, 244
Elephantis: m. of some Danaids, Apd. 2.16
Elephenor: s. of Chalcodon, suitor of Helen, Apd. 3.130, E.3.11, E.6.15b| Hyg. 81, 97.10, 113
Eleusinus: s. of Mercury, king of Eleusis, Hyg. 147, 275.3
Eleusis: king of Eleusis, Apd. 1.32
Eleuther: s. of Apollo, Apd. 3.111| Hyg. 225
Elpenor: companion of Odysseus, Apd. E.7.17| Hyg. 125.11–12
Elysian Field(s): place of happy afterlife for heroes, Apd. 3.39, E.6.30
Emathion: s. of Tithonos, Apd. 2.119, 3.147
Emphytus: Giant, Hyg. Th.4
Enaesimus: s. of Hippocoon, Calydonian boar hunter, Hyg. 173
Enarete: d. of Deimachos, Apd. 1.51
Enarophoros: s. of Hippocoon, Apd. 3.124
Encelados: **I** Giant, Apd. 1.37| Hyg. Th.4 **II** s. of Aigyptos, Apd. 2.16| Hyg. 170
Endeis: d. of Sceiron, Apd. 3.158| Hyg. 14.8 [d. of Chiron]
Endios: husband of Benthesicyme, Apd. 3.201
Endymion: s. of Aethlios, beloved of Selene, Apd. 1.56, 1.57| Hyg. 271 [here s. of Aetolus, perhaps mistake for Aethlius]
Enipeus: river god, Apd. 1.90
Ennomos: s. of Arsinoos, Apd. E.3.35
Entelides: s. of Heracles, Apd. 2.162
Entellus: Trojan, Hyg. 273.17
Envy: d. of Pallas & Styx, Hyg. Th.17
Enyo: one of the Phorcides, Apd. 2.37| Hyg. Th.9
Eone: d. of Thespios, Apd. 2.163
Eos, Aurora: "Dawn," Apd. 1.8, 1.9, 1.27, 1.35, 1.86, 3.147, 3.181, E.5.3| Hyg. Th.12, Th.15, 189, 270
Eous: horse of the Sun, Hyg. 183
Epaphos: **I** s. of Zeus & Io, Apd. 2.8–10, 2.116| Hyg. 145, 149–150, 155, 157, 275.2 **II** early god, Hyg. Th.1 **III** mistake for Epopeus, king of Sicyon, Hyg. 7–8
Epeios, Epeus: builder of the Trojan horse, Apd. E.4.8, E.5.14| Hyg. 108
Ephialtes: **I** Giant, Apd. 1.37| Hyg. Th.4 **II** one of the Aloadai, Apd. 1.53| Hyg. 28 **III** s. of Aegyptus, Hyg. 170

abducts Persephone, 1.38, 1.106 fights with Heracles, 2.38, 2.108, 2.125 & Heracles, 2.142 wounded by Heracles, 3.159, E.1.24 imprisons Theseus & Peirithous, E.7.34 | Hyg. Th.13, 79, 139, 146 abducts Proserpina
Haemon: *see* Haimon
Hagios: suitor of Penelope, Apd. E.7.27
Hagnias: f. of Tiphys, Apd. 1.111
Haimon: **I** s. of Creon, Apd. 3.54 | Hyg. 72 **II** s. of Lycaon, Apd. 3.97 **III** one of Actaeon's dogs, Hyg. 181
Haimonios: f. of Amaltheia, Apd. 2.148
Halcyon Days: Hyg. 65
Halie: Nereid, Apd. 1.11
Halimede: Nereid, Apd. 1.12
Halios: suitor of Penelope, Apd. E.7.29
Halipheros: s. of Lycaon, Apd. 3.97
Halirrhothios: s. of Poseidon, Apd. 3.180
Halocrates: s. of Heracles, Apd. 2.164
Harmodius: Athenian tyrannicide, Hyg. 257.2, 257.9–12
Harmonia: d. of Ares & Aphrodite, wife of Cadmos, Apd. 3.25, 3.39 | Hyg. Th.29, 2, 6, 148, 155, 159, 179
Harpaleus: s. of Lycaon, Apd. 3.97
Harpalicus: one of Actaeon's dogs, Hyg. 181
Harpalus: one of Actaeon's dogs, Hyg. 181
Harpalyce: **I** d. of Clymenus, Hyg. 206, 238–239, 246, 253, 255 **II** d. of Harpalycus, Hyg. 193, 252, 254.2
Harpalycos: **I** s. of Lycaon, Apd. 3.97 **II** king of the Amymneans, Hyg. 193, 252, 254.2
Harpies: Apd. 1.10, 1.121–122, 1.124, 3.199 | Hyg. Th.35, 14.18, 19; *see also* Aello, Ocypete
Harpocrates: s. of Isis, Hyg. 277
Harpyia: one of Actaeon's dogs, Hyg. 181
Hebe: "Youth," d. of Zeus & Hera, Apd. 1.13, 2.160 | Hyg. Th.24
Hecabe, Hecuba: **I** wife of Priam, Apd. 3.148–149, 3.151, E.5.24 | Hyg. 91, 93, 109, 111, 243.1, 249, 256, 270 **II** Danaid, Hyg. 170
Hecate: goddess, d. of Perses, Apd. 1.9, 1.37
Hecato: f. of Calyce, Hyg. 157
hecatomb: sacrifice of a hundred head of cattle
Hector: s. of Priam, Apd. 3.148, 3.154, E.3.30, E.4.2–8 *passim* | Hyg. 90, 103, 106–107, 111–113, 115
Hecuba: *see* Hecabe
Hedymeles: early god, Hyg. Th.1
Heleios: s. of Perseus, Apd. 2.49, 2.59–60
Helen: d. of Tyndareos, wife of Menelaos, Apd. 3.126–129, 3.133, 3.154–155, E.1.23, E.2.15–16, E.3.1–5, E.3.18, E.3.28, E.5.9, E.5.13, E.5.19, E.5.22, E.6.30 | Hyg. 77–81, 92, 98, 118, 122, 224, 240, 249, 270
Helenos: **I** s. of Priam, Apd. 3.151, E.5.9–10, E.5.24, E.6.12–13 | Hyg. 90, 128, 273.12 **II** suitor of Penelope, Apd. E.7.30
Helia: sister of Phaethon, Hyg. Th.38, 154, 156
Heliades: sisters of Phaethon, Hyg. 154
Helice: **I** constellation, Hyg. 177 **II** Danaid, Hyg. 170
Heliconis: d. of Thespios, Apd. 2.164
Helicta: Danaid, Hyg. 170
Helios: the "Sun," Apd. 1.8, 1.28, 1.35, 1.83, 1.113, 1.137, 1.146, 2.88, 2.107, 2.109, 2.119, 3.7, E.7.14, E.7.22 | Hyg. Th.12, Th.36, Th.38, 3, 14.15, 14.20, 14.22, 22, 27, 40, 125.8, 125.15, 148, 152A, 156, 183, 199, 205, 223.3, 244–245, 250, 258, 275.6
Helix: s. of Lycaon, Apd. 3.96
Hellanicos: suitor of Penelope, Apd. E.7.27
Helle: d. of Athamas, Apd. 1.80, 1.82 | Hyg. 1–3
Hellen: s. of Deucalion, eponym of the Hellenes, Apd. 1.49–50 | Hyg. 125.6, 155 [called s. of Jupiter & Pyrrha], 157 [called s. of Neptune & Antiope]
Helymus: Trojan, Hyg. 273.16
Hemithea: d. of Cycnos, Apd. E.3.24
Henicea: d. of Priam, Hyg. 90
Heosphoros, Lucifer: f. of Ceyx, Apd. 1.52 | Hyg. 65, 161
Hephaistine: m. of some sons of Aigyptos, Apd. 3.20
Hephaistos, Vulcan: s. of Zeus & Hera, or by Hera alone, god of the forge, Apd. 1.19 birth, 1.20, 1.26–27, 1.37 Gigantomachy, 1.45 nails Prometheus to mountain, 1.112, 1.128, 1.140, 2.71 gives Heracles breastplate, 2.93, 2.111, 3.25 makes cursed necklace, 3.187–188 attempts to rape Athena, 3.217, E.2.9, E.4.7 makes Achilles' armor E.4.8 fights Scamandros | Hyg. Th.22, 38.5, 48 f. of Erichthonius, 106 makes Achilles' armor, 140 gives Apollo & Diana bows, 142 makes first woman, 148 catches Venus & Mars in bed, gives Harmonia cursed dress, 158 sons, 166 traps Juno in throne, 238
Hera, Juno: d. of Cronos & Rhea, wife of Zeus, queen of the gods, goddess of women & mar-

sos, 3.43, 3.112 birth, 3.112–114 steals Apollo's cows, 3.113 invents lyre, 3.115 reconciles with Apollo 3.181, E.2.6, E.2.12, E.3.2 leads goddesses to Paris, E.3.5 takes Helen to Egypt, E.3.30 fetches Protesilaos from underworld, E.7.16 gives Odysseus *moly,* E.7.38 f. of Pan by Penelope | Hyg.Th.32, 8 stops Zethus & Amphion from killing Lycus, 14.3, 32, 62 takes Ixion to underworld, 92 leads goddesses to Paris, 103 leads Protesilaus back from the underworld, 106 leads Priam to Greek camp, 125.8 gives Ulysses antidote for Circe's magic, 125.16, 125.19 [mistake for Neptune, who shipwrecks Ulysses], 143 creates different languages, 144 binds Prometheus to mountain, 145 kills Argus, 160, 164 stops Neptune from flooding Attica, 173, 179, 195 visits Hyrieus, 200 sleeps with Chione, fathers Autolycus, 201 gives Autolycus ability to steal anything, 224, 225, 241 f. of Cephalus, 251, 271, 273.11, 275.3, 277 invented letters

Hermione: d. of Menelaos & Helen, Apd. 3.133, E.3.3, E.6.14, E.6.28 | Hyg. 122–123

Hermos: s. of Aigyptos, Apd. 2.19

Hero: **I** Danaid, Hyg. 170 **II** d. of Priam, Hyg. 90

Herophilus: Athenian doctor, Hyg. 274.10

Herse: **I** d. of Cecrops, Apd. 3.180–181 | Hyg. 166 **II** m. of some Danaids, Apd. 2.20

Hesione: **I** d. of Laomedon, Apd. 2.104, 2.136, 3.146, 3.162 | Hyg. 31.4, 89, 97.3 **II** wife of Nauplios, Apd. 2.23

Hesperethousa: one of the Hesperides, Apd. 2.114

Hesperia: one of the Hesperides, Hyg.Th.1

Hesperides: nymph guardians of the Golden Apples, Apd. 2.113–115, 2.120 | Hyg. Th.1, Th.39, 30.12, 31.7, 151

Hesperis: one of the Horae, Hyg. 183

Hesperus: *see* Heosphoros

Hestia, Vesta: goddess of the hearth, Apd. 1.4 | Hyg. Th.13

Hestyaea: Oceanid, Hyg.Th.6

Hesycheia: d. of Thespios, Apd. 2.164

Hicetaon: s. of Laomedon, Apd. 3.146

Hierax: reveals Zeus' plan, Apd. 2.7

Hieromneme: d. of Simoeis, Apd. 3.141

Hilaeira: d. of Leucippos, Apd. 3.117, 3.134 | Hyg. 80

Hilagus: s. of Priam, Hyg. 90

Himas: f. of Pluto, Hyg. 155

Hippalcimos: f. of Peneleos, Apd. 3.130 | Hyg. 14.20; also called Hippalmos in Apd. 1.113

Hippalcus: **I** s. of Pelops & Hippodamia, Hyg. 84 **II** f. of Peneleus, Hyg. 97.8

Hippalmos: f. of Peneleos, Apd. 1.113; also called Hippalcimos in Apd. 3.130

Hipparete: Danaid, Hyg. 170

Hippasos: **I** f. of Actor or other Argonauts, Apd. 1.112 | Hyg. 14.15, 14.17, 14.20, perhaps to be identified with **II** s. of Eurytus, Calydonian boar hunter, Hyg. 173 **III** s. of Priam, Hyg. 90 **IV** s. of Ceyx, Apd. 2.156

Hippea: m. of Polyphemus, Hyg. 14.2

Hippeus: s. of Heracles, Apd. 2.161

Hippo: d. of Thespios, Apd. 2.162

Hippocoon: **I** s. of Perieres, f. of the Hippocoontidai, Apd. 2.143, 2.145, 3.123–125 | Hyg. 14.21, 31.8, 173 **II** Trojan, Hyg. 273.18

Hippocoontidai: sons of Hippocoon, Apd. 2.143, 2.145

Hippocorystes: **I** s. of Aigyptos, Apd. 2.20 **II** s. of Hippocoon, Apd. 3.124

Hippocrate: d. of Thespios, Apd. 2.164

Hippodamas: **I** s. of Acheloos, Apd. 1.52, 1.63 **II** s. of Priam, Apd. 3.152

Hippodameia: **I** d. of Oinomaos, wife of Pelops, Apd. 2.36, E.2.4–8 | Hyg. 14.20, 84–88.1, 243.3, 253 **II** fiancée or wife of Peirithous, Apd. E.1.21 | Hyg. 33, 97.14 **III** Danaid, Apd. 2.17

Hippodamus: Trojan, Hyg. 113

Hippodice: Danaid, Apd. 2.20

Hippodochos: suitor of Penelope, Apd. E.7.28

Hippodromos: s. of Heracles, Apd. 2.162

Hippolochos: f. of Glaucos, Apd. E.3.35

Hippolyte: **I** Amazon queen killed by Heracles, Apd. 2.98, 2.101–102 | Hyg. 30.10, 163 **II** another Amazon (=Antiope), Apd. E.1.16, E.5.1, E.5.2 **III** wife of Iphitus, Hyg. 97.10

Hippolytos: **I** s. of Theseus by Amazon, Apd. 3.121, E.1.17–19, E.5.2 | Hyg. 47, 49, 243.5, 250, 251 [called Virbius by Romans] **II** f. of Deiphobos, Apd. 2.130 **III** Giant, Apd. 1.38 **IV** s. of Aigyptos, Apd. 2.17

Hippomedon: s. of Aristomachos, one of the Seven against Thebes, Apd. 3.63, 3.68, 3.74 | Hyg. 70–71A

Hippomedousa: Danaid, Apd. 2.17

Hippomenes: **I** husband of Atalante, Apd. 3.109 | Hyg. 185 **II** f. of Megareus, Apd. 3.210

Ichneumo: one of Actaeon's dogs, Hyg. 181

Ichnobates: one of Actaeon's dogs, Hyg. 181

ichor: fluid running in veins of gods & goddesses instead of blood

Ida: raises the infant Zeus, Apd. 1.5 | Hyg. 182

Idaia: **I** nymph, Apd. 3.139 **II** d. of Dardanos, Apd. 3.200

Idas: **I** s. of Aphareus, Calydonian boar hunter, Argonaut, Apd. 1.60–61, 1.67, 1.69, 1.111, 3.117, 3.135–137 | Hyg. 14.12–13, 14.26, 14.32, 80, 100, 173 **II** s. of Aigyptos, Apd. 2.20

Ideus: s. of Thestius, Calydonian boar hunter, Hyg. 173–174

Idmon: **I** s. of Apollo, Argonaut, prophet, Apd. 1.126 | Hyg. 14.11, 14.26, 18, 248 **II** s. of Aigyptos, Apd. 2.20

Idomeneus: **I** s. of Deucalion, Apd. 3.17, E.3.13, E.6.9, E.6.10 | Hyg. 81, 97.7, 114, 270 **II** s. of Priam, Apd. 3.153

Idothea: d. of Proteus, Hyg. 118

Idyia: m. of Medea, Hyg. 25

Ienios: Giant, Hyg. Th.4

Ileus: *see* Oileus

Ilia: m. of Romulus & Remus, Hyg. 252

Iliona: d. of Priam & Hecuba, Hyg. 90, 109, 240, 243.4, 254.1

Illyrios: s. of Cadmos, Apd. 3.39

Ilos: **I** s. of Dardanos, Apd. 3.140 **II** s. of Tros, Apd. 3.140–146 | Hyg. 250

Iltonomus: s. of Aegyptus, Hyg. 170

Imbros: s. of Aigyptos, Apd. 2.19

Imenarete: m. of Elephenor, Hyg. 97.10

Imeusimos: s. of Icarios, Apd. 3.126

Inachos: river god in Argos, Apd. 2.1, 2.5–6, 2.13, 3.1 | Hyg. Th.6, 124, 143, 145, 155, 225, 274.8

Incest: early god, Hyg. Th.3

Indios: suitor of Penelope, Apd. E.7.29

Indus: **I** river god, Hyg. Th.6 **II** king in Scythia, discovers silver, Hyg. 274.4

Ino: d. of Cadmos, becomes goddess Leucothea, Apd. 1.80–81, 1.84, 3.26, 3.28 | Hyg. 1–2, 4, 179, 184, 224, 239, 243.1, 243.5, 273.8; *see also* Leucothea

Io: seduced by Zeus, transformed into a cow, Apd. 2.5–9 | Hyg. 145, 149, 155

Iobates: king of Lycia, Apd. 2.25, 2.30–33 | Hyg. 57, 243.2

Iobes: s. of Heracles, Apd. 2.161

Iocaste, Jocasta: d. of Menoiceus, m. & wife of Oidipous, Apd. 3.48, 3.56 | Hyg. 66, 67, 70, 242, 243.7, 253

Iolaos: s. of Iphicles (in Hyg. often s. of Iphiclus), companion of Heracles, Apd. 2.70, 2.78–80, 2.127 | Hyg. 14.22, 103, 173, 273.11

Iole: d. of Eurytos, Apd. 2.127–128, 2.156–157, 2.159, 2.170 | Hyg. 31.9, 35–36

Ion: s. of Xouthos, eponym of the Ionians, Apd. 1.50

Ione: Nereid, Apd. 1.12

Ios: m. of Agapenor, Hyg. 97.11

Iphianassa: **I** m. of Aitolos, Apd. 1.57 **II** d. of Proitos, Apd. 2.26

Iphicles: s. of Amphitryon, Apd. 1.68, 2.61–62, 2.70, 2.72, 2.145; *see also* Iphiclos III

Iphiclos: **I** s. of Phylacos, f. of Protesilaos, Argonaut, Apd. 1.100–102, 3.131, E.3.14 | Hyg. 14.2, 97.12, 251 **II** s. of Thestios, Argonaut, Apd. 1.62, 1.72, 1.113 | Hyg. 14.17 **III** in Hyg. for Iphicles f. of Iolaus, Hyg. 14.22, 103, 173, 273.11

Iphidamas: **I** suitor of Penelope, Apd. E.7.27 **II** Trojan, Hyg. 113

Iphigeneia: d. of Agamemnon, Apd. E.2.16, E.3.22 | Hyg. 98, 120–122, 238, 261

Iphimachus: takes care of Philoctetes on Lemnos, Hyg. 102

Iphimede: m. of the Aloadai, Hyg. 28

Iphimedeia: d. of Triops, Apd. 1.53

Iphimedon: s. of Eurystheus, Apd. 2.168

Iphimedousa: Danaid, Apd. 2.17

Iphinoe: **I** d. of Proitos, Apd. 2.26, 2.29 **II** gatekeeper of Lemnos, Hyg. 15

Iphinome: Amazon, Hyg. 163

Iphis: **I** d. of Thespios, Apd. 2.163 **II** s. of Alector, Apd. 3.60, 3.63, 3.79

Iphitos: **I** s. of Eurytos, Apd. 2.128–130, E.7.33 | Hyg. 14.8 **II** s. of Naubolos, Argonaut, Apd. 1.113, 3.130 | Hyg. 14.17, 97.10 **III** killed by Copreus, Apd. 2.76 **IV** f. of Eurynome, Hyg. 70

Irene: *see* Eirene

Iris: d. of Thaumas, Apd. 1.10 | Hyg. Th.35

Irus: **I** f. of Eurydamas, Hyg. 14.5 **II** f. of Eurytion, Hyg. 14.7 **III** beggar at Ulysses' palace, Hyg. 126.6–7

Ischys: s. of Elatos, Apd. 3.118 | Hyg. 202

Isis: Egyptian goddess, Apd. 2.9 | Hyg. 145, 277

Ismaros: **I** s. of Astacos, Apd. 3.74 **II** s. of Eumolpos, Apd. 3.202

Learchos: s. of Athamas, Apd. 1.80, 1.84, 3.28 | Hyg. 1–2, 4

Leda: d. of Thestios, wife of Tyndareos, m. of the Dioscouroi, Clytaimnestra, & Helen, Apd. 1.62, 1.67, 3.125–127, 3.134 | Hyg. 14.12, 77, 78, 79, 155, 224, 240, 251

Leiocritos: suitor of Penelope, Apd. E.7.29

Leiodes: suitor of Penelope, Apd. E.7.30

Leitos: s. of Alector, Argonaut, Greek leader at Troy, Apd. 1.113, 3.130 | Hyg. 97.9, 114

Lelex: f. of Eurotas, Apd. 3.116

Leodocus: s. of Mars & Pero, Hyg. 159

Leon: s. of Lycaon, Apd. 3.97

Leonteus: **I** f. of Ixion, Hyg. 62 **II** s. of Coronos, Greek leader at Troy, Apd. 3.130, E.6.2 | Hyg. 81, 97.15, 114

Leontophonos: s. of Odysseus, Apd. E.7.40

Lernaian Hydra: *see* Hydra

Lernus: f. of Palaemonius, Hyg. 14.19

Lestorides: suitor of Penelope, Apd. E.7.27

Leto, Latona: d. of Coios & Phoibe, m. of Artemis & Apollo, Apd. 1.8, 1.21, 1.23, 3.46, 3.122 | Hyg. Th.10, Th.33, 9, 53, 55, 140

Leucippe: **I** m. of Iphiclus, Hyg. 14.17 **II** d. of Thestor, Hyg. 190 **III** m. of Laomedon, Hyg. 250 **IV** wife of Laomedon, Apd. 3.146

Leucippos: **I** s. of Perieres, Apd. 1.87, 3.117–118, 3.123, 3.134 | Hyg. 80, 173 **II** s. of Heracles, Apd. 2.164 | Hyg. 162 **III** f. of Calchinia, Hyg. 157

Leucon: **I** s. of Athamas, Apd. 1.84 **II** s. of Neptune, Hyg. 157 **III** one of Actaeon's dogs, Hyg. 181

Leucones: s. of Heracles, Apd. 2.163

Leuconoe: m. of Philammon, Hyg. 161

Leucopeus: s. of Porthaon, Apd. 1.63

Leucos: Cretan tyrant, Apd. E.6.10

Leucothea, Mater Matuta: divine name of Ino, Apd. 3.29 | Hyg. 2, 125.17 [called Leucothoe], 224

Leucothoe: Nereid, Hyg. Th.8, 14.20

Liber: *see* Dionysos

Libera: *see* Ariadne

Libya: **I** d. of Epaphos, Apd. 2.10, 3.1 | Hyg. 149, 157 **II** d. of Palamedes, Hyg. 160

Libys: **I** Tyrrhenian sailor, Hyg. 134 **II** s. of Mercury, Hyg. 160

Lichas: herald of Heracles, Apd. 2.157–158 | Hyg. 36

Licymnios: s. of Electryon, Apd. 2.52, 2.54, 2.57, 2.143, 2.156, 2.170

Ligea: Nereid, Hyg. Th.8

Ligyron: original name of Achilles, Apd. 3.172

Limnoreia: Nereid, Apd. 1.12 | Hyg. Th.8

Linos: **I** s. of Calliope & Oiagros/Apollo, Apd. 1.14, 2.63 | Hyg. 161, 273.11 **II** s. of Lycaon 3.97

Lixos: s. of Aigyptos, Apd. 2.19

Lotophagi: *see* Lotus-eaters

Lotus-eaters: visited by Odysseus, Apd. E.7.3 | Hyg. 125.2

Lucifer: *see* Heosphoros

Lucretia: Roman famous for chastity, Hyg. 256

Lucretius: f. of Lucretia, Hyg. 256

Lyammos: suitor of Penelope, Apd. E.7.28

Lycabas: Tyrrhenian sailor, Hyg. 134

Lycaena: one of Actaeon's dogs, Hyg. 181

Lycaithos: **I** s. of Hippocoon, Apd. 3.124 **II** suitor of Penelope, Apd. E.7.28

Lycaon: **I** s. of Pelasgos, Apd. 3.96, 3.99–100 | Hyg. 155, 176–177, 224–225 **II** f. of Pandaros, Apd. E.3.35 **III** s. of Priam, Apd. 3.152, E.3.32

Lycios: s. of Lycaon, Apd. 3.97

Lycisce: one of Actaeon's dogs, Hyg. 181

Lycomedes: king of Scyros, Apd. 3.174, E.1.24, E.5.11 | Hyg. 96

Lycopeus: s. of Agrios, Apd. 1.77 | Hyg. 175

Lycoreus: s. of Apollo, Hyg. 161

Lycorias: Nereid, Hyg. Th.8

Lycos: **I** king of the Mariandynoi, Apd. 1.126, 2.100 | Hyg. 14.26, 14.30, 18, 248 **II** s. of Chthonios or Hyrieus, steward of Thebes, Apd. 3.40–44 | Hyg. 7, 8 **III** s. of Neptune, tries to rape Heracles' wife Megara, Hyg. 31.6, 32, 76, 157 **IV** f. of Ialmenus, Hyg. 97.10 **V** s. of Poseidon & Celaino, Apd. 3.111 **VI** s. of Pandion, Apd. 3.206 **VII** s. of Aigyptos, Apd. 2.16 **VIII** s. of Mars, Hyg. 159

Lycotherses: king of Illyria, married to Agave, Hyg. 184, 240, 254.3

Lycourgos: **I** s. of Dryas, rejects Dionysos, Apd. 3.34–35 | Hyg. 132, 192, 242 **II** s. of Aleos, Apd. 1.67, 1.112, 3.102, 3.105, 3.121 | Hyg. 14.14, 173, 248 **III** s. of Pheres, king of Thebes or Nemea, Apd. 1.104, 3.64–65 | Hyg. 15, 74, 273.6 **IV** s. of Heracles, Apd. 2.164 **V** s. of Pronax, Apd. 1.103

Lydus: s. of Hercules, Hyg. 162

Lying: early god, Hyg. Th.3

Lyncaios: s. of Heracles, Apd. 2.163

Lynceste: one of Actaeon's dogs, Hyg. 181

Melampous: s. of Amythaon, seer, Apd. 1.96, 1.99–103, 2.27–29
Melampus: one of Actaeon's dogs, Hyg. 181
Melanchaetes: one of Actaeon's dogs, Hyg. 181
Melaneus: one of Actaeon's dogs, Hyg. 181
Melanion: s. of Amphidamas, husband of Atalante, Apd. 3.63, 3.105, 3.108–109
Melanippe: Amazon, Apd. E.1.16, E.5.2 | Hyg. 186, 252
Melanippos: **I** s. of Astacos, Apd. 1.77, 3.75–76 **II** s. of Priam, Apd. 3.152 **III** s. of Agrios, Apd. 1.77 **IV** killed by brother Tydeus, Hyg. 69.2, 69A
Melanthios: slave of Odysseus, Apd. E.7.32–33 | Hyg. 126.7–8
Melas: **I** s. of Phrixos, Apd. 1.83 | Hyg. 3, 14.30, 21 **II** s. of Porthaon, Apd. 1.63, 1.76 **III** s. of Licymnios, Apd. 2.156 **IV** Tyrrhenian sailor, Hyg. 134
Meleager: *see* Meleagros
Meleagros, Meleager: s. of Oineus, led Calydonian boar hunt, Argonaut, Apd. 1.65–73 *passim,* 1.112, 2.123 | Hyg. 14.16, 70, 99, 171–174, 239, 244, 249, 270, 273.10
Melia: **I** wife of Inachos, Apd. 2.1 **II** m. of Amycus, Hyg. 17, 157
Meliboia: **I** d. of Niobe, Apd. 3.47 **II** d. of Oceanos, Apd. 3.96
Melicertes: s. of Athamas, becomes god Palaimon, Apd. 1.80, 1.84, 3.28–29 | Hyg. 1–2, 4, 224, 239, 243.1, 273.8; *see also* Palaimon
Meline: d. of Thespios, Apd. 2.161
Melisseus: f. of Adrasteia & Ida, Apd. 1.5 | Hyg. 182
Melite: Nereid, Apd. 1.12 | Hyg. Th.8
Melphis: m. of Meriones, Hyg. 97.7
Melpomene: Muse, Apd. 1.13, 1.18, E.7.18 | Hyg. Th.30, 125.13, 141
Memnon: s. of Eos & Tithonos, Apd. 3.147, E.5.3 | Hyg. 112, 223.5
Memphis: **I** d. of Nile, Apd. 2.10 **II** m. of some Danaids, Apd. 2.18
Menalces: s. of Aigyptos, Apd. 2.20
Menelaos: s. of Atreus, husband of Helen, Apd. 3.15, 3.131–133, 3.137, E.2.15–16, E.3.3, E.3.6, E.3.9, E.3.12 (s. of Pleisthenes), E.3.28, E.4.1, E.5.21–22, E.6.1, E.6.29–30 | Hyg. 78, 81, 88.8, 92, 95, 97.1, 98, 107–108, 112–114, 116, 118, 122–123, 273.13
Menemachos: s. of Aigyptos, Apd. 2.18
Menephiarus: Giant, Hyg. Th.4
Menephron: f. of Cyllene, Hyg. 253
Meneptolemos: suitor of Penelope, Apd. E.7.27
Menestheus: **I** s. of Peteos, Greek leader at Troy, Apd. 3.129, E.1.23–24, E.3.11, E.6.15b | Hyg. 81, 97.11 **II** Trojan, Hyg. 273.14–15
Menesthios: s. of Spercheios, Apd. 3.168
Menetus: f. of Antianira Hyg. 14.3
Menippe: Oceanid, Hyg. Th.6
Menippis: d. of Thespios, Apd. 2.162
Menodice: a nymph, Hyg. 14.11
Menoe-: *see* Menoi-
Menoiceus: **I** Theban, f. of Iocaste & Creon, Apd. 2.50, 2.67, 3.48, 3.52 | Hyg. 25 [mistakenly identified as f. of Creon of Corinth], 67.4, 67.6, 68, 70, 72, 76, 242, 243.7 **II** s. of Creon, grands. of Menoiceus I, Apd. 3.73 | [**I** & **II** are conflated in Hyg. 67.6 and 68]
Menoites: **I** herder of Hades' cattle, Apd. 2.108, 2.125 **II** old man who exposed Oedipus, Hyg. 67.7
Menoitios: **I** s. of Actor, f. of Patroclos, Apd. 1.112, 3.131, 3.176 | Hyg. 14.6, 97.2, 257.1, 270 **II** s. of Iapetos, Apd. 1.8
Mentis: Oceanid, Hyg. Th.6
Mentor: **I** s. of Heracles, Apd. 2.163 **II** s. of Eurystheus, Apd. 2.168
Mercury: *see* Hermes
Meriones: Greek leader at Troy, Hyg. 81, 97.7, 114
Mermerus: s. of Jason & Medea, Hyg. 25, 239
Merope: **I** d. of Atlas, wife of Sisyphos, Apd. 1.85, 3.110 | Hyg. Th.16, 154, 192 **II** wife of Cresphontes, Apd. 2.180 | Hyg. 137 **III** d. of Oinopion, Apd. 1.25 **IV** one of Phaethon's sisters, Hyg. Th.38, 154, 156 **V** m. of Hippomenes, Hyg. 185
Merops: f. of Arisbe, Apd. 3.147, 3.149, E.3.35
Mesembria: one of the Horae, Hyg. 183
Mesthles: s. of Talaimenes, Apd. E.3.35
Mestor: **I** s. of Priam, Apd. 3.152, E.3.32 | Hyg. 90 **II** s. of Perseus, Apd. 2.49, 2.50 **III** s. of Pterelaos, Apd. 2.51, 2.54
Meta: d. of Hoples, Apd. 3.207
Metabus: king of the Volscians, Hyg. 252
Metalces: s. of Aegyptus, Hyg. 170
Metaneira: wife of Celeos, Apd. 1.31–32
Metapontus: king of Icaria, Hyg. 186
Metharme: d. of Pygmalion, Apd. 3.182
Metiadousa: d. of Eupalamos, Apd. 3.204

Metidice: d. of Talaus, Hyg. 70
Metion: s. of Erechtheus, Apd. 3.196, 3.205–206, 3.214
Metis: Oceanid, m. of Athena, Apd. 1.6, 1.8, 1.20
Metope: **I** wife of Sangarios, Apd. 3.148 **II** d. of Asopos, Apd. 3.156
Midamus: s. of Aegyptus, Hyg. 170
Midas: king of Mygdon, s. of Cybele, Hyg. 191, 274.6
Midea: Danaid, Hyg. 170
Mideia: m. of Licymnios, Apd. 2.52
Miletos: s. of Apollo, Apd. 3.5–6 | Hyg. 243.6
Mimas: Giant, Apd. 1.37
Minerva: *see* Athena
Mineus: s. of Aegyptus, Hyg. 170
Minis: suitor of Penelope, Apd. E.7.29
Minos: s. of Zeus & Europa, king of Crete, Apd. 1.83, 1.140, 2.58, 2.94, 2.95, 2.99, 2.100, 3.3–20 *passim,* 3.121, 3.197–198, 3.209–215, E.1.8, E.1.12, E.1.14–15, E.1.17 | Hyg. 14.10, 14.19, 14.22, 39, 40–42, 44, 47, 49, 136, 155, 173, 178, 198, 224, 243.5, 255
Minotaur: s. of Pasiphae & a bull, Apd. 3.11–12, 3.213, 3.215, E.1.7, E.1.9 | Hyg. 38.8, 40, 41, 42, 43
Minyans: collective name of the Argonauts, Hyg. 14.24
Minyas: f. of Clymene, Apd. 3.105 | Hyg. 14.2, 14.24
Misery: early god, Hyg. Th.1
Mist: the first god, Hyg. Th.1
Mnemosyne: Titan, Apd. 1.2, 1.13 | Hyg. Th.31
Mnesileos: s. of Polydeuces, Apd. 3.134
Mnesimache: d. of Dexamenos, Apd. 2.91
Mnesimachus: f. of Hippomedon, Hyg. 70
Mnestheus: Trojan, Hyg. 273.18
Mnestra: Danaid, Apd. 2.18
Moerus: shows meaning of a true friend, Hyg. 257.3–8
Moirai, Parcae: "Fates," Apd. 1.13, 1.38, 1.43, 1.65, 1.106 | Hyg. Th.1, 171, 174, 251, 277
Molebos: suitor of Penelope, Apd. E.7.29
Molione: m. of the Molionidai, Apd. 2.139
Molionidai: Eurytos & Cteatos, conjoined sons of Molione, Apd. 2.140
Molorchos: Heracles' host in Cleonai, Apd. 2.74–75
Molos: **I** s. of Ares, Apd. 1.59 **II** s. of Deucalion, 3.17
Molossos: s. of Neoptolemos, Apd. E.6.12
Molpe: a Siren, Hyg. Th.30
Molus: f. of Meriones, Hyg. 97.7
Moneta: "memory," m. of Muses (= Mnemosyne), Hyg. Th.3, Th.27
Monuste: Danaid, Hyg. 170
Moon: *see* Selene
Mopsos: s. of Apollo, Apd. E.6.3–4, E.6.19 | Hyg. 14.5, 14.29, 128, 173
Mother Goddess: *see* Cybele
Mourning: early god, Hyg. Th.3
Muses: Apd. 1.13, 1.14–18 (named individually), 3.52, E.7.18 | Hyg. Th.27, 165, 224
Musica: one of the Horae, Hyg. 183
Mycon: saved by daughter, Hyg. 254.3
Mygdalion: f. of an unknown son, Apd. E.3.9
Mygdon: king of the Bebryces, Apd. 2.100
Mylios: s. of Priam, Apd. 3.153
Mynes: f. of Pedias, Apd. 3.186
Myrmidon: s. of Zeus, Apd. 1.52 | Hyg. 14.3
Myrmidone: Danaid, Hyg. 170
Myrmidons: men created for Aeacus from ants, Hyg. 52, 96
Myrtilos: s. of Hermes, Apd. E.2.6–8 | Hyg. 84, 224

Nape: one of Actaeon's dogs, Hyg. 181
Narcissus: s. of river Cephisus, loved himself, Hyg. 271
Nasamon: brother of Cephalion, Hyg. 14.28
Nastes: s. of Nomion, Apd. E.3.35
Naubolos: f. of Iphitos, Apd. 1.113 | Hyg. 14.17
Naucrate: slave of Minos, Apd. E.1.12
Nauplios: s. of Poseidon, f. of Palamedes, Apd. 2.23, 2.147, 3.15, 3.103, E.3.7, E.6.7–11 *passim* | Hyg. 14.11, 105, 116, 157, 169–169A, 249, 277
Nausicaa: d. of Alcinoos, Apd. E.7.25 | Hyg. 125.18, 126.1
Nausidame: m. of Augeias, Hyg. 14.15
Nausimedon: s. of Nauplios, Apd. 2.23
Nausithoe: Nereid, Apd. 1.11
Nausithous: s. of Ulysses & Circe, Hyg. 125.10
Neaira: **I** d. of Niobe, Apd. 3.45 **II** d. of Pereus, Apd. 3.102 **III** wife of Strymon, Apd. 2.3 **IV** d. of Autolycus, Hyg. 243.4
Nebrophonos: **I** s. of Jason & Hypsipyle, Apd. 1.115 **II** one of Actaeon's dogs, Hyg. 181
Nebula: *see* Nephele
Neleus: s. of Poseidon & Tyro, f. of Nestor, Apd. 1.91, 1.93, 1.98, 1.102, 1.113, 2.130,

2.142–143, 3.46, E.3.12 | Hyg. 10, 14.14, 14.21, 31.8, 97.5, 157, 244
Nelo: Danaid, Apd. 2.18
Nemean Games: founded in honor of Opheltes, Apd. 3.66 | Hyg. 74, 85, 273.6
Nemean Lion: invulnerable lion, Heracles' first labor, Apd. 2.74–76 | Hyg. 30.2
Nemertes: Nereid, Hyg. Th.8
Nemesis: goddess of retribution, m. of Helen, Apd. 3.127 | Hyg. Th.1
Neomeris: Nereid, Apd. 1.12
Neoptolemos: later name for Pyrrhos, s. of Achilles, Apd. 3.174, E.5.10–12, E.5.21, E.5.24, E.6.5, E.6.12–14, E.7.40 | Hyg. 97.15, 108, 112–114, 122–123, 193
Nephalion: s. of Minos, Apd. 2.99, 3.7
Nephele: "Cloud" **I** (also Nebula) m. of Phrixos & Helle, Apd. 1.80, 1.82 | Hyg. 1–3 **II** (also Nubis) woman created from clouds, m. of Centauros, Apd. E.1.20 | Hyg. 33–34
Nephos: s. of Heracles, Apd. 2.164
Neptune: *see* Poseidon
Nereids: daughters of Nereus, Apd. 1.11–12 (listed), 1.136, 2.43, 3.171 | Hyg. Th.8 (listed), 64, 106
Nereis: d. of Priam, Hyg. 90
Nereus: s. of Pontos & Ge, Apd. 1.10–11, 2.114–115, 3.34, 3.158, 3.168 | Hyg. Th.7–8, 157
Nesaia: Nereid, Apd. 1.12 | Hyg. Th.8
Nessos: Centaur, 2.86, 2.151–152, 2.157 | Hyg. 31.10, 34, 36, 240, 243.3
Nestor: s. of Neleus, Greek leader at Troy, Apd. 1.93–94, 2.142, 3.129, E.3.12, E.6.1 | Hyg. 10, 97.5, 252, 273.12
Niavius: s. of Aegyptus, Hyg. 170
Nicippe: **I** d. of Pelops, Apd. 2.53 **II** d. of Thespios, Apd. 2.164
Nicodromos: s. of Heracles, Apd. 2.162
Nicomachos: suitor of Penelope, Apd. E.7.27
Nicostratos: s. of Menelaos, Apd. 3.133
Nicothoe: *see* Aello
Night: early god, Hyg. Th.1
Nike: **I** "Victory," Apd. 1.9 | Hyg. Th.17 **II** d. of Thespios, Apd. 1.62
Nile, Nilus: river god, Apd. 2.10–11 | Hyg. Th.6
Ninus: husband of Semiramis, Hyg. 240
Niobe: **I** d. of Phoroneus, Apd. 2.1–2, 3.96 | Hyg. 145, 155 **II** d. of Tantalos, wife of Amphion, Apd. 3.45–47 | Hyg. 9–11, 14.14
Nireus: **I** s. of Charopos, Greek leader at Troy, Apd. E.3.13 | Hyg. 81, 97.13, 113, 270 **II** s. of Poseidon, Apd. 1.53
Nisas: suitor of Penelope, Apd. E.7.29
Nisos: **I** s. of Pandion, Apd. 3.206, 3.210, 3.211 | Hyg. 198, 242, 255 **II** Trojan, Hyg. 257, 273.16
Nissaios: suitor of Penelope, Apd. E.7.29
Nomion: f. of Nastes & Amphimachos, Apd. E.3.35
North Wind: *see* Boreas
Notus: a wind, Hyg. Th.15
Nubis: *see* Nephele
Nycteis: d. of Nycteus, Apd. 3.40
Nycteus: s. of Chthonios, Apd. 3.40–3.42, 3.100, 3.111 | Hyg. 7, 8, 155, 157
Nyctimene: d. of Epopeus, raped by him, Hyg. 204, 253
Nyctimos: s. of Lycaon, Apd. 3.96
Nymphe: one of the Horae, Hyg. 183
Nysa: one of Liber's nurses, Hyg. 182
Nysus: **I** raises Dionysus, Hyg. 131, 167, 179 **II** f. of Eurynome, Hyg. 157

Oannes: discovers astronomy, Hyg. 274.16
Oath: early god, Hyg. Th.3
Obrimus: **I** s. of Aegyptus, Hyg. 170 **II** one of Actaeon's dogs, Hyg. 181
Ocean: *see* Oceanos
Oceanids: daughters of Oceanos & Tethys, Apd. 1.8 | Hyg. Th.6
Oceanos: Titan, Apd. 1.2–3, 1.6, 1.8, 1.13, 1.28, 1.32, 1.129, 2.1, 2.39, 2.106–107, 3.96, 3.110, 3.156, E.2.9, E.7.1, E.7.17 | Hyg. Th.3, Th.6, 138, 143, 151, 156, 177, 182, 275.6
Ocitus: Greek leader at Troy, Hyg. 97.13
Ocyale: Amazon, Hyg. 163
Ocydrome: one of Actaeon's dogs, Hyg. 181
Ocydromus: one of Actaeon's dogs, Hyg. 181
Ocypete: **I** a Harpy, Apd. 1.10, 1.123 | Hyg. Th.35, 14.18; also called Ocythoe or Ocypode **II** Danaid, Apd. 2.20
Ocypode: **I** *see* Ocypete **II** one of Actaeon's dogs, Hyg. 181
Ocythoe: *see* Ocypete
Ocythous: one of Actaeon's dogs, Hyg. 181
Ocytos: f. of Gouneus, Apd. E.3.14
Odios: s. of Mecisteus, Apd. E.3.35
Odysseus, Ulysses: s. of Laertes & Anticleia, king of Ithaca, husband of Penelope, Greek leader at

Poeas: *see* Poias

Poemenis: one of Actaeon's dogs, Hyg. 181

Poias: s. of Thaumacos, Argonaut, Apd. 1.112, 1.141, 2.160, 3.131, E.3.14 | Hyg. 14.22, 36, 97.8, 102, 257.2

Polichos: s. of Lycaon, Apd. 3.97

Polites: s. of Priam, Apd. 3.151 | Hyg. 90, 273.12

Pollux: *see* Polydeuces

Poltys: Heracles' host in Ainos, Apd. 2.105

Polus: *see* Coios

Polyanax: king of Melos, Apd. E.6.15b

Polybe: Danaid, Hyg. 170

Polybos: **I** king of Corinth, adoptive f. of Oidipous, Apd. 3.49 | Hyg. 66.1, 67.7 **II** name of two suitors of Penelope, Apd. E.7.29 **III** Argive, Hyg. 14.10

Polybotes: Giant, Apd. 1.38 | Hyg. Th.4

Polycaste: d. of Nestor, Apd. 1.94

Polyctor: s. of Aigyptos, Apd. 2.19

Polydamas: Trojan, Hyg. 115

Polydectes: s. of Magnes, king of Seriphos, Apd. 1.88, 2.36, 2.45 | Hyg. 63–64, 273.4

Polydector: s. of Aegyptus, Hyg. 170

Polydeuces, Pollux: one of the Dioscouroi, s. of Zeus & Leda, Calydonian boar hunter, Argonaut, Apd. 1.67, 1.111, 1.119, 3.126, 3.128, 3.134, 3.136–137 | Hyg. 14.12, 17, 77, 79–80, 92, 155, 173, 224, 251, 273.10, 275.5

Polydora: **I** d. of Peleus, Apd. 3.163, 3.168 (wife of Peleus) **II** Amazon, Hyg. 163

Polydoros: **I** s. of Priam, Apd. 3.151 | Hyg. 90, 109, 254.1 **II** s. of Cadmos, Apd. 3.26, 3.40 | Hyg. 76, 179 **III** one of the Epigoni, Hyg. 71–71A **IV** suitor of Penelope, Apd. E.7.29

Polygonos: s. of Proteus, Apd. 2.105

Polyhymno: one of Liber's nurses, Hyg. 182

Polyidos: **I** s. of Coiranos, seer, Apd. 3.18–20 | Hyg. 128, 136, 251 **II** suitor of Penelope, E.7.27

Polylaos: s. of Heracles, Apd. 2.161

Polymedon: s. of Priam, Apd. 3.153

Polymede: d. of Autolycos, m. of Jason, Apd. 1.107, 1.143

Polymele: d. of Peleus, Apd. 3.176

Polymetus: s. of Priam, Hyg. 90

Polymnestor: king of Thrace, Hyg. 109, 240

Polymnia: Muse, Apd. 1.13

Polyneices: s. of Oidipous, Apd. 3.55–82, E.3.17 | Hyg. 67–72, 76, 243.8, 254.1

Polynome: Nereid, Apd. 1.12

Polypemon: **I** f. of Sinis, Apd. 3.218 **II** another name for Damastes, Apd. E.1.4

Polypheides: king of Sicyon, Apd. E.2.15

Polyphemos: **I** a Cyclops, s. of Poseidon whom Odysseus blinds, Apd. E.7.4–7.9 | Hyg. 125.3–5 **II** s. of Elatos, Argonaut, Apd. 1.113, 1.117 | Hyg. 14.2, 14.25

Polyphontes: **I** one of the Heracleidai, Apd. 2.180 | king of Messenia, Hyg. 137 **II** Laios' herald, Apd. 3.51

Polypoites: **I** s. of Peirithous, Greek leader at Troy, Apd. 3.130, E.3.14, E.6.2 | Hyg. 81, 97.14, 114 **II** s. of Odysseus, Apd. E.7.35 **III** s. of Phthia & Apollo, Apd. 1.57 **IV** suitor of Penelope, Apd. E.7.27

Polyxene: **I** d. of Priam, Apd. 3.151, E.5.23 | Hyg. 90, 110 **II** Danaid, Hyg. 170

Polyxenos: **I** s. of Agasthenes, suitor of Helen, Apd. 3.130 | Hyg. 81, 97.11 **II** king of Elis, Apd. 2.55

Polyxo: **I** nymph, m. of some Danaids, Apd. 2.19 **II** wife of Nycteus, Apd. 3.111 **III** Oceanid, Hyg. Th.6 **IV** Hypsipyle's adviser, Hyg. 15 **V** d. of Atlas, Hyg. 192

Pontomedousa: Nereid, Apd. 1.11

Pontos: "Sea," Apd. 1.8, 1.10 | Hyg. Th.3, Th.5, Th.7

Porphyrion: Giant, Apd. 1.35–36 | Hyg. Th.1

Porthaon: s. of Agenor, Apd. 1.59, 1.63 | Hyg. 14.17, 129, 174–175, 239, 242

Portheus: **I** s. of Lycaon, Apd. 3.97 **II** f. of Echion, Apd. E.5.20

Portunus: *see* Palaemon

Poseidon, Neptune: s. of Cronos & Rhea, god of the sea, horses, & earthquakes, f. of many heroes, Apd. 1.4 birth, 1.7 receives sea as realm, 1.25–28 & Orion, 1.38 Gigantomachy, 1.53 sleeps with Canace, 1.60, 1.90 sleeps with Tyro, 1.93, 1.108, 1.112–113, 1.119–120, 1.144, 2.10, 2.13 dries up Argos, 2.14 sleeps with Amymone, 2.23, 2.32, 2.42, 2.43 sends monster against Ethiopians, 2.50 fathers Taphios, 2.51 makes Pterelaos immortal, 2.67, 2.86 conceals Centaurs, 2.88, 2.94 sends bull to Minos, 2.103 builds walls of Troy, 2.105, 2.109, 2.111, 2.115–116, 2.138–139, 2.147, 3.1, 3.3, 3.8–9 sends bull & grows angry at Minos, 3.75, 3.77 sleeps with Demeter, 3.111 sleeps with two Pleiades, 3.117, 3.156, 3.161, 3.168, 3.170 gives Peleus immortal horses, 3.178–179 contest with Athena over Athens, 3.180, 3.196,

Pyramids: Hyg. 223.7
Pyramus: Thisbe's lover Hyg. 242, 243.8
Pyrante: Danaid, Hyg. 170
Pyranthus: *see* Periander
Pyrantis: Danaid, Hyg. 170
Pyremus: f. of Asterion, Hyg. 14.1
Pyrene: m. of Cycnos, Apd. 2.114
Pyrippe: d. of Thespios, Apd. 2.164
Pyrois: one of the Sun's horses, Hyg. 183
Pyrrha: **I** d. of Epimetheus, wife of Deucalion, Apd. 1.46–49 | Hyg. 142, 152A, 153, 155 **II** name of Achilles incognito, Hyg. 96, 97.15
Pyrrhos: s. of Achilles, Apd. 3.174; *see also* Neoptolemos
Pythia: Apollo's priestess at the oracle of Delphi, Apd. 2.73, 2.130
Pythian Games: games held in Delphi in honor of Apollo, Hyg. 140
Python: guardian serpent at Delphi, Apd. 1.22 | Hyg. Th.34, 53, 140

Quarreling: early god, Hyg. Th.3

Ram of the Equinox: constellation, Hyg. 133
Remus: brother of Romulus, Hyg. 252
Rhadamanthys: d. of Zeus & Europa, Apd. 2.64, 2.70, 3.3, 3.6 | Hyg. 155, 178
Rhea: Titan, Apd. 1.2, 1.4–5, 1.33, 3.154, E.6.16
Rhene: m. of Ajax, Hyg. 97.5
Rhesos: s. of Euterpe & Strymon, Apd. 1.18, E.4.4 | Hyg. 113
Rhexenor: f. of Chalciope, Apd. 3.207
Rhode: **I** d. of Poseidon & Amphitrite, Apd. 1.28 **II** Danaid, Apd. 2.17
Rhodia: Danaid, Apd. 2.17
Rhodope: Oceanid, Hyg. Th.6
Rhoicos: **I** Centaur, Apd. 3.106 **II** Giant, Hyg. Th.4
Romulus: first king of Rome, Hyg. 252

Sagittarius: constellation, Hyg. 224
Sainon: one of Actaeon's dogs, Hyg. 181
Salius: Trojan, Hyg. 273.16
Salmoneus: s. of Aiolos, Apd. 1.51, 1.89, 1.90, 1.96 | Hyg. 60, 61, 157, 239, 250, 254.3
Sandocos: s. of Astynoos, Apd. 3.181
Sangarios: river god, Apd. 3.148; *see Geographic Index*
Sao: Nereid, Apd. 1.11
Sarapis: a form of the syncretized Egyptian gods Osiris-Apis worshipped by the Greeks, mistakenly associated with the Greek Apis at Apd. 2.2
Sardo: d. of Sthenelus, Hyg. 275.6
Sarpedon: **I** s. of Zeus & Europa, Apd. 3.3, 3.5–6, E.3.35, E.4.6 | Hyg. 106, 112–113, 115, 155, 178, 273.12 **II** s. of Poseidon, Apd. 2.105
Saturn: *see* Cronos
Satyros: steals Arcadian cattle, Apd. 2.4
Satyrs: companions of Dionysos, Apd. 3.34
Scaia: Danaid, Apd. 2.16
Scaios: s. of Hippocoon, Apd. 3.124
Scamandros: river god near Troy, Apd. 3.139–140, 3.146 | Hyg. Th.6; *see Geographic Index*
Sceiron: **I** f. of Endeis, Apd. 3.158 **II** s. of Poseidon or Pelops, Apd. E.1.2 | Hyg. 38.4
Schedios: **I** s. of Iphitos, suitor of Helen, Apd. 3.130 | Hyg. 97.10 **II** suitor of Penelope, Apd. E.7.27
Schoineus: f. of Atalante, Apd. 1.68, 1.84, 1.112, 3.109 | Hyg. 173, 185, 206, 238, 242, 246
Sciron: *see* Sceiron
Scylla: **I** d. of Crataiis, transformed into a sea monster, Apd. 1.136, E.7.20–21 | Hyg. Th.17, Th.39, 125.14, 151, 199 **II** d. of Nisos, Apd. 3.211 | Hyg. 198, 255 **III** Danaid, Hyg. 170
Scyrios: f. of Aigeus, Apd. 3.206
Sea: early god, Hyg. Th.2, Th.5
Seasons: *see* Horai
Seilenos: attendant of Dionysos, Apd. 2.83 | Hyg. 191
Selene: "Moon," Apd. 1.8, 1.35, 1.56 | Hyg. Th.12, Th.28, 30.2, 271
Self-indulgence: early god, Hyg. Th.3
Selinuntius: close friend of Moerus, Hyg. 257.3–8
Semele: d. of Cadmos, m. of Dionysos by Zeus, Apd. 3.26–27, 3.30 | Hyg. 5, 9, 155, 167, 179, 224, 251
Semiramis: d. of Dercetis, Hyg. 223.6, 240, 243.8, 275.7
Septentrio major: Hyg. 177, 224
Septentrio minor: Hyg. 224
Sergestus: Trojan, Hyg. 273.14–15
Shield in Argos: games held in Argos, Hyg. 170, 273.2
Siboe: d. of Niobe, Hyg. 11

Tanais: river god, Hyg. Th.6

Tantalos: **I** f. of Pelops & Niobe among others, punished in the underworld, Apd. 3.45, 3.47, E.2.1 | Hyg. 9, 82–84, 124, 155, 245, 273.5 **II** s. of Thyestes, great-grands. of Tantalos I, Apd. E.2.15–16 | Hyg. 88.1, 244, 246 **III** s. of Niobe, Apd. 3.45 | Hyg. 11

Taphios: s. of Poseidon & Hippothoe, Apd. 2.50–51, 2.54

Tartaros: place of punishment beneath the underworld, Apd. 1.3–8, 1.39, 2.4, 3.122 | Hyg. Th.3, Th.4, 139, 146, 150, 152

Tauros: s. of Neleus, Apd. 1.93

Taurus: constellation, Hyg. 192

Taygete: d. of Atlas, Apd. 3.110, 3.116 | Hyg. 155, 192

Tebros: s. of Hippocoon, Apd. 3.124

Tegyrios: king of Thrace, Apd. 3.202

Teiresias, Tiresias: s. of Eueres & Chariclo, Theban seer, Apd. 2.61, 3.69–73, 3.84–85, 3.94, E.7.17, E.7.34 | Hyg. 67.6, 68, 75, 125.15, 128

Telamon: s. of Aiacos, f. of Aias & Teucros, Calydonian boar hunter, Argonaut, Apd. 1.68, 1.111, 2.135, 2.136, 3.131, 3.158–162 | Hyg. 14.8, 14.32, 81, 89, 97.3, 107, 114, 173, 242, 273.10

Telchis: conspirator against Apis, Apd. 2.2

Teleboas: s. of Lycaon, Apd. 3.97

Teledice: nymph, wife of Phoroneus, Apd. 2.1

Telegonos: **I** s. of Odysseus, Apd. E.7.16, E.7.36–37 | Hyg. 125.10, 125.20, 127 **II** s. of Proteus, Apd. 2.105 **III** king of Egypt, Apd. 2.9

Telemachos: s. of Odysseus, Apd. E.3.7, E.7.32–33 | Hyg. 95, 125.20, 127

Telemus: s. of Eurymus, an augur, Hyg. 125.3, 128

Teleon: f. of Boutes, Apd. 1.112 | Hyg. 14.6, 14.9, 14.27

Telephassa: wife of Agenor, m. of Europa & Cadmos, Apd. 3.2–3.4, 3.21

Telephontes: s. of Cresphontes & Merope, Hyg. 137

Telephos: s. of Heracles & Auge, ruler of Mysia, shows the Greeks the way to Troy, Apd. 1.79, 1.146–147, 2.166, 3.103–104, E.3.17, E.3.20, E.5.12 | Hyg. 99–101, 162, 244, 252, 273.12

Teles: s. of Heracles, Apd. 2.162

Telestas: s. of Priam, Apd. 3.152

Teleutagoras: s. of Heracles, Apd. 2.162

Telmios: suitor of Penelope, Apd. E.7.27

Temenos: s. of Aristomachos, one of the Heracleidai, Apd. 2.172–179 *passim* | Hyg. 124, 219

Tenes: s. of Cycnos or Apollo, Apd. E.3.23–26

Tenthredon: f. of Prothoos, Apd. E.3.14 | Hyg. 97.13

Tereis: m. of Megapenthes, Apd. 3.133

Tereus: s. of Ares, Apd. 3.193–195 | Hyg. 45, 239, 244, 246

Terpsichore: Muse, Apd. 1.13

Terpsicrates: s. of Heracles, Apd. 2.164

Terror: s. of Venus & Mars, Hyg. Th.29

Tethys: Titan, Apd. 1.2, 1.8, 2.1, 3.156 | Hyg. Th.6, 177

Teucer: *see* Teucros

Teucros: **I** s. of Telamon, suitor of Helen, Apd. 3.131, 3.162, E.5.5 | Hyg. 89, 97.3, 114 **II** s. of Scamandros & Idaia, Apd. 3.139

Teutamides: king of Larissa, Apd. 2.47

Teuthras: king of Teuthrania, adoptive f. of Telephos, Apd. 2.147, 3.103–104 | Hyg. 99, 100

Thadytios: suitor of Penelope, Apd. E.7.29

Thaleia: **I** one of the Charites, Apd. 1.13 **II** a Muse, Apd. 1.13, 1.18 **III** Nereid, Hyg. Th.8

Thales: one of the Seven Wise Men, Hyg. 221

Thallo: one of the Horae, Hyg. 183

Thalpios: s. of Eurytos, suitor of Helen, Apd. 3.129 | Hyg. 81

Thamyris: s. of Philammon, first homosexual, Apd. 1.16–17

Thasius: s. of Anius, Hyg. 247

Thasos: s. of Poseidon, Apd. 3.3–4

Thaumacos: f. of Poias, Apd. 1.112

Thaumas: s. of Pontos & Ge, Apd. 1.10 | Hyg. Th.7, Th.35

Theano: **I** wife of Metapontus, Hyg. 186.4 **II** wife of Antenor, Apd. E.3.34 **III** Danaid, Apd. 2.19

Thebais: nurse of Jupiter, Hyg. 275.1

Thebe: wife of Zethos, Apd. 3.45

Theia: Titan, Apd. 1.2, 1.8

Theiodamas: **I** f. of Hylas, Apd. 1.117 **II** an oxdriver encountered by Heracles, Apd. 2.153

Thelxiepeia: one of the Sirens, Apd. E.7.18 | Hyg. Th.30

Thelxion: conspirator against Apis, Apd. 2.2

Themis: Titan, Apd. 1.2, 1.13, 1.22, 2.114, 3.168 | Hyg. Th.3, Th.25, 183

Themistagora: Danaid, Hyg. 170

Themiste: d. of Ilos, Apd. 3.141

INDEX OF PEOPLES AND GEOGRAPHIC LOCATIONS

INDEX OF AUTHORS AND WORKS CITED BY APOLLODORUS AND HYGINUS

Acousilaos: important early mythographer of the 6th century BC; *see General Introduction,* Apd. 2.2 (= *FGrH* 2.25a = 25 Fowler), 2.5 (= *FGrH* 2.26 = 26 Fowler), 2.6 (= *FGrH* 2.27 = 27 Fowler), 2.26 (= *FGrH* 2.28 = 28 Fowler) 2.94 (= *FGrH* 2.29 = 29 Fowler), 3.30 (= *FGrH* 2.33 = 33 Fowler), 3.96 (= *FGrH* 2.25b = 25 Fowler), 3.133 (= *FGrH* 2.41 = 41 Fowler), 3.156 (= *FGrH* 2.21 = 21 Fowler), 3.199 (= *FGrH* 2.31 = 31 Fowler)

Alcmaionid: lost 6th-century BC epic poem, Apd. 1.76 (= Bernabé 4)

Apollonios: author of the surviving poem *Argonautica* in four books, concerning Jason's quest for the Golden Fleece, 3rd century BC, Apd. 1.123 (*see Arg.* 2.284–297) | Hyg. 14.8 (*see Arg.* 1.93)

Asclepiades: of Tragilus, wrote the lost *Tragodoumena, (Subjects of Tragedies); see General Introduction,* Apd. 2.6 (= *FGrH* 12.16), 3.7 (= *FGrH* 12.17)

Asios: a poet (perhaps 6th century BC) from Samos, composed genealogies, Apd. 3.100 (= Bernabé 9)

Castor: chronicler of the 1st century BC, Apd. 2.5 (= *FGrH* 250.8)

Cato: author of the lost *Origines,* a Latin treatise on the early history of the Romans, 3rd–2nd century BC, Hyg. 260 (= *HRR* fr. 9)

Cercops: 6th-century BC poet of lost epic *Aigimios,* Apd. 2.6 (= MW 294), 2.23 (= MW 297)

Cicero: 1st-century AD Roman statesman, orator, and part-time poet; wrote the *Aratea,* an adaptation of Aratus' astronomical poem *Phainomena* (3rd century BC), Hyg. 14.33 (= Soubiran 126–138)

Cretica: a Latin poem in hexameters (of unknown date), a translation of Epimenides' Greek poem of the same name (late 6th century BC?), Hyg. 177 (= *FLP* Anonymous 8)

Demaratos: Hellenistic writer of a prose work on the Argonauts, Apd. 1.118 (= *FGrH* 42.2)

Dionysios: nicknamed Scytobrachion, mid-3rd-century BC writer of rationalized mythology; *see General Introduction,* Apd. 1.118 (= *FGrH* 6a)

Ennius: Roman writer, 3rd–2nd century BC, who adapted Greek mythological poems and plays into Latin, Hyg. 8

Eriphyle: lost poem of Stesichoros, early 6th-century lyric poet, Apd. 3.121 (= *PMGF* 194[iii])

Eumelos: author of an early lost epic on Corinth (*Corinthiaca*) and the lost *Nostoi* (*see below*), 8th century BC, Apd. 3.100 (= Bernabé 14 = 7 Fowler), 3.102 (= Bernabé 15 = 8a Fowler), 3.133 (= Bernabé 9 = 6 Fowler) | Hyg. 183 (= Bernabé test. 12 & *Titanomachia* 7)

Euripides: 5th-century BC writer of tragedies, Apd. 2.11 (= *TGF* 881 K), 3.75 (= *Phoen.* 1157), 3.94 (= *TGF* 5.ii K), 3.109 (= *Phoen.* 1162) | Hyg. 4 (= *TGF* 32.iii K), 8 (= *TGF* 12.iii[a] K), 247 (= *TGF* test. 125d K)

Herodoros: 5th–4th century BC mythographer; *see General Introduction,* Apd. 1.118 (= *FGrH* 31.41a = 41a Fowler), 3.45 (= *FGrH* 31.56 = 56 Fowler)

Hesiod: author of the surviving poems *Theogony* and *Works & Days,* among other lost works, probably 8th–7th century BC, Apd. 1.74 (= MW 12), 1.123 (= MW 155), 2.2 (= MW 160), 2.5 (= MW 124), 2.26 (= MW 131), 2.31 (= *Th.* 319), 2.38 (= [*Sc.*] 223–224), 3.45 (= MW 183), 3.71 (= MW 275), 3.96 (= MW 160), 3.100 (= MW 163), 3.109 (= MW 72), 3.183 (= MW 139) | Hyg. 154 (in title) (= MW 311)

Homer: author of the epic poems *Iliad* and *Odyssey,* perhaps the 8th century BC; many other poems were attributed to him in antiquity, Apd. 1.19 (= *Il.* 1.578), 2.25 (= *Il.* 6.160), 2.31 (= *Il.* 16.328), 3.3 (= *Il.* 6.198–199), 3.45 (= *Il.* 24.602–604) | Hyg. 183 (unknown reference)

Little Iliad: lost poem from the epic cycle in four books, attributed to Lesches of Mytilene, probably 7th century BC, Apd. E.5.14 (= Bernabé 8)

Melesagoras: or Amelesagoras, Athenian chronologist, around 300 BC, Apd. 3.121 (= *FGrH* 330.3)

Naupactica: lost anonymous epic poem on an unknown subject, perhaps 6th century BC, Apd. 3.121 (= Bernabé 10)

Nostoi: "Returns," a lost epic poem about the Greeks' travels home after the Trojan War, attributed to various poets, including Eumelos & Homer (perhaps 6th century BC), Apd. 2.23 (= Bernabé 1)

Odyssey: surviving epic poem by Homer recounting Odysseus' journey home after the Trojan War (8th or 7th century BC), Hyg. 125

Orphics: writers of epic poems circulating under name Orpheus, of various dates but generally early, Apd. 3.121 (= Bernabé 365)

Ovid: Roman poet, 1st century BC–1st century AD, author of the surviving poem *Metamorphoses,* Hyg. 183 (= *Met.* 2.153)

Panyassis: 5th-century BC poet of lost *Heracleia,* Apd. 1.32 (= Bernabé 13.1), 3.121 (= Bernabé 26), 3.183 (= Bernabé 27)

Peisandros: unknown mythographer, perhaps Hellenistic, Apd. 1.75 (= *FGrH* 16.1)

Pherecydes: mythographer of the 5th century BC; *see General Introduction,* Apd. 1.25 (= *FGrH* 3.52 = 52 Fowler), 1.32 (= *FGrH* 3.53 = 53 Fowler), 1.76 (= *FGrH* 3.122a = 122a Fowler), 1.118 (= *FGrH* 3.111a = 111a Fowler), 2.6 (= *FGrH* 3.67 = 66 Fowler), 2.62 (= *FGrH* 3.69a = 69a Fowler), 2.148 (= *FGrH* 3.42 = 42 Fowler), 3.3 (= *FGrH* 3.87 = 87 Fowler), 3.24 (= *FGrH* 3.22c, see Hellanicus 51b Fowler), 3.25 (= *FGrH* 3.89 = 89 Fowler), 3.70 (= *FGrH* 3.92a = 92a Fowler), 3.100 (= *FGrH* 3.157 = 157 Fowler), 3.158 (= *FGrH* 3.60 = 60 Fowler) | Hyg. 154 (= *FGrH* 3.74 = 74 Fowler)

Philocrates: author of a mythological poem or treatise on Thessaly, perhaps 4th century BC, Apd. 3.176 (= *FGrH* 601.1)

Pindar: 5th-century BC poet of odes with mythological content, Apd. 2.38 (= fr. 254 Snell-Maehler, but not printed)

Simonides: 6th–5th century BC lyric poet, Apd. E.1.16 | Hyg. 277 (does not seem to have been noticed in collections of Simonides; cf. *PMG,* where it is not found)

Stesichoros: lyric poet of the 6th century BC, Apd. 3.117 (= *PMGF* 227), 3.121 (= *PMGF* 194[iii])

Telesilla: poetess from Argos, writer of hymns, 5th century BC, Apd. 3.47 (= *PMG* 5)

Thebaid: lost epic poem on Thebes, Apd. 1.74 (= Bernabé 5)

tragedians: writers of dramatic plays of myth, mostly 5th century; best known are Aeschylus, Sophocles, & Euripides (only the last is cited by name by Apd. and Hyg.), Apd. 2.5 (*see TGF* vol. 5.1 p. 494), 2.23 (*see TGF* vol. 4 p. 354), 2.25 (*see note on FTG* [Nauck] p. 567)